KILLER
CRITIQUE

Also by Alexander Campion

THE GRAVE GOURMET

CRIME FRAÎCHE

Published by Kensington Publishing Corporation

KILLER CRITIQUE

ALEXANDER CAMPION

KENSINGTON BOOKS
www.kensingtonbooks.com

KENSINGTON BOOKS are published by

Kensington Publishing Corp.
119 West 40th Street
New York, NY 10018

All Kensington titles, imprints, and distributed lines are available at special quantity discounts for bulk purchases for sales promotion, premiums, fund-raising, educational, or institutional use.

Special book excerpts or customized printings can also be created to fit specific needs. For details, write or phone the office of the Kensington Special Sales Manager: Attn. Special Sales Department. Kensington Publishing Corp., 119 West 40th Street, New York, NY 10018. Phone: 1-800-221-2647.

Kensington and the K logo Reg. U.S. Pat. & TM Off.

Library of Congress Card Catalogue Number: 2012934789

ISBN-13: 978-0-7582-6879-2
ISBN-10: 0-7582-6879-3

First Hardcover Printing: July 2012

10 9 8 7 6 5 4 3 2 1

Printed in the United States of America

Encore une pour T, bien sûr. Sans elle il n'y aurait rien.

Acknowledgements

Thanks to Frédéric Pagès who cut the imaginary philosopher Jean-Baptiste Botul from whole cloth then wrote *The Sexual Life of Emmanuel Kant* and attributed it to Botul. The practical joke was continued by Christophe Clerc and Bertrand Rothé who published a work entitled *Landru, Precursor of Feminism: Unpublished Correspondence between Henri-Désiré Landru and Jean-Baptist Botul*. Landru, of course, a serial killer of women, is another invented character.

The hoax was so successful that Bernard-Henri Lévy, certainly the world's most charismatic and mediatized philosopher, enthusiastically supported Botul's philosophy in his work *De La Guerre en Philosophie—On the War in Philosophy*, published in 2010.

Without Botul, Professor Caillot and Caillaud's erudition would have been incomplete.

My profound thanks also to Sharon Bower, paragon of agents, who makes this all possible. Without her, there would be no Capucine and certainly no Alexander Campion.

And deepest thanks to my stepdaughter, Sydnie, who really is as old as Sybille claims to be. Sydnie had the patience to fine tune Sybille's dialogue and make her sound her age. I'm still not too sure how Sydnie knew about Special K, though.

And finally to Basset Hound Micawber who sits under my desk all day long, listening to me read out loud, growling faintly when it doesn't sound right. He's had one cameo appearance in the last book—drinking a beer in front of France's "other" Notre Dame. He's furious he's not in this one. I hope this acknowledgement makes up for the lacuna.

CHAPTER 1

"Is he dead yet?" *Brigadier* David Martineau asked.

"No, not quite. Wait a minute. Hang on. There. Now he's dead," *Commissaire* Capucine Le Tellier replied. The other detectives were struck dumb. Hardened as they were, actually seeing a life escape from its body was deeply moving.

For Capucine the scene was all the more disturbing because the context was so familiar. Gautier du Fesnay, senior food critic for *Le Figaro,* good friend of her husband, Alexandre, senior food critic for *Le Monde,* was—had been—very proud of his blog. He delighted in going to restaurants he was reviewing, placing a miniature camcorder on the table, and making acerbic comments as he ate. He would edit them at home, adding a little background music, blurring out his face, inserting a graphic of the noise level and ambient temperature, winding up with a shot of the check. Even if he loved the meal, he always managed to sound cynical and drop a caustic barb or two.

Capucine knew that Fesnay had taken far more pleasure in these little videos than in his highly polished pieces for *Le Figaro,* which Alexandre claimed were the summum bonum of food criticism.

The clip had started out exactly like all the others. Fesnay had walked jerkily down the rue de Varenne, the street still bright in the summer twilight, swinging the camcorder left and right, making supercilious comments about the austerity of the ministerial façades until, hesitantly, the street blossomed with chic boutiques as it approached the rue du Bac. As if by accident, Fesnay had discovered Chez Béatrice with a little exclamation of joy.

The camcorder had dropped to waist level as Fesnay entered the restaurant and was shown to his table. Once seated, Fesnay had placed it on the table and had twisted the zoom lens to extreme wide angle. Not yet blurred out, his face was aristocratically haughty as he had scanned the menu and wine list, chatted with the waiter, and ordered. There had been a long, slow pan of the room, filled with cheerful well-to-do youths, promising-looking, young bankerly types and their wives, well dressed from *bon chic, bon genre* boutiques but still a few years away from bespoke tailors and forays to Givenchy.

The waiter had appeared with a dish of pâté. "Ah, the famous truffled duck foie gras from the Landes," Fesnay had whispered. He cut a small piece, put it on a piece of toast, nibbled, pursed his lips, and nodded in silent approval.

After a fifteen-minute interval the waiter had returned and placed a large, flat soup bowl in front of Fesnay. The camcorder had been lifted, the zoom homed in on a close-up, and the dish examined meticulously. In a conspiratorial murmur Fesnay had announced, "*Ravioles d'homard—*lobster ravioli—in a sauce of carrot and tandoori spices, served with a mousseline of citrus fruit confit." The dish seemed to consist of three or four oversized raviolis in a copious, thick sauce. Fesnay had held a fork in his left hand and a large spoon in his right and had delicately cut a quarter out of one of the raviolis and scooped it up with a good quantity of the sauce.

"*Pas mal. Pas mal du tout*—not bad at all," Fesnay had stage-whispered conspiratorially.

As he swallowed, he had jerked slightly, as if repressing a hiccup. The camcorder had continued to admire him placidly. He had remained immobile for lengthy seconds, holding the fork and spoon in clenched fists over the sides of the bowl. Slowly, with the solemnity of a marble Roman statue toppling off its base, he had leaned forward, almost imperceptibly at first, gradually accelerating until he had collapsed face-first into his bowl, crating a splashed nimbus of crimson sauce.

It was the interminable wait after the crash that had prompted David's question. Finally, another eternity after Capucine's diagnostic, a hand had appeared, lifted Fesnay's head, turned it sideways, and let it sink back into the bowl. Fesnay stared into the camera with immobile, glassy doll eyes. A piece of ravioli stuck to the tip of his nose.

"So if it's curare, like the guy from forensics thought, he could be alive here, unable to move, crying out his anguish in tormented silence," David said, twisting one of his locks into a tight noose around a finger, intent on the screen.

"Nah, he's dead, all right," said *Brigadier-Chef* Isabelle Lemercier with a snort. "He musta drowned in the sauce. Don't need forensics to tell us that, right, Momo?"

Brigadier Mohammed Benarouche, a giant North African of few words even when he was in a good mood, glowered at his immediate superior.

All four stared at the screen, each horrified in his own way. Absolutely nothing happened. The scene was as static as a photograph. Finally, as if it had been the entire purpose of the cinematographic endeavor, the scrap of ravioli fell off Fesnay's nose. The screen went black.

CHAPTER 2

Five hours earlier Capucine had been awash in bliss, supine on a long wooden bench next to the huge Provençal table that dominated their kitchen, as Alexandre massaged her feet, prattling on about cooking. Her tummy had been pleasantly full of his latest creation, a large scoop of lamb ragù served on a bed of chrome-yellow *risotto alla milanese*. The secret to the ragù, she would have learned had she been listening, was to puree the vegetables in a processor and then brown them to the point of cruelty before adding the rest of the ingredients, and the sine qua non of the risotto was to add the threads of saffron only at the very end, precisely at the moment when the dish's climax was at hand.

The soothing lapping of her husband's mellifluous prose had been interrupted by the shrill note of the phone. Despite Alexandre's insistence that she let the little gremlins of electronic technology deal with it, Capucine had recognized the leaden timbre of the call to duty and snatched the cordless handset off its base.

Contrôleur Général Tallon, her boss's boss and well into the stratosphere of the *Police Judiciaire* hierarchy, was known for his testiness. "*Commissaire*, I hope you weren't planning on an early evening. I'm assigning you to

a case because of your knowledge of the restaurant industry. A man has been killed in a restaurant on the rue de
Varenne in the Seventh called Chez Béatrice. The chef and
owner, a certain Béatrice Mesnagier, called it in, and I
want you in charge."

At the words "restaurant industry" Capucine had beckoned to Alexandre, who had put his ear next to hers
against the receiver.

"I know it's outside of your brigade's sector, but it's
clearly your area of expertise, or at least your husband's.
Good evening, Monsieur de Huguelet."

Capucine resisted the impulse to stare at the window to
see if anyone was peeking in. Tallon's ability to know her
better than she knew herself was always unnerving.

Alexandre smiled. "Bonsoir, monsieur le contrôleur
général." He had met Tallon only twice, but the two had
developed a natural affinity in the way that oil and vinegar
complemented each other.

"The bad news," continued Tallon, "is that you both
must know the victim, Gautier du Fesnay. If he was a
friend, I offer my most sincere condolences. Anyway,
Commissaire, I need you to get right over there with some
of the team from your brigade. The local police are on the
scene, and you know how quickly they can muddy up a
crime scene. Report to me in the morning."

Capucine was numb. They had seen Gautier at a dinner
a week before. He wasn't an intimate friend, but he was
someone they saw frequently at friends' houses, restaurant
openings, and once or twice a year at dinners in their own
apartment. Gautier was unquestionably part of the furniture of their existence.

On her way to the bedroom to change she had called the
front desk of her brigade and had given instructions that
Isabelle, David, and Momo were to join her at the crime
scene. She had stared unseeing into her closet and had finally mechanically chosen a beige linen summer suit. Even

though it was by Christophe Josse and had been the pride of her summer wardrobe the year before, it was now relegated to the role of a work outfit. Behind her Alexandre had stared moodily out of the bedroom window, brooding.

"I feel guilty for having had mixed feelings for Gautier," he had said. "He was a brilliant critic but had a decided haughty streak. Even his rave reviews always had an unpleasant twist to them. I think he made up for it with that blog of his. He spent more time on that than writing for his paper. Somehow he must have felt that those silly videos made him more human."

"You don't think he was just in love with his own image, even if it was blurred out?" Capucine asked as she clipped her Sig Sauer into the back of her pants.

"Possibly. It was a bone of contention with his paper. His blog had a huge following and they felt it pulled readers away. I guess that's not going to be a problem anymore. Merde, I'll miss him, but there are going to be a lot of chefs in town who will breathe a sigh of relief tomorrow morning."

"What about Béatrice Mesnagier?" Capucine asked. "What do you know about her?"

"Her name's not really Mesnagier. She's the only child of Paul Renaud, the owner of that huge drinks business. They've now bought out so much of their competition that they must be the second or third largest producer of alcoholic beverages in the world. A real empire. The story has it that she wants nothing to do with the family and opened her restaurant under the name Mesnagier with money she borrowed from a bank."

"The name sounds medieval."

"It's intended as a joke. A double joke, actually. *Le Mesnagier de Paris—The Paris Housewife*—is one of the first cookbooks ever published. In thirteen ninety-three, if memory serves, supposedly by some bourgeois type hoping to inspire his wife. Renaud might have chosen the name to let her father know that as far as she was concerned, tying her apron strings to a stove was preferable to becoming an executive in the family business. Also the real author of the book was the famous Taillevent."

"Like the restaurant?" Capucine asked.

"Exactly. Since Taillevent is supposed to be the best restaurant in the world, I suspect La Béatrice is hinting that she's aiming at taking their place."

"The things you know. So she's an heir to the Pastis Renaud fortune? And with all those millions she spends her evenings sweating in a kitchen? Well, well, well."

"Don't be so snide, my dear. I seem to recall you infuriating your parents by joining the police just so you could get your hands deep into the nitty-gritty. In her case it wasn't the police, it was the rough-and-tumble of the professional kitchen."

Capucine had pursed her lips in a theatrical pout.

"Good for her, then," she had said. "Can she cook?"

"Can she cook? Very definitely. When she first opened the restaurant, she stuck to a menu based on the dishes of her childhood in the Midi. At her opening I recall starting with a *fougasse* stuffed with a complicated tapenade and then a main dish of oxtail with foie gras. A skilled twist on traditional recipes. Now that her commercial success is assured, her cuisine is becoming more sophisticated and she's edging into the world of genuine haute cuisine. She's definitely someone to keep an eye on."

CHAPTER 3

The three *brigadiers* continued to stare at the black computer screen until Capucine picked up the palmsized camcorder splotched with black fingerprint powder and unplugged it from her computer. She leaned back, producing an outraged squeal from the swivel of the ancient government-issue office chair, and put her legs up on the desk, a gesture that invariably produced an admiring look from Isabelle and a knowledgeable comment about her shoes from David. But this time only Momo spoke.

"Jeez, *Commissaire*, that was the first time I'd ever seen a snuff film. Can't say I want to see another one."

"Momo," Isabelle said testily. "That's not what snuff films are. Snuff films are the worst possible manifestation of female oppression. There's humiliating sex, and at the end—" She stopped short as the three other detectives exploded into laughter.

"All right, *Brigadier-Chef*," Capucine said with a smile. "Walk us through what we have here."

Isabelle read stiffly from her notebook in the litany of police officialese. "Du Fesnay, Gautier, journalist, unmarried, residing at thirty-two rue Cardinet in the Seventeenth Arrondissement, found apparently murdered in a restaurant by the name of Chez Béatrice in the Seventh Arrondissement. The identification of the body is from the victim's identity papers and has been confirmed by *Commissaire* Le Tellier, who was acquainted with him.

"The INPS forensics expert on the scene, *Ajudant* Dechery, believes that the death was due either to a nerve poison or curare since (a) there is a small puncture wound just under the victim's right ear and (b) the victim fell into his plate of food, which was very liquid and, judging from the amount of said food visible inside his nostrils and throat, he continued to breath even though he had collapsed and apparently was unable to move. It is highly likely that the victim died by drowning in the sauce and not from the poison. Such acute muscular failure is typically associated with nerve gases and curare."

Isabelle looked up and said in her normal voice, "Of course, we won't know fuck all until they do the autopsy and all their cultures and whatever else it is they do, but Dechery seemed pretty sure that someone had walked by and either stabbed him or shot him with something that contained a very potent muscle relaxant."

"Time of death?" Capucine asked.

"A few minutes after nine. We have that from the time-clock on the video and the fact that pretty much everyone in the restaurant saw him keel over just after nine. Of course only two people actually admit they saw it happen."

"Actually," Capucine said, wagging a size-six foot comfortably shod in Zanotti flats, thanking her guardian angel for the current trend away from high heels, "I had a word with Ajudant Dechery as they wheeled the body out. He thinks he might be seeing a glimmer of something metallic about half an inch inside the wound. He had no idea what it might be, but certainly not a bullet from a gun."

"Air-gun pellet?" David asked.

"Yes, of course, that's what it could be," Capucine said.

"I hadn't thought of that. Someone could have shot him in the neck as they walked by."

"This case is going to be a no-brainer," Isabelle said. "It had to be someone who was either eating there or was working as waitstaff. No one could have rushed in off the street, and the cooks don't go wandering around the restaurant, right?"

"Except for the chef," Capucine said. "It would have been normal for her to make a little cameo appearance. My husband tells me she loves to press the flesh in the front of the house."

"She did," David said. "But that was half an hour before our stiff keeled over. One of the waiters told me. Those nerve things are supposed to be very fast acting. Does that mean she's off the hook, *Commissaire*?"

"No, not really," Capucine said. "You know how unreliable crowd testimonies are. She could easily have come out again. We'll need to go into that very carefully."

Isabelle snapped through the pages of her notebook noisily. "There were exactly ninety-two people—plus the chef makes ninety-three—who were either customers or worked in the front of the house. One of them has to be the killer. So the perp's name is already right here in my little book. This is an all-time first!"

"Oh, goody," David said. "A locked-room mystery. I've always wanted to work on one of those."

Isabelle glared at him.

"Make that ninety-one people," Momo said with his ponderous logic. "The chef is the boss's husband's pal, and the boss is close buds with one of the customers."

"Let's stick with ninety-three," Capucine said. "Even if Béatrice Renaud were Alexandre's buddy, which I don't really think is the case, she very definitely could still be a suspect. And I was as amazed as anyone else to run into Cécile de Rougemont. It's true she's a very close friend, but that certainly doesn't mean she won't be investigated as thoroughly as anyone else."

Ever so slightly, the three *brigadiers* pursed their lips, moved their eyebrows together, and nodded fractionally in a highly attenuated version of the Gallic expression of ironic incredulity.

"How many of the people in the dining room did you three talk to?" Capucine asked.

Isabelle consulted her notebook. "We had a quick word with all twenty-one of the waitstaff and eleven of the customers. We concentrated on the ones sitting nearest the victim's table, like you said."

"And?"

"And same as always, big nothing. None of the customers saw anything, except two women who saw Fesnay fall over. One of them wanted to get up to help him, but her husband stopped her. And the waiters did what you'd expect them to do; they got that solemn priestly look, like what was going on at their tables was as secret as confession in church."

"But you got their names and addresses and told them not to leave Paris without permission?"

"Of course," Isabelle said. "We even double-checked their identity papers to make sure no one was fibbing. So what do we do now, *Commissaire*?"

"Starting first thing in the morning, you're going to haul each one of the ninety-three down here to the brigade and interview them formally. They're going to be different animals outside of their comfort zone. Feel free to get tough. Use the usual tricks. You know, tell them that someone at the next table swears he saw them get up just before the murder. Scare them. When they get really desperate to get out of the interview room, they'll spill whatever it is they might actually have seen.

"Then start going through their backgrounds. See if you can find anyone who has even the remotest connection with the victim. Same hometown, worked in the same company, you know the drill. If the murderer really is one of the people in the room, we're going to need to find a motive."

"And what do you want us to start doing in the fall?" Isabelle asked ironically.

"Fair enough," Capucine said. "It *is* a lot of work for you three. How many backups do you need?"

"As many as I can get," Isabelle said with a grin.

Capucine shuffled through her duty roster file. "I think I can give you five *brigadiers* for a week. That should give you a start. We'll figure it out from there. By the way, I had already planned a lunch with Madame de Rougemont tomorrow, but I still want one of you three to interview her down here just like the others. What are you so happy about, Isabelle?"

"This case is a slam dunk. I mean, shit, how many times are we absolutely certain we have the perp's name down on a piece of paper on day one? All we have to do is slog through the grunt work and we'll have the guy in cuffs in no time at all."

"Let's hope it's that simple. It might not be. I've been ordered to see the *juge d'instruction* in charge of the case tomorrow."

"Big deal. Aren't those guys just a formality?" David asked.

"Normally they are. But I'm sure you remember the most excellent *Juge d'Instruction* de La Martinière?"

"August-Marie Parmentier de La Martinière?" Isabelle asked. "How could I forget that pompous little faggot? The sun just went out of my life. *Merde,* it makes you want to quit the force."

"Thinking about becoming a nun again, Isabelle?" David asked.

With blinding speed Isabelle landed a short right jab on David's upper arm. The pain was enough to take his breath away.

CHAPTER 4

At lunchtime, La Dacha—a caviar bar smack in the middle of Paris's Golden Triangle, home to the cream of its business world—was the canteen for a select handful of investment banks, management consulting firms, and advertising agencies, the senor staffs of which felt that their expense accounts fully entitled them to lunches as exorbitant as the portions were small. In the evening the fauna expanded to include talking heads from TV news shows and senior officials from government ministries. Cécile de Rougemont was a frequent participant at both servings.

From early childhood Capucine and Cécile had been best friends, with that white-hot intensity that men invariably mistook for sexual glue. Their friendship had survived the cruel watershed when intimacy was transferred to the opposite sex and had even grown as they evolved into womanhood.

As Capucine entered, Cécile rose from the miniscule table to greet her. The two women stared deeply into each other's eyes, embraced, kissed on both cheeks.

"I loved seeing you at work last night. Right out of a movie. So tough, so completely in charge, so ordering people right and left!" Both women laughed. "All I get to do,"

Cécile continued, "is humbly offer my little opinions to my clients."

"Humble. Right. You charge three thousand euros a day and you order your associates around like slaves. If I took that tone with my *brigadiers,* they'd probably shoot me in the leg." Cécile was an associate partner—one small step away from becoming a full partner—at the most prestigious of management consulting firms, Beisdean and Company, a firm so elite that knowing the correct pronunciation—BASE-tchan—separated the winners from the losers throughout the Western business world.

A waiter in a severely starched formal white mess jacket cut off at the waist, trimmed with shiny brass buttons and gold brocade epaulets, came up with the menus. The intended effect was to vaguely evoke Czarist Russia. The menus were entirely superfluous. Both Cécile and Capucine had known the contents by heart for years.

Cécile smiled warmly at the waiter. "Hervé, just bring us a quarter of vodka and give us some time to sort ourselves out."

The vodka came promptly: a small quarter-liter decanter frozen into a solid block of ice in a silver-plated cooler. The cooler has been dipped briefly in very hot water so that the block of ice would come free when the decanter was lifted. The waiter filled two dollhouse-sized crystal stemmed glasses. The liquid was thick and oily from being so close to its freezing point.

Both women raised their glasses and giggled happily. Capucine took a sip. The vodka was so cold, it had no taste at all, just a numbing feeling on the tongue. But once in her stomach it spread with an acid flame that melted the edge of her perpetual angst. Her shoulders relaxed a half a notch. She grabbed Cécile's hand.

"It always does me such a world of good to see you."

Cécile put her other hand on top of Capucine's and squeezed her reply with an earnest smile. Then she broke the moment by tapping the back of Capucine's hand impatiently with her index finger.

"So. Tell me, whatever happened yesterday? What did that poor man die of? Food poisoning? And who was it? Anyone we know of?"

Capucine's answer was delayed by the return of the waiter, who announced that the restaurant had just received a good quantity of beluga caviar that was of a far better quality than he had seen in months. Capucine was impressed. Beluga, the largest grained of the three caviars, was now on the endangered species list and illegal to serve. The fact that the waiter, who knew full well that Capucine was a *commissaire* in the *Police Judiciaire*, felt not the slightest qualm in touting it spoke volumes about the insouciance of an establishment that catered to the upper echelons of politics and commerce.

"Voilà," said Cécile. "We'll each have fifty grams of your beluga with a mountain of toast and worry about the rest later." She was transparently eager for the waiter to leave.

"Come on, *ma belle*, you're tormenting me by not telling what happened last night."

"It was Gautier du Fesnay. You know, the restaurant reviewer for *Le Figaro*."

"You mean the one with the blog that has all those prissy videos of him eating with his face fuzzed out? Who on earth would want to kill that bumptious little man?"

"That's the sort of thing they pay me to find out. Someone seems to have injected him with some form of nerve drug, and he fell over and drowned in his dish of lobster ravioles floating in a nice thick tandoori sauce."

"I had that myself. It was outstanding. Good Lord, the poor man actually drowned in his dinner?" As Cécile thought about it, her face became rigid and she began to tremble. Finally, she could contain herself no longer and erupted in giggles.

"I know it's terrible, and he must have died horribly, but what a perfectly appropriate death for that catty little snob."

Capucine was caught by the mood and knew she was fighting a losing battle with suppressing her own giggling fit. In desperation she took a deep swig of vodka, choked, coughed, and finally broke free from her attack of *fou rire*.

Both women patted the tears out of the corners of their eyes with napkins, careful not to spoil their makeup.

"What was he injected with that killed him so quickly?" Cécile asked.

"The forensics people think it might have been some sort of nerve poison, curare or one of the military versions. The thinking is that it was probably an air-gun pellet tipped with curare. One of my detectives is hoping it was done with a jungle blowgun." Capucine laughed, expecting Cécile to join in.

Cécile looked at her expressionlessly.

"Blowguns don't shoot metallic projectiles," Cécile said with the heavy gravitas of a Beisdean consultant. "They shoot darts made from the stems of the *inayuga* palm, which grows in certain parts of the Amazon rain forest. The stems soak up the curare mixture, which is then dried. The darts remain effective for years."

"And you know this from your *Beisdean Little Consultant's Handbook,* of which you read a few pages every night before bed even if you're a bit tipsy?"

Cécile smiled tolerantly. "No. Oddly enough, I was at a reception last week at the Maison de l'Amérique Latine—you know, that old *hôtel particulier* in the Faubourg Saint-Germain—for some fund or other that protects Amerindians. There was an exhibit of Brazilian Indian hunting weapons with lots of blowguns and darts and bows and arrows and stuff like that. A man from the embassy gave a little lecture about the exhibit."

"Interesting?"

"*Au contraire.* In fact, it was so boring that some of the guests got a little out of hand. A few golden youths who were pretty drunk to begin with decided that it would be great fun to wander off and blow darts into a portrait of the president of the republic that had just been unveiled in the reception room."

"Really?"

"Actually, it's a lot harder to shoot those things than you'd think. I must have smoked too much in my teens."

"You shot darts into the president's portrait? I don't believe it!" Capucine shrieked.

"Certainly not! Whatever gave you that idea?"

"And were there any darts tipped with curare?"

"That's what made me think of the reception. As it turned out, a few of them actually were, even though most weren't. The exhibited items were on pegs on a decorated board. The darts were in little quivers next to gourds used for the poison. But some of them were behind glass in a kind of picture frame thingy to show how the tips were all dark black after they'd been soaked in the curare solution. A couple of the kids managed to pry off the back of the case and grab a handful of poisoned darts. The guy from the embassy was furious and snatched them all back, but I saw he missed the three that had already been shot into the portrait."

"Do you have any idea what happened to them?"

"Nope. The mood of the party had turned sour, so I left right after the incident."

"I'm going to have to look into that. I think I might just drop by the Brazilian embassy tomorrow."

The waiter came up, removed the empty carafe of vodka, and asked them if they wanted anything else. They both opted for smoked salmon on blinis topped with dollops of crème fraîche and a half bottle of Chablis.

Capucine was flooded by a wave of embarrassment. She masked it by staring, apparently entranced, at the woman in the window of the restaurant slicing their salmon with a two-foot-long knife no wider than a wooden pencil. With consummate skill she produced oily pink strips so thin they were translucent. There were questions Capucine needed to ask. Questions that would have been asked routinely in a police interview but that somehow seemed out of place for a friend—even a very close friend.

"I know it's none of my business, but we'll need it for the file. Who is this Honorine Lecanu you were having dinner with last night?"

For half a beat Cécile seemed put out. Then, retreating into the bastion of her adamantine self-confidence, she smiled.

"Honorine is one of my associates. An exceptional young woman. One of the brightest the firm has ever recruited."

There was something in the tone that wasn't quite right.

"And I suppose you were taking her for an expensive night out as a reward for some job well done? I'm going to start doing that with my *brigadiers* every time they solve a case. I wonder if the *Police Judiciaire* will spring for it."

"It wasn't quite that. Honorine and I are . . . well . . . we're having a . . . I guess you'd call it a liaison."

"What on earth do you mean?"

"Oh, Capucine, how can you be so dense? You know it hasn't been going all that well with Théophile. We've talked about that, right? Well, I'm having a fling with Honorine to unload the tension. And just between you and me, I'm finding her a great deal more fulfilling than Théophile."

Capucine was staggered, utterly nonplussed. She had been best friends with Cécile since they were four years old at *école maternelle*. How was it possible she didn't have the first clue about her sexual orientation?

"So what does this mean?" Capucine stammered. "Are you going to divorce Théophile?"

"Don't be silly. You can be such a little girl at times. It means that my life is very complicated right now. I'm at a turning point in my career. I'm at a turning point in my marriage. Théophile is just a big fat lump who's more interested in his wine tastings and his *cave* than anything going on with me. And so I've found a friend. We do things that drain out my tension and leave me fit and productive. It's my way of forging on. Surely you can understand that."

Capucine stared at her, mute.

"Look," Cécile said. "This is nothing. It's like smoking a cigarette or having a drink, nothing more. Don't try to turn it into a big deal. I have to get back to the office. We'll talk soon and I'll fill you in on all the fun details."

Cécile stood up, making the classic writing in the air sign of requesting the check, except that this time it meant that it was to be added to her running tab, and dashed out of the restaurant.

Capucine didn't see it at all. She wasn't revolted. She was just thunderstruck. When her own life became impossible, she automatically turned to Alexandre. And sleeping with a woman! She saw herself as a feminist. Of course she did. Hadn't she studied all the greats: Simone de Beauvoir, Hélène Cixous, Luce Irigaray? Hadn't she put herself to sleep the night before reading Elisabeth Badinter's *Le Conflit?* But there was a vast difference between an intellectual exercise and the necessity of having a man as the mainstay to your life. Anything other than that was as incomprehensible as viewing tripe as a great delicacy. Wasn't it?

Capucine sat, staring, mesmerized by the woman untiringly slicing smoked salmon, until with a jerk she realized she was far more than her usual fifteen minutes late for her appointment with the *juge d'instruction*. It wasn't really important, she told herself, but still, she hated being rude to anyone.

CHAPTER 5

As her brand-new Renault Twingo purred its way across Paris, Capucine thought of the president's portrait defaced by poisoned blowgun darts. She herself was far from a fan of the man. She despised his philistinism—he had publicly announced that reading Madame de Lafayette's *La Princesse de Clèves* was a waste of time—his indifference to gastronomy—an endomorphic, fanatic runner, he took no pleasure at all in restaurants—and, most of all, his trophy wife—a former model whose naked breasts had adorned the popular press for months after their wedding until everyone got tired of the little things.

But one thing about the president pleased her enormously: his recent decision to phase out the function of *juge d'instruction* as part of his overhaul of the French judicial system, which he had labeled archaic and no longer viable in modern society.

From the police's point of view, the *juges d'instruction* were a bane. Not only were they nominally in charge of most investigations, they had a monopoly of control over surveillances, wiretapping, and arrests. It was true that most of the juges had the good sense to recognize their real utility was to ensure that the police assembled all the legal niceties that would guarantee the public prosecutor a conviction, but a small handful seemed to genuinely believe they were running the show.

For Capucine, the most egregious of the latter group was *Juge d'Instruction* August-Marie Parmentier de La Martinière, whose ambition was as boundless as his inhumanity. The police truism was that the only good juges were the ones who thought like flics; the bad ones thought like judges. Martinière thought only of himself.

Capucine trotted a little breathlessly into Martinière's office and apologized profusely for her lateness. His face black with rage, he scowled at his watch and pointed a long bony index finger at a chair, indicating she should sit. Junior in the juges' hierarchy, Martinière had been allocated only a closet-sized office. From her last visit Capucine remembered the excessively ornate Empire desk that took up most of the floor space. Since then Martinière seemed to have transformed the room into a perfect Directoire period piece. Ponderous gilt framed portraits leaned threateningly from the wall at dangerous angles. Modern technology had been purged. The large surface of the desk was conspicuously devoid of a computer monitor and the phone had been banished to a tiny table at some remove from the desk, giving the impression it was very rarely used.

The overall effect was that Martinière hankered to be back in the era of Fouché's notorious police during the Napoleonic reign, when a handful of effete aristocrats ruled over armies of police thugs who accumulated extensive files of purloined letters, spied by insinuating themselves into households as servants, and resolved cases with fists and truncheons in dark alleys.

Wordlessly, relishing the tension he was creating with his silence, Martinière lifted the gold-tooled top of an antique leather-covered blotter with the delighted anticipatory disgust of a small boy lifting a rock in the hopes that something truly awful will come slithering out. He produced a slim file, sheathed in flimsy blue-dun paper, and placed it delicately on his knee. Reaching into his jacket pocket, he extracted a gold fountain pen and used it to tap the top of the file.

"This is a very valuable case. Very valuable indeed. A well-known journalist has been found dead in the restaurant of an heiress to one of the most important fortunes in France. The press will pay a great deal of attention." His tight, close-lipped smile curved into an upward U in satisfaction.

"I'm planning on a rapid arrest, next Friday at the latest, with daily press bulletins this week to announce my progress. In the following week I shall be unstinting in giving interviews about the success of my methodology.

"I know that you agree with me that a rapid arrest is mandatory and eminently feasible. There are only ninety-three possible suspects. I want you and your policemen to screen them all and bring me a list of those who could have had any sort of motive. You are to spare no efforts. If you think wiretaps or close surveillance is indicated, I will approve those immediately." He glanced at Capucine to verify she was following.

"Based on your screening I will convoke the most suspicious individuals and interview them here. I will require your preliminary results so I can begin my interviews in the next two or three days. Is that perfectly clear? I'm confident I will have the culprit identified by the end of the week." He again leaned forward to peer at Capucine, confirming that she had understood.

"*Commissaire*, are you sure you've assigned enough staff to get the work done in the requisite time frame?" His tone was that of a governess questioning the study habits of a wayward young ward.

"Monsieur le juge, I have a total of eight *brigadiers* on the case. I'm planning on having the entire list interviewed by the end of the week."

Martinière sat up straight in his chair and pointed his pen at her as if it was a weapon. "*Attention, Commissaire!* The police are not to interview the suspects, only check their backgrounds. I will interview them myself. This case is too important to be handled otherwise. I'm absolutely determined to make an arrest by the end of the week. This case is providential, both highly visible and rudimentarily straightforward. It's precisely what I need to demonstrate the viability of the institution of the juges d'instruction."

Capucine was incredulous. "Am I correct in understanding that you don't want us to contact any of the possible suspects?"

"*Commissaire,* it's not a question of 'don't want.' I absolutely forbid it. I will do the interviewing. Suspects that have already been interviewed by heavy-handed policemen are of no use to me. They already know all the ins and outs of the case and have prepared their answers. It is imperative I see them first. Have I made that perfectly clear?"

"And what do you expect the police to do, monsieur le juge?"

"Do what the police are intended to do, I suppose. Look into people's bank accounts. Gossip with concierges. That sort of thing." He paused, clearly at a loss for what else the police might be useful for. His face brightened. He'd had a brain wave. "Oh yes, of course, fingerprints. Definitely fingerprints. And don't forget the DNA. We must be up to date. Scrape everything for DNA. It can be very useful evidence. There you are. Create dossiers. Be meticulous. Courts require thick dossiers filled with accurate information. It facilitates the conviction. Is that clear?"

It was the second time that afternoon that Capucine was completely at a loss for words.

CHAPTER 6

The next morning Capucine woke in a bad mood. Over coffee she traced her mood to the fact that, despite herself, she was kowtowing to the juge's strictures. Visiting the Brazilian embassy was infuriatingly within the dictates he had laid down.

Fortunately, as she slid the diminutive Twingo into the middle of a diplomats-only no parking zone in front of the embassy, the imposing, solemn façade of the former mansion of the Schneider family of steel magnates restored her natural equanimity.

The arrival of Wilson de Mello, the embassy's cultural attaché, lit up the gloomy mahogany paneling of the reception room like a Carioca sunrise. As he caught sight of Capucine, he was clearly held in the grips of two conflicting emotions. One she was used to, the exaggerated attention her physiognomy seemed to provoke almost invariably in members of the opposite sex. The other took her a moment to identify. It was fear, and it won out hands down over the first.

Mello was such a perfect caricature of a rich Ipanema Beach playboy that it was obvious he had secured his plum posting by virtue of his family's position. It was easy to imagine him wearing bathing trunks under his well-tailored summer suit, ready for the surf and a *chope* with the *garotas* from the beach afterward. Capucine hoped that the vista of the gray Seine flowing sluggishly on the other side of the cours Albert Premier didn't make him too homesick.

With obvious trepidation, he led Capucine into a reception room filled with Brazilian Baroque antique furniture in lustrous jacaranda and with courtly grace invited her to sit across from him at a very elegant octagonal table. Capucine had to admit that even by French standards his manners were perfect.

"*Senhor* de Mello," Capucine said, "I've come to talk to you about curare and blowgun darts."

"I was afraid that was what it was about, *Madame le Commissaire*. The incident was as inexcusable as it was deplorable, and the embassy extends its most profound and humble apologies. We profoundly hope the French government understands no affront was intended. Quite the contrary."

"You must be talking about those kids blowing darts into the portrait of the president. I heard about that, but that's not what I've come to talk about. As long as the darts weren't going into the president himself, it's hardly a matter for the police. In fact," Capucine said with a smile, "quite a few people would have been a lot happier if the darts *had* wound up in the president's head."

Mello was transformed. He beamed almost from ear to ear. "What a relief. In my country the incident would have been considered treasonous or possibly even some form of lèse-majesté. The ambassador would probably have been recalled. My career would have been over." He leaned over the table and took Capucine's hand with sensual delicacy. "So how can I help you, dear madame? When my secretary told me a *commissaire* of the *Police Judiciaire* wanted to see me, I imagined a big, fat old man with a pipe."

"The look may have changed, senhor, but *Commissaire* Maigret is still our role model. I'm here because we have a case that may involve curare, and I thought you might be able to tell me something about it," she said, beaming her most fetching smile while gently retrieving her hand.

"In that case," Mello said, "you must come up to my office." He winked with a charming parody of a leer. "I don't have any etchings, but I do have all sorts of intriguing Indian artifacts."

Mello's office could equally well have belonged to a museum curator or an editor of a fashion magazine. Almost every inch of wall space held a brightly colored tropical painting and even more were stacked upright in the corners. Bookcases were jammed with multiple copies of cocktail-table books about Brazil, obviously to be used as gifts. The sofa and chairs were heaped with Carnival masks and costumes. One sprawling leather chair, which Capucine recognized as Sergio Rodrigues's famous *Poltrona Mole*, was piled high with Indian handiwork: clothing, jewelry, gourds. On top of the pile, a collection of long bows, eight-foot arrows, and blowguns was poised precariously.

"First things first. We need a *cafezinho* after all that emotion."

"Thank you, but no," Capucine said. "I already had two coffees after lunch."

The attaché laughed his charming, boyish laugh. "*Pas question,*" he said with a perfect Parisian inflection. "The ambassador would never forgive me if I let you leave the embassy without tasting our coffee, particularly now that he is secure in his job once again."

He picked up the phone and spoke briefly. After an impossibly short pause, a servant in a high-collared, starched white jacket arrived with a small silver tray holding two demitasse cups, a silver coffee pitcher, and a small silver sugar bowl. The servant handed Capucine a cup and saucer, proffered the sugar bowl, then poured in the coffee. When it was the attaché's turn, he filled his cup almost half full of sugar, leaving little room for the coffee. Mello stirred the sugary sludge vigorously and then downed the contents in one go. Capucine imitated his gesture. It was several times stronger than even the most powerful French *express,* but rounder in the mouth and with none of the sharp bite. The attaché had been right. That was something not to have been missed.

"Tell me about the reception," Capucine asked.

"It was part of a year-long program we sponsor to raise money for a fund that protects Brazilian Amerindians. The focus is on their art. This is just some of the collection," he said, waving his hand vaguely around the chaos of his office. "The exhibits include objects from prehistoric times to the present. You know, masks, feather finery, jewelry, weapons, statuettes, pottery, musical instruments, that sort of thing." He smiled seductively at her. "But it's the curare darts you're interested in."

Capucine nodded.

"Well then, let me show you." He rooted around in the pile on his beautiful leather chair and produced a glass-fronted wooden case about three feet by two, flat as a picture frame, exhibiting about fifty darts in different stages of manufacture. At the beginning of the series the sticks were rough and irregular, but the last half dozen stood stiff and straight, as if they had come off a Bavarian assembly line.

"It's amazing the skill that goes into making these things. These particular darts are made from the central stalk of the leaves of a palm we call the *inayuga* and are smoothed and sharpened with piranha teeth, then hardened over a fire. Of course, each tribe has its own method. They use all sorts of plants. Some tribes even make the darts from rolled-up leaves. And every tribe uses a different kind of curare. Apparently, you can make the stuff from over seventy-five different plants."

"And when does the curare go on the dart?"

The attaché rooted around in the jumble on the chair and produced an eight-inch quiver holding thirty or so darts. A blackened half jaw with long, thin razor-like teeth—certainly a piranha's—and a six-inch orange gourd with a fibrous stopper dangled on thongs attached to the quiver.

"The piranha jaw is for a last-minute sharpening of the dart. The curare is kept in a gourd like this. The hunter dips his dart in there, twirls it around, and he's good to go. This is what they wind up looking like."

He produced another display case. One end of the back had been pulled from the frame. The tips of the darts were jet black. It was apparent that three were missing from the side of the case that had been pried open.

"The missing ones were shot into the president's portrait?"

"Yes, I was mortified. Two waiters and I escorted the miscreants to the door. I rather lost my temper, I'm afraid."

"And when you got back, you recovered the darts?"

"I pulled seven darts out of the portrait. All of them were plain tipped and had been taken from the quiver. But the three curare darts were no longer there. The worst part is that they would still be quite lethal, even if the curare had been applied long ago." He was visibly abashed.

"Oh," Capucine said tolerantly. "You know how exuberant the jeunesse dorée can be."

Mello smiled gratefully, entirely oblivious to the reference to his own persona.

"Senhor de Mello, can I ask you for one more favor? Would you happen to have a list of the guests at the reception?"

"Of course, chère madame. The hostess made a check mark for the people who turned up. If they brought a guest, she made a note of the name." Mello rooted around in the pile on his desk and produced a large folio-size piece of paper, which he folded, put in a large white envelope embossed with the seal and address of the embassy, and handed to her.

"Senhor Mello, I think you just may have made my life a whole lot easier. I know I'm imposing, but do you think I could possibly borrow your display of darts for a week or ten days?"

"By all means. And when you're done with it, I'd be delighted to come to your office to pick it up and, if you're kind enough to allow me, to take you to lunch. I know a Brazilian restaurant that makes caipirinhas almost as good as the ones in Rio."

"What a charming idea. It would be a perfect occasion for my husband to meet you. He's a food critic and particularly adores Brazilian food. I'm sure you'd love each other."

The attaché's smile remained glowingly effusive. It would have taken the most observant eye to notice it had become just ever so slightly strained.

CHAPTER 7

Capucine hadn't set foot in Le Florian since she was ten. Of course, as it was located on the Champs-Elysées, she had passed it countless times, each time invaded by the damp aura of haunted-house gloom. As a child, her parents would take her there for special occasions. She would sit, itching in a stiff smocked frock that had been painstakingly hand pleated by her mother's seamstress, struggling to swallow the over-seasoned adult food, listening to her parents talk over her head, ignoring her completely save for the one or two times they remembered her presence and made a production of how lucky she was to be sitting outside in the glassed-in terrace, reserved for those known to the management, and not inside in the gloomy gilt purgatory, where the *ploucs* were consigned. Even now, Le Florian represented the absolute epitome of the bourgeois life she had struggled so hard to reject.

"My editor cajoled me into this," Alexandre said testily. "After this horrid place had sat quietly for a hundred years, like a little old spinster too well born to talk to anyone, one of the trendsetting chains finally bought it, turned the upstairs floors into a froufrou hotel, and decided the restaurant was going to be a fashionable hot spot. So naturally we have to review the bloody thing. Thank God you came. I couldn't have faced another meal here by myself."

Alexandre closed his leather menu with an angry whip-crack snap. "I know the damn thing by heart. This is my third time. Their chain's marketing department has taken over from the chef. They think it's an act of genius to hark back to the days when the Champs-Elysées was the center of the French film industry, and have rebaptized their tired old dishes with the names of movie stars."

He opened his menu again and read to Capucine.

"Get this. 'Risotto Robert Hossein, fried whiting Colbert, sea bream Charles Aznavour.' Can you imagine less appropriate eponyms? One was Persian, not Italian, and the other two lived most of their lives in exile far from the sea. You order for me. I can't go through with it a third time."

Hell had no fury like Alexandre's when he had decided he didn't like a restaurant.

A waiter came up and was persuaded to bring a double of single-malt whiskey for Alexandre and a Lillet Blanc for Capucine.

"And no ice, mind you!" Alexandre said sharply to the departing waiter. "They've been deformed by the American trade." Alexandre shook his head in existential gloom.

"Dear Alexandre isn't being fed up to his usual standard. My poor sweetie."

"Nothing is more pathetic than the spectacle of a once noble institution attempting to save itself by bilking the press."

"A sentiment I share wholeheartedly." Capucine paused, chewing her lower lip. "I had exactly the same experience with my juge. For the life of me, I can't understand why these lost causes have such confidence in the press. I mean, here you are, detesting this place, and yet they're pleased as punch to keep you coming back again and again for more. And my dear little juge seems to be utterly indifferent to the risk of opening up his *Figaro* one morning and reading that he has been attacked for obstruction of justice."

The drinks arrived and Alexandre downed his in one go. Its effect on his humor was instantaneous.

"Ah," he said. "There's the rub. This restaurant knows how to use the media, but your juge doesn't. There's no such thing as bad press for a restaurant. What kills them is being forgotten. Your juge is in a much more vulnerable position. If we ran a story tomorrow with a head along the lines of MURDER OF A FAMOUS JOURNALIST GOES UNSOLVED BECAUSE OF A MEDDLING JUGE D'INSTRUCTION, that would be all the president needed to consign the function to the oubliettes. In fact, just say the word. I know exactly who to tip off at the paper."

"I'm sorely tempted," Capucine said with a smile. "I have no idea how to handle the situation. But at least I have my hands full for the next few days, even without interviewing suspects."

She was prevented from elaborating by the arrival of the food.

The waiter presented the dishes with almost comic pomposity. "Poularde de Bresse truffé Brigitte Bardot," he intoned as he tendered Capucine her roast chicken. "Tournedos François Truffaut," he announced over Alexandre's beef fillet.

Alexandre made an exploratory incision with his knife. "François Truffaut *mon cul,*" he said with unusual vulgarity. "This is a plain old tournedos Rossini. A fillet topped with a slab of foie gras and capped with a slice of truffle. Still, it's perfectly cooked and the sauce is excellent."

He speared a piece of Capucine's chicken. "This isn't bad, either. It was a mistake bringing you along. The radiance of your pulchritude has charmed me into an eleventh-hour reprieve for this loathsome place. Quick, distract me with your brilliant progress on the case before I change my mind about this chamber of horrors."

"The preliminary report from forensics came in yester-day morning. For openers there were no clues of any kind. No fingerprints, no floating particles of dandruff, no stray threads of alpaca that comes only from a specific mountain-top in the Andes. The thing that killed Gautier was a plain-vanilla one-seventy-seven caliber air-gun pellet, just under his right ear. A perfectly ordinary hollow-point pellet, ex-cept that the hollow had been packed with a compound that was largely curare paste."

"Largely? And the stuff that wasn't curare?"

Capucine sat up straight and leaned over the table. "That's the interesting part. They were shavings of some sort of plant."

"And it's these tiny particles of this unknown plant that reveal the murderer to Madame Maigret, *n'est-ce pas?*"

"Don't be so snide. It's the first thing we have that might be a lead. As it happened, I had lunch with Cécile yester-day, who was very knowledgeable about blowguns and curare darts. You know how she can get. She said the darts were usually made from some tree called an inayuga that grows in the middle of the Amazon jungle. She learned all this at a reception last week given by the Brazilian em-bassy in aid of Amerindians. There was an exhibition of artifacts. Some of the guests got out of hand and started blowing curare darts at a portrait of the president—"

Alexandre guffawed. "I hope that was practice for the real thing!"

"Pay attention. This is tricky stuff for a dipsomaniac old codger like you. So I immediately bounced this off forensics, who called the *Muséum National d'Histoire Na-turelle*, who not only knew what an inayuga was but actu-ally had a specimen of the tree in question growing in their greenhouse near Rambouillet. And—ta-dah!—the hot news is that it took them no time at all to determine that the veg-etable powder in the pellet was from that very species of tree."

Alexandre finished the last bite of tournedos and made a pantomime of a dullard drawing a conclusion. "And the supposition is that the someone nicked the darts from the reception, shaved the tips, packed the dust into the tip of a dumdum air-gun pellet, and shot poor old Gautier in the neck with it. Is that the idea?"

"Right on, Sherlock. But spare me your raised eyebrow. Where else would the killer have obtained curare? You don't expect me to traipse around Paris, looking for some aboriginal character in tribal beads with a ring in his nose and dessert plates in his earlobes, do you?"

Alexandre raised his hands in mock surrender.

"So I nipped around to the Brazilian embassy this morning and met a bronzed young Greek god making a terrestrial appearance as a cultural attaché. It seems that, as expected, the curare darts in the president's portrait had vanished. He explained all the ins and outs of blowguns and curare-tipped darts. There are as many plants used for the darts as there are different formulas for the poison, so we may be able to get a conclusive match between the poison in the air-gun pellet and the stolen darts."

"Your *juge* is going to be so proud of you."

"Keep it up and I'm going to kick you. The good news is that the Brazilians were very careful about who they let into their reception and kept a diligent list. I got a copy and dropped it off with Isabelle this morning so she could compare it to the names of the people at the restaurant. Voilà, we may get our list of ninety-three down to one. Or two, of course, because we already know that Cécile was at both places."

Capucine was spared Alexandre's sarcastic retort by the shrill note of her cell phone. Capucine flipped it open, listened, and mouthed "Isabelle" at Alexandre. The conversation proved lengthy.

As Alexandre chose a selection of cheeses from the platter and poured the last of the bottle of Château Beychevelle into their glasses, Capucine extracted a leather Hermès notebook from her bag and scribbled energetically with a small silver pencil.

After a few minutes she snapped the phone shut and dropped it back in her bag.

"It's an embarrassment of riches. There are four names in addition to Cécile's."

"Paris may be a village, but that seems like overkill."

"And wait till you see who they are. The most surprising was Béatrice Renaud. She's the last person I would have expected."

"Not if you think about it," Alexandre said. "Even if she's distanced herself from her family, she's still a very wealthy woman, and I can easily see her feeling strongly for the oppressed Amerindians. Also, the timing of the reception probably didn't interfere with her dinner service. Most chefs are desperate to get out of their kitchens at the slightest opportunity."

"Then there was Sybille Charbonnier, you know, that sixteen-year-old, slutty actress, who was there with some sugar daddy called Guy Voisin."

Alexandre exploded in laughter.

"What's so funny?"

"Well, I'm not sure I'd call Sybille Charbonnier an actress. She never says anything in her movies. She pouts a little and then engages in sex that looks more like a cross between kung fu and professional wrestling than anything that happens in real life." He paused for a few beats with a wistful expression. "Of course, she does have absolutely perfect breasts. She puts our first lady to shame.

"And Guy Voisin is hardly a sugar daddy. Of course, he is in his sixties, but he also makes the best rosé in France, Château de la Motte. It's superbly balanced, with a delightfully pronounced note of honey, a hint of passion fruit and peach, and maybe just a slight soupçon of rose—"

"Got it. And the most amazing of all was Gaël Tanguy," concluded Capucine.

"You mean *the* Gaël Tanguy, the author who just won the Prix Goncourt for that twelve-hundred page book about the sordid dystopian end of the world in a vast mud puddle?"

"I'm virtually sure it's him. It didn't register when I saw his name on the list of customers at Chez Béatrice, but if he was also at an exclusive Brazilian embassy reception, it's bound be him."

Alexandre raised his eyebrows and pursed his lips in mock amazement.

"And the best part is that I can't even think of interviewing any of them, thanks to that infernal juge."

"*Oh, là là,*" Alexandre said. "You become such a little girl scout when you get flustered. In the first place, Béatrice Renaud is someone I've seen any number of times. An acquaintance, if you will. Make that a close acquaintance. Hell, let's just say she's a good friend. And Guy Voisin, you could definitely call him a friend. I've even spent the night at Château de la Motte a couple of times. Broken bread with him, as it were. Of course, you were a little toddler at the time, but a friend of your husband's is a friend of yours. There's no law in this country that will prevent you from paying a call on your husband's close friends, now is there?"

"Next you're going to tell me that you've spent the night at Sybille Charbonnier's and she's a wonderfully close friend too."

"Not really. But I'd be more than happy to work on that if it furthers your career. Just give me the nod."

"I won't go that far, but I do think I'll use your name when I announce to Béatrice Renaud I'm dropping by to see her."

CHAPTER 8

The night of the murder the rue de Varenne had been plugged tight with police vans and squad cars, blue lights throbbing. But in the kind early summer light the street was intimate and welcoming. Capucine bounced the nose of the Twingo up on the sidewalk at the corner, her preferred method of parking ever since she had received her license. She had been as indifferent to parking tickets as a university student as she was as a police officer.

The restaurant had also been transformed by the light of day. The dark brown awning and smoked plate-glass windows promised elegance and sophistication. When Capucine pushed open the glass door, a willowy hostess who had been staring, slack-jawed, out the window came abruptly alive, as if a switch had been toggled on an automaton. "Chef's already called twice to make sure you weren't kept waiting," she said with artificial brightness.

Béatrice Renaud hurried out to collect Capucine. She, too, was changed from the distraught, disoriented woman in the grips of catastrophe and the machinery of the police.

Now she was what must be her usual self, lusty, confident, big boned, plump, and hearty. Her round, innocent face, framed by severely brushed mid-length chestnut hair, could have belonged to a farm girl. But the lattice work of scars and burns on her muscular hands and forearms gave testimony to long, ruthless years in professional kitchens.

Béatrice briskly showed off her still-empty dining room, modish in soothing beige fabric wall coverings, tan deep-pile carpeting, crisp lighting from tiny ceiling spotlights.

The kitchen was clearly her sanctum. Hanging domed heat lamps bathed long rows of deeply gouged wooden tables in dramatic chiaroscuro. A dozen or so chefs, all male, all young, in loose-fitting white T-shirts and black aprons, fussed with their *mises en places,* keyed up for the lunch rush.

Walking through the kitchen, Béatrice scrutinized her cooks' set-ups with a critical eye that didn't ignore one or two pairs of her chefs' *fesses.* The lasciviousness of the glances were blatant enough to make Capucine wonder if it wasn't some form of psychological compensation.

The interview took place in Béatrice's miniscule office, barely large enough for a chair at either side of the wooden desk, piled high with loose papers and ring-bound notebooks. The office was glass-walled from waist height up, providing an uninterrupted view of the entire kitchen.

"Lunch is a lot tougher than dinner," Béatrice said. "They arrive all at once, between twelve thirty and a quarter to one, dead sober, set on having a perfect meal in an hour and fifteen minutes. One mistake in the kitchen and it all falls apart. Dinner is a different story. They're mellow from a few *apéros* and arrive anytime from seven thirty to nine. It's their evening entertainment, so if a dish is a little slow in coming, so much the better. Dinner is definitely the meal to cook."

"Wouldn't it have been better if I had come between services?"

"No, this is fine. I've gone over everything with the *chefs de partie* and double-checked their mises. They're all set. Now all I have to do is sit here until someone screws up. That won't happen for at least fifteen minutes. Let me get you something to drink."

She waved over a runner who had been lounging in a corner and told him to bring Capucine a *Kir Royal*.

"I know *Kirs* have become totally démodé, but this one is special. We make it with rosé champagne, a lightly fermented raspberry syrup that comes from a small farm in the Midi, and a half a tot of *alcool de framboise* to give it just a bit of punch.

"Of course, getting you here for the luncheon service wasn't entirely disinterested. I hadn't realized until your call that you were married to Alexandre de Huguelet. I'm counting on you to put in a good word for me. I need all the help I can get."

The *Kir* arrived. It really was in a class apart, bubbly and almost tart, with a slight alcoholic unctuousness.

"So what can I tell you that I didn't already tell your charming policewoman that horrible night?"

It was the first time Capucine had ever heard Isabelle described as charming. Capucine checked closely for cynicism, but apparently there was none.

"I just wanted to go over the events of the evening a little more carefully and make sure we didn't miss anything. I understand you were in the kitchen the whole time and came out only once, about half an hour before the murder."

"Good Lord, no. I'm very much focused on the front of the house. I come out as often as a can, and when I can't, my eye is constantly at the judas in the service door. A chef feels her house like an actress senses the mood of her audience. I need that to cook. Do you understand?"

Capucine nodded.

"Well, that night was a nightmare. The kitchen was hopeless. They kept getting into mess after mess. They were in a tizzy over Fesnay. It was his third and last dinner before he wrote his review. I had to be in the kitchen, but you can bet I was glued to that little window to see how he reacted to his meal. I didn't miss a forkful."

"And did you see anything out of the ordinary?"

"No, nothing at all. The service was perfect. I'm blessed with my maître d'. Fesnay seemed to like his first course, a truffled duck foie gras from the Landes I serve with a celery root fondant and a kumquat confit. Then the sommelier served him his second wine, a Château La Moutonne, and with perfect timing the *chef de rang* presented the ravioles. He took his first bite, and I saw that look in his eyes that makes you feel better than sex. Then I smelled something just beginning to scorch in the kitchen, had the cook replate, and went right back to my window. But Fesnay already had his face in his dish. A waiter was rushing up to help him, and I ran out of the kitchen."

"And did you see anything unusual then? Say, someone coming back from the men's room or something like that?"

"Did I see anything unusual?" Béatrice snorted. "Are you kidding? A man had just collapsed at his table. The waiters danced around with no idea what to do. A number of guests got up to look. In a few minutes the SAMU arrived. Then the police arrived. Then the *Police Judiciaire*. It was pandemonium."

"What I meant was, did you see anyone coming back to his table? You know, someone who might have gone to the toilet or gone outside for a quick smoke?"

"Half the dining room was standing up, edging in for a closer look. There was so much confusion, any number of guests could have walked in or out. The place was such a mess, I didn't even bother presenting the checks. How could I?"

As she spoke, the maître d' began arriving more and more frequently with little white dupe sheets taken from the waiters' order books and stuck them in a circular rack over the service counter. In a few minutes the rack had turned into a Christmas tree of fluttering slips. Béatrice went to the door and peered intently through the little round window. Back in her chair she no longer looked at Capucine but swung her head, relentlessly scanning the kitchen. Her breathing was faster and her cheeks became flushed. She reminded Capucine of a cavalry major surveying his troopers as the enemy appeared on the crest of the hill opposite.

"Shall I tell you the supreme irony?" Béatrice said.

Capucine nodded.

"I'm sure Fesnay would have given me an excellent review. He was much more human than most critics. The first time he came, he had the ravioles and very politely suggested as he left that the sauce was excellent, but it was a bit too 'tight.' It would be much better if I 'loosened' it. You know, made it more liquid. He was trying it a second time to see if I'd taken his hint. If I'd left it the way it was, he might not have drowned in the damned stuff."

"Did you take it off the menu?"

"Of course not. It's all they order now. They love to look at the table and eat the dish he drowned in. Thank God it's such an easy one to prep. It's a Breton blue lobster tucked into oversized ravioles served in a sauce made from lobster fumet, to which I add tandoori spice, carrot, preserved lemon mousseline, wild sorrel, and a spring-onion reduction made with fresh coriander. We make the ravioles an hour or two before the service and freeze them. Then, for each order, we drop the frozen ravioles in boiling water, and they're ready in four minutes. The sauce is kept warm under the lamps and just before it goes on the *ravioles* each portion is *monté* with a *beurre noisette* so it's nice and rich and creamy. Fesnay's idea was to use less butter and add a spoonful or two of pasta water. He was perfectly right. The dish is perfect now. What pisses me off is that they're eating it for entirely the wrong reason."

At the row of stoves a chef was bent almost in half over

a copper pot in a pantomime of intense concentration. His T-shirt, which had been immaculate a few minutes before, was transparent with perspiration and stuck tightly to his skin. His face was bathed in sweat, and large drops fell into the pot.

"What's he making?"

"That is going to be my signature dish. It's a pigeon I get from the Midi that I pan roast in coffee butter and serve on a bed made with quinoa, Medjool dates, and Sicilian pistachios that have been spiced up with arabica coffee. It's served with a sauce that's a little tricky. That's what he's worried ab—"

Béatrice shot out the door of the office, yelling, *"Bordel de merde. Qu'est-ce que c'est que ce souk?"*

Capucine was sure the sin had been the sweat dripping into the sauce. Béatrice shouldered the cook aside roughly, jerked open the stainless-steel door of the oven, yanked the side towel off her shoulder, pulled out a baking tray, revealing an apparently perfectly cooked squab, and banged it noisily on the top of the stove.

"Merde. Throw this out and start again!" she hissed at the trembling chef.

She stalked back to the office, stiff with indignation.

"They get *dans le jus*—you know, into the weeds—over the sauce and forget about the poor little pigeon drying out and losing its soul in the oven. These small birds have to be done just right. A few seconds too early and they're raw, a few seconds too late and they taste like papier-mâché. That one has talent, though," she said, carefully folding her side towel and draping it over her left shoulder. "But he gets flustered too easily for haute cuisine. In his case he doesn't just slide into the weeds. He plunges right into *la merde*. What were we talking about?"

"Supreme irony."

"Yes, that's exactly what it was. Fesnay's death was a tragedy in more ways than one. I'm sure you know that my name is not really Mesnagier and everything about my family and all that."

"Of course."

"Well, getting into the restaurant business has been an uphill battle. My father has always been dead set against it. As far as he's concerned, the entire purpose of my life is to take over his business one day. You can't imagine the scene when I announced I wasn't going to business school but was off to the *école hôtelière* to learn to cook. He only let me go because he was sure I'd lose interest. Then he was disappointed when I was accepted for an internship at Troisgros, but he let me do it because he was sure the brutality of the professional kitchen would be too much for me and would teach me some useful lessons. When I decided to open a restaurant in Paris, he was against that, too, but was convinced it would fail and that the experience would be valuable when I finally took up my position in his company."

"I've been through a bit of that myself," Capucine said.

Béatrice looked at Capucine in surprise. It was not clear whether it was because her élan had been checked or because of the unexpectedness of the comment. After a beat she picked up her narrative.

"Well, I made goddamn sure my place was a howling success. I invited everyone in my address book, got the gossip columns to write about me, and made my food uncomplicated and easy to eat. Naturally, the restaurant became the watering hole for the young gratin of Paris, which was not at all what I wanted it to be, but it nailed my father's mouth shut. Now I'm inching upward. More and more of my dishes are truly *haute cuisine*. I'm hoping to get my first Michelin star before too long and was convinced Fesnay's review would be the turning point."

"Surely your success has palliated your father?"

"It's a double-edged sword. He left me alone as long as he was convinced I was going to fail. Now that I'm a success, he may be so driven to get me back, he'll poke his big stick in the wheel of my little bicycle—which is easy enough for him to do with all his money and power." She paused and looked sharply at Capucine. "Do you know about that part of it, too?"

"Totally. My family was horrified at the idea of my going into the police. I spent years in fear that they would pull some strings and have me thrown out. In fact, it's still something I lose sleep over."

"But you're a *commissaire*. That's a big deal."

"And you're on your way to a Michelin star. That's an even bigger deal."

They both laughed.

"*Ah, non, non, non, non! Bordel. Merde, merde, merde! Qu'est-ce que tu me foutez là?*" Béatrice shouted through the door.

"He's done it again!" she said to Capucine as she ran into the kitchen. Capucine realized it was high time for her to leave and made for the door with a wave at Béatrice who took no notice as she elbowed the trembling cook away from the stove and took over his position.

CHAPTER 9

When Capucine walked into her brigade the next morning, the uniformed receptionist stopped her.

"*Commissaire,* one of those process servers from the City of Paris Administration dropped something off for you this morning. You know, those creepy guys with black uniforms with no insignia. Funny thing was that it wasn't an official document, looked more like a wedding invitation or something like that. I put it on your desk."

The missive in question would have gladdened the heart of Capucine's dear grandmother, now departed to a world where she no doubt continued to spend the day perusing the social register—the celestial one, of course—making acid comments about the inadmissibility of most of the entries.

The envelope was a thick creamy bond with the name of a famous rue du Faubourg Saint-Honoré stationer pressed into one of the folds that would normally be hidden when the flap was sealed. It was addressed with the extreme formality that had gone out of style with Choderlos de Laclos:

A Madame
Madame le Commissaire Capucine Le Tellier
E/V

As her grandmother had explained to her many times, it was necessary to state that the letter was for Madame before actually naming the madame in question. She had no idea why; that was just the way it was done. The "E/V" was to signify that the letter was being delivered *en ville*— in-town, in other words, by hand of servant and not entrusted to *La Poste*. The missive itself was on thick card stock with a beautifully hand-engraved letterhead stating only the street address.

> *Paris, the 10th June MMVI*
> Madame,
> *The presence of Madame is requested and required at 11:00 on the 10th inst. at the offices of Monsieur le Juge d'Instruction August-Marie Parmentier de La Martinière to assist in the interview of Mademoiselle Sybille Charbonnier. It will not be necessary for Madame to be accompanied.*
> *Please allow the undersigned, Madame, to express the assurance of his most perfect consideration.*

The signature was an illegible scribble.

Capucine giggled all the way to the kitchen to get a cup of coffee and all the way back.

Even though Capucine arrived her usual fifteen minutes late at Martinière's office, Sybille was not there yet. Martinière was visibly tense and fretted skittishly with the bibelots on his desk. He placed Capucine on a small stool in the farthest corner of the room, presumably relegating her to the role of keeper of the peace. Capucine wondered if she had been invited only because, as a woman, it would acceptable for her to deal physically with another woman if the need arose.

After many long, fidgety moments the phone rang and Martinière snatched it up. "*Ah, enfin*—finally," he said.

Sybille burst into the room—red eyed, makeup-smeared, her famous corkscrew curls in the matted tangle of a wet sheepdog—utterly unrecognizable from silver screen or glossy magazine page. From her vibrancy, reddened nostrils, and dilated pupils, Capucine surmised she had yet to make it to bed after a long night out in which controlled substances had played a prominent role. Still, to a woman's eye, her beauty and adolescent sensuality were striking even through her disarray.

But Martinière was as crestfallen as a ten-year-old boy who had received the wrong video game for Christmas.

"Mademoiselle," he said through his disappointment, "it's so kind of you to come all the way to my office to see me." In his nervousness, he extended his hand to be shaken, no doubt knowing as well as Capucine's grandmother that it was always the woman who was to initiate the gesture.

Sybille stared at the floor with humming intensity, the proffered hand unnoticed. She sniffed loudly, mopped her nose with her sleeve, and then clawed at her collar to smell an offending armpit under her raised arm. After three long, self-absorbed beats she bleated something that sounded like *"c'fay,"* apparently directed at her high-top sneakers. She drooped in the wooden armchair, splaying out like butter melting in the sun.

Martinière was momentarily at a loss but finally figured it out. "A coffee? Would you like a coffee? Is that what I can get you?"

Sybille nodded distractedly, as if still intently pursuing some private thought. Martinière rose and busied himself at his telephone on the side table.

Capucine began to enjoy herself. The scene had a strong sense of déjà vu. It was obvious that Sybille was playing a role. Capucine wondered how far she would dare go.

As they waited for the coffee, Martinière launched a line of small talk, sounding like a gawky boy from the provinces attempting to pick up a girl on his first visit to a fashionable Paris bar. Sybille did not lift her eyes from the floor.

Once Sybille had downed her coffee, Martinière launched awkwardly into his questions.

"Mademoiselle, you were sitting at the table next to the victim. It's highly possible that—even though you didn't know it—you saw the murder being committed." Clearly he hoped for this dramatic statement to startle Sybille. She continued to stare at her sneakers, apparently obsessed with her thoughts.

"Did you see anyone pass behind the victim just before he died? Think carefully."

Sybille continued to goggle at her sneakers. Capucine was amazed that Martinière missed that she was acting out a part.

After an interminable wait she muttered, in Brando's Method mumble, "*C'hais pas*—I dunno."

Martinière was at a loss. "Mademoiselle, this is a murder investigation, a very serious matter. Your active cooperation is required by law."

Sybille glanced up at him with a withering adolescent sneer, rolled her eyes, and returned them to the floor.

Capucine had had enough. "Sybille, didn't you see the man splash into his dinner? I wish I'd been there. I would have bust a gut."

Sybille giggled and started to reply, but Martinière cut her off with a retort to Capucine.

"*Commissaire*, please do not interfere. This is a very serious interview."

He directed his attention to Sybille.

"This is a capital case. A man has been murdered. You were quite possibly an ocular witness."

Clearly bored, Sybille changed tack. She pulled her chair up to the edge of Martinière's desk, leaned far forward, put her elbows on the top, nestled her chin in her palms, and stared at him fixedly, unblinkingly. Martinière was completely unnerved.

"Mademoiselle, you must pay attention to what I'm saying," he said in a voice that was beginning to become high pitched. "Let me read you what the *Code Penal* has to say about failure to cooperate with a *juge d'instruction*."

Martinière got up and went to a bookcase in the corner and started searching for a law book that eluded him. He wasn't going to find it. Capucine had already noticed Sybille smirking at the red-bound *Code Penal* on the desk. She was a lot less scatterbrained than she sought to appear.

As Martinière rooted through the shelves in exasperation, Sybille picked up his cherished gold pen, stealthily opened the top of his blotter, and began doodling on the immaculate felt-like paper. With unexpected talent she drew a cartoon of a blustery and comically severe egret that was a perfect caricature of Martinière. Capucine was sure that she fully well knew that Martinière would be incensed by someone even touching his beloved fountain pen.

Giving up at the bookcase, Martinière turned around and caught sight of Sybille's handiwork. He shrieked, "Put that pen down. What do you think you're doing? And look at it! You've destroyed my blotter." He grabbed his pen and examined the nib carefully to see if any damage had been done. Capucine could feel him burning with desire to try it out on a piece of paper, while knowing that the gesture would make him utterly ridiculous.

"Mademoiselle, I give up. Since you refuse to talk to me, I'm going to have no alternative but to hand you over to the police," he said, as if this was the most dire threat imaginable. "And you'll see that they are far from being as enlightened as I am. In fact, their techniques can sometimes be quite harsh, believe me."

Instead of being cowed, as Martinière had hoped, Sybille turned and winkled at Capucine, who smiled sweetly back.

Martinière fumed at both of them. "*Ça suffit, mademoiselle*—enough of this nonsense. This interview is at an end," Martinière said with dramatic finality intended to foretell imminent and grave consequences.

Sybille stood up and sashayed out of the office, swiveling her hips, smirking victoriously at Capucine as she passed. Capucine fervently hoped the expression was out of Martinière's range of vision.

The door clicked shut. Capucine waited for the explosion. But Martinière just sat perplexed, looking at his desk.

"*Mais, mais,* that juvenile delinquent has stolen my Limoges penholder. It was my mother's. Or, wait, perhaps I put it in a drawer."

He began opening the drawers of his desk one by one, rooting through them in a barely controlled panic.

Capucine slipped out of the office and caught up with Sybille in the corridor. Laughing quietly, Capucine beckoned with her index finger. Unashamed, Sybille reached into the hand-warmer muff stitched onto the front of her hoodie and handed over a blue and yellow porcelain pen holder.

"I enjoyed your performance. It's always a treat to see a great actress at work. Unfortunately, I'll have to call on you in the next few days to ask the same questions."

"Oh, I'd like that. It'll be fun." Sybille was completely transformed. The sullen adolescent look had been replaced by the look of a gamine with a healthy adolescent love of life.

When she returned the penholder, Martinière looked at Capucine suspiciously, as if somehow she had been the author of the theft. He turned it over carefully in his hands, making sure that it had not been chipped or damaged in any way and then put it reverently on the desk.

"You see, *Commissaire,* contrary to your unjustified suspicions, I'm the last person who would ever deny the usefulness of the police."

CHAPTER 10

Capucine hadn't been back to *La Crim'*, as the *Brigade Criminelle* of the *Police Judiciaire* was known, since she had worked there before passing the *commissaire's* exam, taken the *commissaire's* training course, and had been assigned her own brigade. She couldn't resist forgoing the elevator to walk up the steps to the third floor, Stairway A, the scene of countless movies and mystery novels.

In the days when she worked there, Tallon—then a *commissaire principale*—had had an office overlooking the central courtyard, jammed with police cars and officers milling around like ants in organized confusion. He seemed to spend at least half of his meetings with her staring out the window. She was never sure if it was rumination or if he found the activity in the courtyard more interesting than what she had to say.

His new office was twice the size of the old one and had a sumptuous view of Notre Dame, which was directly across from the prefecture. As she walked in, both casements of the large window were wide open, framing the vista of the façade of the most visited attraction in France.

The gabbling of the crowd of tourists on the parvis filled the room. Tallon read a file with great concentration. Capucine coughed gently to alert him to her presence.

He raised his head with a start. "Ah, *Commissaire*, there you are. I can't hear myself think in here. I keep asking to be moved to the back, but they won't hear of it." With a gesture of irritation, he closed the window.

Capucine did not reply. She knew Tallon hated small talk.

"We have a serious problem with the case."

"The *juge d'instruction?*"

Capucine nodded.

"Something happened?"

"He made a fool of himself with Sybille Charbonnier."

For a split second Tallon's face betrayed a range of emotions, first surprised pleasure, then incredulity, finally curiosity.

He smiled at Capucine. "For a second I thought you were going to tell me he'd made a pass at her. What happened?"

"He convoked her to his office, and me as well—I suppose to act as the heavy and subdue her if necessary. Then he made a complete hash of the interview. She played a role with him. I'm not absolutely sure, but I think it was Anne Parillaud in that Luc Besson film."

Tallon looked blank.

"You know, *La Femme Nikita*, the one where the beautiful delinquent sticks a pencil through the back of the interrogating officer's hand."

"She stuck a pencil in his hand?"

"No, she made a funny cartoon of him on his blotter with his sacred gold pen and then stole his precious Limoges pen stand."

Tallon exploded in laughter. "You have all the fun and then come to me to complain about it."

Capucine joined in the laughter. When you explained it, she thought to herself, it was really pretty comical and not that serious at all.

When they both had caught their breaths, Capucine said, "He's allowing me to interview her, but she's the only one. I'm sure I won't even be invited to the rest of his sessions. You have to do something. I'll never get the case solved if you don't."

Tallon smiled broadly. "Do you want me to go over there and stick a pencil in the back of his hand?" he said and started laughing again.

Capucine crossed her arms across her chest and frowned in a way that might almost have been mistaken for a pout. On her first case with Tallon she had been constantly teased and had suffered a great deal in the process.

"You read my report. I've already interviewed Béatrice Renaud, since she knows my husband and counts as an acquaintance more than a suspect." Tallon's lips tightened almost imperceptibly. "And I was thinking of interviewing Guy Voisin. Apparently, my husband knows him, as well."

"Don't. *Commissaire,* you know the law as well as I do. Your juge is doing exactly what he's empowered to do. As you well know, the function was set up in seventeen ninety, during the Revolution, for the specific purpose of protecting the citizenry from the abuse of the police."

"So that's it? There's nothing we can do? We leave the case in his hands?"

"It's the law. Only the Cour de Cassation, our highest court, can remove a *juge d'instruction* from a case, and that's supposed to be because someone accuses him of partiality. The motion is brought forward by the accused, not a police officer. Unless you're suggesting we claim that he couldn't control himself when faced with the allure of Sybille Charbonnier. And I'm not sure how that would go down at the Cour de Cassation."

Capucine did not respond to the joke.

"And the Cour de Cassation is the only way?"

"*Commissaire,* you know all this. In theory the *Procureur de la République*—the federal prosecutor—can limit the juge's range of investigation, but those cases are extremely rare, and that's certainly not going to happen when the elimination of the function is such a hot topic."

Capucine was about to make a comment about letting a murderer go free but said nothing.

Tallon massaged his chin and, instinctively, threw both casements of the window open and bent forward to look out, crossing his arms and leaning them on the iron safety bar. Capucine stood up to peer over his shoulder. The parvis was packed with tourists in shorts and sandals and brightly colored T-shirts. Children screamed, wives scolded husbands, people shoved and jostled to have their picture taken in front of the eternal façade showing off their toothy rictuses. Tallon was disgusted. Almost imperceptibly, he hiked his shoulders in a shudder. His mood changed with the suddenness of a summer squall. He turned and spoke sharply.

"*Commissaire,* we are civil servants, not prima donnas. In a year your juge will be powerless. You'll catch your killer then. He'll go to ground and still be there, fresh as ever, waiting for you to snap the cuffs on him. Don't waste your time trying to buck the system. Work on other things and let this one sit."

Possibly the most irritating sound to the human ear was the voice of reason. Irked as she was, Capucine accepted that not only was he speaking with maturity and authority, but he was also unquestionably right. What she couldn't know was that this was the one time in his life when Contrôleur Général Tallon would turn out to be dead wrong.

CHAPTER 11

That afternoon Capucine threw herself into the work of her brigade with fiery zeal. She fine-tuned the duty roster and then went through a stack of personnel evaluations, reviewing each one carefully, making notations in the margins. Next, she attacked the training program and made sure that each of her officers would attend at least one course before the end of the year. At that point it was only three o'clock and she was still haunted by the restaurant murder. It was worse than weaning herself from a lover. With strict discipline she banished it from her mind. But, using Sacha Guitry's phrase, she was forced to admit she was telling herself six times an hour that she wasn't thinking about it. She then went through all the open cases on the brigade list, calling in her lieutenants, who were managing them with irreproachable competence, to discuss them in exhaustive detail. Just as their irritation threatened to bubble over, she realized it was almost nine o'clock and Alexandre would be dying to get at his dinner.

After a long drive home through a pummeling rain, she found Alexandre in his study, sitting in his ancient red leather armchair, tapping energetically on a laptop on his knees, a nearly empty glass of whiskey teetering on the arm of the chair. He stopped typing and read over his copy, keeping time to the cadence by waving the stub of his cigar in the air as if he were conducting an imaginary orchestra. He gave a satisfied sigh and banged the RETURN key with élan.

"Done!" he said, throwing the cigar butt in the fireplace. "Another chef d'oeuvre in the gloomy annals of restaurant criticism. You've arrived just in the nick of time. I was beginning to feel faint from hunger."

After Alexandre went into the kitchen to put the finishing touches on dinner, Capucine changed, stripped off her soaking clothes, dried her hair vigorously with a towel, pulled on jeans and a T-shirt, and joined him.

The sight of Alexandre puttering around his kitchen, nudging his copper pots on his enormous stove and poking through his disparate jumble of jars and bottles, looking for the precisely right spices, always filled Capucine with a sense of calm and security. Like the keep of a medieval castle, this was her inviolable bastion.

"What are we having?"

"*Tournedos de canard à l'aillade.*"

"Isn't tournedos beef? It smells like duck."

"It's a *magret de canard* that's been coaxed into the shape of a block of beef fillet with the help of the end of my rolling pin. I'm going to sear it and then cook it for three minutes on each side so it's nice and rare. I've already cooked two apples in duck fat in this skillet, and I'm going to use the remaining fat to cook the duck," he said, putting a much-battered steel frying pan on the high heat section of the central burner. When it was hot enough, he gently placed the two "tournedos" on the pan. They hissed and spat angrily in the duck fat.

"The apples are nice and warm in the oven, and I'm just going to finish the sauce, which has been waiting patiently for you in a tepid bain-marie." He moved the double boiler closer to the hot center of the burner. When the water began to boil, he wrinkled his nose and squinched his eyebrows in concentration, carefully adding two spoonfuls of a dark liquid, which he whisked energetically into the sauce.

"What's that?" Capucine asked, pouring herself a glass of Bordeaux from a bottle that had been breathing on a sideboard. She sat at the long Provençal table, crossed her legs on the bench, and leaned back, supporting herself by holding on to the sides of the bench. Stretching her back sensually, she felt the irritations of the day volatilize.

"Duck's blood. Not easy to find when you're not in the country. Two spoonfuls only. A thickening liaison to give the sauce body."

"Smells garlicky."

Alexandre laughed and brought their dinners over to the table. "That's why it's called an *aillade*."

The dark brown sauce was rich and pungent, almost as if intended for a steak. The thick slab of duck was charred brown on the outside and bright pink at the center. The apples had acquired the taste of duck but had retained their fruity unctuousness. Capucine told herself that she didn't come close to doing Alexandre's cooking justice when she thought of it as a mere palliative.

When the meal was over, Alexandre looked at her with liquid eyes. "You didn't seem your usual bubbly self when you came in. Case getting you down?"

"Not anymore. It's history. Toast. Gone. *Finito.*"

"That might require a word or two more of explanation."

"I went to see Tallon this morning. The main point of the meeting was that he hates his view of Notre Dame. He'd much rather be at the back of the building, where he could watch officers unload detainees. But he also explained that the juges d'instruction have been around since the Revolution to protect the downtrodden citizenry from the ruthlessness of the police."

Alexandre refilled his wife's glass. "And so?"

"And so Martinière is well within his legal rights to refuse to let the police conduct their inquiry. That's all there is to it. He was very philosophical. We'll just wait until the function is discontinued and solve the case then."

"You're just going to drop it?"

"No, we'll finish all the background checking. Of course, there won't be anything that even remotely looks like a motive. We'll write it up and send it to the most excellent juge. He'll parade around for a few weeks and get absolutely nowhere. And that will be that. Yet another unsolved case."

"How frustrating, my love." Alexandre put his lips on her neck, kissed her gently, and muttered something that might, or might not, have been, "The heartbreak of coitus interruptus . . ."

"Did I really hear what I think you just said?"

Rather than answer, Alexandre moved from her neck to her lips and slipped off her T-shirt.

Capucine's cell phone rang. She looked at the caller ID on the screen, then at her watch, and flipped the phone open. Alexandre well knew what ten-thiry calls meant and moved off to collect the dishes and put them in the sink.

"Capu, it's Bruno Lacombe. You know, your pal who runs the *PJ* brigade in the Fourth Arrondissement East, your best buddy at the *commissaires'* school—"

"Bruno, it's nearly eleven at night." The detested nickname made her sharp.

"So it is. So it is. I'm calling from a restaurant called Dans le Noir, on the rue Quincampoix. You know, the little street right next to the Beaubourg. It's a creepy place, and it's even creepier right now because there's a dead guy lying in the middle of it. So I figure this is a case that's gotta be yours. A guy gets bumped off in a restaurant, and I'm already thinking you. When the stiff turns out to be a restaurant critic, I *know* it's yours. Come on down and join the fun. Don't bother to change. Just come as you are."

For once, Capucine decided that, given the hour and her mood, she might as well look like every other female detective on the force and show up in grunge. She pulled her T-shirt back on and decided it was just the ticket, even though it was a Jean Paul Gaultier original and cost far more than she would ever dare confess to Alexandre. The low-heeled Zanottis were probably all wrong, too. But so what? She was never going to be a typical female flic no matter how hard she tried.

"Know anything about a restaurant called Dans le Noir on the rue Quincampoix?" she asked Alexandre.

"*Dans Le Noir?* In the Black? It's that blind restaurant. A supposedly sightless maître d' leads you into a completely dark room, and you get to spill mediocre food all over your shirtfront, or down your décolleté, as the case may be. The only appeal seems to be that they seat you at a long table and you chat away with people you don't know. Seeing them in the light when you leave is supposed to teach you that beauty is not just skin deep, or some nonsense like that."

"Well, a restaurant critic's been murdered there."

"Good Lord, that must be Jean Monteil. He was with the *Le Figaro*. The restaurant was bought out by an international chain, and he was going to review it. He even asked me to go along to keep him company. I decided it would be way more fun to eat with you than to spill bad food all over myself in the dark. Of all the bad luck. If I'd gone, I'd be spending the rest of the evening with you."

He leaned over to kiss Capucine, who pushed him away roughly.

"That's in very bad taste and not funny at all," she said as she stormed out of the apartment, stuffing her Sig into the back of her jeans, not at all sure why Alexandre's comment had upset her so much.

CHAPTER 12

Even though Capucine left the Twingo double-parked directly in front of the restaurant, the rain was heavy enough to soak her by the time she reached the protection of the low black canvas awning over the restaurant's door. She cursed the heavens. Two times in one night was just too much.

Inside the tiny anteroom, decorated only with jet-black felt on the walls, a uniformed PJ officer stood guard in front of a high dark black wooden desk.

"*Commissaire* Lacombe's been waiting for you, *Commissaire*. He's in the dining room downstairs. Go through that door and then the next one. But watch out. The stairs are right after the second door."

A ten-foot hallway, decorated in the same deep black felt as the anteroom, lay behind the first door, which swung shut behind her with the whoosh of a pneumatic door closer. She was in total darkness. The effect was surprisingly discomforting. She inched forward, guiding herself with a hand on the wall, and found the second door, which opened onto a precipitous staircase. The light from below was almost blinding after the dark.

Lacombe was waiting at the foot of the stairs.

"See, you're having a good time already," he said with a deep belly laugh. "Nice setup, eh? There's a pretend blind maître d' who leads the customers down the stairs, whispers the menu in their ears, and then the fun begins."

"The fun?"

"It's a real gas. The food is as liquid and as hard to eat as they can make it. The idea is for the customers to feel as helpless as possible and think they're bonding with blind people," Lacombe said with heavy irony.

Brightly lit, the room was even more depressing than a nightclub when the lights were turned up at four in the morning to induce everyone to go home. The walls were a shabby, faded, and splotched dark green and hadn't been repainted in years. The beige carpeting was streaked with dirt and dotted with food stains. On the tables, once jet-black tablecloths were covered with a mosaic of spots and spatters in varying shades of brown and purple.

"Must look a whole lot better in the dark," Lacombe said. He moved aside to give her a view of the room, revealing a heavyset man slumped over one of the center tables. His body was twisted to the right, his head turned away from them, his ear resting in a deep dish of lumpy, liquid stew.

Capucine was blinded by a spasm of anguish. For a split second she was convinced it was Alexandre. But as they approached the table she gratefully recognized Jean Monteil, whom she had seen many times at cocktail parties and restaurant openings. She breathed again but was still held by the nightmarish sense of déjà vu.

Monteil was wearing the same sort of clothes Alexandre favored, a tweed jacket and gray flannel trousers. His head lay peacefully on the side of what was unmistakably a dish of *bœuf bourguignon*. Unlike the body in Chez Béatrice, there were no splashes of food. Shattering the image of repose, a six-inch metallic tube projected straight up from Monteil's right ear.

Capucine was vaguely aware that Lacombe was asking her something, but she was too captivated by Monteil's body to be able to focus on his question.

The left flap of Monteil's jacket hung limply. Capucine squatted on the balls of her feet and peered, careful to touch nothing. The tailor's label, CHARLES TOLUB, 7 RUE DE THORIGNY, was clearly visible under the inside pocket. Monteil had had his clothes made by the same tailor as Alexandre. The clips of two plastic pens were visible, the words HOTELS COSTES conspicuous on one of them.

"You know him?" Lacombe was asking.

Capucine nodded. "Jean Monteil. He was one of the journalists on *Le Figaro*'s restaurant page. He wasn't a close friend, but I definitely knew him."

There was a moment of awkward silence.

"And that metal thing sticking in his ear? Any idea what that is?"

Capucine's mood broke.

"I have two of them in my kitchen. It's a basting needle. They're used to inject stock or sauce or whatever into meat while it's cooking. See, the plunger's been completely depressed." If this one was anything like Alexandre's, Capucine thought to herself, the needle would be over three inches long and would easily have killed the victim without the need to inject anything.

There was a loud crashing and clanging of metallic tubing from the top of the stairwell. The forensics team had arrived and was having problems getting its gurney down the stairs. Momo appeared, holding the front of the folded aluminum contraption.

In a high-pitched complaint Isabelle's voice could be heard from the top of the stairs. *"Merde,* David, stop pushing me!"

Ajudant Dechery came up to Lacombe and Capucine. "Luckily, we ran into your *brigadiers*. The big one was a godsend with the gurney. Whatever you do, *Commissaire*, don't let him go. Without him, we'll never get the stiff out of here."

Dechery's professional enthusiasm took over as he looked at the body and almost rubbed his hands in glee. "A basting needle stuck in the ear. Now, that's something I've never seen before. Good! If you two will give me a little room, I need to get to work." He waved his assistants over joyfully.

The two *commissaires* stood back and watched as the forensics experts opened their cases, slipped into white plastic jumpsuits, snapped on rubber gloves, and began their grisly work.

Capucine's three officers had joined Lacombe's team, which had herded the fifty or so customers into a corner of the room and were busy taking names and meticulously checking identification papers, an act as sacred to a French policeman as receiving the wafer at mass was to Catholics. The customers hovered patiently but apprehensively in their corner like a small drove of steers who were about to be driven into a chute.

David came over to report. "They've completed the list of the customers, and Isabelle and Momo are starting on the serving staff. The cook staff is waiting in the kitchen. Can I let the customers go home?"

Isabelle rushed up, her pupils black with anger. "Nobody's going home!" she said. "*Commissaire*, you'll never guess who's here."

Capucine looked at her levelly.

"Our favorite movie star and her sugar granddaddy."

Following Isabelle's gaze, Capucine saw Sybille Charbonnier and Guy Voisin talking to Momo quietly on the far side of the restaurant.

"*Commissaire*, you need to talk to the maître d' right away. I'm going to get him to tell you what he just told me. You won't believe it."

Capucine exhaled noisily in irritation. Good as she was at her job, sometimes Isabelle was just too much.

Behind her Lacombe was chuckling happily. "Capu, you really *should* talk to him. It'll make your evening." His protuberant belly shook with laughter.

Capucine frowned. He was the sort of cop who milked his job for gags. She didn't like it, but she could live with it. It was the appalling nickname she had acquired during the *commissaires'* course that was over the top. One of her deepest fears was that the foul sobriquet would circulate in her own brigade. The thought of being called *Commissaire* Capu by her own staff behind her back gave her the shivers.

"Bruno, your guys have done most of the work. There's not much left to wrap it up. It's after midnight. Why don't you and your team go on home?"

"Capu," he said. Capucine cringed. "That's something you don't have to ask me twice. I'm always happy to leave the late-night stuff to the kids." He motioned to his *brigadiers* and they disappeared promptly up the stairs into the rain.

"All right, Isabelle, bring the maître d' over and let's hear this."

Isabelle went off and returned with a round-faced man with the dead eyes of a blind person. But his approach was so confident it was obvious he saw perfectly and had mastered the technique of staring blankly straight ahead while getting around on his peripheral vision.

"This is Monsieur Flétard. He's the maître d'hôtel. His job is complicated because he has to keep everything moving smoothly in the dark. But he doesn't miss a trick. You really need to listen to what he has to say."

Flétard was obviously fond of his blind look. As he spoke to Capucine, he stared unseeingly fifteen degrees off her left shoulder with a lugubrious deadpan.

"Tell her what you saw," Isabelle encouraged, like an outraged grandmother prodding a grandchild to report on the peccadillo of a sibling.

"*Commissaire,*" Flétard said, "as I've already told your officers, I heard one of my waiters shout out in alarm and turned on the lights. It took a few moments for our eyes to adjust, and then I saw that one of the guests had been stabbed, so I called the police."

"Not that part," Isabelle said irritably.

"Well, *Commissaire,* I don't quite know how to put this, but in the midst of the confusion I noticed that one of our patrons seemed to be emerging from under the table."

"From under the table?"

"Yes, and her companion was stretching back in his chair in a gesture that just might have been . . . I can't really be sure . . . but it was as if he was . . . How can I phrase this . . . ? Well, uh, possibly, zipping up his trousers."

"So shall I arrest them?" Isabelle asked breathlessly. She clearly saw no need to explain whom she was speaking about.

Capucine locked her face into the tight, stony look of those trying very hard not to laugh.

"Isabelle, I need the three of you to get back to interviewing the front-of-the-house staff. I'll deal with this little incident myself. Monsieur Flétard, stay right here. I'll be back in a moment. I need to talk to you."

As Capucine came up to Sybille and Voisin, Sybille greeted her with adolescent intimacy. "*Salut!* I was hoping I'd get to see you. I had a lot of fun with your boss the other day."

"He's not my bo—," Capucine started to say sharply and caught herself.

Sybille wore a very short black chiffon dress that fell away from the bustline with X-ratable Empire simplicity. As she rose, her ample breasts swung freely under the flimsy chiffon. Capucine could feel the attraction in the male component of the herded patrons behind her. Her legs were made even longer by high-heeled sandals held tight by a large floppy satin bow around her ankles. Capucine wondered how she could manage to find out where the shoes had come from while remaining professional. An elaborate tortoiseshell comb held Sybille's hair in a large curlicued bun on top of her head, emphasizing the expanse of creamy flesh of her upper torso and neck. The look was summery and astonishingly erotic. Sensing the crowd's eyes locked on her, she extracted the comb and shook her hair free to cascade into a sensuous bedroom mop. There was an audible intake of breath. For the penned-up customers the gesture had transcended the murder. The body was now no more than a minor prop for her performance. It was the first time Capucine had experienced genuine star quality at close quarters.

During this production Voisin leaned smugly back in his chair, so pleased with himself, he strongly invited a bitch slap. But underneath the veneer something was clearly wrong. It was like rust waiting to explode through the carefully waxed finish of an aging luxury sedan.

"Monsieur Voisin," Capucine said, "is there anything you can tell me about what happened here tonight?"

"A great deal! But none of it has any bearing on the crime."

"And don't ask me," Sybille interjected, giggling. "Where I was, it was even darker than in the restaurant."

Capucine looked at them sternly. "Very well. You two are now officially 'persons of interest' to the police. I'll be calling on you in the morning to take your depositions. You're free to go home now, but you must not leave Paris without police permission. If you do, you will be arrested, and the simple fact of having attempted to leave the city will be considered a crime punishable by a prison sentence. Is that perfectly clear?"

Even beneath their alcoholic glow the couple was

shocked enough to be at a loss for words. Capucine turned on her heel and made a disdainful flicking gesture with the tips of her fingers, instructing Momo to get them out of the restaurant as quickly as possible.

"And a few minutes after they're gone, you can let all the other customers go, too," she told Momo. "Then the three of you can finish up with the waitstaff while I do the kitchen staff."

She went back to the maître d' and sat him down at one of the long tables.

"All right. I need to understand how this place works. First off, how do customers get in?"

"There's only one way. Once the hostess confirms their reservation, she buzzes for me and I go up to collect them. We go through a big song and dance, putting their hands on the shoulder of the person in front so they can follow me through the double set of doors and creep down the staircase. Obviously, the two doors are there so the dining room remains completely dark. We have the same thing for the kitchen so the light doesn't shine in there when they bring in the food. Creating the right mood is the basis of the experience."

"And if you're busy, will the hostess ever let them come down by themselves?"

"Of course not. They'd kill themselves on the staircase. And that rigmarole with the hand on the shoulder gives them a three-blind-mice feeling, kicking their evening off. A key part of the experience is making them feel helpless."

"Understood. Then what?"

"I leave the group standing by the door and take them one by one to their seats. Once they're seated, I whisper the menu in their ear. There are always only three dishes. They're chosen to be as liquid and messy as possible. That's all part of the show. Then a waiter serves them just like in any other restaurant, except he makes a big deal out of feeling their backs to know where they are. The other difference is that we have to bring extra napkins." He laughed maliciously.

Capucine pushed through the two sets of double doors separated by a five-foot hallway and went into the brightly lit kitchen. With its stainless-steel tables, greasy stoves, and grill racks, it looked like every other small-restaurant kitchen in Paris, right down to the open doorway into an alley, a haven for smoke breaks and short respites from the heat.

The kitchen staff champed with impatience. Almost without exception they were North Africans. They had been confined to the kitchen for hours, knowing nothing, hearing nothing, forbidden to leave the room.

Capucine introduced herself and started in. "To begin with, I have to tell you that a man was killed in the restaurant tonight. That means the restaurant will be closed tomorrow and probably for a day or two after. I need to talk to you for a few minutes, and then one of my officers will come in and verify your papers and let you go home."

Several of the men looked uneasily at each other and fidgeted.

"I have nothing to do with immigration. As long as you can give some indication of where you live, that's fine with me."

There was an almost audible sigh of relief.

"Who's in charge of the *cuisine?*"

"I am, madame," a swarthy, squat man said.

"Well, Chef, tell me what goes on in here."

"It's very simple, madame. We make just three dishes. They were picked by the management. We never change them, because we have almost no repeat business. Our dishes are *bœuf bourguignon, bouillabaisse,* and *blanquette de veau.*"

"The three Bs," one of the staff said.

There was a round of loud laughter. They were delighted at the idea of two or three days off with pay.

"We make them in a special way," the chef continued. "The dishes are too liquid and the pieces are all in different sizes to make it difficult and messy for the customers to eat. We also add extra liquid to the desserts to make them drip on the customers' laps. They come in big bowls with oversize serving spoons. We do *île flottante*. The floating mound of fluffed egg white is impossible for them to deal with." There was more raucous laughter in the room. "The other dessert is *nage de fruits rouges*—red berries floating in a sweet sauce. We put in some extra-long pieces of pineapple so they'll fall off the serving spoon and make a big mess and nice red stains."

The staff laughed again, childishly malevolent, like schoolboys who had just engineered a very clever prank. It was clearly a happy kitchen.

"Does anyone ever come in through that door?" Capucine asked, indicating the open back door with her head.

"Of course. We all go out there for a smoke every now and then. And naturally girlfriends show up looking for their man, but I never let them come in the kitchen."

"Are you sure they never sneak in?"

"Not a chance. If someone was in here not wearing white, I'd notice it immediately. I always have the whole kitchen in the corner of my eye. Nothing will screw things up faster than an angry girlfriend. Trust me on that!"

There were loud laughs of agreement.

Isabelle, David, and Momo came in and took names and addresses, checking them against immigration cards and driver's licenses, and in some cases letters or addressed advertising flyers that had come in the mail. Three cases, who had no papers at all, were handed over to Momo, who chatted with them in street patois until he finally announced to Capucine that he would know how to find them if need be. In fifteen minutes they were done and the kitchen staff was sent home. Only the forensics team remained, finishing up before they put the body in a bag and took it to the morgue.

Exhausted, Capucine leaned over the metal table in the kitchen with her weight on her elbows. The three detectives joined her, imitating her posture. From her bag Isabelle removed the bright orange octagonal seals that she would place on the locked front and back doors after they left, leaving the exterior in the care of a lone uniformed officer. They could not go before the seals were affixed. Listlessly, Capucine signed and dated them. They waited, staring at each other with slack mouths.

David drummed his fingers gently and said, "MO's a carbon copy of the last case. And it's another closed-room mystery. The good news is that this time there are only two suspects."

Capucine glanced at him and returned her gaze to the far wall where a small cockroach proceeded serenely toward an air vent.

She stood up straight and gave the table a hard double rap.

"Got it," she said. "There's something wrong with this picture. Momo, you stay here. You two come with me."

She led the two *brigadiers* into the dining room.

"Ajudant Dechery. I hate to interrupt you, but I'm going to need to turn off the lights for a quick minute. David, go over to the circuit box and kill them."

The room was plunged into utter darkness. For a few seconds brightly colored images danced on their retinas, but then those too disappeared and the blackness settled around them like a heavy mantle. The dinginess of the room was transformed into elegance.

"All right, Momo, come in here!" Capucine yelled.

Momo came out briskly. As he came through the second set of double doors, the first doors still swung very slightly on their spring hinges admitting the faintest pulsing glimmer. It lasted for only a few seconds but it was enough to shine on the tables closest to the door and shatter the mood.

"Momo, they must have some sort of subdued light in the kitchen during the food service. Can you go back in there and see if you can find it?"

He returned briskly in less than thirty seconds. This time no light at all was visible through the doors.

"Those low-hanging lamps in there turn out to have red bulbs, like in an old-style darkroom. Come see," Momo said.

In the kitchen, cones of dim ruby light lay over the worktable and the row of stoves. Everything not under the light was cloaked in deep shadow.

"Anyone could have come in through the door. As long as he was wearing a white coat, no one would notice," Isabelle said.

"And in this rain all you'd have to do is show up at the back door, slip off your raincoat so you'd be in your white jacket, walk through the kitchen, do your deed, nip back into the kitchen, put your raincoat back on, and walk away. Nobody'd be any the wiser," David said.

"Of course, they'd have a hell of a time getting around the dining room," Isabelle said.

"You can buy army surplus night-vision glasses real cheap in the Arab part of the flea market," Momo said.

Capucine smiled. There was no doubt at all in their minds. They now were sure they knew exactly how the murder had been committed. The only thing Capucine had no doubts about was that—juge or no juge—she needed to get cracking on the case.

CHAPTER 13

Capucine spent the night writhing and squirming, prodded without mercy by the horns of the two challenges she faced. One was the moral imperative to disobey the order of a direct superior if she was to prevent a murderer from walking away free. The other was more compelling: the desperate need to eliminate the escalating threat to Alexandre.

The phone rang. Capucine glanced at the red LED display of the clock on her night table. Seven o'clock, right on the second.

"*Commissaire?* I'm calling to put your mind at rest."

"You're up early, *monsieur le contrôleur général.*" Capucine could never understand how he read her mind so perfectly.

"I like to get here before the crowd invades the parvis. It's the only time of day I can open the window and think straight. I was happy to see that *Commissaire* Lacombe called you last night. Good man, Lacombe. Gave you the chance of seeing the crime scene while it was fresh. You're now officially in charge of this case, so you're free to interrogate anyone you want. Of course, you were going to do that, anyway."

"What about the *juge d'instruction?*"

"No juge has been appointed yet. I need to polish the case notes before I send them over to the magistrates' hall. No way I can get around to it today. My appointment book is packed solid. The way things are going, it'll take me a few days to get to them. And, of course, it will take the magistrates a few more days to see the link between this case and the last one. So you've got at least a week."

"So you think they're linked."

"Linked?" he snorted. "Of course they are. The second one is almost identical to the first. But let's not waste your morning chatting away. You've got work to do." He hung up without saying good-bye.

It was five minutes after seven. Capucine went into the kitchen and bullied the Pasquini into producing a café au lait.

At eight she picked up the kitchen phone, called the Hôtel Plaza Athénée, and asked for Monsieur Voisin's room. Sybille picked up with a whispered hello.

"Mademoiselle Charbonnier, this is *Commissaire* Le Tellier."

"*Salut,*" Sybille answered, yawning. "S'up?"

"I'm going to come around at ten thirty to see you and Monsieur Voisin."

"Ten thirty? Today? Can't we do it tomorrow? And later in the day? I have a ton of stuff to do, and Guy's not going to be up at ten thirty." There was a pause. She had looked at her clock. "Christ! Do you know what time it is? Don't you ever go to bed?"

"Mademoiselle, I can either come to your hotel at ten thirty or send a squad car to have you both picked up. In that case you might have to spend some time in a detention cell, waiting for me to finish my business. It's up to you."

"All right. All right. *Merde,*" Sybille mumbled. There

were sounds of her sinking back into the pillows. She hung up. It was just not a morning for good telephone manners.

Punctual for once, Capucine walked through the marble and gilt rococo extravagance of the Plaza Athénée exactly at ten thirty with Isabelle and David in her wake.

David knocked politely on the door. There was no reply. He waited a moment and banged loudly.

A distant male voice shouted irritably, "I'm in the shower. Come in. The door's unlocked. I'll be out in a second."

The suite's cavernous sitting room was over full with brand-new Louis XVI–style furniture, shiny with thick varnish and polished marble tops. A large silver tray with three cups, a basket overflowing with croissants and *petits pains au chocolat,* and ornate pots of coffee and milk sat on a black-onyx-topped coffee table, presumably for the two inhabitants of the suite and Capucine. The three detectives milled around the room, waiting for Voisin to emerge.

Isabelle heard it first. She froze, her cheek muscles swelling as she clenched her jaws.

Then Capucine heard it. A barely audible, rhythmic, rasping breathing that gradually became louder and faster. David smirked. Capucine shook her head slightly and plumped down in an armchair next to the coffee table.

She poured herself a cup of coffee and indicated to her *brigadiers* to follow suit. David served himself, but Isabelle sat rigid, round eyed, staring, jaw clamped.

Capucine examined one of the tiny jars of jam from the tray. "Confiture Christine Ferber, Niedermorschwihr, Alsace," she read. "I've heard this is absolutely fabulous stuff. *Tomates vertes à l'orange aux épices de pain d'épices*— green tomato with orange and gingerbread spices. I've got to try that."

David rooted through the selection and opted for violet-scented raspberries.

"Try the *prune de Damas*—damson plums. You'll love it," David said to Isabelle as he slathered a piece of croissant with luminous red jam.

Isabelle glared at him. "Shut the fuck up!" she hissed.

The noise level from the bedroom increased as the breathing escalated into hoarse panting, punctuated by long, tortured "ahhhs" and "*ouis.*"

Isabelle rose to her feet, swayed slightly in her rage. "I'm going to put a stop to it. This is completely unacceptable."

"Sit down, Isabelle," Capucine said. "Think of it as a performance. Imagine they're in there watching the morning news on TV."

The deep panting accelerated until it culminated in the eructation of a prolonged wavering moan. David made a silent mime of clapping his hands. Isabelle launched a stream of daggers at him with her eyes.

After a short pause, the door opened and Guy Voisin strode out, looking very pleased with himself, knotting a terry cloth bathrobe ostentatiously embroidered with the Plaza Athénée coat of arms.

"My goodness, monsieur, what an energetic shower you take," Capucine said.

Voisin smirked. "Sybille will be out in a moment. She's going shopping, and we can have a cozy little chat. I'm ordering some champagne. Would you like some?"

"I'm afraid it's too early for a working girl, but you go right ahead. By the way, I'll need to see Mademoiselle Charbonnier, as well."

Voisin shrugged his shoulders with Gallic fatality. "Good luck with that. Sybille usually does exactly what she wants." He busied himself with the telephone. Halfway through the call he put his hand over the mouthpiece and looked down at Capucine. "Are you sure I can't get you anything? More coffee? How about a sandwich?" he asked, widening his gaze to include the other two detectives. His uncertainty of the previous evening had vanished completely.

After he hung up, there was a long moment of awkward silence as they all waited for Sybille to emerge from the bedroom. Isabelle was the first to run out of patience and, growling, started to rise, obviously intending to go into the bedroom to get her. Just as she got on her feet, there was a loud knock on the door and, simultaneously, Sybille rushed out of the bedroom in a gauzelike summer sundress and a pair of high-heeled, open-toed bright red sling-backs with enormous bows barely covering her toes. Capucine was almost sure they were by Valentino.

Sybille went up to Voisin, who was opening the door for room service, and kissed his cheek. As if she had suddenly noticed Capucine, she turned, flashed a broad smile, and said, "My favorite *commissaire!* I'd love to stay and chat but I'm late already. I have to buy a dress for a party tonight. I have nothing, but really nothing at all, to wear."

Capucine could hear Isabelle grinding her teeth.

"Mademoiselle, I'm afraid I'm going to require you to stay. This is an official police inquiry."

Sybille started as if she had been slapped. Both sides of her upper lip curled in the snide adolescent sneer she had shown the juge. "If it's about last night, you know I was in no position to see anything."

Voisin laughed uproariously.

"Anyway, you can't make me do anything I don't want to do!" she said petulantly. "I really, really need to go shopping, and you can't make me stay. If you try and stop me, I'll—I'll—I'll just call my lawyer. That's what I'll do!"

She moved toward the door. Isabelle started to rise. Capucine shook her head at her.

"I'll tell you what," Capucine said, as if talking to a child. "Why don't you go shopping and come see me at my brigade after lunch? That way you can get everything you need for your party and we can still be friends. I also want to see what you buy. And we need to have a serious talk about shoes. I'm in love with the ones you were wearing yesterday. They were Valentinos, weren't they?"

"So are these! I like them way better. Don't you?" she said with childish delight, showing off her foot.

Capucine breathed an inward sigh of relief. She had no authority to detain an individual in her own home—and a hotel counted as home. The *juge d'instruction* was bound to go into conniptions if he received a complaint from Sybille's lawyer. Not to mention that Voisin preening in front of her and her constant asides to him would have made both interviews less than useless. Trying to see them together had been a bad idea. Very bad.

Capucine got up and walked to the door. "See you at three, then," she said, handing Sybille her card with a smile.

Voisin refilled his champagne flute and dropped into a gray silk armchair. He crossed his legs, adjusted his robe, and flapped the sole of his hotel terry cloth slipper against the heel of his foot making an irritating little slapping noise.

"*Commissaire,* I saw the *juge d'instruction* the other day and told him I had noticed nothing out the ordinary at Chez Béatrice until that poor man collapsed on the table. It was a very short session that lasted no more than ten minutes, and I had the impression the juge was entirely satisfied. I saw even less yesterday. It was pitch dark in that restaurant, as you know."

"Monsieur, the working hypothesis for the moment is that the two deaths are connected. The curare that caused the first death has been traced to artifacts that were stolen at a reception given by the Brazilian embassy, at which you were present. There are only two people who were present at Chez Béatrice, the embassy reception, and Dans le Noir last night. You and Mademoiselle Charbonnier. That makes you both of great interest to the police."

Voisin put both feet on the floor and swallowed hard, saying nothing. He downed his flute of champagne and filled it again from the bottle in the cooler. The sloshing of the ice was the only sound in the room.

"Monsieur, this is just a preliminary interview but any falsehoods will be deemed to be perjury and could result in a criminal sentence. Let's start with your background. Your full name is Guy Arnaud Voisin. You were born in Aubagne, in the *département* of the Bouches-du-Rhône, in nineteen forty-eight. You are sixty-two years old. You are *président–directeur général* of a company, Château da la Motte S.A. Is that correct?"

"Not quite. My son took over as managing director five years ago. Now I'm just *président,* and he's the *directeur général.* I no longer get my hands dirty," he said in an attempt to appear self-satisfied, pouring himself another glass of champagne.

"And is Château da la Motte a successful business?" Isabelle asked.

Voisin pursed his lips and tightened his throat. "Successful, Officer? That's a very relative term. Is this a philosophical interrogation? All your juge wanted to know was what I had seen in the restaurant, but you want to talk about economic theory instead?"

"It's a simple enough question, monsieur," Capucine said. "Is the company profitable, or is it not?"

"La Motte is one of the most prestigious wine producers of the Midi," he said defensively. "In fact, I think I can say we produce the finest rosé in all of France and Navarre." Finally comfortable, Voisin launched into the subject like a dinner party bore. Capucine let him have his head. It was the best way to get people to talk.

"From well before the birth of our Savior and all the way into the sixteen hundreds, almost all French wine was rosé. Stupidly, in modern times the French public has lost its love for rosé. The modern generation has turned its back on our viticultural heritage."

"So that means the company's losing money, right?" Isabelle asked.

"No, it does not, Officer. It's true that about fifteen years ago our volume fell off a bit. But I saved the situation. I introduced a range of second-label wines, which I branded Le Chevalier de la Motte. All the Bordeaux châteaux have second growths, so why not us? They were sold at a very reasonable price and enhanced our profitability considerably."

"I understood," Capucine said, "that you were accused at the time of abusing a venerable name to sell a very inferior wine at inflated prices."

Voisin jumped up. "Madame, that's a villainous lie! The Chevalier line has always been excellent. In fact, it received a gold medal for rosés only last year."

"Did the Chevalier label win any awards when you were managing the business?"

"The wine industry is very conservative. It takes them years to overcome their resistance to something new. But in the end they reward quality when they see it." He poured the last of the champagne into his glass.

"How is it, monsieur, you are lucky enough to be able to spend so much time in Paris?" David asked sweetly, as if to defuse the tension.

Voisin smiled at David and moved to the phone to order more champagne. "Once my son had learned the business well enough to take over operational management, I was only too happy to concentrate on defining the corporate strategy and acting as . . . well . . . ambassador to the industry. As it happens, I'm here to see my tailor and, of course, for a little bit of innocent amusement." He waved his arm vaguely in the direction of the bedroom and gave David a broad wink.

Isabelle grunted in anger.

In a few minutes room service returned. Voisin seemed oddly relieved. He was plainly exasperated at the ostentatious care the waiter took in opening the bottle and encouraged him with nervous gestures. When the cork popped he breathed an audible sigh. Once his glass was in hand, Capucine picked up the thread of the interview.

"I see in your file that just before you stepped down as directeur général, criminal and civil charges were brought against you by a young woman."

"Statutory rape," Isabelle said, filling in. "You like them young, don't you?"

Voisin filled his glass and downed it in one go. All of a sudden the wine seemed to affect him. His eyes became red, and he made a clear effort at focusing. Capucine suspected he was seeing double.

"Those charges were dropped," he said, just barely slurring his words.

"The business bought her out. Is that how it was done?" Isabelle asked.

Voisin shook his head slightly. "There *was* a pecuniary consideration. But only a very small one."

"And because of that you were asked to step down?"

Voisin had had enough of the back and forth. He was tired of them. "No. But it was the last straw. It was really about the wine. It had nothing to do with the girl and her absurd claims. It happened like this. The Chevalier line was doing well, very well. But it was being sold in supermarkets and the wine snobs can't have that, now can they? My son graduated from business school at HEC and started working in the business. He had all these highfalutin conceptual views he had learned there.

"To use his language, he felt that the difference in quality between our two wines created a 'vacuum' that damaged both brands. He insisted on improving the Chevalier de la Motte label and bringing it closer to the excellence of

Château de la Motte. I thought this was a huge mistake. I was afraid of cannibalizing the first growth with the second. I wanted Château de la Motte to stand alone, uncontested, without any competition, least of all from its own house. Do you understand?"

All three detectives nodded.

"But an improved second label would result in more revenue and better margins, I imagine," Capucine said.

"That was exactly Damien's view. He went on a lobbying campaign with the family. They own most of the stock. He made me appear a doddering old fool. He, of course, was a young genius who had just graduated from the best business school in France and had all the answers. I was polluting the historical image of the château to make vulgar money. But he was going to preserve the nobility of the *vignoble*'s tradition *and* the glory of the family while making even *more* money. For the family it was a highly attractive proposition. But in spite of that they still stuck by me." Voisin paused.

"And then that stupid girl had to get into the act with her idiotic suit. I could have talked her out of it, but Damien jumped in and paid her off behind my back. It was all the ammunition he needed. He got his way with the family."

There were a couple of long beats of silence.

"You know, I've always thought that Damien put her up to it. He engineered the whole thing. It's exactly the sort of thing he'd do."

This time the pause was longer.

"Young man," Voisin continued, "you wanted to know why I spend so much time in Paris. I'll tell you why. When I go to my own *vignoble,* I can't get past anyone's secretary. No one will give me the time of day. Damien runs the business like a tyrant and keeps me locked out. But, of course, every time the new Chevalier de la Motte—his Chevalier de la Motte—wins an award, Damien insists I go to receive it. He can't find enough salt to rub in my wounds."

He sighed a deep sigh of the long-suffering, so profound that bats could be heard flapping their wings in his lungs.

"So I amuse myself as I best I can under the circumstances," he said with world weariness to David, as if only a man could understand the true depths of suffering.

There was another long pause, which Capucine finally broke.

"Let's get back to last night at the restaurant," she said. "It seems an odd place for you to want to go."

"Exactly. Like way too down-market a place to take a movie star," David said.

Capucine was amazed that he actually seemed to have formed an affection for Voisin.

"Ah, my friend, you underestimate my little Sybille. She recognized the restaurant's potential," he answered with the hint of a wink. "It was her idea."

"And you really didn't see anything?" David asked.

"You know, it's funny you should ask," he said, as if it was the first time the question had been aired. "As my so-called meal was progressing, I had the impression that there was a very faint green spectral aura floating through the room. At the time I was sure it was my guardian angel. Then I shut my eyes. I'm sure you can imagine why. And when I opened them, the aura was gone. That girl really has a spectacular talent."

Capucine was so delighted with this piece of news that she was completely oblivious to Isabelle's low growl.

CHAPTER 14

It was nearly one in the afternoon by the time Capucine battered the Twingo into an impossibly tight space on the rue de Ménilmontant, a few doors down from her brigade. She realized she was ravenous.

"Do you think we can still squeeze into Benoît's? I'm starving," Capucine asked Isabelle, sitting next to her in the front seat.

"A little *casse-croûte* would be wonderful. All that vintage hot air has given me an appetite, too."

David opened his mouth to say something but thought better of it.

All three of them knew that a *casse-croûte*—a quick snack—was out of the question at Benoît's, the local restaurant of choice for the brigade personnel. It was a full meal, eaten and savored at leisure, or nothing. Benoît's was one of the last handful of genuine working-class bistros, which now existed only in the outlying arrondissements, like the Twentieth. The fare was only simple classics, but they were prepared with love and pride.

Inside, the detectives extracted their napkins, changed once a week, from a long rack of pigeonholes labeled with the names of regular patrons. The restaurant's sole waitress, Angélique, a matron of prodigious proportions, shepherded them to a table in the corner, eulogizing the day's selection.

"Since it's Friday we have two fish dishes, *quenelles de brochet* and *raie au beurre noir*. And for the men, since they're rarely religious," Angélique said, looking severely at David, "we have a *paupiette de veau* that you'll tell your mother about." Behind her, a slate blackboard proclaimed a list of six or seven dishes. They all existed, but Angélique was adamant about choosing for her patrons. Few dared argue with her.

Angélique produced her order pad. "So, *Commissaire*, the pike for you. The sauce is very delicate, perfect for someone of your sensitivity. And mademoiselle *brigadier-chef*, you'll enjoy the skate—"

"You know what?" Isabelle interrupted. "I'm going to have the veal paupiettes instead. My mother forced skate cooked like that down my throat when I was a child. All those bones and that nasty dark butter sauce with that vinegar." She gave a histrionic shudder, shaking her head. "The veal, please. Definitely."

"*Pas question!*" Angélique said. "Your mother was absolutely right. Skate is excellent for the complexion and that beautiful hair you have."

She stroked Isabelle's butch-cropped dark blond hair. Isabelle jerked away.

"*Oh, là laaaà,*" Angélique said in mock alarm. "You should let it grow. You could be very pretty if you took a little better care of yourself." The skate was clearly not up for debate.

"And *monsieur le brigadier* will have the paupiettes, *bien sûr,*" she said, not even looking at him for approval. "I'm going to give you a nice rosé. It's a Domaine Tempier, from Bandol, perfect for both the fish and the veal."

At the word *rosé,* the three detectives shot glances at each other.

"What now?" Angélique asked in a pantomime of irritation. "All of a sudden we don't like *rosé?*"

"Of course we do," Isabelle said. "Do you have any Château de la Motte?"

"Mademoiselle, where do you think you are? This is a restaurant for honest working people. We don't serve Bordeaux. We don't serve *any* fancy, rich-people wine." Angélique stalked off in a huff.

The detectives made small talk, gossiping themselves into a sense of contentment with acronyms and police jargon. When the food came, Isabelle waited until Angélique turned her back, and switched plates decisively with David.

"*Voilà pour toi, monsieur le brigadier* male chauvinist pig," she said.

"*A vos ordres, Brigadier-Chef,*" David replied with a grin and a smart salute. Capucine knew he hated sausage in any form. The paupiettes were a thin wrapping of pounded veal cutlet covering a big lump of sausage meat, held together tightly with string. It was the last thing he would have ordered for himself.

The exchange flooded Capucine with a wave of contentment. It was for moments like this that she had incurred the wrath of her parents to join the police. She smiled as she imagined her mother at their table. The pigeonholed napkins would have been bad, David's fey locks would have been worse, Isabelle's multiple ear piercings and butch haircut would have been an affront, and the very notion of eating proletarian paupiettes would have sent her running out the door.

The trill of her cell phone cut off her reflections.

She flipped it open, turned slightly sideways in her chair, offering a three-quarter profile, and flapped her hand over the table to indicate the two officers should begin.

"*Allô.* Dechery here. I have some preliminary information for you on last night's stiff. Is this a good time?"

"What did you guys find out?"

"The pathologist is just doing the autopsy now," Dechery said loudly over the shrieking whine of an electric saw. "But we already have a bunch of news that's going to interest you. We extracted the baster first thing this morning. First interesting fact, no prints, naturally, but we did find faint ridging on the surface that had been wiped."

"Ridging?"

"The baster had been held by someone wearing loose-fitting plastic-film gloves. Most likely the kind they use in food stores." He paused to see if she had a question.

"Got it. What else?"

"The needle on the baster was three and a half inches long and must have gone into the primary auditory cortex and probably into the cerebrum itself. That alone would have caused immediate death. There was also a residue of thick brown liquid that looked like it might have been injected. We'll know about that when the autopsy is complete. The pathologist is just lifting off the parietal and frontal—"

"Dechery, remember you're talking to a layperson here."

"The front and back of the top of the skull. He saws it off and lifts out the brain. He's doing it now."

Capucine pushed away her plate of lumpy white nuggets of fish in a liquid yellow sauce.

"Then we'll know how far in the needle went and be able to determine how much of the liquid was injected. But here's the punch line. We analyzed the residue in the baster this morning. You'll never guess what it was."

Capucine drummed her fingertips on the table, refusing to rise to the bait.

"A solution of ground-up castor beans!" Dechery was delighted. "Not only did your perp kill the victim with a basting needle but he also injected a castor-bean solution. Two firsts for me in one go. It's made my day."

"Castor beans? Is that some kind of poison?"

"Oh my dear! You kids of today have missed out on so much. Thirty years ago every child in France was regularly dosed with castor oil. It's a mild laxative."

"The murderer wanted to give the victim diarrhea?" Both Isabelle and David looked up at Capucine quizzically.

"There's an urban legend that castor beans are a deadly poison. You know, like the myth that eating rhubarb leaves will kill you instantly. I imagine the castor bean one comes from the fact that they contain ricin, which really *is* a lethal poison. They use it in biological weaponry. But you need a chromatographic protein laboratory to extract ricin from castor beans. This stuff was just crushed mush that had been boiled down. Nothing lethal about it at all." He paused. "Unless, of course, you inject it into someone's brain."

"But you're guessing the murderer probably didn't know that."

"Guessing's your job, *Commissaire*, not mine. But there's more."

"*Oui, Ajudant.*"

"Before we started the autopsy we did a thorough examination of the body with hyperspectral light. There was latent bruising on the left side of the face. Four small circular bruises, which almost certainly came from fingertips. We were able to get a very tight estimate of the time of the bruising and put it within half an hour of the death. It looks like someone came up behind the victim, held his head, and shoved the needle in his ear."

"Are you sure?"

"Of course I'm sure. The hand was very strong. That was why the pressure was on the fingertips and not the palm. Given the spacing between the bruises, it was probably a man's hand. It must have been a sudden, violent gesture."

When Capucine flipped her phone shut, David looked up from his plate and asked, "Death by diarrhea? This case just keeps getting better and better."

CHAPTER 15

They walked into the brigade at three fifteen. Capucine was sure that Sybille, if she came at all, would be at least half an hour late.

But she was already there, sitting in utter dejection on the hard wooden bench by the door. A baggy hoodie, two sizes too large, reached halfway down her black-legginged thighs. Despite the fact that the look was marred by a discreetly embroidered gray-on-gray LV on the hoodie—announcing a Louis Vuitton product—she was still perfectly convincing as a waif from the *banlieue* projects, living from one-night stand to one-night stand and from fix to fix. It was definitely clear that she had a fondness for Anne Parillaud roles. Incongruously, a small, expensive-looking shopping bag labeled SERGIO ROSSI stood arrogantly upright on the seat next to her.

"*Salut, Commissaire,*" Sybille said in a little voice.

"Mademoiselle has been here for nearly half an hour," the uniformed receptionist whined. He was so starstruck, he was unable to divert his eyes from Sybille even when addressing his *commissaire*.

Capucine led Sybille to her office, nodding at Isabelle to

follow and dismissing David with an almost imperceptible flick of her fingers.

Before they sat down, Sybille was transformed by one of her kaleidoscopic mood shifts. Bubbling with excitement, she pulled a shoe box from her shopping bag, extracting a pair of pumps for Capucine's approval. They were bright red sling-backs with outrageously high stiletto heels, a tiny opening in front for a big toe to peep out coyly, and inch-high platform soles. Capucine picked up one of the shoes admiringly.

"What do you think?" Sybille asked breathlessly. "They're Sergio Rossis, and they make me look six feet tall."

Isabelle was ostentatiously bored.

"I could never pull these off," Capucine said. "But they're going to be fabulous on you."

The two women giggled and embarked on a discussion of the dress that was to accompany the shoes. Both women called each other *"tu"* in flagrant violation of the police protocol that officers were to be addressed as *"vous"* and potential miscreants by the condescending *"tu."* Isabelle fidgeted and looked uncomfortable.

Like a skipper coaxing a very refined but capricious yacht into a jibe, Capucine nudged the conversation in a new direction.

"Sybille," she said, "it seems that the murder last night is probably connected to the one at Chez Béatrice."

Sybille looked at her blankly, as if she didn't quite understand what this had to do with her.

"And the curare that killed the victim at Chez Béatrice came from a Brazilian reception that you attended with Monsieur Voisin."

"And since I was there last night too, I'm a hot suspect. I love it! Totally." Sybille shrieked with joy.

"Wise up, kid," Isabelle said, outraged. "With your arrest record, the *commissaire* is being very kind interviewing you in her office and letting you go out shopping for ugly shoes. You should be in a detention cell right now."

"My arrest record?" Sybille said with a childish pout. "I've never been arrested in my life," she added, as if fighting back tears.

"Our records show that you've been charged with shoplifting sixteen times."

"Charges, smarges. They were all dropped."

"You paid the store owners off. Without your money you'd be in a juvenile center right now. You don't get what a serious position you're in."

"Officer, you're the one who doesn't get it. You shoplift because you're bored," Sybille said. "Why else would you bother? It's a kick. You walk by a counter, grab something, and stick it in your pocket. You get a mild rush. I always throw that stuff in the trash the minute I get out of the store. Like I really need another pair of sunglasses." She rolled her eyes. "If I weren't such a fucking celebrity with all the bullshit that goes with it, I wouldn't be shoplifting and getting bleeding noses from snorting coke, now would I?"

Isabelle checked, momentarily speechless.

"And I'll tell you another fucking thing. If you 'steal' a two-hundred-euro pair of Armani sunglasses and throw them in a Dumpster and then tell your lawyer to pay the store owner a thousand euros so he'll go away, do you really think that counts as a crime?"

Even though she knew it must be flawed, Isabelle was defeated by the logic.

"But, *Commissaire,*" Sybille continued, flashing Capucine a smile that she pulled out of an acting drawer labeled EARNEST LOOKS, "I really, truly didn't see anything at either restaurant. The first time I was just eating my dinner, which was actually pretty good, and I looked up and there was this old guy taking a nosedive into his grunts. Guy and I thought it was hysterical. We thought he'd zoned himself out on hooch or blow. But it turned out he was dead. Bummer for him.

"And the second one, as fifty Web sites will now tell you in glowing detail, I was fooling around under the table, and even if I hadn't been, I couldn't have seen anything in that goddamn place anyway."

"Aren't you ashamed of what you were doing? And with that phallocratic old man?" Isabelle asked.

"You know, 'Officer,' " Sybille said, the last word in heavy ironic quotes, "you just don't get much at all, do you? 'Phallocratic.' Phallo-*fucking*-cratic! Christ. Phallo-fuck *you!*"

There was a long three-beat pause. Isabelle didn't know what to say and Capucine was waiting for the rest of it.

"Do you have any idea at all where my big fucking success came from?" Sybille asked with a tone clearly implying that no one over the age of eighteen was capable of understanding anything. "It came from that awful movie. The movie where they raped me."

Capucine raised an eyebrow a quarter of an inch in interrogation.

"*The Black Horror of the Catacombs of Paris.* Remember? That's the one where champagne is squirted on my face after a big, heavy music buildup, implying that I was supposed to have—what's that neato word you like to use in the police?—'*fellated*' the forty-year-old star. Do you know how that was done? Wanna hear about it? I was fourteen at the time. I was told to get on my knees and read a prayer to the fucking world-famous lead actor. It was supposed to be a black-magic initiation rite. Then, two weeks later, we shot a party scene, and I was told that someone was going to open a bottle of champagne. I had no idea it was warm and they'd shook it up and it was going to go all over my face. When I went to the premiere and saw the cut with all those awful people there in those fat-cat clothes just loving it, I cried. I just sat there bawling. It was worse than having been raped. Way worse."

Despite the obvious antagonism toward her, Isabelle looked at Sybille in tender empathy, another defenseless victim abused by the phallocratic society all women are subjected to.

"How did you wind up in the movies?" Capucine asked.

"It was my father. He always told me I was very beautiful. More beautiful than anyone he had ever seen in the cinema. Ever since I was a small child, he made sure I was in all the school plays. By the time I was ten, I was famous in our village as an actress. When I was twelve, he took me to Paris. A friend of his had a cousin who worked at Gaumont and the man was going to give me a screen test. Gaumont put me on contract, and the rest is history," she said with heavy cynicism.

"Doesn't your father deserve some credit for recognizing your talent?" Capucine said.

"My talent? Right. You know what my fucking talent was? My dear old dad left me with this fat old boozehound at Gaumont and told me to be 'real nice to him.' Do you have any idea what that means?"

Capucine was so taken aback, she spoke without thinking.

"Are you sure your father really suggested that?"

"Jeez, *Commissaire,* you must have the best plastic surgeon in the world. What are you? Eighty? How do you think he came to suggest something like that?"

Capucine was utterly nonplussed.

"Look. When I was a really little kid, like three or four or five, my father spent more time with me than my mom. He'd wash me in my bath and then dress me and all that stuff. Getting the picture?"

"How can you possibly remember that?"

"Easy. My mother told me. And he got 'closer' and 'closer' to me right up until she left him." The word *closer* was said with heavy irony.

"Your mother left your father? And you didn't go with her?"

"She left with some guy who didn't like kids, so I was stuck with dear old Dad."

"That must have been very difficult for you."

"No. I was under contract and the euros were cascading in. He was all lovey-dovey."

"And are you estranged from him now?"

"Estranged? Does that mean, do I still see him? You better believe I do. He's my goddamn manager. In fact, he's the only guy in the world I really trust. He's my *man*. I don't go to the toilet unless he okays it."

"I see. Can we talk about your relationship to Guy Voisin?"

"Guy? What's there to say? He's fabulous. Or do you want hot pictures? I have a bunch I could give you. You could post them on your bulletin board. How cool would that be?"

"Where did you meet him?"

" 'Where did you meet him?' Sure, Mommy. If you really want to know, I met him three or four months ago at *Les Bains*."

"Where?" Isabelle asked.

"Oh, God. *Les Bains Douches*. You know, like, the club. Duh."

"And he was there dancing the night away?" Capucine asked.

"Guy? Not even close. I was downstairs with a bunch of assholes who were making me want to barf, they were so boring. On top of it all they'd run out of blow. I really needed to get out of there, but I didn't have any money."

"No money? How could you not have money?" Isabelle asked.

"You're not going to take a bag or anything to a club, are you? Normally, I stick a hundred euro note into my panties in case something comes up except I wasn't wearing any that night. So I went upstairs to the restaurant to see if there was anyone I knew. And there was my sweet little Guy, having snackies with some geriatrics. He looked at me and I looked at him and he knew right off what I wanted."

"What you wanted?" Isabelle asked. "It was love at first sight?"

Sybille gave Isabelle another withering look and examined the ceiling carefully from end to end.

"So we did a bunch of lines on top of the toilet seat in the ladies' room—that's a great way to get to know people in a hurry. You ought to try it sometime. And that was that."

"Meaning?" Capucine asked.

"Meaning he said he had some stuff called Bolshoi Grand Battements back at his place and asked me if I wanted to try it. Obviously I did."

"Ballet moves?"

"Hey, *Commissaire,* you know, it's like you look kind of a little hip, but when you start talking, wow! BGB is like blow, but way, way better. Maybe someday I'll bring you some and you can see what it does. It might change the way you see things, like in a very good way."

"Sybille," Capucine said, "Monsieur Voisin is sixty-two and you're eighteen—"

"Christ, don't tell anyone *that!* My agent wants the world to think I'm sixteen. I'll be sweet sixteen forever. He thinks that makes me sexier."

"How can you have a sexual relationship with a man old enough to be your grandfather?" Isabelle asked. "Don't you find it disgusting that he preys on you like that?"

Sybille produced her withering look again. "You two really do sound just like everybody's mother and grandmother rolled into one. You know what? Just because I didn't finish the lycée and don't have my *bac* doesn't make me an ignoramus. It just so happens I've read Freud and know exactly what you're getting at."

Capucine looked at her with just the hint of a sympathetic smile and said nothing.

"You think I'm with Guy because he's some sort of father figure and I need an old fart to protect me because I'm some sort of retard, don't you?"

Capucine increased the sympathy in her smile by half a notch.

"That's because you don't understand *anything*. If anyone's doing any protecting in our thing, it's me. That's the whole point. Guy's flat broke. *I* pay for the dinners. *I* score the blow. *Merde,* I even paid to have his fat-cat, humongous Mercedes overhauled last week. What do you think about that?" She leaned back with the self-satisfied smile of someone who has scored a major point.

"But isn't he chairman and part owner of a large *vignoble?*" Capucine asked.

"Maybe he is, but he still doesn't have two euro coins to rub together in his jeans. And I'll tell you why. You think I'm a complete retard, but I'm *so* not. I asked my lawyer to check him out. It seems Guy's shares, as well as the rest of the family's, are in some sort of trust. The way it works is that the family votes on everything and they decide how the money gets doled out. He's got lots of shares but not even close to a majority. So he doesn't ever get any gelt from the company. Got that, *Commissaire,* or is this too complicated for you?"

"But he still gets a salary," Capucine said. "So why do you have to pay for his dinners?"

"Who the hell cares? I dunno where his shekels go. And I don't give a rusty fuck. Maybe Guy has another little honey on the side. Hey, there's an idea. We could do a threesome. How cool would that be? But he hasn't come clean on that one yet." She rooted around in her oversized handbag, pulled out a pack of Marlboro Reds, lit one, and blew a thick stream of smoke through her smile.

"Okay if I smoke?" she asked rhetorically. Capucine pushed an ashtray toward her.

"So what do you see in him?" Isabelle asked.

"What do I see in him? What *don't* I see in him? Guy's my little puppy dog. He's pleased as shit to follow me around all day. He never asks for anything. Well, yeah, a little small change maybe, but so fucking what? Sometimes he's like, 'Let's go to such and such three-star restaurant tonight' or 'I need a new suit. Let's go get one at Chaumet,' but that's nothing. It doesn't even count as money. And the best part is he doesn't even like sex. Guys my own age are all over me all the time. You can't even get a decent night's sleep. Guy, man, his head hits the pillow and he's gonzo. It's great!"

"That's not the impression you two give."

"Don't tell me you fell for that crap. You're *so* like somebody's grandmother. That started out as a joke, and now everyone just assumes that's all we do. Take that crazy blind restaurant where the guy was killed. Everyone, and I mean everyone, had his mind in the gutter as to why I was under the table. Well, duh, I was railing a few lines of Special K down there. And, hey, try that one in the dark." She laughed happily.

"Ketamine. A veterinary tranquilizer," Isabelle said, entirely unnecessarily, for Capucine's benefit.

Sybille rolled her eyes.

"You know, that place got really old after about three minutes with the bad food and people making a mess and squealing and all. What the hell else was there to do? K's something you should definitely try, Officer. It gives you a nice mellow outlook on life. You could really use that."

"Have you always liked older men?" Capucine asked.

"Duh. Who wouldn't? They're not childish like guys my age, and I know just how to get what I want from them. My daddy taught me all about that."

CHAPTER 16

Even though Parisians—with the help of a good bit of wishful thinking—prided themselves on their lack of materialism, most of them shared one common object of unbridled desire. This was an apartment on the quai opposite the place de la Concorde. Every night its brightly lit, two-story-high semicircular window sneered down at the traffic stalled in the square. Exasperated motorists inching forward toward their humdrum dinners and domestic squabbles imagined an enormous living room with a spectacular view, populated by a select handful—remarkable physically, sartorially, and intellectually—sipping *martinis américains* in tiny cone-shaped crystal glasses while prattling on with brilliant insouciance.

As it happened, the apartment in question was owned by Capucine's cousin Jacques, who had purchased it when the serendipitous confluence of three substantial inheritances coincided with the apartment's appearance on the market.

Jacques was the closest thing Capucine had to a brother. They had been inseparable companions since early childhood, and now that Jacques held some vague but apparently august position in the DGSE, France's intelligence agency, they shared a loose professional bond. In fact, Jacques had bailed her out on more than one of her cases.

In keeping with his mercurial personality, Jacques redecorated the flat at least twice a year. Capucine was convinced there was some deep Freudian significance to this contrived instability but didn't have the slightest inkling of what it might be.

He had called her the week before with an invitation to a dinner party—a *dîner en ville,* as he had described it—in honor of the latest refurbishment. Capucine was to come at seven, an hour and a half before Alexandre and the other guests, so he "could catch up on all his nubile cousin's little peccadilloes" while he supervised the preparation of dinner.

For a split second after she arrived, let in by one of the catering staff, Capucine thought the new furniture had been delivered that afternoon and was still covered with dust cloths. Every single piece in the cavernous room was draped in fabric tinted in a blue so pale it took an effort to perceive the hue.

"You hate it, of course," Jacques said, entering the gigantic room, foppish as ever in a light brown silk suit, the fourth button on each sleeve conspicuously unbuttoned, a dark blue silk shirt open to mid-chest, giving him an aggressively relaxed, rock-star look. "It was done by a decorator who is profoundly influenced by Christo and Jeanne-Claude. You know, the couple who drape bridges and islands and things."

"It's quite . . . interesting," Capucine said.

"No it isn't. The only appeal is that every time someone sits on anything, the decorator has to come back the next morning to redrape the cloth, while glaring at me in reproach." He emitted a loud cackle halfway between a hyena's snicker and a donkey's bray. "Truth be told, it's been this way for a week and I'm already more than a little sick of it."

He sidled up to Capucine with a burlesque of a Lothario leer. "It's delightful to see you, *ma petite cousine*," he murmured and embraced her in a hug that began with an exploration of her back and proceeded gradually south. When his fingers reached her waist, Capucine pulled away and slapped him playfully on the cheek.

He winked and took her by the hand.

"Come with me *mon petit chou*—little cabbage of my life. We're needed in the kitchen."

The kitchen was also brand new. The ceiling had been raised into the floor above to form a perfect cube. Every surface, including floor and ceiling, was covered in apparently seamless, gleaming white lacquer, like a squash court from hell. No appliances or kitchen utensils were visible. The room was completely bare save for a long brilliantly white marble table in the exact center.

"Hideous, isn't it?" Jacques said. "I can't wait until Alexandre sees it. He'll be apoplectic." He neighed his demonic laugh.

Three women in white aprons unloaded aluminum boxes onto the center table, taking particular care not to scratch the surface. A fourth, who looked vaguely familiar to Capucine, wandered around feverishly, searching the room frantically. In a flash Jacqueline de Sansavour's photo from a *Figaro Madame* article the week before popped up in Capucine's consciousness. Apparently, she was officially the ne plus ultra of the Paris catering scene.

"Excuse me," Madame de Sansavour said nervously. "There must be a stove, *non?*"

"Of course," Jacques said. "Right here. Just push the panel and the door opens up." He pushed. The panel slid upward, disappearing with a discreet sibilant hiss, revealing a professional brushed-steel range.

Madame de Sansavour breathed a deep sigh of relief.

"Enough of all this domesticity," Jacques said to Capucine. "Come and have a drink. We have a good hour and a half until Tubby Hubby arrives. I'm sure we can pass the time in all sorts of creative ways."

She followed her cousin into what he called "his room," a cramped, cluttered student's studio with disordered bookshelves along one wall, a particularly messy desk, an unmade single bed. The room was categorically off-limits to decorators and Capucine knew it was where Jacques spent most of his time when at home, almost never wandering out into the rest of the huge apartment if guests weren't present.

An overturned wooden wine crate held a small array of bottles, a few glasses, and a bottle of Krug champagne in a dented tin ice bucket. In a maternal gesture, Capucine straightened the sheets on the bed, pulled the covers up, and sat, knees primly together, on the edge.

Without asking, Jacques poured Capucine a flute of champagne and two fingers of Japanese whiskey for himself. Furtively, he added an ice cube.

Putting his index finger to his lips and sitting next to her on the bed, he said, "Not a word to Portly Partner. He'd never forgive the desecration of the whiskey he taught me to drink.

"I see from the scraps of paper that flit across my desk that you're working on an amusing little case. A restaurant critic who's been snuffed out in flagrante critico, as it were. What fun. And it seems that you're giving that poor, valiant *juge d'instruction,* August-Marie Parmentier de La Martinière, such a hard time, it borders on insubordination." He cackled loudly.

"And I also understand that your suspects include a delectable, barely pubescent sexpot movie star, the current winner of the Prix Goncourt, the owner of one of the most well-known wine domains in France, the heiress to one of the great fortunes of France, who is amusing herself by dabbling in the restaurant business, and our dear childhood playmate who now hobnobs with the government's ministerial cabinets."

"You do get that kind of dramatis personae when murders happen in haute cuisine restaurants," Capucine replied with studied nonchalance. "Your little scraps of paper seem to be particularly well informed. Your people wouldn't happen to be bugging the *PJ's* phones, would they?"

"Bug? I wouldn't even know what such a vulgarism might mean. But when you're entrusted with the protection of the patrimony of *La Belle France* from the onslaught of the philistine invasion, your weapons must be very well honed indeed."

Capucine did not smile at this. Jacques frowned in mock concern.

"Oh, stop fretting. Be kind to your dear little juge. Underneath it all, you know he loves you. He's a little shy. Just don't lend him any money. He'll be unemployed by the Saint-Sylvestre," Jacques said, using the French term for New Year's Eve.

"That's not it at all."

"Oh, how dim of me. You think Corpulent Consort might be on the murderer's list. Could that be it?"

"More or less. I'm concerned that there's some chance these are not rational, motive-driven murders. Some deranged person may be engineering some sort of vendetta against journalists or restaurant critics or something like that."

Jacques hee-hawing laugh exploded. "A serial killer in France! Can you imagine? You've been watching too much American TV. Serial killing is just not our thing. The only one we've ever had who didn't ride a horse was Eusebius Pieydagnelle. And he only killed hot young women, presumably because they laughed at his name. If my parents had saddled me with a moniker like that, I'd probably try to take out as much of the population as I could, too."

"Be serious, Jacques. Two critics have been killed while

reviewing restaurants. In virtually identical circumstances. Of *course* it makes you think. And the worst part is that the *juge d'instruction* is making it impossible for me to take any action on the case. I feel so impotent."

"I'd have thought you'd be used to that with Geriatric Gastronome."

"Jacques, please! I need to talk to you about this."

"All is not lost. My little pieces of paper also tell me that the PJ was naughtily negligent in the way they reported the second murder to the magistrates. Fingers will be rapped with the administrative ruler in due course, but you still have a few days' grace before your juge reappears on your horizon."

"But he'll be back. And then I won't be able to do a thing. I may need you to pull some strings for me one more time."

"*Cousine,* even the DGSE doesn't dare stick its blood-stained fingers into the magistrates' hall. You know what's inscribed over their door. '*Lasciate ogni speranza, voi ch'entrate*'—'Abandon all hope, ye who enter.' This time, I'm afraid you're on your own." His hee-haw was so piercing that Jacqueline de Sansavour appeared at the door, alarmed.

"Is everything all right?" she asked with wrinkled brow.

Jacques favored her with an enigmatic smile.

Madame de Sansavour proffered a dinner plate on which the perfectly browned carcass of a small bird lay on a bed of dark green sauce, surrounded by almost fluorescently orange baby carrots and brilliant green, undersized string beans.

"I thought I'd show you what you're serving tonight," she said her voice lowered conspiratorially. "It's a recipe I pinched from Béatrice Mesnagier."

Capucine and Jacques darted each other a conspiratorial glance.

Mistaking their look for a lack of recognition, Madame

de Sansavour said, "She's the up-and-coming star of the Parisian restaurant world. The *tout Paris* talks only of her. This is quail stuffed with foie gras on a bed of *pistou,* accompanied by carrots and *haricots primeurs.* Of course, they're not really primeur this late in the season. I have a supplier who plants late to make them look like early spring vegetables. What do you think?"

Both Capucine and Jacques peered intently, sniffed as energetically as hound puppies and beamed idiotically.

When she left, Jacques looked at Capucine thoughtfully. "You know," he began, "this *juge* of yours—"

Jacques fell silent, cocked his head, eyebrows raised, ears piqued at the door.

In a loud theatrical voice he said, "Quick, *ma cousine,* slip your panties back on and pretend nothing happened. That always works."

Alexandre walked into the room scowling. Biting her lip, Capucine tried very hard not to giggle. Alexandre was such a sucker for Jacques' gibes.

Capucine could never come to grips with her husband's jealousy of her favorite cousin. True, Jacques loved to tease Alexandre with veiled double entendres of implied past sexual episodes between him and Capucine. True, too, that in the years since their marriage Jacques had refined his repartee to a degree that he could enrage Alexandre with the vaguest of references. But surely Alexandre could see that it was all just affectionate ribbing. Inexplicably, he never did.

"So you've taken to cooking, have you?" Alexandre asked Jacques a little coldly.

"I have indeed. I've been sweating like a navvy at my stove all afternoon and right now have a few helpers cleaning up the kitchen before the guests arrive."

Alexandre harrumphed. "I just ran into Jacqueline de Sansavour. I wrote a piece on her a few weeks back. Her catering is the current rage. I wouldn't have thought you'd have the good taste to hire her."

"So, Jacques," Capucine interjected hastily, "who's coming tonight?"

"As Françoise Sagan used to say, 'The four sexes will be represented.' A novelist whose stories all take place in Japan, a poet who writes only in classic alexandrines, a sculptor who does delightfully nasty things with steel, and a dancer who has elevated the tango to new heights."

"I see," Alexandre said. "And I take it Capucine and I are here to represent the other two sexes, is that it?"

"And so there will be seven at the table?" Capucine asked, a little more loudly than necessary.

"Oh, yes," Jacques drawled, aping a Sixteenth Arrondissement accent. "I've given the matter of the optimum number of people at a dinner party a great deal of thought. Conventional wisdom has it that eight is the ideal number. But it strikes me that an odd number is far superior. Five is too few. There is just a single cumbersome conversation. Seven is perfect. The conversation fragments, regroups, and fragments again. And with an odd number everyone tries to guess who's the odd person out. That creates a delightful creative tension."

"The odd person out?" Alexandre asked. "Surely that can't be the host?"

With dismay Capucine saw the direction Alexandre was attempting to take. He never seemed to accept the impossibility of defeating her cousin at his own game.

"Hardly."

"Does that mean this may be the evening we are finally to be introduced to a significant other? Should the family prepare itself for a blessed announcement?"

"My dear cousin-in-law, when I told you the four sexes would be represented, I was simplifying for a general audience. As I'm sure you know, there are now really eight.

Possibly ten, if you count fastidiously. It's the principal progress our civilization has achieved since Sagan's day. Don't you think?"

Despite himself, Alexandre struggled with the mental gymnastics of identifying ten different sexes. Capucine bit her lip once again to keep from giggling.

Jacques put his hand affectionately on Alexandre's upper arm. "When the dinner is over, why don't you tell who you think my putative consort is and to which of the ten groups 'he' or 'she' belongs?"

Alexandre glared at him.

"If you guess right, and give me your blessing, I might even be tempted to bring 'him' or 'her' to the *Dîner en Blanc*. Or perhaps not," Jacques said with the smarmiest variant on his Cheshire grin.

"The *Dîner en Blanc,*" Alexandre said with the relief of a drowning man clutching a life ring. "I'd forgotten that it was next week. I know it's a little passé, but I still think it's great fun to dress up in white and descend en masse for a picnic in some part of Paris like some sort of culinary flash mob."

Capucine wondered if his emotion was elation at the upcoming dinner or relief that the subject of multiple sexes had been abandoned.

"Pardon, monsieur," Madame de Sansavour said, peeking timidly through the door. "I think your guests are here." From behind her a wave of bourgeois phonemes rolled into the room.

Jacques's dinner was an undeniable success. It turned out the novelist and the sculptor were women and the poet and and the dancer were men. They had all whetted their epigrams well and the conversation tintinnabulated like rapiers ringing against each other at a duel. Alexandre's eye bounced back and forth across the table continually, as he vainly attempted to discern the slightest attachment between Jacques and one of the guests. It was only when the

quail stuffed with foie gras arrived—it really was superb—
that he gave up his futile quest.

Well after midnight, just as the conversation was coast-
ing comfortably toward its perigee, someone raised the
topic of Gaël Tanguy in the context of being the darkest
possible horse in history to have ever received the coveted
Goncourt. Tanguy was a source of acute frustration for
Capucine as he was one of the suspects who remained tan-
talizingly beyond her reach. The conversation flared. The
novelist and the poet launched into an argument of fulmi-
nating violence. The poet decried Tanguy as a charlatan
who had nothing to say and who was revolting merely to
be the focus of the press. The novelist hotly compared him
to Baudelaire and accused the poet of being incapable of
comprehending a work easily equal to *Les Fleurs du Mal.*
The dancer and the sculptor joined the fray. It wasn't until
Jacques adopted his Sixteenth Arrondissement drawl and
said, "Say what you will, but Tanguy has awakened my
erotic interest in my coffeemaker. He's added a whole new
dimension to my life," and followed it up with an earsplitting
rendition of his braying laugh, that the table was brought to
order and calm restored.

The dinner ended in the warm, embracing, multihued
cloud of good fellowship that is the ultimate object of every
Parisian *dîner mondain.* Only Capucine remained on edge
as the worm of frustration tunneled inexorably through
her innards.

CHAPTER 17

At ten the next morning Capucine was deeply immersed in the bitter waters of one of her brigade's case files. An SDF—police jargon for *sans domicile fixe,* a homeless person—had been savaged viciously by a dog at four in the morning as he was sleeping in the doorway of a Carrefour supermarket. The lieutenant in charge of the case suspected it was the work of a gang of youths notorious for breeding and arranging fights for illegal pit bulls. He had a few good leads. He needed more support to run them to ground.

The phone rang. Immersed in the lengthy and grisly description of the victim's wounds, Capucine picked up the receiver mechanically.

"Commissaire? Hi! It's Béatrice. From the restaurant."

"Béatrice. *Ca va?* How are things?"

There was a short pause.

"*Pas mal*—just fine. I was calling because, well, I hadn't spoken to you in over a week and was wondering if you had any news on that killing in my restaurant."

"We're making satisfactory progress on the case."

Béatrice snorted a polite guffaw. "Capucine, it's me,

Béatrice, your favorite chef, not the press. You don't have to feed me a line."

"Sorry." Capucine laughed. "But it's not really a line. Police work is mostly slogging and even when you've been at it for weeks there's often not all that much to talk about."

"Poor you. That must be really frustrating sometimes. Listen. I was also calling because I want to ask you to do me a favor. Will you do something for me?"

"A favor? What's up?"

"I want you to be my guinea pig."

"I don't understand."

"I'm trying out something new in the restaurant, and I want you to tell me if it works or not. See, a lot of restaurants put a table for two right in the kitchen. The guests get to sit in the middle of the action. No barrier at all between chef and diner. I'm dying to do that, but my maître d' tells me I'm too foulmouthed."

"And you want to try it out on me? Is that it?"

"If you could. I'm going to clear out my office and put a table in there just to see how it works. See, you'd be the distinguished guest, but since you're really a pal, it would be okay if the experiment doesn't work out."

"Count on me. I'm game. Just tell me when."

"Tomorrow night, if you're free. And I'm also going to try out a new dish on you. I've been working on it for months. It's a big departure from what I usually do, but it's totally fabulous and I want it to be my signature piece. You'll be the first person outside of my kitchen who's tasted it."

"I wouldn't miss this for the world."

With great formality Capucine was shown into Béatrice's tiny office by the black-suited maître d'. The desk piled with papers and notebooks had been replaced by a

small two-person table covered with an immaculate white
tablecloth set with stemmed glasses, the restaurant's gold-
rimmed plates, and monogrammed silver flatware. As the
maître d' eased her into the chair, a waiter arrived with a
flute of champagne.

"Before we start," the maître d' said with the gravity of
a croupier, "Chef would like to show you the preparation
of your appetizer. I think she'll be ready in a minute."

Béatrice stood at the corner of a table surrounded by
four cooks in brilliantly white T-shirts set off by black
aprons. The cooks were bent over intently, brows fur-
rowed, staring at something on the stainless-steel table as
Béatrice lectured them, wagging a finger in the air. In the
contrasting light and shadow from the overhead lamp, the
tableau looked like a scene from an eighteenth-century
medical dissection.

Béatrice looked up and pointed at the maître d'.

"I believe Chef is ready for you now," he said.

Béatrice beamed and kissed Capucine on both cheeks.
"We're about to assemble our little masterpiece. If you
don't tell me it's the best thing you've ever put in your
mouth, I'll . . . I don't know . . . cry, probably."

The center of attention was a shiny, solid-looking sepia
tube that appeared to be made of industrial plastic, possibly a component of some mechanical apparatus. A one-
inch hole had been bored through the center and was filled
with a gelatinous sludge the color of crankcase oil. It was
anything but appetizing.

As Béatrice extracted a long-bladed chef's knife from a
stainless-steel beaker filled with water, there was a collective intake of breath. With great care she cut a sliver from
the end of the tube. The knife slid through the substance as
if it was warm butter. One of the chefs scooped up the initial slice and removed it. The tension around the table increased a notch.

Béatrice dipped the knife back in the beaker of water

and cut a second slice—this one a good inch thick—and placed it reverently on one of the restaurant's plates. An acolyte produced a plastic squeeze bottle and—with great concentration—made an artistic squiggle of black sludge around the supine disk.

A waiter appeared and, under the hawkeyed gaze of the maître d', took the plate to Capucine's table. Capucine followed, trailed by a procession of white-clad cooks, who hovered, almost farcically nervous, when she sat.

A waiter ceremoniously placed a small silver bucket on the table containing points of brioche toast peeking coquettishly out of a napkin.

"What am I supposed to do here?" Capucine asked. "Eat it like foie gras?"

"Of course. It *is* foie gras," Béatrice said.

It certainly didn't look like any foie gras Capucine had ever seen. She cut a small section and put it on a piece of the toast.

"Put some of the sauce on it. That's very important," Béatrice said.

As Capucine put the morsel in her mouth, the four chefs stared at her intently, waiting for the verdict. The scene reminded her of that coffee advertisement where the entire village waits breathlessly for the decision as the gringo taster samples their beans. She suppressed a giggle, and then the taste hit her. It was a lobe of foie gras, no doubt at all about that, but as she held it in her mouth, the flavor continued to grow and grow and grow in a crescendo that culminated with far more intensity than any foie gras she had ever eaten. As the detonation subsided, she recognized a delicate fruity sweetness. Fig? Yes. The sludge was some sort of fabulous fig sauce.

"It *is* the best thing I've ever eaten. Without any doubt at all. But what on earth is it?"

The four chefs beamed. A mariachi band played loudly. The gringo would buy the coffee. The village was saved.

"The magic of the laboratory," Béatrice said. "Molecular cuisine. Food is deconstructed and then reconstructed so that it tastes even more like itself. Like sorbet, but carried to new heights."

"But how did you make this?"

"The lobe is first put in a bag, which goes into a vacuum machine that sucks out all the air. Then it sits in a precisely controlled water bath the precise temperate the inside would reach if it was grilled on a pan. That way the entire lobe reaches the ideal temperature. If it's cooked in a pan, the outside is overcooked so the middle comes out right."

"Is that what they call *sous vide?*"

"Exactly," Béatrice said in a tone halfway between an older sister and a schoolmarm. "After four hours it's ready. Then it goes into a special high-speed blender that transforms it into an unctuous cream. We inject that under pressure into a steel cylinder, which is flash frozen with liquid nitrogen. When it's rock hard, it's released and kept frozen for a day until it's allowed to thaw very, very slowly. The freezing process further accentuates the taste."

"And the sauce?" Capucine asked.

"Now that's a little tricky," Béatrice said.

Her four chefs laughed politely in adulatory agreement.

"It's made with fresh Persian figs with a number of Indian spices and a hint of ginger. It's cooked only just enough to marry the components but not to reduce it. The trick is that instead of boiling it down, which would sully the flavors, I reduce it in a chemist's centrifuge, which separates the liquid from the solids. That's why it tastes more figgy then figs do. It's harder to pull off than to describe."

"I'm beyond impressed," Capucine said.

Béatrice laughed. "So are we. We had some exciting moments with that liquid nitrogen. I'm amazed we all still have ten fingers left."

The chefs continued to beam.

"All right," Béatrice said. "You just sit and enjoy your

molecular treat while I get these guys off their high and sorted out for the dinner service. Then I'll be back and we can catch up."

As Capucine drifted beatifically with her foie gras and the glass of Sauternes that had appeared unnoticed, the kitchen began to pick up momentum as the restaurant filled slowly for the dinner service. The noise level escalated, and the air filled with steam, pungent odors, and urgent, coarse invective.

Once the kitchen choreography stabilized and the noise level dimmed, Béatrice arrived with the main course, the quail stuffed with foie gras Capucine had been served at Jacques' dinner.

"Normally, I'd never serve foie gras on top of foie gras, but you're like family and I wanted you to taste this. It's my signature dish, the staple of the restaurant."

Even though it appeared identical, and had presumably been made following an identical recipe, the quail was so superior to Madame de Sansavour's, it seemed like an entirely different dish. Capucine decided Alexandre was going to have to explain how that was possible.

"So, still no breakthroughs on the killing in my restaurant?" Béatrice asked.

Capucine shook her head, relishing her quail. "This is really unbelievably good."

"Yup. The problem is that we cook it so often, the chefs do it by rote now. That invites mediocrity. I'm going to have to take it off the menu. And what about the murder in that blind restaurant? Do you think it was the same guy?"

"Might have been," Capucine said. "The MO was almost identical."

"It was?"

"The victim was stabbed fatally with a basting needle but he was also injected with a concentrate of castor beans."

"It's totally lethal, right?"

"No. That's an old wives' tale. To extract the poison from castor beans, you need a complicated chemistry lab."

"Well, I convinced my mother it was poisonous and got her to stop making me take that awful castor oil. It was the only time I ever convinced her of anything."

Both women laughed.

"And how do you go about solving these cases? Is it like television, where very somber and intense men determine the identity of the killer from a single microfiber found in the victim's nose?"

"We have those somber, intense guys, all right. But they haven't found anything. So it's going to be good old flat-footed police work, pounding the pavement, looking for a motive."

"Motive?"

"Ninety-five percent of all police work is so-called motive-driven. Find out who would benefit from the crime and you're three quarters of the way to finding the culprit."

"Motive. I never would have thought of that. I thought it was all about clues—"

Béatrice jumped up. *"Bordel de merde, Jean, qu'est-ce que tu me fous la!"* She dashed over to one of the chefs and pushed him away from his station with her hip. Peering down into a copper pot he had been whisking, she shook her head in disgust.

"Putain de merde," she shouted. *"C'est dégelasse. Dé . . . gueu . . . lasse!*—Vomit! Start over!" The cook stood abashed, trying to hide under the stove.

As the loud, heavily spiced, remonstration continued, the maître d' appeared at Capucine's table, his croupier's veneer cracked, his brow wrinkled by lines of concern.

"Ça vous convient, Madame? Is everything all right? Is Madame enjoying her experience of eating in the kitchen? Madame doesn't find it too troubling?" He looked ner-

vously at Béatrice, who continued ranting, red-faced, at the cook. When it was finally over and she started to return, the maître d' intercepted her and whispered urgently in her ear.

Béatrice arrived at the table, blowing exasperated puffs of irritation.

"He's telling me that I won't be able to talk to my chefs like that if I'm going to have patrons eating in the kitchen. How the fuck does that smart-ass think this stuff gets cooked? This isn't some fucking TV show where sweet, fat old ladies make coq au vin while they prattle on about their stupid grandchildren. *Merde!*" Béatrice kicked the table leg. Capucine's empty plate jumped, and she grabbed her glasses before they toppled over.

Béatrice took a deep breath and sat down. "Some cheese?" she asked Capucine with forced sweetness.

Capucine nodded, feeling a rush of sympathy. How many times had she fought to master her own irritation and frustration? How often had she been tempted to shake an officer by the scruff of his neck?

"The table in the middle of the kitchen might not be the best idea, after all, right?" Béatrice asked.

Capucine squeezed her hand. "Maybe in good time. Or maybe not." Capucine smiled at her. "You know, the genius of your cooking really doesn't need support from any gimmicks."

Capucine smiled and then burst into laughter.

"What's so funny?" Béatrice asked with a hint of irritation.

"I was thinking about my mother. I once got spanked for saying something we had been served at dinner was *dégueulasse.*"

"Spanked? You got off lightly. I was deprived of dessert for a week for saying that!"

In the midst of their laughter Capucine crossed over a watershed.

"You know," she said. *"The Dîner en Blanc* is next week. We're setting up a table for six. Just a few close friends and my cousin, but it would be totally fabulous if you could join us."

"The Dîner en Blanc? What's that?"

"It's this silly tradition—actually kind of fun, though— that's been going on for years. It started when about twenty or thirty people dressed up in white outfits and had a picnic in some public place in Paris. You know, like the courtyard of the Louvre or someplace like that. They'd arrive, throw a big white tablecloth on the ground, and gobble up their picnic before the police arrived. Over the years it just got bigger and bigger, and now it's a huge production with rented buses and thousands of people. The location is still kept secret even though it's officially 'tolerated.' "

"So how do you know where to go?"

"They announce a meeting place—usually somewhere in the Bois de Boulogne—where the buses are lined up. Last year five thousand people showed up. You bring folding bridge tables and dress as extravagantly as you want, but it has to be all in white. And, of course, you bring fabulous food and wine."

"How did I miss this?"

"Probably because you were in the South, but you won't miss it this year."

Béatrice looked crestfallen. "I'd love to go, but there's just no way I can leave the restaurant. You've seen the way the cooks get. One disastrous dinner and I'm toast. But . . . wait. Let me cook dinner for you guys. How about that?"

"Béatrice, I can't let you do that."

"Of course you can. I'll give you my molecular foie gras as an appetizer. It will impress Alexandre. Maybe some of his restaurant critic pals will stop by, and you can give them a taste. I need all the press I can get. Every little bit helps."

Capucine squeezed her hand. "Béatrice, that would be absolutely fabulous. I can't thank you enough."

"Do you have any idea where it's going to be held this year?"

"Of course. The press always knows beforehand. Alexandre told me. It's going to be at the Arc de Triomphe. The tables will spill all the way down the Champs-Elysées."

"Is Alexandre going to review the event?"

"No. He never does human interest pieces. But there are always loads of reporters. *Le Figaro* always sends a fashion reporter, and some photographers take pictures of all the kooky white outfits for their 'Living' section. And most of the other papers send food critics and photo teams."

"Perfect. Then I'll definitely get the right kind of publicity."

CHAPTER 18

Even though it had changed almost beyond recognition over the years, Capucine still delighted in the annual *Dîner en Blanc*. While still in university she had seen the event as something mildly countercultural, meaningful in its derision of bourgeois convention and its flirtation with lawlessness. Now, even though the dinner had become an established event on the Paris social calendar, the closing item on the eleven o'clock news, it still gave her a frisson.

In recent years the event was organized by professionals, who announced the "secret" staging ground by e-mail, rather than whispered word of mouth, which had been the rule in earlier years. An e-mail had announced they were to board the buses at precisely seven o'clock the next evening at an intersection deep in the Bois de Boulogne.

The evening air was still hot and the sun still far from setting as Capucine and Alexandre lugged Béatrice's two surprisingly heavy plastic containers in search of bus D-24. Alexandre wore white linen slacks, a white shirt opened down to the third button, and an enormous Panama hat with the brim turned down all around. With a cigar in his mouth he fully achieved the intended look of a Cuban roué.

Capucine was glowingly summery in a daringly short,

pleated frock made from white cotton tulle as light as tissue paper. She felt deliciously naughty in her outfit. It wasn't just the brevity of her dress. She had finally summoned the courage to break free from the *Police Judiciaire* rule requiring officers to carry a regulation sidearm even when off duty. The directive made dresses impossible for women, an irritating sartorial constraint for Capucine.

Determined to wear what she wanted on her own time, she had purchased a quick-draw holster that could be attached to her inner thigh with a strap of soft foam rubber and had fitted it with a Beretta 21A pocket-sized pistol so tiny it looked like a child's toy. True, it was not an officially sanctioned weapon and fired a derisory .22 caliber bullet, universally deemed useless for police work but still she was armed as required. She had never had the need for a side arm when off duty anyway and most important, it was finally at long last truly summer so what difference did it really make? And the best part was that Alexandre had told her the thigh holster was the sexiest thing he had ever seen her wear. It had been a miracle they made it to the buses on time.

The turnout at the *Dîner en Blanc* seemed even larger this year. A throng of thousands swarmed joyously. The bois was punctuated with shrieks, laughter, and whoops of greeting. The outfits seemed more extravagant: hats were bigger and floppier, dresses were either skimpier or more billowing, and costume jewelry cascaded more copiously. The event had turned into a fashion parade.

After an interminable search—made all the longer by the need to stop and greet and air kiss every few seconds—Capucine and Alexandre finally found bus D-24. Jacques, sans companion—immaculately turned out in a white linen suit that could have been made only by a Milanese tailor—detached himself from a group happily shouting gossip at each other and latched on to Capucine, theatrically ravishing her with caricature Lothario eyes. He stroked her thigh with an index finger, hiked up the hem of her dress, and hooked a finger under the strap of her holster.

"Freud would have had a great deal to say about this," he murmured in her ear, giving the strap a gentle tug.

Capucine broke free and struck a coquettish pose, showing off her shapely leg. From behind she could hear Alexandre grinding his teeth.

Capucine's friend Cécile, in an ankle-length, high-necked, almost diaphanous dress, clearly inspired by a Victorian nightgown, reclined languidly on the steps of the bus side by side with her husband, her arm limply through his. She looked more comfortable in her skin than she had been in months. Théophile sat stiffly upright, a proprietary foot on a large wicker hamper. Despite his reputation as something rather less than an intellectual luminary, he prospered effortlessly at The Société Générale, selling stocks and bonds to his family's connections. His only interest in life, other than his wife, was wine, a subject in which his expertise—as even Alexandre readily acknowledged—was beyond question.

Alexandre conferred with Théophile earnestly about his choices for the evening, selected from Théophile's extensive *cave* and now secure under his foot. Alexandre clapped Théophile warmly on the back. The oenological success of the dinner was assured.

Béatrice's bins and Théophile's hamper safely loaded in the belly of the bus, the dinner party clambered aboard, cresting on a wave of joviality. The noise level in the bus rose. Even though Capucine didn't actually know anyone, they all looked like they must have been guests in common at a dinner party or two over the years. Someone passed plastic flutes of champagne. The hilarity escalated.

As the long line of buses emerged from the Bois and cruised majestically up the avenue de la Grande Armée, pedestrians stopped to gawk and were waved at and toasted jovially by the occupants. Champagne corks popped continually. The buses circled the place de l'Etoile, parking in two circular rows, like covered wagons preparing to stave off an Indian attack. The immense horde of white-clad revelers was disgorged. Organizers appeared and consulted clipboards, orchestrating the placing of tables.

Not a single blue uniform was in sight, but Capucine knew that the event had been coordinated with the Paris police and a contingent of black-clad CRS riot police, vastly larger than necessary, was tucked into buses on a side street, a knee-jerk official reaction whenever large crowds assembled that had persisted from the somber days of the Revolution.

Following the instructions of the organizers, Capucine's party toted their containers, hampers, bridge tables, and folding chairs a hundred feet down the Champs-Elysées to a spot directly in front of the glass façade that had been installed to spruce up the aging Publicis building like a layer of too-thick pancake makeup on the face of a dowager. While they set up camp, the laden, white-uniformed army soldiered cheerfully on in front of them, making its way down the length of the Champs-Elysées. Capucine suspected Alexandre had somehow pulled culinary rank to obtain a spot so close to the Arc de Triomphe. The location turned out to be a mixed blessing. The endless white tide contained legions of friends and acquaintances, a good number of whom stopped for a chat and a sip of champagne.

Théophile was incensed when the first bottle of champagne he opened was depleted in less than a minute. He had an excited, whispered discussion with Alexandre. Capucine could hear only snatches. *"Voyons!" . . ." "Deutz Rserve de Famille . . ." "A truly extraordinary millésime . . ." ". . . Far worse than throwing pearls before swine . . ."*

With the gesture of an oriental sage, Alexandre extended his arm, pointing, sending a beaming Théophile off into the Publicis building. Théophile reemerged ten minutes later with two heavy orange shopping bags decorated with bright yellow suns.

"What a blessing Le Drugstore is. Anything you need available twenty-four hours a day," Théophile said happily as he pulled ten frosty bottles of Cordon Rouge from his bags and set them in a row on the table. He kissed Cécile on the cheek and breathed a sigh of relief. "Crisis resolved, *chérie*," he said to her. "The Deutz must be sipped with concentration. Cherished. Adulated. The Mumm will be just the thing to restore our thirsty *copains*."

For another half an hour the shimmering procession continued past their table in full force. Théophile disappeared into Le Drugstore twice more. A small clutch that seemed to consist mainly of Alexandre's cronies—mainly food critics and journalists—clustered around their table, drinking far more than their fair share of Théophile's *Cordon Rouge*.

Capucine had only a limited tolerance for congregations of the gentlemen of the press. Their preening and pretentious flaunting of bons mots rankled.

One of the swarm—a man well into his sixties, with the sad, knowing eyes and the loose facial folds of a shar-pei puppy—greeted Capucine with a kiss on each cheek. Arsène Peroché, the senior food critic for the *Nouvel Observateur*, a left-leaning weekly that was the darling of the liberal intelligentsia, was one of the handful of Alexandre's professional colleagues she genuinely appreciated.

"I must apologize for our little crowd's intrusion. But don't worry, I'm about to lead them off into the wilderness and let you get to your dinner. After all, we're here to work and not to get soused on your champagne," Peroché said with an endearing lopsided smile.

Capucine put her hand on his arm. "Please, you're all more than welcome. You know, you must come to us for dinner very soon. I haven't seen you in ages. Are you writing a human interest piece tonight, or are you rooting for culinary treasures?"

"I'm afraid it's to be a snide human interest piece," Peroché said with his sad look. "I don't know how I let myself get roped into these things. The editor wants the theme to be something along the lines of 'BoBo Two-Dot-Oh—The Second Generation Of Bohemian Bourgeois At Play.' Makes you cringe, doesn't it?"

Capucine laughed.

"Off I go. I'm going to lead them back to the Etoile. I had so much champagne on the bus, I forgot my camera bag in the overhead rack. Then right down to the Rond Point at the bottom of the avenue, and then back up again on the other side so we don't miss a single precious morsel of human interest."

As Peroché marshaled his colleagues, Alexandre announced to Capucine that he was going to walk with his cronies up to the Etoile but would be back well before they got to the fabled foie gras. Capucine was untroubled by this announcement. Alexandre could always be counted on not to be late for dinner, particularly if it had been prepared by an up-and-coming chef.

After the clutch of journalists left, the river of humanity flowing past Capucine's table gradually thinned to a trickle. Most of the tables were now filled, and there was a long, thin line of immaculate white tablecloths and gleaming white outfits on both sides of the Champs-Elysées, stretching all the way down the one and a half miles from the Etoile to the Rond Point.

A group of late arrivals, three couples in their early twenties, struggled timidly down the avenue with their bridge tables and baskets of food. It was a group that might have emerged from some doctoral class in cybernetics at the Sorbonne. Almost without exception, their eyes were vague behind oversized wire-rim glasses, their hair was badly cut and in need of a generous application of shampoo, and their clothes baggy over ungainly, rangy frames.

Recognizing Cécile, the group stopped and greeted her cheerfully. Cécile whooped joyfully. "They're associates from the firm," she said to no one in particular and ordered Théophile to give them champagne.

As they approached, one of them—a young-looking, slight blonde with small, almond-shaped, rimless glasses and two large adolescent acne pimples glowing volcanically from her neck and cheek—hung back from her friends.

Catching sight of her, Cécile exclaimed, "Honorine. What a surprise! You're the last person I expected to see here."

For a split second Capucine didn't place the name, even though the face looked vaguely familiar. Then it hit her. This was Cécile's paramour, or lover, or *amante,* or whatever the damn word was. She prepared herself for a scene.

Honorine looked like she might bolt. Cécile grabbed her by the elbow and led her up to Théophile, who automatically handed her a glass of champagne. "Look who's here, Théo chéri," Cécile said. "Do you remember Honorine Lecanu? You know, she's the star at the firm I'm always telling you about."

Théophile, immersed in the process of meticulously opening three bottles of Bordeaux so they could breathe, barely glanced up, quickly returning his attention to the underside of a cork. Honorine shuffled her feet, hurt by the imagined rebuff, and looked at Cécile for support. Cécile glanced hopefully at Capucine, as if she could somehow smooth over the situation. For a long moment there was complete silence at the table, punctuated twice by the gentle popping of corks. A sense of inexplicable awkwardness spread through the group like a thick green gas. Only Théophile was spared.

It took the cool breeze of Alexandre's exuberant return to blow the mood away and restore joviality.

As Honorine and her friends resumed their trek down the Champs-Elysées, Capucine felt another stab of frustration. Here was an important witness—even, technically, a possible suspect—and Capucine was being held at such length from the case that not only had she never interviewed Honorine, but even recognizing her was a rusty process.

"What an eventful little sortie that turned into!" Alexandre said. "You'll never guess what we saw." He gratefully accepted a flute of Deutz from Théophile.

"Well, there we were, walking past the buses, and in one of them the most beautiful pair of legs began waving rhythmically in the window. Of course, we stopped to admire. In a few seconds the waving stopped and Sybille Charbonnier—it really was her—appeared in the window."

"The movie star?" Théophile asked. "The one with all that curly dark hair and those luscious . . ." He caught himself and glanced guiltily at Cécile. Capucine was amazed he had any interests at all other than wine.

"She winked at us. And gave us all a delightful smile. And then"—Alexandre paused dramatically to take a sip of champagne—"her beau's head appeared, and he waved at us, too."

"Distinguished-looking older fellow with well-brushed white hair?" Capucine asked.

"The very man, except that his hair was in a bit of disarray." Alexandre chuckled. "Now, there's a couple who will figure largely in the gossip columns of tomorrow's press."

"Let's eat," Jacques said with a leer. "All this salacious gossip makes my appetite perk right up!"

Alexandre frowned at the double entendre.

Théophile inflated and took over center stage. "Capucine told me we were going to start with an extraordinary lobe of foie gras. So I brought some bottles of Château Climens—the year two thousand, of course." He turned to Cécile. Despite considerable evidence to the contrary, Théophile persisted in the belief that his wife was as passionate about wine as he was. "It's from Barsac, of course, even though it says Sauternes on the bottle. To my mind the mechanical balance between the acid and the unctuous is absolutely perfect, possibly rivaling even Yquem's—"

Capucine cut him off with a loud "Voilà!" as she produced the foie gras. Cécile smiled in gratitude.

There was a dismayed silence as the industrial starkness of the foie gras was revealed. But when it was served, even with an amateurish dribbling of the sauce, it was as superb as at the restaurant. For a long moment the dish overwhelmed the table. The surrounding crowd, the traffic on the avenue, even the rising yellow and roseate hues of the early evening, all faded into the distant background as the flavor soared up to its crescendo. They spent a good half an hour eating two helpings while talking of little else.

"This is quite a revelation," Alexandre said. "I need to take that young woman even more seriously. This is going to be quite a meal. What's next?"

"Capucine has already told me," Théophile said. "And finding the right wine was quite a challenge. In the end I picked a Château Chasse-Spleen, the two thousand again, naturally." He turned to Cécile. "It's a Moulis, of course, and there's an interesting little controversy over whether the name comes from Baudelaire or Lord Byron. In my op—"

Capucine cut him off again by reading from the little card that had come with the food. This time the smiles of gratitude came from the entire table.

"This is called 'la poularde de Marcel Meunier' and is a pan-roasted fattened hen—presumably raised by this Monsieur Meunier—served with blue lobster tail, green asparagus, morels, and a lobster reduction."

There was a murmur of appreciation and approval.

As Capucine began to unpack the container and

Théophile poured wine with great concentration, a faint commotion was heard from the Etoile. Was it just merry-makers whooping, or was there the note of a girl screaming? Capucine fell silent, cocking her ears, analyzing the noise, instinctively placing her hand over her crotch, preparing to grab her firearm. Jacques was equally alert but couldn't resist smirking at her gesture and giving a knowing wink.

The tumult at the top of the avenue increased in volume. Someone yelled, *"A l'aide! Police! Police!"* Capucine got up and ran up the hill.

When she reached the Etoile, a large knot of people had gathered around one of the buses, talking loudly to each other, spilling out into the roundabout, slowing traffic. Angry motorists vented their rage with their horns. Four uniformed Paris police officers approached at a rapid, self-important walk from the opposite direction. In the distance Capucine could hear the faint double note of the *pan-pon* of police sirens coming up the avenue de la Grande Armée.

Capucine pushed through the crowd. The epicenter seemed to be in the tight alleyway created by two buses parked in parallel. Gawkers peered in from either end. A dark lump lay half under one of the buses.

The four Paris police officers appeared behind Capucine and ordered her away. She produced her tricolor police card. They saluted smartly. She ordered two to stand at either end of the corridor between the buses and the other two to clear the *Etoile* of people and restore the flow of traffic. They moved off readily. Traffic control held no secrets from them.

Capucine inched down the narrow space. The buses were so close to each other that the area was shrouded in deep twilight. In the exact middle of the alleyway, a man lay prone half under one of the buses, his head and face hidden by the chassis. The body was completely immobile. She knelt down and felt the carotid for a pulse. Nothing.

With two hands she gently turned the head toward her. It was a grotesque parody of an African headhunter's trophy about to be shrunk in hot sand. The cheeks billowed out, horribly distended. The lips had been pulled tight over an open jaw and sutured shut with white string. The mouth had obviously been crammed to the bursting point with something. Clumps of green leaves protruded from between the sutured lips. The eyes bulged, lifeless, beginning to glaze like a bad fish's. A cord had bitten deeply into the neck, leaving a blackened depression.

In the half-light recognition came slowly but surely. It was Peroché. Without any doubt whatsoever.

CHAPTER 19

By the time Capucine arrived home, it was nearly one in the morning. It had been a long night.

After her examination of the body she had immediately called her brigade and given orders for Isabelle, David, and Momo to be found, wherever they were, and sent to the crime scene, along with a contingent of uniformed officers and the forensic unit.

As she'd waited for the troops to arrive, she had called Tallon's cell phone to give her report. They had a long conversation, frequently punctuated by Tallon's salty invective. When she had announced that a van of Paris police had arrived, Tallon had said, "*Bon sang*, get off the phone and deal with them before they destroy your crime scene. We'll finish this discussion in my office in the morning."

The van had disgorged eight uniformed officers with the cloth badges of the Paris police on their arms. She had flashed her card and had directed them to get the names and addresses of the people who had been gawking when she arrived and to cordon off both buses. A broad yellow tape marked POLICE—ZONE INTERDITE had been hastily

wrapped twice around the two buses with the enthusiastic
zeal of a child wrapping an oversize Christmas present.

The driver of the bus farther from the curb had arrived
on the scene and was outraged at being denied access by
the officer guarding the front of the buses. The driver's
wallet was in the jacket hanging on the back of his seat,
and he needed it to have a bite in a café. Sullenly obdurate,
the officer asked for the driver's *papiers*. In a rage, the driver
explained with mordant irony that his national identity
card was in his wallet in his jacket on the bus, which he
had not been allowed to get. Just as Capucine was about
to step in to quash the escalating confrontation between
irresistible and unmovable, the local Paris police commissaire and one of his lieutenants arrived—imposing in blue
uniforms dripping with silver trim—in a midsize Renault
police car, self-importantly announcing itself with an arrogant *pam-pom-pam-pom*.

"*Eh bien, voilà!*" the *commissaire* had said with a broad
grin. "Now, this is something you don't see every day. Normally, we arrive at the crime scene and stand around for
hours cooling our heels, doing fuck-all waiting for the *PJ*
to turn up. But here you are first! This is something I'm going
to have to tell my grandchildren, if either of my daughters
ever have the wit to get married."

In a few minutes two vans of uniformed *Police Judiciaire* officers rolled up and took over the crime scene. Capucine dismissed the Paris police and got busy with her
men.

They taped off a wider perimeter using yellow tape
marked POLICE JUDICIAIRE—ZONE INTERDITE and removed
the tape from the buses, clucking at the sloppy application. Just as they finished taping, two TV vans and a dozen
reporters appeared. Capucine delegated them to David,
who was a past master with the press. Skillfully, he gathered them in a tight clutch, let the cameramen get set up,

and made a statement so crisp and upbeat, he might have been a professional actor. Although he spoke for ten minutes, he revealed nothing at all, not even the victim's name, and left the residual impression that the death was most likely from natural causes without actually having specifically made any such statement. Artfully, he fed them a story that wrote itself so easily none of the reporters felt the need to ask the obvious question of why the *Police Judiciaire* was present in such force at the scene of a humdrum food poisoning.

Despite the commotion, the *Dîner en Blanc* continued merrily on from a point five hundred feet down from the Etoile. In the morning the diners would read that some poor reveler had collapsed under a bus and would mutter an only mildly interested, "*Tiens!* So that's what that was all about," to their spouses.

A large van with double rear wheels, painted in police colors but marked only with the letters INPS, swept up majestically. Capucine smiled. The Institut National de Police Scientifique never seemed to be able to make up its mind if it was the police's forensic department or an independent academic function.

The van disgorged Ajudant Dechery and five of his *agents spécialisés,* who lost no time in cordoning off an even larger crime scene area using yellow tape marked POLICE TECHNIQUE ET SCIENTIFIQUE—ZONE INTERDITE.

In less than five minutes Dechery came up to Capucine. "You know the drill, my dear. Can't say anything with certainty until the autopsy is done, tests performed, etcetera, etcetera, but I can certainly point out the obvious. The victim was killed by strangulation. Someone slipped a cord around his neck, held both ends in his fist, and twisted. I can tell that from the mark of the cord and the bruising at the nape of the neck. It's a good way to kill someone. Takes about ten seconds for the victim to lose consciousness—compressed carotids—and then the murderer has no trouble keeping the pressure on for five to ten minutes, while he waits for the victim to die.

"From the look of it, the stitching was done after death. No blood from the wounds. The murderer must have crammed the mouth full of something that had leaves on it and then sewed it shut. Never seen that one before. *Commissaire,* you get some good ones, no doubt about that."

It took another two hours for Dechery's team to complete their analysis of the crime scene; for the uniformed officers to scour the area around the buses, only to find nothing; and finally, for the buses to be released. Capucine was tempted to ask the disgruntled driver if he eventually managed to get something to eat, but thought better of it.

Walking into her apartment later that night, Capucine had been sure that Alexandre would be pottering around in the kitchen or reading in his study. She was astonished to find him in the sitting room, immersed in a game of backgammon with Jacques on an antique ebony and ivory board that she had bought Alexandre on the rue Jacob as a Christmas present the year before.

When she walked into the room, Alexandre tipped over his dice cup, declaring a forfeit. Both men stood up and greeted her warmly. There was a feeling that something was a little off. More than a little off.

"I'm starving," Capucine said with strained brightness. "I've been on my feet since seven, and other than two bites of foie gras at dinner, I haven't had a thing to eat."

"But what a foie gras it was!" Alexandre said with genuine admiration. "That girl's a genius."

"And Monsieur Meunier's *poularde* was not only sublime but also seemed to be engaged in a deliciously complicated maneuver with a crustacean. You know, Alexandre, that makes me think there are really twelve sexes, not just ten."

Neither Alexandre nor Capucine responded. They both had worried eyes only for each other.

"So, *cousine,* I understand the victim was that poor man Peroché you were chatting with. Did you find out what kind of leaves were in his mouth?"

Capucine looked at him levelly. "How do you know about that? Do your little slips of paper flit by even when you're not at your desk?"

"Of course." He reached out in a pantomime of grabbing a passing butterfly.

"It was Peroché!" Alexandre exclaimed, visibly upset. *"Merde, double merde, triple merde!* He was the most gentle person I'd ever met. Capucine, this really has to stop."

No one said anything for a very long moment.

Alexandre put his arm around his wife's waist.

"*Chérie,* forgive me. It's just that I always had such regard for Peroché. Let's go in the kitchen. I'll make you an omelet with dried *cèpes* and *confit* duck *gésiers,* and you can tell us what happened."

They settled in the large kitchen. With its long table topped with Provençal tiles, its huge La Cornue professional range, and its walls festooned with utensils and strands of hanging peppers, sausages, and garlic, the room was normally a temple of calm for Capucine. But tonight even the very core of her hearth seemed threatened.

While Alexandre beat eggs in a bowl, Capucine shared the meager findings from the crime scene.

"Peroché must have gone back to his bus to retrieve his camera bag. When he left our table he mentioned he'd forgotten it. We found the bag in the overhead rack, so it looks like he never made it onto the bus. The murderer garroted him with a cord and, when he was dead, stuffed something in his mouth and sewed it shut with kitchen twine."

Alexandre put the bowl down and stared at the wall.

"And that's it?" Jacques asked.

"I thought you knew everything."

"Just checking to see if you'd understood all the nuances."

"I had a long cell phone chat with Tallon. He's far from pleased. This is going to be classified as a serial killing. The technical definition is three or more deaths, presumably by the same hand, with at least a three-day interval between each."

"So what does that change?" Alexandre asked from his stove.

Jacques leaned back, smirking his all-knowing smirk.

"What changes is that serial killers are viewed as deranged. Or at least they are driven by something abnormal, and not by the usual motives of revenge, sex, money, or what have you," Capucine said.

"So, can't Tallon do what he did the last time and just delay in reporting the case to the magistrates?" Alexandre asked.

"No, this time he can't," Capucine said. "The case will require psychological profilers and under French law only a *juge d'instruction* can assign people who aren't members of the police to a case. So Martinière will have full charge of whatever experts he chooses, and he doesn't even have to report their findings to us."

"Good for you, *petite cousine,* you *do* understand," Jacques said, lazily running a finger up and down Capucine's thigh under the table, well out of the range of Alexandre's vision.

Lifting his hand away from her leg, Capucine said, "I can't even guess who Martinière will pick. The man who lectured us on profiling at the academy was an American. I think there are some professors at the Sorbonne the *PJ* has consulted in the past, but I have no idea who they are."

"Ah, the Americans," Alexandre murmured, serving Capucine her omelet. "They've created the McDonald's of the crime world. They really do understand how to do things on a broad scale. We poor French know nothing about serial killing."

"I don't know about that," Jacques said, mimicking the drawling tone of a Saint-Germain intellectual argument. "What about Gilles de Rais? What about the unforgettable Eusebius Pieydagnelle? What about Henri-Désiré Landru, killer of ten women but who is recognized as the precursor of feminism by that great philosopher Jean-Baptiste Botul?"

Capucine tucked into her omelet with relish. Things were finally getting back to normal. "Alexandre is absolutely right," she said. "Legendary historical figures don't count. It's true we've had a small handful of multiple killers in this century, but serial killing really is an American thing. Something we know next to nothing about in this country."

After they finished their omelets, they each had a tiny thimbleful of Armagnac.

Alexandre looked at his watch. "Good Lord, it's nearly three in the morning."

"Time for me to hop into my pumpkin and leave you lovebirds twittering in your feathered nest," Jacques said with a loud cackle. "*Cousine,* walk me to the door and I'll give you some tips on how to tickle some life into geriatrics with one of those cute pink feathers."

At the door, in an unusually serious voice, he said, "Two things. If I were you, I wouldn't let Alexandre go to restaurants at night without a . . . ah . . . professional escort."

"I'd already figured that one out myself. And the other?"

"A couple of weeks ago, when you were pedaling away in choucroute, you begged me to tug on some of my moldy little strings and extract you." He cackled loudly enough to wake the neighbors. "And now you're going to get your wish. I'm going to pull you out well before your adorable little dabtoes start stinking of cabbage."

"What do you mean?"

"I'm going to introduce you to someone. A very special expert who's going to solve your case for you."

Capucine deflated. "An expert? A profiler? I'm sure Martinière will find enough of those." She smiled tiredly at Jacques. "You're sweet. But I'm sure I'm going to be up to my eyeballs all week. Why don't I call you next weekend and we can set up a date for me to meet your friend?"

"No need for that. You know me. You can never tell when I'm going to pop up. Don't bother to call me a cab. I have one or two members of my fan club waiting downstairs. I'm sure they'll be delighted to give me a lift home."

CHAPTER 20

A s Capucine tried to busy herself at her brigade the next morning, she was on tenterhooks waiting for Tallon's secretary to call with the time of their meeting. The hours oozed by as sluggishly as an overcooked *sauce brune*. At eleven Dechery phoned.

"*Commissaire,* we've finished our analysis. As I expected, the victim died from asphyxiation several minutes after he lost consciousness from the garrote compressing his carotid arteries. The suturing was definitely done after death. The substance in the buccal cavity—"

"In the what?"

"Mouth. It was stuffed with the leaves of a cassava plant."

"What kind of plant?"

"Cassava. Manioc. Yuca. It's a staple in Latin America and Africa."

"Is it a poison?"

"Yes and no. Cassava contains two different cyanogenetic glucosides, which can be result in serious food poisoning or even death if eaten in sufficient quantities. The concentration is highest in the leaves. All the cultures that eat it regularly know the importance of removing the glucosides, and their recipes invariably involve some form of soaking, cooking, or fermentation, all of which will purify the plant effectively."

"So the leaves *could* have been poisonous."

"I'm sure those leaves would have given the victim quite a tummy ache if he'd swallowed them. Maybe even killed him. Who knows? But that doesn't make any difference. The leaves were put in his mouth after he was already dead."

At eleven fifteen a very testy Tallon called.

"*Commissaire,*" he said through gritted teeth, "you and I have been convoked to the offices of *Monsieur le Juge d'Instruction* August-Marie Parmentier de La Martinière." He rolled the syllables of the name off his tongue with a satirical snarl. "This afternoon at two thirty. Note that I did not say 'invited.' I said 'convoked' because that was the word monsieur le juge used with me."

"Does he have the power to convoke a *contrôleur général?*"

"Of course not. He can only request specific investigations from the police officers directly assigned to him. But the constraints of the law are insignificant when compared to the ambition of our good juge."

"And you're going, sir?"

"*Certainement, Commissaire.* We're both going. This case is going to be difficult enough without a loose cannon rolling through the middle of it, and I intend to put chocks under the wheels of that cannon. Don't be late."

Capucine arrived at Martinière's office punctually at two thirty, patting herself on the back for her diligence. She wondered if Tallon would be on time. He had been famous at the Quai for his love of dramatic appearances well into the process of whatever was going on.

Martinière sat, even more puffed up than usual with self-importance, with his back to his ministerially ornate desk. He was in his glory, listening intently to two men who resembled each other so closely they must have been twins.

"Ah, *Commissaire,*" Martinière said, consulting his watch. "You're on time for once. Let me introduce Professor Barnabé Caillot and Professor Dieudonné Caillaud. They're renowned worldwide as criminal profilers."

"It must be very pleasant for brothers to work together," Capucine said.

"*Commissaire,* you have a foreigner's ear for our glorious language. Their names are completely different, CA-YO and CA-YOo," Martinière said, lingering the merest hemidemisemiquaver on the final imagined phoneme of the second "YO." "They're obviously not related."

Professor Caillot bestowed a closed-lipped smile on Capucine. "People often make that mistake. I can't imagine why. Professor Caillaud and I both lecture on criminology at the Université Panthéon-Assas. We have published a number of books together, most recently a scholarly biography, accompanied by a critical bibliography, of the well known historical sociopath Eusebius Pieydagnelle."

"And we are currently working on a reevaluation of Botul's famous work on Landru," said Caillaud.

"Oh yes, *Landru, the Precursor of Feminism.* My husband was discussing it with me just the other night. He's a great reader of Botul."

"A seminal work," said Caillaud.

"I'd say even more, pioneering," said Caillot.

Capucine, who had looked up the Botul in question, began to enjoy herself. Irritating as Martinière was, the sessions with him definitely didn't lack in entertainment value.

"These gentlemen have spent the last two hours sharing their insights with me, and our plan of action is now clear. Let me summarize," Martinière said.

He turned to face the two professors, completely ignoring Capucine.

"You confirm that the perpetrator meets the formal definition of a serial killer. At least three murders at least three days apart. You have explained that there are two types of serial killers. One is uneducated and of less than average intelligence and kills haphazardly in what you have termed 'unstructured' crimes. The other type is well educated and of above average intelligence and kills with premeditation in carefully structured crimes. You believe our killer is of the second type. Strongly driven by a delusion of some sort. The crimes are 'ordered' and the deaths have been carefully planned out and are carefully executed."

That much was obvious, Capucine told herself.

"You also confirm that this type of killer cannot be apprehended by conventional police methods."

"Why is that?" Capucine asked sweetly.

"Ah," said Martinière, as if he had just scored a decisive point. "Because his motive will stem from a deranged perception of reality, which will be unintelligible to a normal person. He will also certainly be geographically unstable and will begin to hunt in a broader and broader territory, moving around France and possibly even abroad. This is why this type of serial killer often takes years to catch. Am I correct, gentlemen?"

"Perfectly," said Caillaud.

"Absolutely," said Caillot.

"So how do you propose to apprehend him?" Capucine asked.

"The technique is straightforward," Caillaud said.

"Completely straightforward," added Caillot.

"We develop a profile."

"A detailed profile."

"To publish in the media."

"To alert the general public."

"Who will inform the police if he is seen."

"So he can be arrested."

"This is how this type of murderer is apprehended."

"Invariably."

"And how do you develop the profile?" Capucine asked.

"Much of the work is already done," Caillaud said.

"The killer is male, almost certainly with homosexual tendencies. Possibly effeminate, so he will dress outlandishly in bright colors," said Caillot.

"How can you possibly know that?"

"Oh, it's really quite simple. Serial killers are almost invariably male. It's true there have been a few females but they always kill for money—you know, owners of boardinghouses who have an eye on their boarders' possessions, that sort of thing. This is obviously a male," Caillaud said.

"But he has a low masculinity coefficient. Males generally have a strong component of violence in their killings. There has been an element of poison—a purely feminine choice—in all of the three killings. That gives us a masculinity coefficient of about zero-point-six-five," said Caillot.

"Specifically in a range between zero-point-six-three and zero-point-six-seven," added Caillaud.

"And," continued Caillot, "the profile will become more and more detailed as the crimes evolve."

"By way of example," added Caillaud, "the killer will almost certainly have shown signs of the Macdonald triad. As we progress, that will help in identifying him."

"He is a fanatic of le triple-decker hamburger?" Capucine asked. She was now enjoying herself hugely.

"No, no, *Commissaire,*" Caillaud said with a show of great patience. "It has been noticed that this type of serial killer almost invariably has a childhood history of enuresis, animal cruelty, and pyromania. That is what is known as the Macdonald triad."

"Enuresis?"

"Yes," Caillot said. "Bed-wetting past the age of early childhood."

"The other important feature, *Commissaire,*" said Caillaud, "is that this type of killer is also almost invariably peripatetic. That is what makes him so hard to catch."

"Precisely," said Caillot. "They are intelligent, they have means, and they operate over a very broad territory."

"There you have it, *Commissaire,*" said Martinière. "Our path is clear. There will be further killings, most likely in other cities in France. The police throughout the nation need to be alerted and the profile circulated and recirculated as it evolves. We will also liaise with Interpol to determine if the murderer is active abroad. We will need to appeal to the press. Perhaps even run advertisements if they are not sufficiently responsive. Suspects need to be brought in. Eventually, we will close in on the killer. That is why I have convoked *Contrôleur Général* Tallon. His role will be to coordinate the national effort. Under my direction, of course."

As if on cue, the door opened violently and Tallon strode in, his back ramrod straight, his shoulders squared. When Capucine had worked directly for him, his bulk, his reputation, his rank were invariably enough to silence any group and suck up all the attention in the room. This time he was ignored—utterly and completely. Caillot and Caillaud continued on with their statistics and Martinière barely glanced up at him, lifting an index finger for silence. When the two profilers had finished Martinière looked at Tallon and then at his watch.

"Monsieur *le contrôleur général,* you were convoked for eleven thirty. It is now after twelve. You have missed a very important exposé by our two profilers and my definition of the expanded role I expect the police to play in this investigation. We're now going to have to backpedal to bring you up to speed. That is unacceptable.

"*Commissaire,*" Martinière continued, addressing Capucine, "could you run down the hall and see if you can find a chair for *Contrôleur Général* Tallon?"

Tallon lifted a hand, ordering Capucine to remain seated. As he advanced into the room he seemed to inflate. His anger was palpably that of a man who had spent a life awash in violence. Martinière recoiled in his chair, his physical fear of Tallon at war with his vanity and ambition. Physical fear won the first round.

"Enough of this nonsense, Martinière. There's going to be no expanded anything. These are crimes that clearly exceed your competence. I will allow *Commissaire* Le Tellier to keep you informed of the progress on the case, but you are not to interfere with her work in any way."

Affronted at the abuse of his surname, some of Martinière's arrogance returned. "But *Monsieur le contrôleur général,*" he began in a rush, "Professors Caillot and Caillaud, who have been appointed by me to the case, have explained that they expect the killer to expand his geography and that it will be necessary to mobilize the police throughout the country and most likely alert the population through the media."

"Martinière, be very careful here. There will be no mobilization of the national police and most certainly not the media. If that happens, we will be deluged with false confessions and possibly even copycat crimes. If you involve yourself actively in any way and there are any crimes of imitation, rest assured that I will have criminal charges brought against you and I'll damn well make sure that they stick. I would advise you to sit in your office and amuse yourself with your two *plaisantins* and leave the police work to the police."

The disdain of the threat was too much. Martinière was red in the face. "Monsieur, we will see what we will see!"

"That we will. *Allez, Commissaire.* We have work to do."

Capucine followed Tallon as he marched down the hall, radiating animal energy. When he reached out to push the elevator button, his finger trembled. Noticing the tremor, he burst out laughing.

"Problem solved!"

Capucine hoped he was right.

In the street Tallon continued to pace on imperiously, sucking Capucine into the slipstream of his wake. He made for the nearest café.

"*Calva. Deux,*" he said to the man behind the zinc bar.

When the Calvadoses came, he tapped his miniature snifter against Capucine's and said, "*Tchin-tchin.* I haven't had this much fun since I got my fucking promotion." He downed his drink in one go and looked up at the barman. "*Encore deux.*"

"Did those two cretins have anything useful to say? I wouldn't have thought they would."

"So you don't believe in profiling?" Capucine asked.

"Of course I do," Tallon said. "I'm a very modern *flic.* I'll even give you my own profile of this perp. It's someone who likes good food."

CHAPTER 21

"And he actually made the juge cringe?" David asked incredulously.

As Capucine, her feet on her desk, procrastinated by regaling her three *brigadiers* with the tale of the previous day's meeting with Martinière, she beseeched her guardian angel to bestow her with just one good idea that would break the case out of its apparently ironclad box.

Despite her almost boundless confidence in Tallon, Capucine doubted the respite from Martinière would be anything but short-lived. In a burst of élan she had ordered Isabelle and David to collect Honorine Lecanu and interview her at the brigade that afternoon, while she herself planned to interview Gaël Tanguy in his apartment. But despite those efforts Capucine was still deeply frustrated.

The meeting was proving painfully typical. David admired her shoes—a pair of Jimmy Choo platform slingbacks—Isabelle her legs, and Momo ruminated, glowering.

The door opened stealthily. Capucine assumed it was one of the uniformed officers with a message. But instead Jacques slipped in, dapper in a featherweight wool suit, pink silk shirt, and navy blue rough silk tie.

"How did you get in here?" Capucine asked.

"Oh, you know me. I have my little ways," Jacques said, smiling knowingly at the three *brigadiers*.

"Children, I've come to take your mama out to a very chic lunch to cheer her up. If you play nicely together, she may bring you back a doggie bag."

"Jacques, we're in a meeting."

"I think the one with the curls has admired your shoes as much as he needs to, and if the one with the muscles stares at your legs anymore, she's going to start to drool, and the big one is going to take a very long time to figure out what he really wants. So let's get going."

On the way out the door Capucine said, "This is my cousin." And then, sotto voce, "The one in the DGSE." She thought she heard, but really couldn't have, the three of them respond in a whispered chorus, "We figured."

The Twingo's close confines invited confidence. As they headed toward the center of Paris, Jacques removed his seat belt, leaned over, put his hand on Capucine's neck, and drew her ear close to his mouth. He began to whisper very quietly. At first she thought it was one of his eternal passes, but no, he was being genuinely conspiratorial.

"I'm going out on a long, shaky limb here," he susurrated. "But as they say in the ads, 'you're worth it.' We're going to see a man who is what we call in tradespeak a 'hidden deeply asset.' Only a small handful of people know he even exists. You must not talk about him to anyone, most particularly not to anyone in the *Police Judiciaire*. Do you understand?"

Capucine nodded. "Who is he?"

"A philosopher. A psychiatrist. A former operative. How's that for a combination?" Jacques gave an attenuated version of his cackle. "He was instrumental in a critical project a few years ago that, ah, didn't turn out as well as it might have. For him or for us. We've kept him on the roster of hidden assets ever since."

"What kind of psychiatrist?"

"He's a follower of Lacan. Remember him from school?"

"Vaguely. Wasn't he the shrink who was the big pal of the surrealists?"

"The very one. But Lacan was more than a shrink. He was a philosopher and literary theorist who was one of the people who put surrealism on the rails."

"So you're taking me to see a surrealist psychologist who is going to solve my case for me. And you really think my time will be better spent doing this than actually working on it with my team?"

"You'll see."

"So where exactly are we going?"

"Don't ask so many questions. Keep driving. Turn left here. Merde, *cousine*, left, *left!*"

Capucine followed Jacque's lefts and rights until she reached the Pont Marie, which led to the Ile Saint-Louis, that marvelous bark of an island that eternally navigates the waters of the Seine untouchable by the passage of time.

"Stop! Pull over," ordered Jacques.

"We're in the middle of a bridge. I can't stop."

"Of course you can. We're here. You're not going to get a ticket. You're a *flic*."

They walked under tall poplars a few feet down the peaceful quai lined with elegant seventeenth-century *hôtels particuliers,* until they reached a cut in the ancient stone parapet. The sun shone; the river murmured; birds chirped. It was a picture postcard of a Paris that had never really existed.

"Down," instructed Jacques.

They descended the vertiginously steep stone steps and emerged on the stone walkway at the river's edge, a few feet away from the arches of the bridge. Jacques labored under the weight of a heavy-looking olive drab metal box painted with a long number in large black characters.

Uncharacteristically, Jacques hesitated.

"Better let me go first. You wait here. I'll be right back."

He disappeared under a stone arch, then appeared immediately with a broad smile, waving Capucine forward.

Under the low protective dome of the arch, four metal police barricades, obviously purloined, had been used to define three cubicles. Each was meticulously neat, housing immaculately made-up cots, small pieces of furniture, a few books, a picture or two. One of the cots had a cute stuffed kangaroo next to the pillow.

How perfectly surrealist, how perfectly appropriate, Capucine thought to herself.

In the farthest cubicle, a tall, gaunt, aquiline man in a well-cut tweet jacket, far too thick for the season, stood awkwardly, his deep-set, hunted eyes squinting at her in concerned suspicion. As Capucine advanced a step, he retreated deeper into his cubicle like a cornered rodent.

"You're taking me to see a hobo!" Capucine hissed in Jacques's ear. "You think a homeless surrealist is going to solve my case for me! Have you taken complete leave of your senses?"

"Don't be such a stuffy old prude," Jacques hissed back. "This man is going to change your life."

As they approached, the man retreated even farther, nervously looking left and right, as if for a means of escape, backing into the rigid galvanized-steel police barricade. He reminded Capucine of a young deer at bay, surrounded by hounds.

In a faux hearty cocktail party voice Jacques said, "Docteur Vavasseur, may I present my little cousin, Madame Le Tellier. She's the police officer I told you about. Do you remember? I'm afraid she is deeply troubled and very much in need of your help."

He stepped forward and deposited the metal box on the cobblestones at the foot of the bed. At Jacques's approach the man retreated even farther, bending his back over the barricade.

"Well," Jacques said breezily, "now that the introductions are made, why don't I just leave you two to get on with your lunch?" He sprang jauntily up the steep stairway.

Vavasseur stared anxiously at Capucine. Like a cinematographic Western gunfight, the moment was lengthened by the tense silence. Gradually, his breathing slowed and his shoulders dropped in relaxation.

"We might as well see what they brought us today. Sometimes it's actually quite palatable," Vavasseur said, his eyes on the container.

Capucine retreated a few paces. Vavasseur walked timorously up to the metal box and snapped open the lid. Taking a deep sniff, he smiled in contentment and read a menu card that had been placed on top of the contents.

"Ah, risotto. Wonderful. It cooks for over twenty minutes. I'm particularly partial to thoroughly cooked food. In fact, I believe they've exceeded themselves. It's a lobster risotto. One drinks champagne with that." He beamed. "And I have just the one to go with it." His joy in the meal was childlike and eclipsed the threat Capucine seemed to represent.

Vavasseur busied himself removing the objects from his pedestaled night table, putting them carefully on the large, irregular paving stones on the ground. He moved the table opposite the midpoint of the bed and set his single chair opposite.

"Now, you just sit comfortably on the bed, and I'll go get the wine from my cellar." Little by little he was morphing into the perfect host. Capucine sat on the edge of the bed, which smelled pleasantly of laundry soap. Vavasseur walked to the edge of the walkway, where a steep stone embankment sloped off into the river. Four or five lengths of thin rope had been tied to an ancient iron ring. Vavasseur selected one and drew it in with great care.

"Perfect." He smiled broadly. "Got it on the first try."

He held up a squat dark bottle of champagne with an under-sized dark gold label.

"A Krug Clos du Mesnil nineteen ninety-five. Not quite their Clos d'Ambonnay, of course, but almost."

He pulled a wooden box from under the bed, produced two champagne flutes, opened the bottle with a pop discreet enough to have met with Alexandre's approval, and lovingly filled both glasses half full.

"One of the many nice things about living here is that I have a perfect cellar. Dark, constant temperature, no vibration. *A votre santé, madame,*" he said, touching Capucine's glass with his.

"And the symbolic purity of the water must appeal to a psychiatrist," Capucine ventured.

"Symbolic purity. I never thought of that. The river is a means of escape. That's why it's so satisfying. But enough philosophizing. Let's see what we think of the ministry of defense's lobster risotto." He was like a child impatient to get at his Christmas presents.

Vavasseur dove under the bed again, coming up with plates and cutlery. He then extracted a plastic storage container from the canister, opened it, and sniffed approvingly.

"This should be quite edible once we heat it up." He emptied the contents into a small skillet, placed it on a butane gas ring, lit it with a plastic cigarette lighter, and stirred the contents gently as they began to heat.

"My cousin was absolutely right," Capucine said. "You have the best view of the Seine in Paris."

"Possibly. Of course, I share it with a good number of friends."

"Where are your flatmates?" Capucine asked.

"They're not as fortunate as I am and have to spend most of the day foraging for food and, I'm embarrassed to say, occasionally even actually begging. I have the luxury of being able to remain here all day with my books and my thoughts. And a good thing, too. The consequences of leaving a prime location like this unattended can be dire."

Warmed, the risotto fully lived up to its expectations. Capucine and Vavasseur ate and sipped contentedly, as at ease as if they were at a luncheon in an elegant Fourth Arrondissement apartment. At one point a dapper man with a perfectly conformed black Labrador appeared on the walkway on the opposite bank and waved cheerfully. Vavasseur waved back, but his mood seemed to have soured slightly.

"Nice fellow. Very attached to his dog. He lives in a cardboard refrigerator carton under the arch on the other side of the bridge. It's roomy enough, I suppose. But the thought of being confined like that . . ." Vavasseur shuddered. "Nothing beats being tucked in under a warm blanket with the cold air on one's face. Even in the middle of the winter. Pure bliss."

The meal went on and on: salad, cheeses, very elegant pastry for dessert, a thermos of strong espresso, even a small vial of excellent Armagnac. When it was finally over, Vavasseur piled the dishes in a plastic bin he produced from under the bed.

"I'll get to those later. Now let's focus on you. Your cousin, Monsieur de la Fournière, told me you needed some counseling in unraveling a problem that troubles you a great deal. Is that correct?"

"Yes. He said that you had unparalleled expertise."

"He's too kind, but there are many analysts who are easily as skilled as I am."

Vavasseur's metamorphosis was complete. He had tucked in his chin and arched the back of his neck, eminently credible as a practicing psychiatrist.

"I think it would be best if you were to lie on the bed so you can relax completely. That was one of the many things Freud was so right about. The act of lying down, completely at ease, makes it so much easier to explore one's feelings."

With hesitation—she was still young enough to be able to feel utterly embarrassed—Capucine steeled herself, took off her shoes, and stretched out on the bed, her head on the snowy white pillow. Vavasseur moved the little table and his chair out of her range of vision. She half expected Jacques to pop up, screeching his cackle at the success of a hugely funny practical joke, but decided that since she had come this far, she might as well see the farce out to the end.

"It's about a serial killer—"

"Ah, my little specialty, as I'm sure your cousin told you."

"No, he told me nothing at all about you. Nothing."

"Just as well. Let's get back to your concern. Tell me about it."

Capucine spoke steadily for half an hour, systematically detailing the three murders, the interviews of the suspects, the background checks her officers had undertaken, winding up with a summary of the two police profilers.

"Ah yes, the good professors Caillot and Caillaud. I've read their books." Capucine could hear the chuckle in his voice. "Their latest one is really very entertaining. I'd lend it to you, but one of my flatmates is reading it.

"Let's focus on your case. It's far too early to even guess at an etiology, but I think you can begin to draw some conclusions."

"Me?"

"Of course. The solution can come only from *your* head. Certainly not mine. Why do you think the deaths all take place in restaurants or, in the case of the third one, a quasi restaurant?"

"I have no idea. I hadn't thought about it."

"Wouldn't it have been far more easy to kill these people somewhere else?"

"Obviously."

"Good. If you search out the reason, if you understand the symbolism, you will be a good way toward the solution."

"What do you mean?"

"Lacan explained that much of the effort in human comportment was directed at a validation of what he called the Mirror Image. Man is unlike the animals because he can see and recognize his image in the mirror. It is from this image that he forms a perception of himself. His life is a quest to prove the reality of this perception. It's close to Freud's notion of ego but more complex."

"I think I remember that from school. But isn't there something that can block that validation?"

"Yes. Very good. Lacan called it the big Other. It is a transcending symbol that actively prevents the little other, the patient, from becoming his or her true self, the Mirror Image. It can be any governing force, a person in a position of power, a social system, even language itself."

"I thought the big Other is supposed to be the father."

"The father is the most frequent example, but it can also be any number of other things. What is important is that the big Other can prevent the patient from attaining his Mirror Image, his true, desired, self. That blockage can be so psychologically crippling that the patient will go to any lengths to remove, or at least weaken, the big Other."

"Even serial killings."

"Precisely."

"So you don't agree that the killer is a man with possible homosexual tendencies who likes to dress in bright colors and who has a masculinity index of precisely zero-point-six-five?"

"I'd agree with that only if you wanted to inculpate your cousin."

Capucine attempted to stifle her giggles. She chalked it off to the half bottle of Krug she had just consumed. Losing the battle, she erupted in an explosive *fou rire*. After a few seconds Vavasseur joined in.

Capucine was the first to become serious. "So it's impossible to form a stereotype at this stage?"

"I'm afraid so. Of course, there's a wealth of data, most of it from the Americans. But we live in a very different world from them. The key point is that the killer is acting out a personal form of intense psychodrama. It is the reaction of his audience that is all-important to him."

"Audience?"

"Of course. If the murders were committed in a vacuum, there would be no point to them. The murderer needs someone to assure him that they are effective for his psychological needs. Ironically, frequently the police are often viewed as the best audience, and the classic etiology often includes a desire to establish a relationship with the investigating officers."

"You mean like Raskolnikov?"

"Just the opposite. Raskolnikov sought the release of confession. The serial killer wants the adulation of a knowledgeable specialist. If his murders are perceived to be brilliantly executed and unsolvable by an expert, it significantly enhances their symbolic psychological value to him."

Capucine nodded.

"Let's talk about the poison aspect of the murders. What do you think about that?"

"That puzzles me. The poison killed only in the first case. In the second two they seem purely symbolic."

"Of course, but symbols of what?"

"I have no idea."

"It's good that you're so frank with yourself. Let's keep an eye on that aspect. It may turn out to be highly relevant."

"Turn out? Do you think there will be more killings?"

"I'm sad to say your case is still very young. Serial

killing is a form of addiction. It is the consumption that makes the addict. It's quite possible his appetite will grow. Particularly as the killer becomes more and more skilled at adapting his method to his psychological need."

"What do you think about the perpetrator killing outside of Paris?"

"What do *you* think?"

"I'm not sure. It takes a great deal of specific knowledge to commit these crimes. It's obviously someone who knows the Paris restaurant scene extremely well. But of course, most of the restaurant personnel here started elsewhere. It seems possible that the killer would know enough about the restaurant world in the town where he started out to kill there."

"That's a very valuable observation. You're making a great deal of progress."

Vavasseur looked up sharply.

"Come and see me whenever you like. Right now, I'd suggest you be on your way."

"Why? I thought we were just getting going."

"Indeed. But two members of the Paris constabulary are coming down the walkway. They invariably ask for papers. I think they would find it highly amusing that a *commissaire* of the *Police Judiciaire* was stretched out on my bed."

Capucine leaped up and ran up the steep stairway and paused halfway to wave at Vavasseur, thank him loudly, and blow him a kiss. One of the officers ran after her, shouting, ordering her to stop, but stopped short at the bottom of the steep stairs. One look at his belly told her she was completely safe from pursuit.

CHAPTER 22

Capucine barely remembered Tanguy from the night of the murder at Chez Béatrice. In preparation for her interview, she had read his book that had won the Prix Goncourt. It turned out to be a grotesque, dystopian, end-of-the-world tale, populated with malfunctioning, rusting androids slogging aimlessly through mud, slime, and charred, burning vegetation, morbidly fascinated with the spectacle of festering, dying animals screaming their last in muddy, excrement-filled shell craters. It had given Capucine nightmares.

Responding to her knock, he opened the door, blinking myopically, revealing a flat moon face made distinctive by an enormous pair of perfectly round tortoiseshell glasses.

"Com . . . Commissaire Le Tellier?" he asked with a slight stammer. "Please come in. I've been waiting for your call. I saw the murderer. I tried to explain to *that juge d'instruction* who convoked me to his office, but he thought I was joking with him. I'm so glad you're finally here. Please come in."

Tanguy's apartment was the antithesis of his book. True, it was a fifth-floor walk-up in the drab Eleventh Arrondissement, but once there the rooms were large and white, the sun streamed in, the furniture was pleasantly minimalist—brilliantly colored directors' chairs, large bright vases holding two or three elegantly arranged branches, a long glass table with a huge, flat-screened computer, a single thick book by its side, the almost catatonically boring *Le Bon Usage,* the canonic manual of French usage and grammar.

They sat face-to-face in the middle of the stark room. But the second Tanguy eased himself into his chair he jumped up.

"How rude of me! I'll be right back." He disappeared into the kitchen.

Tanguy reappeared, holding two short-stemmed Spanish *copita* sherry glasses filled with a flaxen liquid.

"Wine is my *péché mignon.* This is an *Amontillado fino.* It's a pale sherry that has been aged in Canadian casks for a short while. It's halfway between a true *fino* and an Amontillado. A friend of mine in Cáadiz sends me a case every Christmas. I find it vastly better than the usual flinty fino."

Just as he handed Capucine her glass, he jerked it away. "Oh, I'm so s . . . sorry!" he said, blinking and stuttering. "In mystery novels police officers are not allowed to drink on duty."

Capucine laughed. "The police in mystery novels have very little to do with real *flics,* I'm afraid," she said.

The liquid was the color of raw umber, opaque and murky, what Alexandre would have called "troubled." It tasted as delicious as promised. The fact that Tanguy was able to converse in Alexandrespeak was somehow even more surprising than his anodyne appearance.

"So you saw the murder?"

"Oh no. Not the murder, the *murderer.*"

Capucine understood immediately. "One of the people

you examined that night must have done the killing. Is that the idea? Looking at it that way, I saw him, too. But it doesn't put me any closer to an arrest."

Tanguy peered at her like an owl through his enormous glassed eyes but said nothing.

"You were dining alone that night. Do you frequently go to expensive restaurants by yourself?"

"Of course. I have no one to go with. And it's important for me to observe the bourgeoisie. You see, I write about them and so I need to understand them."

"And you gain your insights from just observing people eat their dinner?"

"Naturally. That great American turned Englishman, Henry James, said that if a virginal young girl, if she was really a writer, walked by an army barracks and heard just a snatch of expletive-laden conversation, she would be able to write an entire novel about army life. And he was perfectly right. I understand the bourgeoisie perfectly. Would you like some more sherry?"

Capucine laughed in delight as she accepted the sherry. She was going to have to grit her teeth and finish his book.

"And in material terms, what did you see that night?"

"There was a cacophonous symphony of chatter and a jerky ballet of bourgeois motion."

"You mean people talking and the waiters moving around."

"Not just the waiters. The customers moved about during almost the entire meal."

"Are you sure? Almost all the customers we interviewed insisted that they had not seen anyone leave the tables."

"The bourgeois are blind to life. When I was a child, my father always told me to make a pee-pee before I went out, but I always forgot. I still do. So I had to go to the WC between courses. There were two other people waiting when I got there."

"What did they look like?"

"I have no idea. My eyes were glued to the dining room. It's the interaction among people that matters. Not their appearance."

"I see. And how long before the victim keeled over was this?"

"Not long. Five, ten minutes. It's hard to keep track of the time when there is so much to observe."

"And so you stood patiently as these two gentlemen waited for the WC?"

"I'm not really sure. Perhaps they had already left when I arrived at the WC, and I only saw them waiting from my table. Who knows? What difference does it make?"

Capucine decided to take a new tack.

"Your family must be extremely proud of your award, aren't they?"

Tanguy recoiled in clear distaste. He got up, collected their glasses, and left the room.

In a few minutes he returned with more sherry. His stay in the kitchen seemed longer than necessary to refill the two glasses.

"There's only my father left," Tanguy said. "My mother died when I was a child. My brothers and sisters have moved away. We don't even exchange Christmas cards. Our childhood was not happy." He gave Capucine an intense, emotionally charged look that was indecipherable, other than the fact that she might possibly be to blame for some unnamed sin. "My father was beyond thrilled. He told all his friends at the factory, even though none of them had any idea what he was talking about. Of course, he didn't either."

"Your father still works?"

"Naturally. He's only fifty-five. In a steel mill in Lorraine. I was born when he was eighteen."

"And your mother passed away?"

"She died when I was nine. Cervical cancer. My father remarried. He needed someone to cook and clean and look after his children for him. None of us could stand our stepmother. Happily, the feeling was mutual. But despite all the yelling, accusations, slammed doors, and whippings, I'm still my father's pride and joy," he said, frowning. It was impossible to tell if he was being cynical.

"Really?"

"Oh, yes. My father's a die-hard Communist, a militant. He sees me as an intellectual in the Marxist definition of the word. Marx placed value on intellectuals, so the fact that I won an award for my book pleases him."

"That must be satisfying."

"It would be more satisfying if he related in any way to what I write. But he's never read a single word. In fact, I doubt he's ever read a book in his life. Can you imagine his reaction if he ever cracked one of my books open?

"Actually, I don't know if you've read *La Nature des Particules,* but the vision comes from my father's steel mill. Ever since I was a child the *clair-obscur* of that light of the fires drowning in the smoke seemed to me what the end of the world would be like."

"But there are no screaming animals and piles of excrement."

Tanguy smiled happily. "There are. You just don't know how to see them. But enough about my books. I hate authors who feel obliged to explain their works. I want to hear about the case. Is it true that the murderer I saw with my very own eyes committed two more crimes?"

"It's very likely."

"I think so, too. I've been reading the press very carefully. The symbolic content of the crimes is very appealing to an author. Do you want to hear my views?"

Assuming the answer would be automatically affirmative, he went back to the kitchen for more sherry. As she waited, it struck Capucine that the two director's chairs resembled a stage set for a TV interview. It was as if they were slightly angled toward an imaginary camera. It was not clear who was intended to be interviewing whom.

"I think," Tanguy said, sitting down and handing Capucine her glass, "you need to look at the case through a writer's eyes. The MO is evolving very gradually. In the first case there was a component of violence—the shot from the pellet gun—but it was the poison that killed the victim. In the second case, it was the violent act—the stabbing with the basting needle—that killed the victim, but the poison was also potentially lethal. In the third case, the poison was purely symbolic since the victim had already been strangled. The progression is very clear. The poison has evolved progressively from being the active agent to becoming entirely symbolic. Clearly that is the message. Did you notice that?"

"I did, actually. But I'm not sure it's all that important. Why do you see it as so vital?"

"Writers don't always have to know the meaning of what they write. Like musical composers they know what works and what doesn't. And this story works for me. It really does."

CHAPTER 23

Cécile looked longingly at the little domed plastic dish of sushi as it traveled down on the little conveyor belt. It was an *asatsuki shake*—salmon tartare. Just as she reached out to grab it, she caught sight of a *tal shiso*—sea bream dotted with salmon eggs. She hesitated indecisively, reached out for the bream, pulled away, extended an arm toward the salmon, pulled back, and then it was too late. Both had gone by.

"*Merde, merde, merde!*" she said, almost shouting. "I can never make up my mind in this place. Capucine, I don't know why on earth I suggested we eat here. I don't know why you let us come. It's like being trapped in an evil video game."

In Japan, *kaiten*-style sushi restaurants were distinctly at the bottom end of the spectrum, but somehow a Paris restaurateur had succeeded in elevating the technique to the ne plus ultra of chic. Little dishes of single sushis snaked slowly down a counter on a miniature conveyor belt. Customers chose what they liked and stacked the color-coded saucers for a waiter to tot up when they were ready to go. At the head of the conveyor five chefs cut fish and wrapped rice balls feverishly, making sushis, popping them into little black bowls, topping them with clear plastic domes, depositing them on colored dishes, and placing them on the belt, where they sallied forth bravely like railroad cars of an endless electric train.

Cécile focused on another little plastic dome, *uni*—sea urchin eggs. She raised her hand, lowered it, raised it again. Her lower lip began to quiver, and tears formed in her eyes. As the sushi passed in front of Capucine, she snatched it up with the vigor of a bear clawing a salmon out of an Alaskan rapid and, with her other hand, grabbed a *negi maguro*—chopped tuna topped with finely julienned leeks—tooting along bravely behind. She placed the tuna in front of Cécile.

"I've never really been all that fond of leeks," Cécile said, her plaintive voice stammering through a quivering smile.

"Cécile, just taste it. You'll love it."

"You can't just taste sushi. You have to put the whole thing in your mouth. And then it's too late," Cécile said. "Can we swap?"

Capucine exchanged the little plastic bowls and scowled at her friend, whose lower lip began to tremble again.

"I'm coming apart," Cécile almost wailed. "I really am. If this keeps up, I'm going to have a nervous breakdown."

"You're dating yourself. Nowadays they're called 'depressive syndromes,'" Capucine said, smiling because she had just caught sight of another *asatsuki shake* finally coming down the conveyor. She had no intention of letting this one escape.

"Aren't you the little psychiatric expert all of a sudden?"

"This is about your paramour with the granny glasses and the problem skin?" Capucine asked.

"That was unkind. Very. Anyway, it's over. At least to all intents and purposes."

"Which means it's still on, but you're bored with it."

"Not exactly, but close enough. She's sweet. She's sensual. She's too awed to even think of judging me. But you miss that male vigor, you know, that power they have. And you're so right! There's that skin." Cécile shuddered histrionically.

Capucine looked at her expressionlessly.

"I have no idea what's really bothering me. That's why I wanted to have dinner with you. I was hoping you could tell me," Cécile said.

Capucine said nothing but expertly gripped the *asatsuki* with her chopsticks and placed it elegantly in her mouth, raising one eyebrow in interrogation.

"The firm is making noises that they'll put me up for election to the partnership in the fall."

"Congratulations! That's quite a coup!" Capucine moved to hug her friend, but Cécile blocked her with her shoulder.

"Do you know what that means? You can't imagine how awful it would be. Two partners would be assigned to my case and would review every second of my past six years at the firm. Everything! Project performance appraisals. All those psychological assessments they always do. Interview my clients. My peers. My subordinates. Everything! And on top of that they would investigate my private life. Even poor, defenseless Théophile would be put under the microscope. Think of the poor dear! And they'd probably even find out about Honorine. It would be like being thrown out of my apartment stark naked so all those awful people could look at me and see how ugly I really am and laugh at all my warts and moles."

She began to cry in earnest. As the sorority of women required, Capucine took Cécile in her arms but her heart didn't go out to her. She had already spent far too many meals dissecting Cécile's Machiavellian career moves. Also, an *unagi*—grilled eel—Capucine's absolute favorite, bumped down on the conveyor and she was powerless to grab it.

"So you're going to say no to the firm?"

"Why would I do that?" Cécile awkwardly negotiated a sushi, which fell apart. When she had finally consumed the fragments, she brightened.

She leaned closer to Capucine. "I'm going to tell you a deep, deep secret. You won't breathe a word of this, will you?"

Capucine remained silent.

"I've been talking to a headhunter about a possibility of becoming the head of strategic planning for Nestlé." She paused. "To tell you the truth, I've been to three rounds of interviews in Switzerland and I'm pretty sure they'll make me an offer."

"Are you tempted?"

Cécile raised an arm vaguely in the direction of a domed sushi but let her arm drop listlessly. She sighed deeply.

"Capucine, I am *so* coming unglued. I really am. Nestlé would be like Honorine on a larger scale. Relaxing. Pleasant. Even satisfying at a certain level. But it would be far away from the flame. And how could I ask dear Théophile to move to Vevey? He would want to bring his fifteen thousand bottles of wine with him. Can you imagine!"

"What's this about a flame?"

"My life is all about flitting around a flame. Trying to get closer and closer without sizzling to a crisp. Honorine was a respite from that. Vevey would be too."

"I would have thought Théophile would be relaxing and tranquilizing. Isn't he?"

"Of course not. I married him for the same reason you married Alexandre. He's a judge. When he tastes a wine the severity and cruelty of his decision is absolute. Just watching him picking up a bottle and examining the label with that scowl of his is an erotic experience. You must feel that way with Alexandre's judgments of restaurants. Doesn't reading his reviews excite you?"

"I'd never thought about it that way." Capucine

paused. "So the choice is move to Vevey with Honorine and tend your garden or stay in Paris and flirt with the flame."

"Don't mock me. Not flirt. Try and become one with it without perishing in the process." She looked at Capucine with the merest hint of a sneer. "But of course you don't understand. You wouldn't. You couldn't."

Capucine said nothing. She was beginning to find Cécile beyond irritating. Here was a girl who had been handed all the gifts the world had to offer from the moment she uttered her first howl, who had never faced the doubts and anguish that she—or, for that matter, Béatrice—had had to deal with all her life. And now, when the cornucopia of her good fortune tipped over even further, showering ever more of its bounteous flow, she was on the edge of a nervous breakdown, or a depressive syndrome, or whatever the hell it was supposed to be called.

"You know, I envy you," Cécile said. "You're perfectly content with an undemanding husband and a relatively simple job, the main merit of which is that it's iconoclastic and a symbolic wedge between you and the bourgeois life you claim to despise."

Capucine glared at her.

"I'm sorry. You *do* have your little mysteries to solve. Of course, they have none of the complexities of a management consulting strategic assignment, but there must be a certain challenge. I'll grant you that. How *are* you doing with your case?"

Capucine remained silent, her eyes dark with anger.

"If I were smart," Cécile continued, "I'd follow your example. Go to Vevey. Cart Honorine along with me to keep me company and leave Théophile in Paris with all his precious dusty bottles. He'd never notice I was gone. I'd have marvelously boring lunches with wonderfully boring Swiss executives, gaze out serenely at boring Swiss cows, with their boring bells, chewing their boring cud next to that boringly big lake they have, and have nice, tender, boring sex with boring Honorine. And I'd never be judged again." She paused and her face tightened into a rictus of anger.

"But I'd kill myself—or someone else—before I ever let that happen."

CHAPTER 24

The next morning Capucine was aghast when she saw *Le Figaro's* front page. An above-the-fold, four-column headline screamed, JUGE ANNOUNCES NEXT RESTAURANT KILLING WILL BE IN PROVINCIAL TOWN. Martinière had apparently given a press conference. A picture of him—attempting to look grim and determined, but coming across as severely dyspeptic—ran across all four columns. The caption under the picture stated that he had warned the entire nation to be on its guard since "the restaurant killer" was likely to strike again without warning anywhere in the national hexagon, even though he had the case "firmly in hand."

Below the fold, under the photos of professors Caillaud and Caillot, *Le Figaro* had included a box detailing the murderer's profile in clever graphics. Just as Capucine began reading, her phone rang.

Without preamble Tallon launched into a smoldering imprecation against Martinière and the two professors, frequently using the term "criminal charges."

As he ranted, Capucine skimmed the profile. "Effeminate . . . possibly homosexual . . . works in a menial position in a restaurant or hotel . . . childhood history of

cruelty to animals, bed-wetting, pyromania . . . public to inform local police immediately if seen . . ."

Capucine realized Tallon had concluded his rant and had moved on to the substance of the call. "And then it seems he followed up his press conference with phone calls to the editors of the major papers in Lyon and Marseille. Obviously, every newspaper in France had a field day this morning."

"Has there already been an impact?" Capucine asked.

"Impact?" Tallon growled. "Most of the provincial police switchboards are already jammed. Everyone who dislikes a neighbor is calling in to report him as a gay bed wetter who is cruel to animals and behaves suspiciously. There are also calls from feuding restaurant workers, denouncing their colleagues. Next we're going to get complaints from the restaurant owners' association and at least three gay-rights movements. Trust me on that."

"Won't this be enough to get Martinière removed from the case?"

"I don't know about removed, but I think I finally got a muzzle on him that he won't be able to slip out of."

He paused dramatically.

"This morning someone very senior in the police hierarchy made a call on the minister of the interior's chief of staff to discuss *la situation Martinière*. I believe he will be speaking to the minister of justice later today. I trust that call will prevent a repetition of this debacle."

"Let's hope so."

"And for good measure I put in a call myself to the doyen of the Université Panthéon-Assas to make sure those two clowns don't appear in public again."

Capucine couldn't help but feel that even if Martinière had had the door successfully slammed in his face, he would still be snooping around the house, searching for an unlocked window.

"Now we need to get to work," continued Tallon. "I've

set up a task force here at the Quai to evaluate calls made to the local police forces. It's not impossible that our murderer will actually strike outside of Paris. In theory the task force will keep that information from drowning in the tidal wave of misinformation Martinière has created. They'll make their first report tomorrow morning at eleven. I'll need you here for that."

The next morning Capucine rushed down the third-floor hallway her usual fifteen minutes late. Isabelle was at her side, fretting and muttering about their lateness, as David and Momo trailed behind. Capucine assumed they would slip into the conference room unnoticed and melt unseen into seats against the wall.

"*Enfin, Commissaire,*" Tallon boomed as they walked in. "How kind of you to come. Now we can begin our meeting."

Isabelle tried desperately to hide behind Capucine.

"Come sit up here next to me. We've been making progress."

The conference room was packed. Tallon's task force was far larger than she expected. There were a handful of *commissaires* she knew slightly and a large group of more junior officers, most of whom she knew by sight only.

"A special switchboard has been set up, and these gentlemen are in charge of collating and triaging what comes in. *Lieutenant* Cornudet," Tallon said, nodding at a man sitting at his left, "has been appointed as the secretary to the task force."

Capucine smiled at him in acknowledgment.

"All right, *lieutenant*, let's hear what you've got so far."

"Oui, monsieur le contrôleur général," Cornudet said, consulting a notebook. "As of ten thirty this morning, three hundred and thirty-one people have called various local police forces, reporting suspicious individuals. Also, eleven people have called various police departments, confessing

to the Paris murders. Five others called to confess to other homicides of which we have no record. And . . ." He paused for effect. "Several regional police have informed us of thirty-two criminal incidents they feel may have been perpetrated by the Paris murderer."

"Thirty-two?" Capucine asked.

Cornudet laughed. "They're calling in anything that's happened in or near a café or restaurant, fights, lovers' quarrels, the occasional mugging, stuff like that. Nothing that's even remotely connected to your cases."

"But," said Tallon, "it all has to be checked out, particularly the unreported murders. That's what these gentlemen are here for."

He indicated the other participants at the table. "We owe *Monsieur le Juge* Martinière a vote of thanks. We finally have something to fill up our days."

There was a polite ripple of laughter from around the table.

"*Commissaire* Bertoli, tell us about the confessions," Tallon said.

"*Oui, monsieur le contrôleur général,*" said a lantern-jawed man with close-cropped hair. "All of the eleven have been interviewed by my men. None of them knew any details of the murders that hadn't been reported in the press. They were very carefully interviewed in this regard. They have all been given psychiatric examinations and appear to be compulsive confessors. However, when confronted with the fact they were not credible as the author of the Paris killings, four of them confessed to other murders. It appears that one of them may possibly have committed at least two murders three years ago. One of the victims was a waiter, but there doesn't appear to be any connection with the Paris cases. The suspect has been placed under *garde à vue* and the *Police Judiciaire* in Lyon has opened up a full investigation."

"Excellent, Bertoli. Excellent," Tallon said.

"Now, *lieutenant,* tell us about your *pièce de résistance.*"

"Yes, sir," Cornudet said. "The Lille *Police Judiciaire* has reported that last night a man was murdered, shot in the head with a shotgun at close range, in the garden of a restaurant in Seclin, a few miles south of Lille. The restaurant is in an inn." He glanced at his notes. "Called Le St. Jacques de Lorraine. Apparently a very up-market place. Affiliated with the Relais & Châteaux and given one star in the Michelin *Guide.*"

"I know the place," said Capucine.

"I was sure you would," Tallon said.

Cornudet glanced anxiously at Tallon and Capucine to see if the interruption would blossom into a conversation. The nuance of the exchange had eluded him. Seeing that it was over, he continued his report with the relentlessness of a hound questing after a scent.

"The victim was a local journalist. He wrote for the main Lille paper, *La Voix du Nord.* Mainly filler pieces, human interest stories, book and movie reviews, and every now and then a restaurant review. In fact," Cornudet said, "last night he was at the restaurant, working on a review. It was the last of three visits before he wrote his piece."

Everyone in the room sat up straight.

"How was the murder committed?" Capucine asked.

"Shotgun," Cornudet said. "He walked out of the restaurant, took a few steps, and someone shot him in the head from about three feet away. Killer fired both barrels, probably a twelve-gauge, number six steel shot. Not much of his head left. The local gendarmerie found footprints in the shrubbery next to the door. Looks like the murderer was crouched down and rose to fire when the victim walked out."

"So he was hit in the back of the head?"

"No," Cornudet replied. "The head was almost facing

the gun. The victim must have heard something or the murderer spoke to him."

There was a long moment of silence.

"What do you think, *Commissaire?*" Tallon asked.

"The essential ingredients are there. A restaurant critic undertaking a review killed in or close to a restaurant. It's definitely the right MO."

"Of course, it could be a copycat killing. I'm actually amazed we haven't had more of those," said one of the officers halfway down the table.

"Good point," Tallon said. "Still, it has to be investigated thoroughly. We can't leave this to the Lille people. How quickly can you get up there, *Commissaire?*"

"I'll leave right after the meeting, sir," Capucine said.

As the session broke up, Tallon signaled Capucine to remain. The two sat silently at the table. Tallon pivoted in his chair, looking for a window. Finding none, he massaged his chin, staring into space.

"You don't think it's our killer, do you?" Tallon asked.

"I can't really say why, but you're right. I don't. I think it's the absence of poison that bothers me. Other than that, the MO is identical. Even the escalation of violence is right on track."

"If it's him," Tallon said, "he's right on the Belgian border. He could have moved north. Belgium or Holland could be his next stop. The last goddamn thing I want is to get Interpol involved."

"Lille is only an hour away by the TGV. High-speed trains make it an easy day trip. And there'd be no trace. He could have paid for his ticket in cash. But that's not what bothers me."

Tallon looked at her gimlet-eyed.

"If this isn't our guy," Capucine said, "that means he hasn't killed for over three weeks."

"Three weeks and four days. And your point?"

"What if he never kills again? We'll have lost him. We have nothing on him so far. Not a single clue. Not a single shred of evidence. That whole business of the short list of the people who were present at both the first killing and the embassy reception seems to be a red herring. If the killer stops now, the cases would be filed and forgotten."

"Things like that happen," Tallon said with the ghost of a wry smile. "Jack the Ripper was active from the end of August to the beginning of November, a little more than two and a half months. Then he never killed again. And the Brits still haven't caught him."

Capucine started to respond to his joke but couldn't find anything to say.

"I understand you've been seeing a Docteur Vavasseur," Tallon said. "What does he say? Does he think our killer is possessed by an insatiable thirst that will keep driving him until he's caught?"

Capucine started slightly. Tallon's apparent omniscience never failed to unnerve her. With an effort she succeeded in responding to the question as if it had been perfectly anodyne.

"Vavasseur says the killer has defined his modus operandi so minutely, it may be becoming extremely difficult for him to find suitable opportunities. He thinks that may be the cause of the long intermission."

Tallon grunted. "I hope you're enjoying those lunches of his. I understand they're three-star quality."

"Sir, is there anything you don't know?"

"I don't know the important things. Like who the killer is."

CHAPTER 25

Capucine had gone directly from the Quai des Orfèvres to the Gare du Nord and had scrambled onto the twelve fifty-eight TGV high-speed train to Lille with only seconds to spare. That she hadn't had time to pack a bag was immaterial since she planned on being back in Paris for dinner. That she hadn't had time to stop at the station to buy a ticket including a full hot meal delivered to her seat was definitely very material. She was ravenous.

As the train rocketed through the dark gray suburbs, she swayed her way to the bar car, disgruntled that her lunch was going to consist of a cottony, cellophane-wrapped ham and cheese sandwich with a tiny bottle of toxically tannic red wine. She was further dismayed when she found the door to the bar car locked. Through the glass she could see the barman industriously setting up his wares. He smiled at her and made a victory sign with thumb and index finger to let her know he would be opening up in just two minutes.

As she waited, leaning up against the side of the gently oscillating railway car, Capucine reflected on how much Lille depressed her. It was a city that had recently reinvented

itself, becoming heavier, more plodding, and even less French
in the process. In previous generations, the capital of the
North had been the locus of France's booming coal, min-
ing, and textile industries. Fortuitously, just as these activ-
ities had waned, the TGV, the tunnel under the Channel,
and the European Union seemed to arrive almost simultaneously, transforming Lille into the nexus of Europe's two
financial capitals, London and Brussels. Almost overnight,
rotund, prosperous bosses of heavy industry became run-
ner-lean, gym-hard, sharp-elbowed, obscenely wealthy wiz-
ards of finance.

After a trip that lasted precisely the scheduled one hour
and two minutes, Capucine was greeted at the Lille-Eu-
rope station by Lieutenant Tirmont of the Lille *Police Judiciaire*. With his James Dean slouch and worn leather
jacket, he overdid the movie look of a Paris *PJ* detective.
But, wardrobe effects aside, there was no doubt Tirmont
was a thoroughly professional flic.

Deferential to a Paris *commissaire*, Tirmont suggested they
go first to the crime scene, chat with the general manager of
the inn, then view the body in the morgue, and afterwards,
interview the victim's boss at the newspaper, whom Tirmont had only spoken to briefly when he identified the
body at the morgue. Then it would be up to Capucine to
decide what to do.

As they drove down a departmental road through Lille's
neat suburbs, Tirmont detailed the facts of the case.

"The perp was hiding behind a bush next to the door,
waiting for the victim, Didier Rocher. His footprints in the
soft, turned soil tell the story. He must have been crouch-
ing, waiting for his man, and stood up to take his shot
when the guy walked out. He made a noise or called out.
When the victim turned, he let him have both barrels of a
twelve- gauge shotgun in the face. Blew half his head off."

"Any doubt about the ID?"

"None. There was enough face left to match him to the

photo on his national identity card, and, anyway, his editor made him out straight off at the morgue."

"Any idea how the killer got away?"

"No problem there. No one seems to have heard the shot, so he must have walked back to his car and just driven off. The first people who came out the door raised the alarm, but according to forensics, he'd already been dead for fifteen to twenty minutes."

"Rocher was a journalist at *La Voix du Nord,* right?"

"He wasn't a salaried employee. He was what the editor calls a stringer. They'd publish his freelance pieces, but only if they liked them. The editor doesn't seem to hold him in high esteem."

When they pulled into the meticulously raked gravel courtyard of Le St. Jacques de Lorraine, the long, low stone building looked like every other Relais & Château country hotel, blatantly expensive despite its ostensible simplicity.

The area in front of the elegant rustic oak double doors to the inn had been cordoned off with yellow police crime-scene tape. A large, professionally-lettered poster-board sign propped up on an easel directed patrons to enter by the side door.

Ten feet in front of the closed door, a small rust-brown stain indicated where the victim had fallen. Given the size of the stain, he had clearly already been dead by the time he landed. Capucine ducked under the tape and stood next to a four-foot-high laurel bush flanking the door. It was a perfect spot for an ambush.

The general manager, a Monsieur La Farge, a round-faced clone of Bibendum—Michelin's roly-poly avatar—was waiting for them behind the marble-topped reception counter.

La Farge led them down a long hallway covered in gray watered silk dotted with Piranesi prints in artfully gilt frames. A thick velvet curtain covered the entrance to the dining room.

"You can see why no one noticed the shot," Tirmont said.

They walked through the dining room where a cleaning crew was vigorously vacuuming and stripping the immaculate white cloths from the tables and sat at the outside terrace overlooking the garden. An immense lawn rolled out flawlessly into the middle distance, broken only by the occasional round bed of tall perennials in carefully coordinated pastel colors.

La Farge beamed at them using only the bottom of his face, panting and mopping his brow with a handkerchief, fidgeting nervously as only a fat man can.

"Are you going to remove your tape?" he asked urgently.

"The crime-scene tape? Why is that so important?" Capucine asked.

"*C'est une catastrophe.* Lunch today was off by nearly thirty-five percent. The patrons have the feeling that something sordid has happened. When they see your tape, they get back in their cars and drive off." He threw up his hands in an exaggerated gesture of despair.

Tirmont looked at Capucine, who nodded. "Feel free to remove the tape at your convenience," he said.

La Farge beamed. This time with his whole face. He made a beckoning gesture with his stubby fingers at one of the staff, who rushed off after a brief whispered discussion.

"That's an enormous load off my mind," he sighed. "And now, how can I be of service to you?"

"We'd like to talk about Didier Rocher, the man who was killed here last night." Capucine said.

"What a shabby little person. He started out as a minor inconvenience and wound up as a major problem." La Farge mopped his face energetically with his handkerchief. "I should never have allowed that tacky little specimen on the premises in the first place."

"I would have thought you'd welcome a review in *La Voix du Nord*," Capucine said.

"Frankly, madame, I'd prefer not to be reviewed at all. Most of our customers are Lille companies who know us well and have their executive meetings here. They've been with us for years. We don't need any help from the press. As it is, we're almost full all year round. Still, *La Voix du Nord* is a very powerful paper. When this man Rocher called me, I just couldn't afford to risk antagonizing them."

"Of course," Capucine said.

"But when this Rocher came the first time, he didn't look quite right. His clothes were shabby, even for a journalist. He was arrogant with the staff. He sent dishes back. He drank a good deal of very expensive Armagnac after his dinner. In short, he was an insult to the restaurant. And then he had the impudence to claim that he couldn't write a review unless he had dined here three times. He wanted to come back two more times. Can you imagine!"

"What did you do?"

"I checked up on him. It's easy with the Internet. It turned out he'd never written an haute cuisine review for *La Voix du Nord*. So I called his paper. It seemed he was a freelancer. I was furious, but I was still stuck. If I threw him out, he might have succeeded in publishing a disastrous review. I was powerless." His face crinkled like a baby on the edge of tears.

With its wall of gleaming stainless-steel refrigerated lockers and hydraulic lifting tables, the Lille morgue was far more up to date than the one in Paris.

The pallid, wiry remains of Didier Rocher, rapaciously vulpine even in death, lay naked and obscenely vulnerable. Utterly insensitive to the sacrosanctity of human clay, a forensic technician sat comfortably on the middle of the table, his buttocks abutting the cadaver's hip, flipping through his file, looking for the right page.

A deep Y-shaped incision had opened the body from shoulders to scrotum. A quadrant of the head was missing, the open surface black with dried blood, except for the section where pale gray brain matter was clearly visible.

The technician snapped the file shut. "Both barrels of a twelve-gauge. Can't tell if it was a side by side or an over and under. Most of the shot went straight through, but a couple of pellets lodged in the cranium. Steel. Impossible to identify the manufacturer.

"Nothing noteworthy in the autopsy. He was in good health. Out of shape. Drank and smoked too much but no significant health problems.

"Alcohol content in the blood was high enough to make waking difficult for him. His stomach was full. He'd just finished a large meal. His scrotum was partially emptied, a condition consistent with someone who had ejaculated four or five hours prior to death."

"What can you tell us about the angle he was shot from?" Capucine asked.

"That's very straightforward. Given the position of the body, he was shot when he was a foot or two out the door of the restaurant. He had turned his head to face his attacker. The line of fire is about fifteen degrees off center. The attacker seems to have partially missed, which is why the blast hit the right part of the head, not the middle."

"Can we see the personal effects?" Capucine asked.

The technician produced a large cardboard box labeled CAS NO. 8144-732. The contents were meager, a pair of pointed loafers, scuffed and down at the heels; a lightweight gray summer jacket with too-thin lapels, dotted with stains; a pair of dark blue cotton trousers that looked like they would have been tight around the legs of even such a skinny body; a white shirt with decorative embroidery down the front; a black knit tie that looked like it had been stretched considerably and bore the faint traces of a good number of meals.

A plastic bag contained the victim's possessions: a much-dented steel-capped Waterman fountain pen, a wallet containing a national identity card, a Carte Bleue bank card, seven business cards imprinted with the *La Voix du Nord* logo, eight credit card receipts, and a ten- and a five-euro banknote.

Capucine picked out a new-looking steel wristwatch and examined it carefully.

"Looks cheap enough," Tirmont said.

"Not if it's genuine. It's a Cartier. One of the Santos line they brought out to commemorate the centennial of the Brazilian pilot's death."

The numbers and the engraving on the back had the feel of authenticity.

"How much would it have cost?" Tirmont asked.

"About five thousand euros if it's not a knockoff. Doesn't quite go with the shoes or the clothes, does it? Do you think you can have someone check out if it's real?"

It was true that Aristide Callies, the editor who screened Rocher's submissions, didn't hold him in very high regard.

"There's not a lot that I didn't tell Lieutenant Tirmont yesterday," Callies said. "Rocher had been a stringer for the paper for about five years. Sooner or later, most of these stringers wind up with a full-time contract. But not Rocher. He was lazy and he cut too many corners. He didn't hesitate to make up a fact or two if it suited him. That kept him from being assigned to anything serious."

"What sort of pieces did he write?" Capucine asked.

"He did the stuff the full-time staff thought was beneath them. Reviews of children's movies. Book reviews of mystery novels. Cute puppy-dog human interest stuff. And the occasional restaurant piece about down-market places. The last one he did was on Charolais Allô when they opened in Lille." Callies paused and looked at Capucine. "You probably don't know who they are. It's a fast-food chain that specializes in beef."

"I know them all too well," Capucine said with unexpected emotion. "So how did he get assigned to review a Relais & Château restaurant?"

Callies laughed. "He hadn't been assigned. The first I heard about it was from Lieutenant Tirmont. He must have called the restaurant and got them to comp him a fancy meal. Even if he'd gotten around to actually writing a review, I doubt we would have run it."

"And he had no family, no wife, no children?" Capucine asked.

Callies shook his head.

"Any girlfriends?"

"He wasn't gay, if that's what you're asking. I know he'd had one or two flings with women here at the paper, but I don't know anything else about his sex life." Callies chuckled. "He had a pretty stormy breakup a few weeks ago with one of our fact-checkers that kept too many people gossiping at the coffee dispenser. I actually had to speak to the girl about it." Callies laughed. Capucine frowned. Callies tilted his head at a woman who had just passed his cubicle, indicating she had been Rocher's paramour.

Capucine had noticed her walk by the cubicle several times during the interview—a blowsy, home-dyed redhead who must have been fetchingly buxom as a young girl but who was now edging to the slatternly—to all appearances waiting to consult with Callies on some urgent matter. Capucine had no difficulty in imagining her creating a public ruckus over a failed office romance.

The interview over, Tirmont proposed they have a beer in the Grand'Place, in front of *La Voix du Nord*. He assured Capucine it was one of the great architectural marvels of Europe and a perfect place for them to sit and plan out their next moves.

In the hallway the redhead was pacing back and forth impatiently in front of the elevator bank, her stiletto heels clicking loudly on the white tile floor.

"You're the police, aren't you?" she asked Capucine as they came up. "And you're asking questions about that asshole Rocher, right?"

"Did you know him well?" Capucine asked.

"He spent most of his nights in my apartment for six months. Does that count as 'well'?"

Capucine replied with her most empathetic smile. "Can you tell us anything that might help with our investigation?"

"Girlfriend, can I ever. But not here. I knock off at six. Can you meet me at one of the café tables at the opposite end of the square?"

Capucine and Tirmont killed the half hour drinking *demis* of beer while Tirmont swelled with pride as he launched into a recitative of the glories of the vast Grand'-Place. To Capucine's eye the pink wedding cake buildings dripping with curlicued white trim looked like they belonged in Belgium, not France.

Tirmont was specially proud of a large bronze statue of a crowned woman that dominated the square from the top of a pillar. "That's La Déesse—the Goddess of the North. The statue was cast to go on the top of the Arc de Triomphe." Capucine shuddered at the thought. "And those," he said, pointing to a number of dark spots, like blackheads, in the white trim of the square's buildings, "are Austrian cannonballs from the attack on the city in seventeen ninety-two. Isn't that amazing?"

He was almost disappointed when the redhead bustled up, cutting his lecture short.

"Natalie Duchamp," she said, extending her hand aggressively.

Capucine completed the introductions, asked her to sit, ordered another round of *demis*.

"You were Rocher's girlfriend?" Tirmont asked.

Natalie looked at him sourly. "His mark. That would describe it better."

"Tell me about it," Capucine said gently.

"He was in it for what he could get. We got friendly one night, after someone's retirement party, and he started staying over at my place four or five nights a week. I knew he was coming over because he was too broke to buy himself a meal in a restaurant, but I still liked the company. I like to cook. He liked to eat. It was nice. Then we'd do a little 'sheeeet,' " she said the word in Frenchified English— apparently outdated American slang for recreational drugs was still cool in the North—"and get cuddly. Like I said, it was nice."

"Why was he so broke?" Tirmont asked.

"I never did figure that out. He didn't make much from his pieces at the paper, but he must have had enough to live on. I think he was blowing the little he had on women."

"What makes you say that?" Capucine asked.

"For one, he just couldn't get enough. The minute he walked into my apartment, he was all over me. It was hard as hell to cook with him around. He'd keep me up until late and then wake me up again at three in the morning. In the beginning it was fun, but the sleep deprivation got to be too much."

"Just because he found you so attractive doesn't mean he went out with other women," Tirmont said.

"Right." Natalie shot him an irritated glance. "I caught him in the act."

"Poor you," Capucine said. "What happened?"

"One evening I saw him in a café, sitting with a girl, leaning over and whispering in her ear. Two nights later he came by for his free meal and free fuck and—can you believe this?—he actually convinced me the girl was just a friend." She shook her head in self-disgust. "So we kept on going. Business as usual."

A heavy silence lasted for two long beats.

"Then it happened. About a month later he comes over and I cook up his favorite dish, *rôti de porc au maroilles*." Natalie paused. She was on the edge of tears.

Embarrassed, Tirmont jumped into the breach. "Maroilles is the best cheese of the North." He bunched his fingers together, kissed them, and opened them up toward the sky, as if releasing a divine spirit. "The dish is a Northern classic, pieces of pork roasted in a cream and cheese sauce."

"Not just any cream," Natalie said, giving him another acid look. "Crème fraîche. It's the bite of the crème fraîche and the onion that make the dish work—"

Capucine cut her off by putting two fingers on the back of her hand.

"What happened after he ate your *rôti de porc au maroilles?*"

"What do you think happened? We went to bed. Actually, we didn't even make it to bed." She smiled happily and then paused, frowning.

"So, the next morning I see that he's putting the things he has at my place—two or three shirts and some shaving stuff—in this plastic bag. 'What are you doing?' I ask him. 'I'm breaking this off. I've found someone else,' he says, just like that. I was drying the breakfast dishes and started throwing them at him. The little coward was so scared, he ran out the door and left his pathetic little bag."

"So then what?" Tirmont asked.

"I threw it out the window after him."

"No, I meant, did you see him again other than at the paper?"

"Not the way you mean," Natalie said with barely suppressed rage.

"Maybe it was because I missed him a little. And the bed part, too, I guess."

She looked at Capucine to see if she understood. Capucine nodded fractionally and raised her eyebrows.

"He was really very good in bed. I have to say that for him. Good *and* imaginative. He taught me all sorts of new stuff. Like that wonderful thing you do with the whisk—" She caught herself.

"So I'd follow him after he left work. It took me all of two days to figure out what he was up to. The first day he goes to this expensive bar. It was in a narrow street, and I couldn't hang around looking like I was a street walker, could I? So I followed him again the next day and he winds up right here!"

"Here?" Tirmont asked.

"Not at this very table, obviously. That one over there. So, anyway, he's with this woman. Older. I don't know how old, but more than fifty. One of those bourgeois types. Suit. Hermès scarf. Lots of jewelry. Big boobs and a big butt, but old, old, old. I couldn't quite figure it. They're sitting there drinking, all stiff and formal-like, and I didn't really know what the hell was going on. But I sure found out fast. Do you know what they did?"

Capucine shook her head with a sad smile.

"They got up and walked down the rue de Paris to the Hermitage Gantois. I followed them, of course."

"That's the most expensive hotel in town," Tirmont said. "It's about two hundred yards down that street over there."

"So here's the good part. I waited outside exactly ten minutes to let them check in and then used a trick reporters like. I went rushing into the hotel waving this manila envelope full of stuff I was going to check out at home that night. I go up to the desk real panicked like and say to the guy, 'Can you deliver this immediately to Monsieur Lepoutre. It's urgent and he forgot it on his desk at the office.' The guy checks his computer and of course there's no Lepoutre. So I say, 'He just checked in right now. He was with a very elegant woman older than he was.' The guy doesn't even look at me, but he takes the envelope, bangs the bell on the desk, and this kid runs up in a fancy uniform with a pillbox hat like they had in the twenties. 'Madame Debruyne, *chambre* two oh seven' he says to the bellhop and then looks at me like I'm a piece of shit and goes, '*Voilà*' meaning, 'Get the hell out.' "

She leaned back in her chair with a gloating, self-satisfied look and drained her beer.

Capucine ordered another round.

"Then what?"

"I ran after the bellhop, told him I had made a mistake and it was the wrong envelope, and went back to the office. It took me all of four minutes to find out who Madame Debruyne is—a certain Camille married to a guy called Matteo Debruyne who is financial director of a company called Sofinor."

"It's one of the larger finance houses in Lille. They specialize in complex infrastructure financing," Tirmont said to Capucine.

"Exactly," Natalie said. "I checked the company out, as well. It's very big. So, there, that's my story. Sleazebag dumped me to fuck a geriatric. Sure makes me feel good."

There was another awkward pause. The mood had changed, as if storm clouds had arrived unexpectedly. Natalie became evasive, refusing to meet either of the detectives' gazes. She shuffled her feet under the table and looked at her watch. "It's nearly seven. I've got to get going."

"Not so fast," Tirmont said. "We need to hear the rest of the story."

Capucine shot Tirmont a glance, ordering him to remain silent.

"You must have been devastated," Capucine said. She put her hand on Natalie's. "Were you in love with him?"

Natalie's eyes filmed with liquid. "I . . . I don't know.

Maybe." She paused, snatched her hand from under Capucine's, banged it on the table. "No! How could I have been in love and done what I did?"

Capucine saw Tirmont filling his lungs to ask a question and shot him another look. There was another long silence.

"Did he deserve it?" Capucine asked.

"Of course he did. He deserved far worse."

"You called the husband?"

"That would have been vulgar. I sent an anonymous letter. It took me a whole day to get the wording right."

CHAPTER 26

The Debruynes lived in the pink-bricked and white-iced place Louise-de-Bettignies. One of the most exclusive addresses in Lille, Tirmont had explained, even though it had never been peppered with cannonballs.

Monsieur Debruyne, who could be no more than a year or two away from retirement, answered the door when they rang at nine thirty that night. He wore a dark gray flannel double-breasted suit that accentuated his large belly. When the detectives showed their ID wallets, he turned without a word and led them into a living room crammed oppressively with fussy antiques.

Camille Debruyne sat on a silk upholstered Louis XVI settee, wearing a formal beige dress, a double string of pearls, and alligator shoes with two-inch heels. Her red-rimmed eyes intensified a sense of carnality that was at odds with her matronly outfit. Even though she was fifteen pounds over the current canon of beauty, Boucher would have snapped her up as a model. Like a seed pod about to pop, she was ready to explode in erotic passion at the slightest touch. Although she was probably into her fifties, she could have passed for being in her forties, or even less in younger clothes.

It was obvious the couple had been deep in discussion.

"The police," Debruyne announced tonelessly to his wife.

Camille burst loudly into tears.

"We need to ask you some questions about the death of a man called Didier Rocher. Did either of you know him?" Tirmont asked loudly over her sobs.

"Please sit down, Officers," Debruyne said, pulling two elaborately gilt chairs closer to the coffee table. He shot a now-see-what-you've-done look at his wife and sat at the opposite end of the sofa from her.

"Yes," Debruyne said, "my wife was a friend of Monsieur Rocher. We were just discussing their acquaintance when you arrived."

Camille Debruyne began to sob again. This time soundlessly. Tears ran down her cheeks and dripped on her lap. She made no effort to blot them.

"Would you care to share that discussion with us?" Capucine asked.

For the first time Debruyne was unsettled. He avoided Capucine's gaze.

"My wife is upset at Monsieur Rocher's death," he said in a low voice. "We were discussing the nature of her affection for him. I doubt that would be of much interest to you."

"Do you own a shotgun, Monsieur Debruyne?" Tirmont asked.

"Of course. What Frenchman doesn't? Would you like to see it?"

"Please."

The very fine English gun was disassembled into its two component parts and stored in an elegant leather case. Tirmont extracted the barrel component and scrunched up his face to peer through the tubes with one eye. Then he removed the stock-and-lock component from the case, examined it carefully, and fitted the gun together with a loud snap. The room was deathly still. Meditatively, he caressed the side of the lock with his finger. Surely it was Capucine's imagination, but the smell of oil seemed to fill the room.

"When did you use this last?" he asked.

"Oh, in the fall, I suppose. I have a friend who has a pheasant shoot in Wallonia. We go once or twice in the season, don't we, dear?"

Camille Debruyne could not take her eyes from the gun.

Tirmont smiled and said pleasantly, one hunter to another, "Belgian pheasant are one of the great attractions of the North, aren't they?"

Debruyne did not reply.

"You take very good care of your gun, monsieur, but I'm afraid you use too much oil. Eventually, it will gum up the action. Although this oil," he said, rubbing his thumb against the tip of his index finger, "feels quite fresh." Tirmont glanced at Capucine, requesting permission to continue.

"Thank you, Monsieur Debruyne," Capucine said briskly. "This has been very helpful. It's enough for tonight. Of course, you understand we'll have to continue our discussion tomorrow." She turned to Camille and said, "*Madame, mes excuses*. It was unpardonable of us to intrude so late."

As they walked back to Tirmont's car, he asked, "You didn't want to arrest him tonight?"

"No. He has some things to settle with his wife, and he'll confess more freely once he's done that. We'll pick him up in the morning."

"And you don't think he'll bolt?"

"He's the sort of man who is incapable of traveling without his credit cards. If he ran we'd have him in half a day at the most. And, anyway, you're going to post men around the building all night, aren't you?"

Tirmont laughed.

*　*　*

Capucine spent the night in an inexpensive Novotel that had no room service. She had skipped dinner and, with only the TGV sandwich in her stomach, was famished. She filled a white cardboard bucket with ice from a machine down the hall and gleefully attacked the minibar, putting four cubes of ice in the bathroom glass, followed by two mignonettes of vodka. Then she proceeded systematically to consume the entire comestible contents of the bar, starting with the chips and nuts and winding up with the chocolate. When the feed was finally over, she was nauseous but still felt hungry and marveled at how that was possible.

She poured herself another drink—this time gin, since there was no more vodka—and dialed the apartment in Paris. Her only meager consolation for spending the night away from Alexandre was the freedom to drink her alcohol so cold it made her teeth hurt, a practice Alexandre condemned as an American solecism to be strictly avoided.

Alexandre picked up at the first ring. "I can hear ice tinkling. You must be celebrating your arrest."

"We're making the arrest in the morning. He's having his last evening with his wife, who is the one who really should be behind bars. It's one of these heavy Northern stories filled with depression, beer, brown bread, and dishes gluey with cheese. I'm not celebrating. I'm drowning my sorrows."

"When are you coming home?"

"I'll be there for dinner. You'd better make me something specially nice. All I've had to eat today is a TGV sandwich and the contents of my minibar."

"Good Lord!" Alexandre was genuinely appalled. "The next time you leave Paris, I'm going to send you off with a proper picnic basket. Tomorrow night I have a restaurant to review, but I'll leave you something worthy of your return in the oven."

The announcement that Alexandre would not be at

home when she got back, on top of the contents of the minibar, made Capucine toss and turn for most of the night.

Tirmont and a wrinkled and unmade-up Capucine collected Debruyne as he left his building to go to work in the morning.

"Monsieur, I thought we would finish our discussion at the *Police Judiciaire* brigade, if you don't mind," Capucine said.

"I expected nothing less, *Commissaire.*"

It was over in forty-five minutes. Debruyne had prepared himself. He handed over Natalie Duchamps's anonymous letter and told his story. He had had a private detective follow his wife. When the detective confirmed the liaison, Debruyne had ordered him to tail Rocher continuously. After Rocher's first solitary meal at Le St. Jacques de Lorraine, the detective had gone to see the general manager, ostensibly about organizing a conference at the hotel, and had learned about Rocher's three dinners to write a review. On the fatal night the detective had followed Rocher and Camille to the Hermitage Gantois, where they stayed until seven. He had reported by cell phone to Debruyne, who had instructed him to stick with Rocher. Debruyne had had dinner with his wife at home, had dismissed the detective by phone, and had driven out to Le St. Jacques de Lorraine.

At the inn, Debruyne had parked his Mercedes 500 in the lot behind the hotel and had waited behind the bush for Rocher to come out. As he emerged, Debruyne had shouted out an epithet—"I just couldn't shoot a man in the back," he had explained—and had let him have both barrels as he turned. He had then walked to his car, the shotgun broken open over his arm as if walking home from a bird shoot, and had calmly driven back to Lille.

"One of the happiest hours of my life."

If the confession had gushed forth like the bubbling waters of a cool rocky mountain brook, the paperwork certainly didn't. It was not until late afternoon that the police file was complete and Debruyne was sent off to Séquedin Prison to await his trial and thence to return to serve out his sentence, which was unlikely to be very long—two years at the most, with a release halfway through for good behavior—since even in the North courts took a very Latin view of crimes of romantic passion.

On the six-thirty TGV back to Paris Capucine smiled to herself over Tirmont's scorn of the naïveté of the amateur criminal. If Debruyne had blown his wife's lover's head off when they were actually in bed together at the Hermitage Gantois, a skilled lawyer—and Debruyne had the money to hire the best—would have had no trouble at all convincing the court to exonerate him completely and he would undoubtedly have even received the court's apology for his pretrial detention. And witnessing the act would have put the fear of God into his wife for the rest of her days.

Capucine knew Tirmont was wrong. She was convinced Debruyne was sitting peacefully in his cell, master of his life, smiling contentedly, a Sisyphus following a very small stone down a very small hill.

CHAPTER 27

Capucine's wry pleasure with the Lille case volatilized as the train surged smoothly southward. All that remained of what had seemed like an anachronistic comedy of manners was the image of the victim's grisly mutilated head. As she stared out the window with unfocused eyes, the rocketing scenery an impressionist oil in greens and browns, the ruined head became Alexandre's.

Capucine felt trapped in the train. She couldn't eat a full dinner so early in the evening. She couldn't face the aseptic metallic bar. She had no book to read. She had only her thoughts, and they were unwelcome travel companions. If the TGV going north had been propelled by a rocket, on the way back it was pulled by a leaky steam engine.

Capucine cursed herself for her thirty-six-hour abdication. She had known from the beginning that the Lille case was a digression. Tirmont would have taken at most a day or two longer to solve the crime, and if she had stayed in Paris she might have made some progress on her own case. And she certainly wouldn't have let Alexandre go out to a restaurant on his own. There was no doubt about it. A minute away from Paris was a minute wasted. She execrated the train for its slowness.

As these thoughts festered, the horizon filled with dark, looming clouds. Capucine's heart lifted, welcoming the catharsis of a violent storm. The first squall broke as the TGV entered the outskirts of Paris. By the time it eased into the Gare du Nord at seven thirty-two, precisely on time once again, rain drummed on the train car's roof so loudly, they might be in the tropics. Still, the storm only distracted; it brought no relief.

In the seconds it took her to sprint to the Twingo, Capucine was soaked to the skin. The realization that she would have to fieldstrip and oil her Sig Sauer the minute she got home took her over the top. She kicked the front tire of her diminutive car and howled in dismay and frustration.

The empty apartment mocked her. She peeled off her sopping clothes and shapeless shoes and left them in a soggy pile by the front door. She dropped the holstered Sig on top, a brown cherry capping a bitter sundae—let the damn thing rust—and made for the shower.

Twenty minutes later, her face rosy from the heat of the blow-dryer, she emerged from the bedroom in a pair of ancient jeans and an extra-large T-shirt with a wine merchant's logo so faded it might have been a ghostly advertisement from a previous century on the side of a building deep in the Marais. Her desire for Alexandre was so intense it made her stomach ache.

In the kitchen she found an opened bottle of Ott rosé in the door of the refrigerator, poured herself a glass, and remembered Alexandre's promise to leave her something delicious in the oven. Sure enough, he had made her a Comté and artichoke-heart quiche, which was still lukewarm. She returned to the refrigerator and discovered he had also made her an endive, escarole, and frisée salad and had left a jam jar next to it filled with a lemony vinaigrette punctuated by suspended motes of finely chopped tarragon.

She took her plate of quiche and salad along with the glass of wine into the living room. The first bite of quiche moved her profoundly. It wasn't just that he had known exactly what she would have wanted, it was that the quiche was a perfect emanation of Alexandre. It was almost as if he was in the room, looking over her shoulder, watching her eat. The link was so powerful, consuming the quiche and salad bordered on the sexual. Where the hell was he? *Merde.* It was only a quarter to nine. She imagined him sitting in a restaurant, she had no idea where, scowling critically at his meal before forming his opinion. Maybe he'd be home by ten.

The quiche and salad consumed, Capucine continued to glance at her watch every five minutes while she snapped through the pages of a small pile of *Marie Claire*s and *Vogue*s on the coffee table, simultaneously flipping through the endless cable channels on the television. The inchoate bites of disjointed information escalated her malaise. Angrily, she turned off the TV and dropped the remote on top of the disorderly pile of magazines on the floor.

She poured herself a good measure of vodka, added three ice cubes—happily imagining Alexandre scowling at her philistinism—and picked up her copy of Gaël Tanguy's *The Nature of Possessives.*

It was true the man could write. The verisimilitude of Tanguy's vistas of pockmarked mud stretching without relief to a horizon where a brown sky met a black earth was compelling enough to suck her out of her funk and into his. But the magic carpet of narrative transfer plummeted when Capucine came to a graphic scene in which the android protagonist, with its sparking circuit boards, sought desperately to become a living creature in a fumbled fornication with one of the decaying half-dead animals, incanting, "*Coito, ergo sum,*" which she guessed meant "I copulate, therefore I am." Capucine was so revolted she threw the book at a wall.

So where the hell was Alexandre? It was almost ten. Like a black-clad Provençal grandmother working her rosary beads, she counted off the minutes of his evening. He would have left the apartment at eight. Arrived at the restaurant at eight thirty. Been seated by eight forty. Sipped a flute of champagne while he studied the menu. That would have taken at least ten minutes. No, sometimes it was even more. So, let's call it eight fifty-five—She stopped, the exercise was pointless. He wasn't going to be home before eleven and that was that. She looked at her watch again. Three minutes to ten.

She went to the window. But definitely not to see if he was coming. Definitely not. Sheets of rain made ghostly curtains around the streetlight. Her cell phone trilled. Capucine snapped it open.

"*Allô, Commissaire. C'est David.*"

Capucine snorted in exasperation.

"I'm soaking wet, but that's not why I'm calling." The cell phone connection crackled. David hesitated.

"David, out with it. I'm expecting an important call."

"Well, I'm tailing Charbonnier and Voisin like you ordered and they wound up at the *Hôtel* Costes, you know, the *place on the rue Saint Honoré where all the celebs go—*"

"David, I know where the *Hôtel* Costes is and who goes there. Trust me on that. Why are you calling?"

"Well, I'm standing here soaking wet and all of a sudden Sybille Charbonnier—Sybille Charbonnier herself!—comes out with this doorman holding this huge umbrella over her. And she says that she and her dear friend Monsieur Voisin had noticed that I was following them and they felt very bad about leaving me in front of the hotel getting wet. So they wanted me to come into the restaurant and eat something, where, as she said, 'I would be dry and could keep an even better eye on them.' "

"Are you calling me because you don't like having your

leg pulled or because you think you need my permission to knock off some victuals at their expense?"

"Neither. That's not it at all. Of course I'm going to eat in the restaurant. Who would pass that up? But my hair's a mess. I mean really a mess. Totally. I look like an Afghan Hound that's been left out all night. What would you do?"

Despite her anxiety, Capucine's laughter erupted.

"The ladies' room has hair dryers. There's an attendant—Josette, I think her name is—who's very good with hair. Give her a good tip. You can put it on the expense account. Enjoy your evening."

The oily bubble of mirth blew away all too quickly as the storm clouds returned.

The problem, she decided as she stared out into the black night, was double edged. The killer could only be caught if he kept on killing. But that would be like Russian roulette. If he kept on killing, sooner or later Alexandre would be the target. There was no amount of protection she could possibly provide to guarantee that wouldn't happen. Look at how easy it was to kill a head of state.

So it would be better if he stopped killing—as he seemed to have done. But then maybe he'd start up again one day. And it might be Alexandre's turn. A sword of Damocles would hang eternally over their heads. The joy would be sucked out of their lives. They would never, ever walk into a restaurant again without feeling susp—

Capucine heard the most glorious sound the world could produce, the C major click of a key in the front-door lock, which in its one single note carried an entire symphony of love, joy, and happiness. Alexandre was home!

"Where the hell have you been?"

Capucine's eyes filled with tears of rage. She looked at her watch. It was eleven minutes after ten.

"You knew perfectly well I was worried about you and still monsieur decides to dawdle over his dinner and then flirt with the hostess and come home virtually in the middle of the night." Tears streamed down her cheeks and splattered on the floor.

Alexandre came up to her and attempted to sweep her into his arms. She pushed him away violently. He plastered an opéra bouffe look of confusion and hurt over a hint of a wry smile. Capucine kicked him in the shin with her bare foot.

Alexandre backed off, pretending to limp. "You're right. I should have left earlier. It was a Corsican restaurant. I had a rather boring *fressure de cabri sautée.*"

"A what?"

"It's made with four different kinds of entrails from a goat kid—the liver, the sweetbread, the heart, and the lungs. They're stewed in pork caul with some cubed salted pork, garlic, and a fistful of Corsican spices." Capucine made an exaggerated grimace of disgust. "Actually, it can be excellent," Alexandre went on. "But this was merely bland."

For a split second Capucine looked deep into Alexandre's eyes to see if she was being kidded. One of Alexandre's fortes was making girls shriek at dinner parties with invented grotesque recipes. But he seemed perfectly serious.

"And Adenia, the hostess, is involved in a tragic dispute with her fiancé. I certainly would never have even thought of flirting."

"Well, it's good that you got your Corsican review done with."

"Why do you say that?"

"Because Momo hates Corsican food. And I fully sympathize with him."

Alexandre looked lost.

"Momo?"

"Of course, Momo. He's going to be your constant dinner companion from now on."

CHAPTER 28

Two days later Capucine found herself inching crablike down the vertiginous stone steps to the Seine. The three-inch-heeled Max Kibardin Rosette Sandals, delectable as they were with their delicate leather roses decorating the straps, had definitely been a mistake, particularly if one was laden with an impossibly heavy metal canister.

After all the time she had wasted in Lille she had had misgivings about devoting an entire half day to Vavasseur, who, truth be told, hadn't really produced any earthshaking revelations the last time she had seen him. On top of that she had been loath to run the gauntlet of Jacques' gibes in order to get him to set up the appointment. In the end she had capitulated, more from a neurotic desire to leave no stone unturned than out of any real conviction.

Jacques has been even more snide than expected, but, as always, his barbs had been directed at the more robust areas of her id.

"I knew Docteur Vavasseur would find a willing patient in you," he had said. "All that effort you expend puffing up Meaty Mate's libido must be completely draining. I often think I should offer you a *cinq à sept* myself to ease the tension."

"*Cher cousin,*" Capucine had replied, "it's a thought. We could meet for a quiet drink and I could tell you all about Alexandre's savoir faire. You might pick up some useful pointers."

"No thanks. I'm not even close to the stage where I need to attempt to make my embonpoint appear seductive," he had replied. "When you trot along to Vavasseur tomorrow for lunch you might check if he has any Lacanian insights on pepping up limp Life Partners."

When she reached the bottom of the stairs Vavasseur was as diffident as at the first meeting. At her approach he eased cautiously away until he butted up against the police barricade. It was only when he noticed the olive drab canister that he began to relax.

Vavasseur took a tentative step forward. "I see you brought our lunch. Just put it down so I can have a peek and see if I have a wine that will do it justice."

Capucine placed the container gently on the cobblestones and backed off five paces. Vavasseur scuttled forward, grabbed the canister, and retreated to the safety of his alcove. Keeping her in his field of vision, he snapped the container open and sniffed deeply. The aroma of the food seemed to imbue him with confidence. He beamed.

"Langoustines, definitely. They know I like fish best because it comes from the water and the water is safety. And something else. A fowl of some sort. Quail. Yes, it's definitely quail." He fanned the aroma to his nostrils with an open hand. "Good. I have a very nice two thousand five Côte de Vaubarousse that should just be at the right temperature. Perfect for the langoustines, although I have some doubts it will be full-bodied enough for the quail, but life is all about compromise, isn't it, after all?" His breathing had slowed to normal. He was almost completely relaxed. Food definitely did the trick for him.

"Why don't we have a little *apéro* before we get to our

lunch and after we can talk about all the things on your mind?"

He produced a bottle from under the bed. "This is Yamazaki. It's actually a far better single malt than most of what the Scots produce. The Japanese have succeeded where the Californians have failed in making a better product than the mother country's."

The notion that the Japanese had managed to attain the pinnacle of single malts while the California wines, even though excellent, could not even come close to matching the best of Bordeaux was one of Alexandre's favorite themes. Capucine wondered if the notion had reached Vavasseur through Jacques, who she knew was a far greater admirer of Alexandre than he would ever admit.

They sipped their whiskey standing beside the Seine, which flowed quietly but powerfully, with almost frightening inexorability. The man on the far bank emerged from his cardboard crate, stretched, waved at them, and made off with his perfect Labrador to wherever it was that he went during the day. Vavasseur drew a deep breath.

"Seeing him escape from that box is such a relief." He sighed contentedly. "Let's see what they've sent us today," Vavasseur said, rummaging around in the container. "*Pas mal!*" he said, reading from a little card. "We start with *langoustines* in a crispy crust with basil *pistou* and for a main course have *caille en brochette caramélisée sur un frou frou de légumes révélés de wasabi*—skewered caramelized quail on an amusing bed of vegetables made exciting with wasabi. The Chablis will be perfect with both." Vavasseur pursed his lips in appreciation.

"Is your food always this good?" Capucine asked, impressed.

"Oh, yes," Vavasseur answered, a little taken aback, as if she had asked him if he changed his socks every day. "Why wouldn't it be?"

The meal was superb and the wine perfect, greenish yellow and deliciously full. As they ate, they chatted aimlessly, happily; the sun danced off the relentlessly questing river and a cool breeze flowed under the arch of the bridge. The meal was as serene as it was estival.

"Well," said Vavasseur after he had cleared away the dishes. "Why don't you relax on the bed and share your thoughts?"

Without awkwardness this time, Capucine stretched out, kicked off her dainty shoes, and let them fall on the cobblestones. She wriggled her toes sensuously, taking inordinate pleasure in their release from the bondage of shoes straight out of the box. The whisper of a warm zephyr brushed a lingering kiss across the soles of her feet. She started to float away and brought herself back with a sharp snap.

"I'm not getting anywhere with the case. I think I understand even less than when I came to see you last time."

"Tell me more."

"I have no leads, nothing. When I started I had a list of suspects but that's meaningless now. And the worst part is that the killer seems to have gone to ground. He hasn't manifested himself for over four weeks. I don't know if he's extending the gap between murders or if he's simply disappeared. Is it possible he's really stopped killing?"

"As we've already discussed, the killer may have defined such complicated conditions for his murders that it is very difficult for him to find suitable venues."

Capucine nodded but said nothing.

"And then it's also possible that he is finding his fetishes more and more effective in prolonging his sense of satisfaction and wholeness that he now needs to kill less frequently."

"Fetishes? You mean like men who want their women to wear garter belts and black stockings?"

"It's a bit more complicated than that. The value of the

fetish stems from the nature of desire in Lacanian terms. For Lacan desire could never be satisfied."

"That doesn't make any sense. Of course desire can be satisfied."

"You have a need for your husband to love you, don't you?"

"Obviously. It's by far my greatest need."

"And are you confident he really does love you?"

"Yes, absolutely."

"And how many times a week do you ask him if he does?"

Capucine laughed. "At least five. Sometimes more."

"That's an expression of the fundamental unfulfillability of need, which, Lacan explained, results in permanent, unquenchable desire. As he put it, desire takes up what has been eclipsed at the level of need."

"So you're saying that the killings satisfied the killer's need temporarily, but the desire remains afterward."

"Yes, precisely, but it's not immediately apparent to him. Let me explain. When you make love to your husband, your need is fulfilled for a moment, but soon the desire manifests itself again."

"That's for sure," Capucine said with feeling.

"The killer may be able to palliate that unquenchable desire with a fetish, something tangible that represents a surrogate of his fulfilled need."

"And what would this fetish be?"

"It could be almost anything. Most likely it will be something personal and intimately connected to the victim. A shoe. An item of underwear. A lock of hair."

"But nothing like that was missing from the victims. Our forensic teams are fabulously thorough."

Capucine thought for a moment and then shook her head. "But let's say, for discussion sake, that there were fetishes. For how long would they be effective?"

"Impossible to say. An hour. A day. A month. But not forever."

"So you're sure he'll kill again?"

"Nothing in life is sure, but it's more than likely the value of his fetish—if he has one—will fade quickly. And if his constraint is finding a suitable scene for his crime, that, too, is just a question of time.

"I'm inclined to think the fourth murder is overdue. Well overdue. And also I have a feeling this one will contain all the information you need to identify the murderer."

CHAPTER 29

Two days later Capucine received another one of Martinière's beautifully written notes. Now that he had been officially sanctioned, Capucine viewed the juge almost affectionately, like an ill-tempered house cat that had been declawed and could now be picked up and stroked without risk.

Despite his disgrace, at least on paper Martinière seemed to have lost none of his arrogance. The note "convoked" her peremptorily to his office the next day at eleven. As Capucine admired his handwriting, she wondered if the juge was even capable of turning on a computer or if he ever arrived in his office before ten thirty.

She arrived at the meeting her customary fifteen minutes late. Martinière looked at his thin gold watch and shrugged with a small sigh. He seemed to have shrunk and sat with rounded back at his ornate desk, as if he was trying to achieve a fetal position.

"*Commissaire,* you're fifteen minutes late," he said almost listlessly.

"Yes, I stopped to have a coffee, because I knew you wouldn't offer me any."

"You should have brought me one," he said plaintively. "The coffee here is execrable."

Capucine smiled sweetly at him.

"*Commissaire,* I'm dismayed you chose not to tell me personally about your case in Lille. I had to find out about it from an official circular."

"*Monsieur le Juge,* that murder had absolutely no connection to the serial killer. It was a complete red herring."

"Are you sure? A restaurant critic was killed in a restaurant where he was working on a review, exactly like the other three murders."

"Pure coincidence. It was a crime of passion. An irate husband killed his wife's lover after she had had a tryst in a hotel."

Martinière made a caricatural grimace of doubt. Stealthily, he extracted a thin file covered in flimsy blue paper from under the tooled leather cover of his blotter. He opened it carefully on his lap, withdrew a gold pen from his inside breast pocket and held it upright between his thumb and his first two fingers. The pen seemed to give him strength. He pivoted the pen to the horizontal and jabbed it repeatedly at Capucine as he spoke.

"*Commissaire,* my credulity is strained."

The familiar gesture with the pen had always made Capucine think of someone miming a pistol firing bullets. Now it seemed entirely phallic. She repressed a smirk.

"A restaurant critic killed performing his function—precisely the same modus operandi as the other three killings—please. There simply must be a connection. Let's review this case carefully."

He uncapped his pen and made tick marks in the margin of his file.

"And I'll tell you another thing," he said as an afterthought. "If the Lille murder wasn't our killer at work, that means he's been inactive for well over a month. And that's something I just can't accept."

"*Monsieur le Juge,* the victim wasn't really a restaurant critic. He was just a failed journalist who worked as a stringer, writing pieces that no one else could be bothered with. He wasn't even really writing a review of the restaurant. He was conning them out free meals."

As she spoke Martinière took copious notes with his pen.

"And the perpetrator was an older man in a rage that a wife fifteen years his junior was having a fling. It was a banal crime of passion."

Martinière put down his pen and raised his index finger to indicate she should wait until he finished his note before continuing. She noticed traces of blue ink on his thumb and first two fingers.

"The man shot his wife's lover with his shotgun. He confessed freely. That's all there was to it. How many times have we seen that?"

Capucine smiled as Martinière continued to scribble zealously. These leaky fountain pens were completely ridiculous. Why spend a fortune on obsolete, defective technology? Of course, she had a gold pen too. Dented, but still gold. Her parents had given it to her when she'd passed her *bac*. So did Alexandre. So did everyone, when you came to think about it. It was an entirely foolish affectation.

Martinière capped his pen ostentatiously as a sign she was to continue her narrative.

Capucine sat bolt upright in her chair.

"Did you check carefully that this alleged perpetrator was not in Paris on the dates of the restaurant murders?"

"*Monsieur le Juge,* it absolutely wasn't necessary. There was clearly no connection between the crimes."

She stood up.

"What's the matter?"

"*Monsieur le Juge,* I'm afraid I have an urgent appointment I completely forgot about. Thank you for your time." She bolted out the door.

Waiting for the elevator, she punched the speed dial for her brigade on her cell phone and reached Isabelle.

"I need the complete inventories of the personal effects of all three victims on my desk by the time I get there, which will be in twenty minutes."

The first victim, Gautier du Fesnay, had had a well-worn gold Waterman. Capucine remembered seeing it in his left inside breast pocket. The inventory listed it as "yellow-metal Waterman pen, used condition" and gave no other description.

Jean Monteil, the second victim, had had two pens in his possession, a plastic Pilot Fineliner fine-point felt-tip and a white ballpoint marked HÔTEL COSTES on the clip.

So much for the theory of pens as a fetish. It had been nice while it lasted.

The third victim, Arsène Peroché, had had no pen. But he had had a small spiral-bound Clairefontaine notebook in his right outside jacket pocket. She had forgotten about that.

Capucine went out to the squad room floor and into Isabelle's cubicle.

"Can you get someone in forensics to bring me Peroché's notebook this afternoon? There's something I don't understand."

Sure enough, Peroché notebook was filled with his impressions of meals, written in a spiky hand with indelible black fountain pen ink. It took some time for her to decode, but in the end she got it. The notebook was filled with notations like, *"R de V: p trop d."* Which was obviously, *"Ris de Veau: pas trop dégueulasse*—sweetbreads: not too disgusting." That was the easy part. The tricky question was what had happened to his pen.

CHAPTER 30

While Capucine dealt with the juge, Alexandre had been dealing with his first haute cuisine restaurant review since Capucine had returned from Lille. The venue had been Le Grand Véfour, the doyen of Paris three-star restaurants, which, cradled in its lavish ormolu décor, had throned over the Palais Royal since the mid-seventeen hundreds. The occasion had been the launch of a new "bold and daring" menu, and the restaurant was to be packed with critics and the usual Paris *beau monde*. Capucine had originally planned to accompany him, but when the juge's convocation arrived, she had assigned Momo in her stead. Despite her misgivings, she had issued her fiat without waiting for Alexandre's response.

Momo had returned to the brigade at three thirty in the afternoon. When pressed for details of the lunch, he had replied monosyllabically in terse army jargon, "RAS"— *rien à signaler*—nothing to report—and had lumbered off to his desk.

Far less than sure that Alexandre was not a volcano building up pressure to erupt, Capucine arrived at the apartment at seven, a good hour earlier than usual. From the front door she could hear him singing in the kitchen. She kicked off her shoes and tiptoed down the long hallway, stopping a few feet short of the kitchen. Seriously off-key, he attempted Liporello's catalog aria from *Don Giovanni,* counting Don Juan's conquests.

"*Madamina,*" Alexandre sang loudly, "*il catalogo è questo*—Little madam, this is the catalog. Italy six hundred forty. Germany two hundred thirty-one. Turkey ninety-one. Spain one hundred but in France already one thousand and three—*ma in Francia son già mille e tre!*"

On the butchered final tremolo of "*treeeeeeee!*" Capucine entered the kitchen.

"You've got it wrong," she said. "In France it's only a hundred. The one thousand and three are in Spain. I know because I wrote a paper on Kierkegaard's interpretation of the aria when I was at Sciences Po."

"I'm not wrong. Mozart was wrong. It's obvious Don Juan's preference would have been for French women. Don't be silly."

"You're in an exceptionally good mood."

"I'm always in a good mood when I've had a superb lunch and I get to spend the evening closeted with"—he broke into song again—"youuuuuuuu!" He kissed Capucine lasciviously.

She pushed him away. His insouciance was maddening. She had spent the whole day worrying about him and he had gone about his life utterly indifferent to the dangers he was facing—not to mention the extent of her concern. She hoped Momo had been a thorn in his side. He so richly deserved one.

"I was sure you'd be in a pet because I made Momo go to your luncheon with you."

"*Au contraire.* Momo is an exemplary companion. I might even hire him as a permanent assistant. Not only does he have the delicacy to remain silent during the meal—no mean accomplishment—but he has a highly developed palate."

"He does?"

Alexandre went to the refrigerator, produced a bottle of Deutz champagne, deftly opened it with the merest burp of a pop, and poured them both flutes.

"He acted more like a restaurant critic than I did. I thought he would want to stand behind my back, glowering at the waiters as they came up, making everyone feel ill at ease. But he didn't. He just sat down next to me at the long table where the critics were placed and said nothing at all. Of course, in that crowd they mistake silence for profundity so he was a great hit."

"I'm amazed."

"And he certainly knows how to order. For the appetizers he jumped on the duck foie gras served on a slice of pickled watermelon and left me to the quail eggs and caviar. Then for the main course, with a deadpan face, he beat me to the blue lobster with a sauce of tomato, bell pepper, and cucumber, sprinkled with a vinaigrette made from nasturtium petals. I had to console myself with a sole fillet served with a shellfish emulsion."

"Poor baby. How you must have suffered."

"Actually, it was rather fun. He let me snitch forkfuls from his plate. And it was the first time I've ever had a bodyguard. So, here I am, safe and sound, returned to the family foyer, getting ready to cook you dinner."

"More cutting edge haute cuisine?"

"No, tonight we're having a night off. I'm going to make you a simple tournedos wrapped in thick bacon, the perfect backdrop for an excellent Saint-Emilion that's been breathing happily, waiting for you to lap it up. But it's at least an hour before dinnertime."

"And how are we going to fill that hour?"

"I had formulated a little plan if you came home early, but instead I think I'll make you a béarnaise and some *pommes de terres persillées*."

"Oh, I can easily do without butter sauce and potatoes."

Alexandre clucked his tongue. "It's true that Baudelaire
said that man can live for three days without food but only
three seconds without poetry, but that was only because he
had never tasted my béarnaise. Sit and tell me about your
case while I whip this up."

With an old nailbrush he vigorously scrubbed two
large handfuls of inch-wide, perfectly spherical potatoes.
"*Grenaille*—grapeshot—from Brittany. I found some at
the market this morning," Alexandre said.

He selected an enormous chef's knife from a magnetic
wall rack and began chopping tarragon with great élan.

"So what's new with the case?" Alexandre asked, yelling
over the din.

"I saw the shrink again yesterday. He succeeded in con-
fusing me even more."

"That's better than I can do," Alexandre said, admiring
his meticulous green pile.

"He kept talking about the big Other and Mirror Images and a lot of things I didn't fully understand."

"Ah, I'll bet he's into Lacan's famous jouissance" Alexandre said.

"Doesn't jouissance mean 'getting it off'?"

"Not for Lacan it didn't. It was all about fulfillment so
intense it's painful and unsettling," Alexandre murmured,
absorbed with his sauce.

With the concentration of a watchmaker he chopped a
shallot into minuscule cubes, cutting into it horizontally,
then vertically, and then making precisely aligned slices.
He threw the diced shallot into a venerable copper pot,
splashed in a sprinkle of tarragon vinegar, and added two
pinches of the chopped tarragon. While he waited for the
concoction to come to a boil, with the dexterity of a con-
jurer, he tossed a nut of butter on a hot skillet, then put the
potatoes in a Pyrex dish, added some sprigs of rosemary,

topped it with a thin stream of olive oil and a sprinkle of *fleur de sel*, and placed it carefully in the oven.

As he put the tournedos on the sizzling skillet, he asked, "And that's what you do with this fellow? Hang around and discuss Lacan's arcane theories?"

"No, of course not. We also eat. We had *langoustine en papillotes* with basil *pistou*. I made an effort to remember just so I could tell you."

"You know, that sounds very much like something from Joëlle Robuchon's summer menu. You don't mean to tell me that the DGSE is having its hamper filled at Robuchon's twice a day just to feed some intellectual hobo?"

"No wonder it was so good. And he's not just 'some hobo.' He's a brilliant psychiatrist who seems to have had serious problems on an assignment for them that resulted in a degree of, well, psychological disarray."

Alexandre apparently decided that the ingredients in his pot had done what he wanted them to do and placed the copper saucepan in a round steel bowl filled with ice water.

"So that was it?"

"No, no, of course not. There was a *caille en brochette caramélisée sur un frou frou de légumes révélés de wasabi*."

"That's not what I meant."

"The wine was a Côte de Vaubarousse."

"That's not what I meant either. But the Vaubarousse must have been exceptional. What year?"

"Two thousand and five."

"Ahhh. A bit early to drink a *grand cru* like that. *Dommage*."

The base of the sauce had apparently reached the desired temperature in the ice bath and Alexandre put it back on the stove, added three yolks, and began whisking them with intense concentration. Capucine knew the look. Nothing would distract him from his task until the sauce was done. At some point—known only to alchemists—he deemed the yolks done and began whipping in small pieces of butter. His frenzy must have been rewarded because he exhaled deeply, emitting a *"Voilà."*

"Voilà quoi?" Capucine asked.

"It took. That's always the tricky moment. The rest is pure mechanics." He continued, stirring in small pieces of butter. "And your brilliant hobo had nothing to say about the crimes?"

"We talked a lot about fetishes."

"I fervently hope the message got through. I've always had a hankering to see you in a bustier with a garter belt and mesh stockings. Possibly even with a long whip. Did he give you any sharp pointers?"

"Actually he did. He seemed to think the murderer might collect symbolic fetishes from his victims to prolong the feeling of relief the crimes give him. The only problem with that theory is that nothing seems to be missing from the bodies."

"Hmm," Alexandre said, again distracted by his sauce. He whisked in the last lump of butter, then a pinch of salt and three twists of white pepper, tasted, and nodded happily with a French moue of contentment. He threw in a large double pinch of chopped tarragon, whisked violently, and put the copper pot back in the now almost tepid ice bath.

"Voilà. Let's see how our potatoes are doing." He pricked one with a paring knife, pronounced them ready and slid the tournedos onto a serving dish.

"Madame est servi," he said with a flourish of an imaginary plumed chapeau.

For a long moment the meal created a hiatus in the conversation. But halfway through Alexandre looked at Capucine and asked, "And is your al fresco genius capable of predicting the date of the next murder?"

"No. But he did seem convinced that there would be one. Which, in a way, was a relief."

"Really? I would have thought the contrary."

The meal over, they moved to Alexandre's study for an Armagnac. Capucine realized she still had her Sig and handcuffs tucked into the back of her trousers. She put the holstered pistol on a table and twirled the handcuffs coquettishly on her index finger.

"I had no idea you felt that way about fetishes," she said.

Alexandre rose, his eyebrows histrionically raised, put one arm around Capucine's waist, and caught the handcuffs in mid-rotation.

"Be careful with those," Capucine said. "I've lost the key."

Alexandre nuzzled her neck. Capucine leaned into him. Her cell phone rang.

Capucine flipped it open and listened intently for thirty seconds while Alexandre stared blankly at her.

She put her hand over the mouthpiece and said, "This time it was Sébastien Laroque. He's still alive but only barely. The SAMU are with him."

Alexandre mouthed, "Where?"

Capucine put her hand over the mouthpiece again. "That awful restaurant, Dong, you know, where the *jeunesse dorée* go to be seen and eat badly. Hang on. They're putting the SAMU medic on."

She listened again, thanked whoever it was who had spoken, and cupped the bottom of the cell phone again. "They found him in one of the stalls in the men's room. His dinner companions became alarmed when he didn't return after twenty minutes, and asked the waiter to investigate. The SAMU have him on a respirator but it doesn't look like he's going to make it."

Capucine said, "*Merci.* I'm on my way," and snapped the phone shut.

"*Merde,*" said Alexandre. "I had lunch with Sébastien only two or three weeks ago. He was bitching about that

review. His magazine, the *Nouvel Observateur,* had assigned it weeks ago. They wanted him to dis the place because it offended the *Nouvel Obs'* liberal notion of what
restaurants are supposed to be. He was putting it off because even though it's totally moneygrubbing and commercial, the young chef is supposed to be a genius when it
comes to Asian-French fusion." Alexandre spoke barely
above a whisper.

Capucine took Alexandre in her arms and stroked his
back. Her husband's pain soaked into her. The last thing
she wanted to do was leave him. She squeezed, wrenched
herself away, crammed the Sig and the handcuffs back into
her waistband, and walked out the door without a word.

CHAPTER 31

The restaurant Dong, the scene of the crime, was just across the Seine, normally a ten minute drive. Capucine clapped the pulsing blue dome light on the dashboard of the Twingo, put her foot to the floor, and made it in five. During those few minutes her cell phone was in constant use, occupying her left hand, leaving her right to cope alternately with gearshift and steering wheel, a demanding feat on the twisting streets of the Marais.

She called the front desk of her brigade to make sure a contingent of uniformed officers was on its way to the crime scene and that the forensic squad had been alerted. As she was punching in the speed dial for Isabelle she received a call from the central Police Judiciaire switchboard: Sébastien Laroque had died and the SAMU were leaving the scene. Isabelle answered on the fourth ring in a whisper as if she were trying very hard not to wake someone. Next Capucine called David, who seemed to be in a nightclub with ferociously loud background noise. As they spoke the noise faded and then disappeared. David was already out the door on the street and on his way. She knew Momo would be asleep, but he picked up in the middle of the first ring as alert as if he had been waiting for her call.

Capucine had been to Dong once, when she went with Alexandre to the opening. It was the latest in a long string of overpriced, overdecorated restaurants created by a famous television impresario. Dong was his most extravagant to date. He had leased the top floor of a nineteen thirties department store on the Seine's quai overlooking the Ile de la Cité. The entire front of the site was covered in a glass dome, which—undeniably—had a magnificent view of the City of Light. Then he had hired Georges Orné, the celebrated designer, to conjure up an unforgettable décor. Orné had lived up to his reputation, creating a room full of glowing, bottom-lit Lucite chairs and tables infused with light pastel hues that changed continually throughout the evening in a ballet of muted colors. Even Alexandre had had to admit that the *mise-en-scène* was a perfect complement to the view through the glass dome.

It was the food that had sparked the controversy. The impresario had hired the brilliant young Japanese souschef of one of the fabled three-star restaurants to come up with a Japanese-French fusion menu. The dishes sounded hokey enough: Belle and Zen Duo of Foie Gras, Yellowtail Carpaccio, Glam-Chic Tomatoes, but—truth be told— they were far better than expected.

Still, it had become the official restaurant Parisians in the know loved to hate.

Capucine arrived at the downstairs front door of the restaurant just as the forensics squad was unloading its gurney and aluminum containers of equipment from their van. She rode up in the elevator with Ajudant Dechery who intoned in his basso profundo, "We're seeing altogether too much of each other, *Commissaire*. You need to put a stop to this or people will begin to gossip." Capucine suspected he was using his seniority to be assigned consistently the series of restaurant murders.

As they walked into the dining room, the seventy or so diners fell silent and turned to stared at them, their bottom lit faces as eerily luminous as Degas' ballet dancers. Five uniformed Paris police officers milled, trying hard to look purposeful.

One of them came up to Capucine, saluted importantly, and said, "The body's in the WC back there." As Capucine followed Dechery in the direction of a door decorated with a garishly painted Kabuki mask of a ferocious warrior, she saw Gaël Tanguy, the novelist, sitting by himself at a corner table. He caught her eye and smiled furtively. Ill kempt and shabbily dressed, he looked decidedly out of place surrounded by golden youths preening in their finery. His neighbors caught the exchange of glances and their looks of derision hardened into outright opprobrium for Tanguy.

Anxious to view the body before Dechery's experts commandeered the scene with their plastic evidence bags and aluminum fingerprint powder, Capucine ignored Tanguy and pushed on to the toilet.

The room was surprisingly large. The walls and ceiling were jet-black, and the only lighting came from tightly focused halogen lamps recessed in the ceiling, creating pools of brilliant light surrounded by dark shadow. A row of six urinals had been painted to represent the faces of voluptuous blond women with mouths expectantly wide open.

Dechery shook his head in dismay. "I already have enough problems with my prostate without even thinking of coping with something like that."

Laroque's body sat, pants on, on the seat in one of the toilet stalls. His head was bent back, his mouth wide open, brilliantly lit by a halogen lamp. Except for the fact that his fly was unzipped and his penis hung out, he might have been sitting in a dentist's chair, stoically waiting for the drill.

Dechery bent over, snapping on a pair of latex gloves. He peered intently at the victim's head from all angles and then picked up one of the limp arms, examining the hand closely.

"Why don't you take my usual little speech—you know, the one about nothing being known until the autopsy, the biological cultures, our magical light exam, yada yada—as read, and I'll point out what's plain to see.

"This guy was whacked on the back of the head and then someone forced open his mouth and rammed a Japanese *fugu* fish down his throat."

"This is not the time for kidding, Dechery."

"I'm not kidding. It's crystal clear. There's a laceration on the back of the head that bled profusely. That alone would tell us the blow didn't kill him, but of course, since the SAMU spent a lot of time working on him, he obviously wasn't deceased. The reason his mouth is open like that is because the SAMU stuck a respirator down his throat and only removed it after he was dead."

"So what's this business about a fish?"

"The SAMU pulled it out and left it with one of the Paris *flics,* who handed it over to me." He pulled a plastic evidence bag from the side pocket of his jacket and waved it at Capucine. It contained a bug-eyed fish about three inches long, dark gray with white dots on its back and a pasty white belly.

"I thought blowfish were bigger."

"The ones the Japanese eat are actually a couple of inches longer than this one. But there are at least a hundred and fifty species of Tetraodontidae and this may be a small variety or a juvenile. I'm a forensics expert, not an ichthyologist, but there's no doubt this is a blowfish. After all, they're the second most lethal animal around. That's the sort of thing we know about."

"So he was killed by the fish's poison?"

"Of course not. He suffocated. A goldfish would have been just as effective if it had been crammed down his esophagus. It's pretty clear how it was done."

Dechery lifted the head and turned it to the left. There was a deep gash. Profuse barely clotted blood thickened the hair on the back of the head.

"If you want my guess, he was taking a pee in the toilet bowl—probably because he couldn't deal with the artwork on the urinals—and someone whacked him from behind, stunning him or possibly knocking him unconscious. Then his mouth was forced open. Look at the bruising on the cheeks. Someone pinched him on the maxillary line to force the jaw open. When he opened up, the fish was shoved deep into his throat. You can see the bleeding from where the SAMU extracted it."

"And the fish's poison wouldn't have affected him?"

"It's the liver that contains most of the tetrodotoxin. As you probably know, that's taken out before the Japanese eat the damn thing. The amount of tetrodotoxin that's left in the fish is just enough to give a tingling sensation in the lips. Supposed to be a big thrill. But, anyway, you'd have to eat it for it to have any effect. Having it lodged in your throat wouldn't introduce any toxicity at all."

Capucine nodded.

"Also, there's abundant evidence he suffocated. Look at the blue color of the lips."

Dechery picked up one of the victim's arms and pointed to the cuticles.

"See these blue half-moons at the base of the nails? That's a symptom of prolonged oxygen starvation."

"Prolonged?"

"He suffocated slowly. Some air must have gone past the fish but not much. At a guess, I'd say he was suffocating for a good half an hour before the SAMU got the fish out and the respirator in. Probably my last choice of a way to die."

They both fell silent as they conjured up visions of Laroque's agony.

"I need to get to work," Dechery said. "You know the drill. It's all guesswork until we do our stuff."

"I want to check one thing first. Lend me a pair of your gloves."

Dechery pulled a pair of latex gloves from a cardboard dispenser in his kit and handed them to Capucine, who snapped them on.

The victim's jacket was held shut by the middle button. She opened it and examined the inside pockets. Next she slid her gloved fingers into the outside breast pocket, then the side pockets, and finally patted down the sides of his pants. Shaking her head, she pulled the gloves off and handed them back to Dechery.

"Checking to see if his wallet was taken?"

"No, I was looking for a pen. He doesn't seem to have one. When you do the full inventory can you call me if there's a writing implement of any kind?"

"Sure. Would it be okay if we got rolling or do you want to have a peek at his underwear to check the brand?"

Capucine stood up, wondering why forensics experts were invariably so ill-tempered.

Breathlessly, Isabelle rushed into the WC. "Sorry it took me so long to get here," she said without explanation.

"No problem. While I finish up I want you to go back to the dining room and move Tanguy away from the other customers. I don't want him swapping stories with them."

"Tanguy?"

"Didn't you see him sitting right by the door?"

Isabelle shook her head.

Both women rushed out of the men's room, elbowing the arriving forensics experts aside.

Tanguy's table was empty and it took no more than a glance to determine he was nowhere in the room.

CHAPTER 32

Capucine sprinted for the elevator with Isabelle in her backwash. She tapped the DOWN button and glowered intently at its red glow as if she could suck the elevator up with her willpower.

"It's my fault," she said. "I should have stationed one of the Paris uniforms at the door and told him specifically not to let anyone out. Tanguy probably noticed no one was looking and just walked away." Capucine jabbed impatiently at the button.

"That doesn't help," Isabelle said.

"Of course it does." The elevator door began to open. "See."

Momo stood impassively inside the elevator car. Capucine and Isabelle stormed in. Capucine stabbed repeatedly at the RDC button for the ground floor. Scowling at the button, she explained the situation to Momo.

"Gaël Tanguy was at the restaurant when the murder happened. The Paris flics let him slip out when I was in the WC, examining the body."

Momo emitted a low growl of commiseration.

A uniformed Paris police officer stood hunched over at the street door of the restaurant, lost in the vagaries he had taught himself over the years to numb the boredom of endless guard duty where nothing ever happened. As the three detectives rushed up to him, he turned toward them sluggishly.

"Did you see a man leave the restaurant about five minutes ago?" Isabelle asked.

"I saw a guy, yeah. So?"

Isabelle snorted. "And you didn't think to stop him?"

"No one told me to stop anyone," the officer said dolefully.

"And what did he do when he left?" Capucine asked.

"He walked to the corner and hailed a cab." The second part of the answer—"What the fuck did you think he would have done, flap his wings and fly off?"—although left unsaid, was so lightly suppressed it hung in the air, clearly visible to his three interlocutors.

"Did you get the cab's number?" Capucine asked.

The policeman looked at her, his eyes slightly widened in disbelief at the stupidity of the question. "It was a Taxi Bleu. I wasn't told to write down the license plate of every passing car."

A white van with blue and red stripes pulled up with its blue light flashing and its siren wailing its deafening *pan-pom-pan-pom*. As it screeched to a stop, the driver turned off the siren, leaving them in the sudden, deafening quiet. The van disgorged a half dozen uniformed *Police Judiciaire* officers.

Capucine flipped open her phone, hit the speed-dial button for her brigade, and began spewing out a volley of instructions.

Putting her hand over the mouthpiece, she said, "Isabelle, get back up there with these guys, and get this fucking show back on the rails. Depositions from the victim's companions. Who saw what. Names and addresses . . ."

"Durand, this is *Commissaire* Le Tellier. Patch me through to Taxi Bleu. . . ."

"Momo, go get the Twingo. We're going to pick him up. . . ."

"Taxi Bleu, this is *Commissaire* Le Tellier of the *Police Judiciaire*. One of your cabs just picked up someone on the quai de la Mégisserie. I need to know where it's headed."

Momo drove up and tapped the horn of the Twingo. As Capucine opened the passenger door, Momo indicated the back of the car with his head. Two bulletproof vests, a Beretta Model 12 submachine gun, and a bag of spare clips lay on the backseat. Capucine was about to make a comment about excessive zeal but realized the equipment, which Momo must have taken out of the van, was required by police procedure when apprehending a fugitive suspect. Momo looked at her, his broad face expressionless as ever except for an almost unnoticeable upturn of his lips.

As the Twingo pulled away from the curb, Capucine continued her multiple staccato dialogues over the cell phone. Finally she snapped it shut.

"The cab just pulled up at the Restaurant Drouant in the rue Gaillon in the Second. We need to get there fast. I asked for a backup squad car but I want to get there first."

"No problem," Momo said, the first words he had spoken that evening.

After a short but bucketing ride that required Capucine to hold on to the handle above the passenger door with both hands, Momo double-parked in front of the restaurant. A valet parking attendant approached but disappeared when he saw Momo emerge from the car with the submachine gun.

They both donned their vests, Velcroed them shut, and walked into Drouant's elegant oak-paneled foyer. The hostess, a trim woman in her late forties, her dark blond hair meticulously coiffed in a bun, recoiled at the sight of the two armored police officers.

"Did a man in a checked shirt just come in here?" Capucine asked.

Wide eyed, the woman stammered, "Y . . . yes. A very shy man. He was looking for a friend."

Capucine and Momo pushed past her into the main dining room. At the sight of them the patrons fell silent, slowly turning toward them like cows facing the wind in a pasture. It was obvious at a glance that Tanguy was not there.

"Upstairs," Capucine said.

The hostess stood in the middle of the foyer, fretting.

"Are there dinners going on in any of the private dining rooms?"

"No. Not tonight."

Momo and Capucine, pistol drawn and machine gun at the ready, crept up the famous staircase, familiar from TV news shots of the Goncourt committee descending gravely to announce that year's winner of the country's top literary award.

The floor above them was dark. If Tanguy was armed, Momo and Capucine were at a dangerous disadvantage, facing an invisible opponent while silhouetted by the backlight from the main floor.

Momo put out an arm, blocking Capucine, and inched soundlessly up the stairs in front of her. Capucine knew better than to try to argue with him.

They reached the second floor and stood immobile, flanking the staircase, waiting for their eyes to adjust to the faint penumbra of street glow coming from under the closed dining room doors.

It took a full three minutes for their pupils to dilate fully. Seven oak doors were visible. Five bore small brass plaques—Capucine assumed these were the private dining rooms—two had larger square plaques, certainly the men's and ladies' toilets.

Wordlessly, they began opening the doors one by one,

Capucine hugging the wall, pistol raised, while Momo inched the heavy oak door open with his foot, pointing the machine gun on extended arms. To their sensitized eyes the luminescence coming through the windows was more than ample.

The first four rooms were empty. As Momo eased the door to the fifth open, the brass rectangle was readable, SALLE GONCOURT. An immobile pyramidal lump in the middle of the large circular table stood out, black against the window's glow.

"Welcome *Commissaire* Le Tellier and friend," Tanguy said.

As they moved closer, wide-legged, arms at the ready, they could see that he was sitting cross-legged in a lotus position in the exact center of the table.

"I apologize if I caused you any inconvenience. But sitting in that restaurant, being judged—and condemned—by philistines, was too much for me. I needed to come here, where I have already been judged, and found not wanting."

His head swiveled around the table, nodding at each seat, naming the committee of ten great French authors, "Françoise Chandernagor, Tahar Ben Jelloun . . ." finally arriving at ". . . Bernard Pivot and Didier Decoin," whose names were just readable on little brass rectangles on the backs of their chairs.

"How I would have liked to be the proverbial fly on the wall," Tanguy said. "Which of them praised me? Who attacked me? Did any of them really make sense of my book? And the burning question of the evening: will their bloody gong goad me to new heights or will it destroy me?"

Capucine holstered her pistol. "*Monsieur Tanguy, je suis désolée,* but fleeing a murder scene, particularly when you are such an obvious suspect, is a rather serious crime. I'm afraid I'm going to have to take you into custody."

Tanguy shrugged his shoulders.

"Were you spying on the bourgeoisie again?" Capucine asked. "Is that what you were doing there?"

A *pan-pom-pan-pom* wailed in the distance as the backup squad car Capucine had ordered approached.

"Do you know about Mary's room?" Tanguy asked.

This was hardly the moment for Saint-Germain cocktail chatter but she might as well listen to him while they were waiting for her men.

"Okay, I'll bite."

"It's a logical construct that was intended to demolish physicalism. You know, the notion that existence is ultimately purely physical."

"So?"

"So, Mary is an extremely learned scientist. She holds six PhDs. Actually, she's also a luscious blonde with enormous boobs—"

"That part sounds excessively physicalist to me right there."

"You're right. She's plain, pimply, and flat chested. I was embellishing. But she really does have four PhDs. You can't take those away from her."

"On with it."

"All right, all right. So for reasons we don't know, Mary is held prisoner in a room entirely decorated in black and white. She has a black-and-white television and, of course, an extensive library that is all black and white because the covers of the books have been removed. She is an expert in the human nervous system and knows all there is to know about sight. Still with me?"

"Just get on with it, Tanguy."

"So, if, for example, she reads something about the bright red poppies in the field, she knows all about the wavelength that produces red on the retina. In fact, she has an absolutely perfect theoretical understanding of the color red."

"I hope that makes up for her poor complexion and flat chest."

"It does. Yes, it does. One day she discovers the door to her cell is open and walks out. And what do you suppose she sees?"

"Epiphenomenal qualia?" Capucine asked. Even in the half-light she could see Tanguy's lower jaw descend a half inch.

"We read Frank Jackson at Sciences Po. Let me cut to the chase. You're trying to tell me that you're an un-pimpled Mary and you were in that restaurant tonight to take a *bain de bourgeoise* to see if the real world has any more substance than the world you see in your Mary's room of a head. Is that it?"

Tanguy nodded, at a loss for words.

"So tell me, Monsieur Tanguy, was your qualia really enhanced? That's really the burning question of the evening. What exactly did you see?"

"I . . . I had no idea you felt so strongly about this sort of thing."

"I do. I'm allergic to bullshit. It's one of the many reasons I joined the police."

The room quietly filled with uniformed officers, all in bullet-proof jackets, all carrying machine guns.

Tanguy looked down at the table, pouting slightly. "Well, it's important to me. My books are all about qualia."

"Before these gentlemen take you off to our own version of Mary's room, I really need to know what you saw this evening."

"Nothing. Absolutely nothing. I sat in my corner, watching the people, eating my meal, which was really more bizarre than good. And all of a sudden the room filled with police officers hovering around the WC. I thought the toilet must have overflowed or something horrible like that.

And the next thing I saw was that everyone was looking down their noses at me and hating me. So I just left."

Capucine nodded at one of the uniformed officers who hauled Tanguy roughly off the table, handcuffed him, and led him out the door.

CHAPTER 33

On Friday night Capucine decided she would sleep in the next morning. If Alexandre could sleep until ten, so could she. And why not? Tanguy had been released after a short interview. It was abundantly clear that he knew nothing about the murder. And she had nothing but administrative tasks on her calendar for the next morning. Investing in an extended sleep might bring some clarity to the case and seemed like a definitely worthwhile endeavor. She dreamt of a carousel of amorphous, comestible clouds. She was starving. But each time she reached out to grab one, it disintegrated.

As she lunged desperately at a particularly appetizing cloud, a large bumblebee attacked her relentlessly, buzzing aggressively.

She half opened one eye. The gray of the night might have lightened just a smidgen. It must be a little after five. The buzzing continued. Not the *"tiout, tiout, tiout"* of her cell phone. That was good news. Capucine relaxed back into her pillow and tried to fall asleep again. The buzzing continued. It wasn't the artificially resonating pre-war ring of Alexandre's cell phone. *Merde.* It was the house phone on her night table.

Eyes shut, she stabbed at it, knocking the cordless receiver off its stand with a clatter.

"Who was killed this time?" Alexandre mumbled, barely audible between two pillows.

Capucine managed to locate the TALK button and get the receiver to her ear.

"*Oui!*" she said, halfway between a bark and a sigh.

"Capucine, it's Béatrice. Are you up? You said you were an early riser."

"Not this early," Capucine said, unable to keep the irritated tone out of her voice.

"Well, you're up now and that's the important thing. What if you came out to Rungis with me?"

"The food market? Sure. Good idea. I've always wanted to go. Let's talk after lunch and figure out a date."

"No. Now. Right now. My car won't start and I need all sorts of things for the lunch service. I remember you saying you'd always wanted to see the market and I thought this would be a great opportunity."

Capucine lifted herself up on one elbow. Alexandre snorfeled deep in his nest of pillows. "Béatrice, there are several excellent taxi companies in Paris. Why don't you just call one? I'd recommend Alpha Taxis. They'll be there in five minutes."

"Very funny. I was hoping we could spend the morning together at the market. Then we could have breakfast and catch up on our gossip. I have a sizzler that I really want to share. And I know the place that serves the best croissants in Paris."

Capucine was dismayed to find that she was fully awake. Now she would never get back to sleep.

"Béatrice. It's five eighteen. No one goes shopping at this hour of the morning."

"Rungis opens at six thirty, and you have to be there right at the very beginning to get the best stuff."

"You're impossible. You really are!"

"And you're fabulous. Pick me up at the restaurant as soon as you can."

"On the condition that you bring some coffee. Coffee strong enough to get my other eye open."

Capucine slipped on a very old pair of jeans and a brand new pair of Miu Miu suede ballet shoes decorated with tiny glass beads. Without thinking, she slid her holstered Sig into the back of her jeans and buttoned on a loose patterned silk blouse that would hide it.

As she breezed through the empty streets of Paris toward the Sixth, Capucine thought about a course in urban planning she had taken at Sciences Po that used the Paris wholesale market as the ultimate example of urban disasters.

It was claimed in the late sixties that Parisians' ravenous appetite for food had outstripped the capacity of the ancient and hallowed Les Halles Market in the First Arrondissement—Zola's *Stomach of Paris*—and it was decided to move the market to a vast site in the outskirts of Paris near the Bourget airport. Capucine's professor had explained that the real reason for the move had been the exponentially exploding rat population that defeated even the most aggressive efforts of exterminators.

The urban catastrophe had been the vacant site left in Paris. A five-story-deep hole was dug, and the barren crater remained a conspicuous eyesore for nearly a decade. *Le Trou des Halles*—the Halles Hole—became a notorious cause célèbre, the embarrassment of Paris. Eventually, a graceless underground shopping mall was built on the site, and it was hoped the area would become a new Saint-Germain. Instead Arab *banlieusards* took over. Police patrols, supported by vicious Alsatians, now made over fifty arrests a day. One of Paris's most charming quartiers had been irretrievably destroyed.

Somehow the new Halles was never mentioned, even though it had become the largest wholesale distribution center in the world and apparently the absolute acme of meticulously organized food facilities management. Now, *that* was going to be something worth seeing.

Béatrice piaffed impatiently on the sidewalk in front of her restaurant, next to a young man in jeans and an olive drab T-shirt made lumpy by gym-inflated muscles. "Béranger, my fish chef," she said by way of introduction as they scrambled into the Twingo.

Béranger bobbed his head and mumbled a shy "M'd'me."

"Capucine, *ma chérie,* we really have to step on it. It's nearly six, and we have a long way to go."

They hummed down the *voie sur berge,* then onto the *Périphérique,* and finally onto the A6—the Autoroute of the Sun, which led ultimately to the glorious Riviera—and arrived at six thirty-seven. Capucine could feel Béranger fretting in the backseat.

The market was the size of a small city. Squat warehouses with trucks backed into loading gates went on and on infinitely in either direction. They parked the Twingo in a parking lot that seemed to stretch to the horizon, and made off at a trot. Béatrice took Capucine's arm to hurry her along.

"I had no idea the market was so large," Capucine said.

"It's bigger than Monaco," Béatrice said with a laugh, breaking into a trot. "But we really need to get our skates on. The fish we're after is usually gone in a few minutes. But I think we're going to make it, right, Béranger?"

Béranger shrugged his shoulders in an attempt at Gallic insouciance, which he was not quite able to pull off.

The building they targeted was five long rows away. After a breathless run they pushed through a screen of hanging plastic strips. The building was cavernous, stark white, overbright from endless rows of fluorescent tubes. The din of vendors shouting to assistants reverberated, augmented by the warning cries of warehousemen pushing electric carts stacked with plastic boxes of produce. The scene was as dramatic as a Puccini opera.

They pulled up in front of a small area under a large white banner marked KIYOTO TANSAIUMA, followed by three rows of Japanese characters. The final line was in French, PATENTED OWNERS OF KAIMIN KATSUGYO.

Béranger searched nervously up and down the rows of piled Styrofoam containers, questing like a spaniel, until he stopped in a point, smiling and peering down at a pile of boxes.

"Chef! We made it in time. Come look at these."

Capucine and Béatrice hurried over. The cases Béranger now guarded proprietarily were divided into twelve compartments, each lined with loose, crinkled plastic film. A scant inch of water lay at the bottom of the sections, which contained round pale orange fish with sharply pointed tails and serrated dorsal fins. The fish brimmed with health, their eyes crystal clear, almost sentient. But despite their sanguine glow, they were as rigid as if dead.

"*Dorade*—sea bream," Béatrice said. "The prince of fish. They're going to be the pièce de résistance for our luncheon menu. These come from Japan. Far better than the Mediterranean variety. They're the absolute best sea bream available."

Béranger was picking up the fish reverently one by one and examining them intently. Two Japanese men had flanked him and bowed repeatedly with stiff smiles that did not reach their eyes. Béatrice held a muted, urgent conversation with one of them.

"I've just bought twenty *dorades*," Béatrice said to Capucine. "That will give us forty fillets. We might do a few more, but if we don't, I wouldn't want to waste fish of this quality." She picked up one of the bream and showed it to Capucine. It was astonishingly fresh, smelling only of the sea, not a hint of fishiness.

Béatrice took Capucine's hand and guided it into a pinching position just behind the fish's gills.

"Squeeze gently."

"Good Lord. Its heart is still beating. How can they survive all the way from Japan in so little water?"

"It's a sort of Japanese zombie thing," Béatrice said with a laugh. "They call it *kaimin katsugyo,* which apparently means something like 'live fish sleeping.' I guess it's really a form of acupuncture. They inject a needle in a very secret spot and the fish goes into some sort of hibernation. It doesn't move, it passes almost no water through its gills, but its heart still beats. Actually, it still keeps beating when we cut the fillet out but it doesn't notice a thing. Or if it notices, it doesn't say anything." Béatrice and Béranger sniggered with laughter.

"That sounds like something out of a grade B horror movie," Capucine said.

"Not when you eat them," Béatrice said. "They cost an arm and a leg but the taste is unique. Imagine a fish on your table that was alive five minutes before you start eating it. The fillet still quivers."

That was something Capucine would rather not have imagined.

"Enough of this," Béatrice said imperiously. "*Gambas,* Béranger—shrimp! Where was that place we found those amazing *gambas* the last time?"

"Right down here, Chef," Béranger said, moving off rapidly.

Capucine assumed that the bream would be left in situ, in their comatose limbo, until the car was driven around and they were picked up for the final leg of their long journey to Paris.

They arrived at a concession several hundred yards away, at the other end of the warehouse, that apparently dealt exclusively with shellfish. There was a profusion of oysters, clams, *oursins,* and dark blue French lobsters. In a far corner, stacks of Styrofoam crates contained giant luminous orange langoustines easily eight inches long.

Béranger carefully examined three or four from different crates, turning them over and pulling gently on their legs. He leaned over to Béatrice and whispered, "*Ils sont superbes!*"

Béatrice motioned to a man who had been following behind with a pad.

"We'll take eighty. No, wait. Make that eighty-eight."

She turned to Capucine. "The extra eight are for your lunch. It's the least I can do for having rousted you out of bed at the crack of dawn."

Capucine hesitated for a beat, about to object. After a second the moment had passed.

Even if the gift of eight shrimp was far less than compromising, Capucine felt unaccountably embarrassed. She had scrupulously avoided labeling Béatrice as either *copine*—pal—or suspect. If the latter, Capucine's presence on the outing was unconscionable, if the former, her hesitation over the modest gift was far worse than ungracious.

On the way back Capucine wound up with a bulky crate of *gambas* under her legs, requiring her to deal with the pedals on tiptoe. The crates filled with the bream had filled the Twingo's tiny trunk and the vacant back seat. The *gambas* had been piled on Béranger's and Béatrice's laps, reaching to the roof. The only place left for the remaining crates had been the floor of the driver's side. Despite the air-conditioning, the funk of *gambas* filled the tiny car. As the ride back progressed, Capucine's anticipation of lunch plummeted.

Back at the restaurant Béatrice marched through the door with a stack of crates up to eye level, Béranger with a slightly smaller stack, and Capucine, slightly embarrassed, with only two of the light Styrofoam boxes. Once the crates were stacked in the walk-in refrigerator, Béranger disappeared promptly out the back door, no doubt to get some sleep before his service in the kitchen began. Béatrice threw her morning's receipts into a wooden out-box in her office and surveyed her deserted domain happily. Her satisfaction was palpable.

"Breakfast! Nothing happens before eleven when the cooks start to come in. Of course the prep staff gets going in about half an hour but the last person they want to see is me. How about a café au lait and some croissants before we get going on our Saturdays?"

They found themselves at a tiny café table around the corner. A napkin-lined wire basket of croissants arrived with the coffee. As they pulled the doughy, yeasty crescents apart, eating them nugget by nugget, brightly scrubbed, freshly made up people and perky little dogs on leashes paraded purposefully across their field of vision. Le weekend was off and running. True to Béatrice's word, the croissants were exceptionally good.

"So, is the case solved yet?" Béatrice asked.

"I wish. It just keeps getting more and more complicated. But tell me your news."

Béatrice leaned over the table, took Capucine's hand, and whispered conspiratorially. "You can't breathe a word of this. Promise?"

Capucine bent close to Béatrice and nodded eagerly.

"I think I'm about to get my first Michelin star. I really do!"

"How do you know?"

"There's been a rumor going around for over a month. Three weeks ago one of their inspectors came for dinner. They always announce who they are. Another came for lunch last week. That's a very good sign. And last night they called up, asking for a reservation on Wednesday. Isn't that incredible!"

"That is *such* good news," Capucine said. "I really hope it works out."

"Oh, it will. You have to have faith in life. But what about your case? You must be making some progress."

"Not really. You must have seen the press about the murder the other day."

"At Dong," Béatrice said. "I read about it. What an awful place that restaurant is."

"Alexandre's sentiments exactly."

Béatrice's spoon clattered in her saucer. "Someone shoved a baby blowfish down the victim's throat, right?"

"Yes, apparently the SAMU found it almost impossible to get it out. The fish has spikes that point backward and they lodged in the throat."

"And he was killed in the toilet?"

"Yes, sitting on the toilet seat."

"How awful." She leaned forward. "With his *pipi* hanging out! How gross was that? Capucine, you really must catch this murderer. I can't get over the fact that the person who killed someone in *my* restaurant is still on the loose."

"What about the three victims in other people's restaurants? Isn't that just as bad?"

"Just as bad? Of course not. It wasn't my restaurant." Béatrice seemed almost affronted.

Breakfast over, Capucine moved the box of *gambas* from the driver's floor to the cargo space in the back of the Twingo and made her way back to the Marais. In the heat of the morning the odor of the shrimp intensified. It was far from unpleasant—they were still perfectly fresh, after all—but it was definitely overly-present. Capucine couldn't make up her mind if her reaction was because sea food didn't sit well on top of croissants or because her unconscious mind had finally deemed the gift unethical.

Parking in front of her building, Capucine crossed the street—the *cageot* of *gambas* in her hands—and walked into a shop that sold magazines and books. She picked up the fat Saturday edition of *Le Figaro* and the *Nouvel Observateur*.

As she paid, she said to the owner of the little shop, "Someone took me to Rungis this morning and gave me these. Unfortunately, we're going out for both lunch and dinner. Would you like them?"

The shop owner was so delighted Capucine was almost embarrassed.

CHAPTER 34

One of the tenets of her marriage's folklore was that Capucine loathed the Salon des Vins de Bordeaux but still insisted on going every year, purely as an act of altruistic solidarity with her husband. In actual fact, Capucine adored the salon, not only because she was fond of Bordeaux but also because of the comic value of the tribal behavior of the oenological elite.

The salon's program was straightforward. The top end of the Bordeaux châteaux gathered in Paris to present their most recent vintage to the owners, chefs, and sommeliers of the city's best restaurants. Naturally, the event was also populated by the usual crested gratin as well as the press.

Since the vintage would not reach its prime for nearly a decade, the châteaux also proposed a selection of their more notable past *millésimes*. Somber men in somber blue suits made long boring speeches to grave gaggles collected around their tables, who vigorously slushed the wines in their mouths and then spat them genteelly into chromed spittoons placed in the center of each snowy white belinened table. For Capucine the gesture was somehow both farcical and profoundly erotic.

Spitting was clearly only a partial palliative to inebriation—Alexandre explained that it was really about "ownership," not staying sober—and by the time they arrived, the crowd had become tipsy enough to resemble passengers on a transatlantic liner weaving as they aimed for the dining room in a swelling sea.

Capucine and Alexandre gamely jumped into the fray, sipping, spitting, nodding at commentary. By the time they reached their third stand, Capucine had sealed her lips shut like an amateur poker player, trying hard not to giggle.

As they sauntered around the room, it was obvious to Capucine that Alexandre had acquired the luster of a celebrity. He was endlessly buttonholed, greeted effusively, loudly bestowed with nuggets of culinary gossip by people he clearly had never seen before. The elephant in the room pursued him as closely as if his jacket pockets were filled with peanuts. Not only had his métier been knighted by the scandal of murder, but Alexandre himself had become irresistible with the notoriety of being the most likely next victim.

Capucine felt a sharp pang of guilt. If she had the slightest skill at her job, she'd already have the killer behind bars. But instead, she was playing a waiting game, counting on the killer to make a mistake. But even though the killer had winked at her, she was not even close to an arrest.

Compounding her feeling of guilt, Alexandre seemed utterly oblivious to his new appeal. Serene, he guffawed and chortled happily with his cronies, delighted to be splashing in the bath of his element.

As they approached the Château Haut-Brion table Capucine heard a shriek.

"But it's *Commissaire* Capucine! Darling, let's go have a drink with her."

At the egregious solecism of "having a drink" when referring to the holy ambrosia of Bordeaux, Alexandre scowled, raising both eyebrows, turning to identify the source of the unbridled philistinism. When he identified the author, his eyebrows elevated to even greater heights.

"Dear," Capucine said to Alexandre, "let me introduce Mademoiselle Sybille Charbonnier and Monsieur Guy Voisin."

Alexandre took Sybille's hand, bent slightly from the waist, and performed a perfectly executed *baisemain,* air kissing the back of her hand with his lips a good two inches away from any contact with skin. Sybille giggled, wrinkling her nose like a preteen. Capucine was impressed. Alexandre seemed so taken by Sybille's pulchritude that he completely lost sight of the stricture that *baisemains* were absolutely not to be bestowed on maidens.

"Mademoiselle," Alexandre said, "I am a great admirer of your thespian assets. They are truly exceptional."

He turned suavely to Voisin. "Monsieur, I'm an equally great admirer of Château de la Motte. Actually, I think we've met once or twice. You know, we were just tasting a Château de Parenchère *clairet* and I was telling my wife that despite it's reputation, it can't hold a candle to your wine."

"The last time I had the honor to speak with madame," Voisin said with a wry but friendly smile, "she told me that you were very critical of my second wine, Le Chevalier de la Motte."

"*Mais non, mais non, pas du tout,*" Alexandre said, taking Voisin by the arm and leading him off fraternally, their kinship as colleagues in the same métier fully established. As they sauntered away, Capucine heard Alexandre saying, "*Mon cher* Voisin, bulls are expected to run after toreadors when they wave their capes, *n'est-ce pas?* But the bull doesn't bear the matador any ill will at all. He's just doing his job. It's the same with food critics. If we weren't critical, we'd merely write recipes, and who would read that?" They both laughed tipsily.

Capucine and Sybille followed twenty feet behind.

"This is the most boring afternoon I've spent in years! Decades even!" Sybille said. "These people all look like undertakers. And this stuff they drink. No wonder they spit it out. I'd kill for a yac and Coke or a Malibu and ginger. Even a glass of champagne would be better than this crap."

She pouted, dragging her heels as she walked.

"I know what! I think I have four, maybe even eight, lines of blow left in a my bag. Let's find a john and do a few bumps and see if we can make ourselves feel a little better."

"Don't forget I'm a police officer," Capucine said with a smile.

"Police officer, smolice officer. You're my *copine*. I know you are. Come on, it's Saturday. I can't snort alone. That's just too *triste*. If I take Guy, he'll want to do that ghastly pretend-sex charade of his, and I couldn't handle that after all this boredom. At least come and keep me company."

Despite herself Capucine chortled delightedly. She imagined Isabelle's reaction and exploded into laughter. Automatically, Sybille joined in.

"You two seem to be in high spirits," Voisin said. He had broken away from the clutch around a tasting table. Catching sight of Sybille, half the group joined him, surrounding her. As if a switch had been thrown, Sybille abandoned the petulant tween role she had been playing for Capucine and assumed the persona of a smoldering vamp. The group thrummed.

Alexandre appeared by Capucine's side and whispered in her ear, "I've had about as much Bordeaux as I can take for one day. Let's get out of here. What if we went and drank something nice and strong and then went to dinner and played footsie under the table?"

"Sybille has been dying to find someone to take her out for a Malibu and ginger ale."

"That might be a bit more than I could handle."

A man pushed into the circle, grabbed Voisin's upper arm, and began hammering him with loud bonhomie, clearly a performance for Sybille's benefit. The man winked salaciously at Sybille and intensified his kidding of Voisin to underscore the depth of their intimacy.

"Voisin, no wonder your wine is always in the papers. You're a shameless suck with journalists. I'll bet you Huguelet here will have nice things to say about you in tomorrow's *Monde.*"

Creases appeared in Alexandre's forehead and between his brows, the closest he ever came to a frown.

The man continued on relentlessly. "And remember that time that you took me to lunch at Taillevent with Druand from the *Nouvel Obs* and that other guy—what's his name?—the one from *Le Figaro,* Gautier du Fesnay? I'll bet you got a ton of press out of that."

Sybille slid her foot back and forth impatiently on the floor. She tugged on Voisin's sleeve. "*Chéri,* could you help me find the ladies room? I"—and she lowered her voice to a clearly audible stage whisper—"desperately need a pee."

"Of course, my little pet," Voisin said. "I think it's right down there."

As Voisin and Sybille trotted off, whispering to each other, Alexandre asked Capucine, "Ready for our drink and early dinner?"

"Very ready. Let's do something a little démodé. How about the Ritz?"

"Their garden bar would be delightful."

"I was thinking their somber little Hemingway Bar. We could get tiddly on outrageously expensive brown things."

"Celebrating, are we?"

"*Au contraire*, I'm going to drown my sorrow over my obtuseness at having missed the obvious for so long and also try to find the Dutch courage I'm going to be needing so desperately."

CHAPTER 35

As luck would have it, the Hemingway Bar at the Ritz had been taken over by a book signing. The small, almost oppressively intimate room was packed to the bursting point with a high-spirited crowd, who were funneling thirty-euro cocktails down their throats as fast as the bottlenecks of their esophaguses allowed. The instant Capucine and Alexandre peered through the door they were aspirated into the melee as if by an industrial-strength vacuum cleaner.

Clutching Alexandre's elbow, Capucine found herself shoved roughly up against the oak bar by the press of the crowd. The serene face of the Hemingway Bar's celebrity bartender twinkled down at them convivially.

"Monsieur and Madame de Huguelet. How good to see you again. What will be my pleasure to serve you?"

"The mood is exasperation. You decide," Capucine said. The bartender was famous for his ability to concoct a drink that perfectly matched the drinker's humor.

The bartender returned in a minute and reverently placed two martini glasses in front of them. "Picasso martinis," he said. "Guaranteed to evaporate exasperation. The secret is to have the gin—only Tanqueray Number Ten will do—at precisely sixty-five degrees Fahrenheit and then insert a small cube of frozen Noilly Prat vermouth."

By conventional standards, the martini was impossibly warm. Cool rivulets of melting vermouth lapped at their lips as they sipped. But, as promised, Capucine's exasperation did seem to volatilize.

Capucine insisted to herself her protean mood shift had nothing to do with the drink. She had finally reached a decision.

"Picasso? Because of the cube?" Capucine asked the bartender.

"Of course," he said, with an engaging smile.

"Don't be so judgmental, Dear. It's a great pleasure to drink a cocktail that allows you to taste the content and doesn't threaten to crack your teeth," Alexandre said.

They took their martinis and explored the room. The author was a shy young woman whose only distinguishing feature seemed to be her oversized, perfectly round, jet-black sunglasses. Capucine picked up a copy of her book, which turned out to be a mystery novel, and flipped through the pages. Every third word seemed to be a shocking profanity. She decided it was exactly the sort of thing Gaël Tanguy should read at the beach, assuming, of course, he ever went to the beach. The thought brought her back to the beatitude of her decision.

"Let's go have a quiet drink in the garden. I need to hear tinkly ice cubes and bask in summer quiet."

In the garden Alexandre and Capucine sat at a table covered in a floral print with matching cushions tied on to white painted wrought iron furniture. The area was dotted with brand-new reproductions of Greek sculpture and potted shrubs so perfectly trimmed and maintained they seemed to be made of plastic. It was so quiet she could hear birds chattering complaints at each other as they quarreled over crumbs on the marble tiles.

Alexandre seemed mesmerized by the change in scene. As their gin and tonics arrived—never mix grape and grain was one of Alexandre's canonic maxims—Capucine made off to the interior section of the bar without word of excuse. She never ceased to marvel at the sanctity with which all males seemed to regard the manifold imperatives of women's "plumbing," even in this age of pugnacious obliteration of all taboos.

The over-elegant bar with its pale wood and tapestry paneling was completely deserted. Capucine flipped open her cell phone and pressed Jacques' speed dial. Despite her love for her cousin, she gritted her teeth.

"I'm happy to see my delicious older *cousine* is developing such very round heels," he said once she had made her request. "I have erotic visions of you lying on your back on that good doctor's bed." The cell phone emitted a high feedback whine Capucine knew was his full-volume braying.

"Jacques, be serious. This man is enormously helpful. I think I'm about to close in on this killer but I definitely need Vavasseur's advice."

Jacques became mock serious. "As you wish, my dear. Tomorrow it is then." He paused. "I have noticed, though, that your embonpoint seems to be developing at an extraordinary rate with all these lunches. I think a *déjeuner minceur* is going to be in order, *n'est ce pas?*"

Capucine hung up on him.

As she minced down the treacherous stone steps the next day, she found Vavasseur waiting for her wearing a warm smile.

"They no longer tell me you're coming. They just deliver an extra large food container. I think I've developed a Pavlovian response to the pleasure of your visits." He dropped his head and stared dejectedly at the rough paving stones. "I suppose that's a very bad thing for an analyst."

Mercurially, he brightened. "But it's true I enjoy your visits very much. And, of course, they *do* excel themselves with the wine when you come. Actually, the food is considerably better too." He beamed.

Capucine wondered if Vavasseur's fascination with fetishes stemmed entirely from Lacan. He seemed to have a rather pronounced food fetish of his own. Of course, who was she to gainsay. It was his tip about those fetishes that had solved the murder for her, wasn't it?

Anxious as she was to air the issue that had brought her, Capucine knew that if she jostled the luncheon ritual, she stood the risk of losing Vavasseur to his shell.

She let him proceed with the elaborate ceremony of clearing off his bedside table, pulling up the chair, and creating a seating for two. Then he carefully snapped open the olive drab container and extracted a cream card with the menu in a florid italic hand. Capucine wondered if the DGSE actually had a calligrapher on its payroll.

"They've spoiled us today. Pan fried sea bream on an *étouffé* of young leeks."

"Sea bream, what a coincidence. I was at Rungis the other day buying *kaimin katsugyo* sea bream."

Vavasseur recoiled in horror. "These fish can't be Japanese." He began to tremble. The card fell out of his hand.

"Of course not, *Docteur*. Sea bream is a Mediterranean fish. It's as French as . . . as . . . *tarte Tatin*. I was talking about something else entirely."

"*Tarte Tatin*," Vavasseur said, reassuring himself. Cradling himself with the phrase, he said it again. "*Tarte Tatin*."

"Did they send us a nice wine, Docteur?" Capucine asked, as if speaking to a child.

Vavasseur rummaged through the container.

"They have! They have indeed," he said delightedly. "A two thousand six Joseph Drouhin, Bâtard-Montrachet. They've outdone themselves. I never get anything like this when you're not here. You must come more often. You really must." The gaffe about Japan had metabolized. Still Vavasseur's phobia of Japan intrigued her. She chalked it off as one of life's many mysteries that would never be unveiled.

The squall had passed, and the sun shone as Vavasseur bustled happily with his luncheon preparations, putting out plates, sampling the wine, and finally devoting his whole being to the meal.

Capucine had to admit it was not only delicious but undoubtedly slimming. As they finished, as if on cue, the neighbor from across the river emerged from his packing crate and began his day with his picture-perfect Labrador. They both waved enthusiastically and were waved back at with equal enthusiasm. The sun became heavy. The river scent rose, pleasantly musky. The stillness of the heat drew their minds to the Midi with its clink of steel *boules* and licorice fragrance of pastis.

"Could I tempt you with a little Ricard?" Vavasseur asked.

"Do you read minds as well as heal them?"

"One can't do one without the other.

"You think you came back to discuss the murderer, but it's really something else that's troubling you deeply that you want to talk about, *non?*" he asked, dropping half-melted ice cubes from the food container into two tumblers holding an inch and a half of the clear dark yellow liquor. Like a magic trick, as the ice melted, the liquid turned as opaque and white as milk. Vavasseur tipped the container and filled the tumblers with melted ice water. "*Tchin-tchin,. Vive l'été!*" he toasted, touching his glass to hers.

"I'll never be able to drink this while lying on my back," Capucine said. "Do I really have to lie down?"

"I think we've progressed beyond that. So tell me, what's bothering you?"

Capucine sat up straight. "You were right. It only took one more murder for me to understand who the killer is. And, of course, the fetishes were the key."

"Congratulations. They should have sent us some champagne."

"Identifying the identity of the murderer is hardly the same thing as being able to make an arrest."

"Ahhh. That's a professional concern. Instead, why don't we talk about why it's such a personal issue?"

"I'd like to very much, but first I need to understand the role of the poison a little better."

Vavasseur nodded and then looked out over the river, stroking the wattle under his chin, saying nothing for what seemed like an inordinately long time. Just as Capucine thought he had lost interest in the conversation, he spoke.

"Yes, of course. I understand why that's so important to you. The complexity here is that we are trying to understand the psychology of someone we have never met. So nothing can be sure. We can only deal with the likely, not the reality. Will that be enough?"

"In the country they like to say, 'If you don't have a dog, you hunt with a cat.' "

"I think we can do better than that. I suspect your real question is whether or not the murderer would let the poison do the killing. Is that it?"

"Of course."

"The poison completes the mise-en-scène for the killer. The victim must be extinguished in the act of committing his crime, in other words, while he is judging. But he must also be punished, at least symbolically, by the substance of what he is judging, which is to say food."

"And why, other than in the first murder, has the death never been from poisoning?"

Vavasseur lost himself in the river and his wattle again. After a long minute he returned.

"The real question is, would the killer kill with poison

alone? And the answer must be, yes, if the opportunity presented itself. But it must be very difficult to introduce poison into a restaurant meal."

"That's not at all what I hoped you would say."

"I'm aware of that. But let's address what is really bothering you. The conviction to do what you know you must do. Isn't that it?"

Capucine downed her Ricard and thrust her glass awkwardly at Vavasseur. "Do you think I could have another?"

As he poured out another Ricard, he said, "The gestalt of the altruistic avenger has been central to Western culture from Homer to Mickey Spillane. It also happens to be the gestalt you have chosen for yourself. Surely you understand that one of the tenets of the model is that the altruism be without limit."

Tears filled Capucine's eyes.

It was a good thing that Vavasseur did not charge by the hour, because the session lasted until well after a rather large man in a loose-fitting dark suit came down the steps with another container of food.

CHAPTER 36

Nearly a month went by. The exhilaration of early summer—with its warm, heady breezes beckoning to the world of café terraces and leisurely walks in the parks—was overcome by the oppressively leaden heat of midsummer. Paris drooped and grumbled, counting the sultry, dusty days until it could finally flee to its *grandes vacances*.

Capucine took to seeing Vavasseur three times a week or more. The level of the river lowered daily. Weed-slimy stone steps now had to be descended to retrieve wine bottles held by their cords in the shrunken Seine. The aroma of river and bank blossomed, its muskiness, sharpened by an ammoniac tang of urine.

Capucine and Vavasseur abandoned the police barricade cubicle and ate their meals on their laps, their legs dangling over the river. After, they continued drinking Portuguese *vinho verde*—cool, green, tart, one step shy of sparkling, thin with its weak level of alcohol. Capucine unburdened herself as she hadn't since her early teens. Most afternoons ended in tears.

Painful as they were, Capucine became hopelessly addicted to the sessions by the river's edge. It was only there

that she could think clearly. It was only there that she had
an appetite. It was only there that the wait became en-
durable.

When it was over she asked herself what she had
learned in all those hours. Certainly nothing more about
the murders—what else was there to know? A handful of
insights about her feelings toward her parents—but that
had nothing at all to do with the case. And, of course, a
metaphysical acceptance of what she knew she must do.
The abstract logic was as robust as those of the silly false
dilemmas of her lycée days: if the Devil promised you the
entire world would be free of hunger for one whole year if
only you would allow him to kill three people you had
never met in a distant country, would you do it? But that
was a very far cry from actually putting a pistol to the
head of one of these people with your own hand, wasn't it?

As ever, Alexandre was masterful in dealing with his wife's
crisis, even though Capucine was convinced he couldn't have
the slightest inkling of its substance. Naturally, his first
concern was her diet. Instinctively, he divined that Capucine ate well only when she was with Vavasseur and he
intuited this must be due to the quality of the meals. He
took her on a tour of the twelve three-star restaurants in
Paris. But this proved ill-fated. Capucine only picked at
her food and when the dishes returned to the kitchen
barely touched there was serious concern over the apparent opprobrium of the wife of one of the nation's most
well-known restaurant critics. The third time a starred
chef came out into the dining room wringing his hands to
consult with him, Alexandre knew he would have to
change tactics.

His next tack was more successful. He and Capucine
began to explore the restaurants of the Ile de la Jatte, the
once lightly grassed sandy bar in the middle of the Seine at
the very edge of Paris' town limits. It would be completely
unknown to the world today were it not for Georges Seu-

rat's pointillist vision of the petit bourgeois taking their Sunday ease on the then deserted island. In the last decade the island had been overrun by real estate developers. Ramshackle warehouses and lopsided wooden garages had disappeared one after the other to make way for six-story luxury condos made all the more luxurious by their river views. But a handful of restaurants still remained with terrace seats only feet away from the water, cool in the shade of poplar trees. These became their nightly haunt.

None of them were particularly good, at least from Alexandre's point of view; but Capucine ate. And both of them found it pleasant enough to finish a bottle of Sancerre as the sky's azure deepened to purple and a fresh breeze lifted off the Seine.

Still, there was no question that Capucine was becoming slightly gaunt. The wait was unquestionably taking its toll.

The call that Capucine so keenly anticipated and so deeply dreaded finally came. She knew she would get only one arrow and she would have to choose carefully. But this one was so straight and true it was impossible to pass up. The problem was that she could not muster the courage to pull back on the bowstring. It was going to take more than the encouraging advice of a professional. Without the comforting embrace of an old friend, she doubted she would ever find the resolve.

She squeezed the buttons of her cell phone to call to Cécile.

"Capucine, *ma chérie,* I literally had my hand on the phone to call you! I need to have lunch with you. Today! Cancel whatever plans you have. You absolutely *must* minister to your best friend in her hour of need."

"Of course we'll have lunch today. Actually, there's something I need to talk to you about myself. It's really very important. I want your advice before I make my final decision."

Inevitably, lunch was at La Dacha. At first Capucine bridled. Even though her appetite had been hamstrung, she was repelled by the notion of upmarket grazing where the only substantial offering would be the check. Still, she acquiesced.

La Dacha hadn't changed. It never would. If Gaël Tanguy's dystopia ever came to pass, rusty automatons might copulate with festering animals in the street, but La Dacha would manage to extract the last hundred grams of beluga caviar from the last moldering sturgeon in the hopelessly polluted Caspian Sea and serve it—with an insufficient amount of toast—for an obscene price.

Capucine scoured the menu. Perversely, she was extremely hungry. As it turned out, if you actually took the time to read it—which, of course, was hardly the done thing—real food could be found. Capucine ordered the borscht with three pirogies on the side to be followed by beef Stroganoff, and a half bottle of a Côtes du Rhône that she had heard Alexandre praise.

"Are you pregnant?" ejaculated Cécile, genuinely alarmed. "Now that I look at you, you do seem different. But thinner, not rounder. What's the matter?"

"Nothing. I just need a bit of support. And a spoonful of fish eggs on toast isn't going to do it for me."

Cécile's concern lasted for almost three seconds before she refocused on her own life.

"I've made up my mind! You'll never guess what I decided."

"You're quitting the firm, leaving Théo and your girlfriend, and going to Switzerland to start life anew."

Cécile deflated like a badly knotted party balloon. "How did you know? I haven't told a soul."

"It was obvious." Capucine dove into her borscht and ate a pierogi, which was superb, cooked to an authentic

Russian recipe, the unleavened dough fried until it was crisp and the interior redolent with potatoes and onions.

"No, seriously, tell me. How did you know?"

"Bolting was the only thing on your menu that excited you." Capucine picked up another pierogi and nibbled on it. "Your interest in your firm had dwindled. It was really only the politicking that challenged you anyway and once you had grabbed the brass ring, nothing was left. The girl-friend was all about the shock value. And poor Théo bored you even before you were married. All he's ever been is a scenic backdrop. Vevey doesn't sound all that longterm but it has the virtue of being something com-pletely new. And that makes it more exciting than the other options."

"How well you know me. Is that how you catch your little criminals, by reading their minds?"

"No. What it takes is spending all night in the rain look-ing up at peoples' apartment lights. In fact—"

"Aren't you excited for me? I feel like I'm about to climb up on a Conestoga wagon and discover a whole new California. Or even join the crew of one of Columbus's ships and not be able to sleep at night for fear of sailing over the edge of the world."

The waiter came up with Capucine's Stroganoff and asked Cécile if she wanted more caviar.

"Please, but I think I'll have the osetra this time." In an aside to Capucine she said, "When you get right down to it, it's by far the best of the three, even if it is the cheap-est."

"Have you stocked enough caviar on your Conestoga wagon to last the whole journey?"

"You're being mean, and that's so not like you. I thought you would be happy that I've made my decision and my agony of uncertainty is over."

"I *am* being mean. It's just that I'm faced with an enor-mous decision mys—"

Cécile squeezed Capucine's hand, comforting her. "I understand. It's difficult for you to understand the enormity of my challenge. You're *so* right. Vevey won't last forever, so I don't want to burn any bridges behind me. I'm going to tell Théophile it's a temporary assignment so he'll feel comfortable staying here, and, of course, I'll come and visit often. Who can stay away from Paris? There are hardly any shops in Geneva, much less Vevey."

Capucine's Stroganoff was perfect, the sauce rich and creamy, the beef satisfyingly rare.

"What is that vile concoction? Some sort of stew? And you're eating it in the middle of the summer. Capucine, are you sure you're not pregnant? Where was I? The worst part of it is I'll need an entire fall wardrobe and the shops still only have summer things. And on top of it all, Théo insists on going to his parents' house on the Ile de Ré for a month. An *entire* month, can you imagine? It's a purgatory of boredom but I feel morally obliged to go. When I get back I'll only have a week for shopping and dealing with Honorine, but one does what one has to do, *n'est-ce pas, ma chérie?* One copes."

The lunch dragged on for another twenty minutes. Capucine stopped listening and contemplated the little lamp on the table with its tasseled red silk shade. At first she could not understand why Cécile was so ebullient. Then it struck her. Because she had finally stopped weighing her alternatives and had committed herself to a course of action. Unlike Capucine, she didn't need a validation of her decision; she merely wanted a witness to her joy.

Capucine unglued herself from the lamp and focused on her friend who was going on about not needing evening clothes in Vevey and what a relief that was. Capucine stood up.

"*Ma belle,* have a wonderful time on the Ile de Ré. After all this you *so* deserve a vacation. I'm sure we'll find a moment to finish catching up when you come back."

"Of course, and then you'll really have to tell me what it is that's on your mind. I must hear about that. Why on earth are you leaving so soon? Don't you want to finish your goulash or whatever it is?" Cécile asked with a grimace.

"I have to get going with an arrest. It's the sort of thing that really can't wait."

As she walked out of the restaurant Capucine knew Cécile would always be part of her life's furniture, if only as an archivist of her early memories. But she also understood that the rift between them would gradually continue to widen until eventually they would do no more than run into each other occasionally at dinner parties and make sincere plans, which would never materialize, to have lunch at La Dacha and rekindle their closeness.

CHAPTER 37

Her decision finally made, Capucine boiled with impatience. On the street corner in front of La Dacha she flipped open her phone and pressed Alexandre's speed dial. He picked up immediately.

"Where are you?" Capucine asked.

"I'm at the paper. In an intensely boring editorial meeting." Alexandre spoke in a sibilant whisper, his hand obviously cupped around his mouth and the receiver of his cell phone in a gesture he recently affected from a movie about Colombian drug dealers.

"Damn!"

"What's the matter?"

"Nothing. It's just that I'm in the Eighth Arrondissement and the Thirteenth is at the other end of Paris. I wanted to see you right away."

"I'll hop in a cab and encourage the driver so vigorously with word and gesture I'll be at your side in a flash."

"Why don't we meet in the middle? The Sixth. How about Les Editeurs? You know, in the carrefour de l'Odéon?"

"Les Editeurs?" Alexandre asked. "I'm sure we could find someplace more amusing."

"Don't be such a snob. Last one to arrive pays the bill."

Capucine flipped her phone shut and smiled for the first time that day.

But in the heat of the unair-conditioned taxi her resolve melted and plopped on the floor like a child's ice cream cone undone by the seaside sun.

Les Editeurs, with its bought-by-the-yard book-lined walls, was pleasant enough, but the unfathomable vagaries of the Saint-Germain intelligentsia had nevertheless deemed it irrevocably infra-dig. Capucine had picked the spot precisely because there was absolutely no chance of running into anyone they knew. She bitterly regretted her choice. There would be no escape for her here.

As if he had read her mind, Alexandre had rejected the welcoming awning-covered terrace and had retreated inside, choosing a table in the farthest recess of the deserted bar–dining room. Grinning happily, he read from an open volume propped up against a small pile of books on the table and sipped whiskey from a glass with a single ice cube.

When he saw Capucine's approach he leapt to his feet and took her into his arms, searching deep in her eyes. She had no idea what he read there but with a jerk he broke the mood.

"I can't for the life of me imagine why no one comes here," Alexandre said as they sat down. "These shelves contain a rich lode." He held up a book and read the title, *"The Astonishing Digestive Tract of the Burgundy Snail."*

Despite herself Capucine grinned.

"And how about *Proceedings of the Thirty-Eighth Annual Congress of Growers of Root Vegetables of the Southwest* or *Guinea Pig Husbandry for Fun and Profit?"*

Capucine began to laugh. "Stop, please."

"It gets even better. *Collectible Swizzle Sticks—A Pictorial Overview.* And my absolute favorite, *The Wit and*

Wisdom of Recipients of the Order of Commander of the Decoration of Maritime Merit."

Capucine's hoots of laughter squeezed out tears. Alexandre leaned forward and kissed her eyes.

"*Chérie,* your problem is that you don't drink enough." He raised his finger imperiously and a waiter scuttled over. Even far off the beaten track of the cognoscenti, his reputation had preceded him. "A double vodka with lots of ice for madame and another one of these for me," he said, shaking his almost empty on-the-rocks glass, making the nearly melted ice lozenge tinkle.

"I'm sorry. I got upset because we need to have a serious talk and you were making jokes," Capucine said.

"Serious talk, eh?" He fell silent as the drinks arrived.

"Very serious. It's about . . . well . . . you see . . . It's sort of hard to explain."

"I'm guessing the word you're looking for is *appât*—bait."

"Bait? No, not that. No. Never."

"How about 'tethered goat,' then? I think that's what lion hunters call it. Would that be better?"

Capucine's eyes filled with tears again.

"Now you're being silly. If you don't stop, I'll take your big black gun away from you and give you a good spanking. Right here."

"You wouldn't dare!"

"Try me."

"It's Jacques, isn't it? You found out from him. That horrible Docteur Vavasseur must have told Jacques and Jacques told you. Men can never keep secrets."

"Oh, please. Jacques didn't tell me anything. I figured it out weeks ago. I know nothing about criminals, thank God, but I know all there is to know about you. And, of course, a rumor has been going around the staffs of the food pages of the big dailies that the *Police Judiciaire* is making inquiries about restaurant openings. The connection wasn't all that hard to make."

Capucine burst into tears in earnest. A waiter poked his head around the door and then retreated. It was the great thing about restaurant service in France, no matter how pretentious and incompetent the management, the waitstaff were always professionals.

When the waiter left, Alexandre asked, "Where was I?"

" 'Oh, please'-ing."

"Exactly. It was obvious. You did what you always do. You let your intuition solve the crime, but since your intuition can't produce evidence, you can't make an arrest."

"There is no evidence. None at all."

"Oh, please. That truism had permeated even my geriatric, alcohol-pickled brain."

"Oh, please. No more 'oh, please'-ing."

Alexandre laughed. Capucine giggled. He picked up her hand and kissed it.

"I'm glad that's finally over," Alexandre said. "Now let's hear this plan of yours. I've been waiting for weeks. You know how I love amateur theatricals."

"It's going to be next Saturday. On the Eiffel Tower."

"Of course!" exclaimed Alexandre, rapping the table with his knuckles. "It's perfect. You're a genius." He kissed his wife happily on the forehead.

After a never-ending month, Capucine was finally reunited with Alexandre. She felt like crying again. In the dusty, over-air-conditioned, empty room, Paris and its oppressive blanket of heat were forgotten. They were like two children in the corner of an attic, eagerly sharing a secret.

Elated, Capucine described her plan. The reopening of the Restaurant Jules Verne on the second level of the Eiffel Tower had long been touted as the restaurant project of the season, if not the decade. Originally the opening had been planned for September—the crowning event of the *rentrée,* when life exploded back into the City of Light after the long dead summer—but it had been moved up to the third week in June. Wags opined this was because the project had run seriously over budget and the investors wanted to tap into the summer revenue from fat-walleted tourists.

There was no doubt the project was magnificent. Even though the restaurant had existed from the construction of the tower, it had become increasingly mediocre over the years, eventually declining to a level where not even American and Japanese tourists were willing to put up with its extravagant prices.

A group of investors had contracted Georges Delmas, the most starred and most ambitious of the French chefs, to revamp the décor and create a level of cuisine that would guarantee one Michelin star at a minimum. But it was no mean undertaking. The new furniture had had to be cleverly designed to meet the tower's draconian weight limits. The kitchen was so tiny it could hold only a handful of cooks and all the prep work would need to be undertaken in the basement of a nearby building and shuttled up to the restaurant in a dedicated lift.

On top of it all, the opening had been billed as the event of the summer. A hundred and twenty highly select guests had been invited to dinner, including representatives of the senior echelons of the government who would be there to celebrate the burnishing of France's most cherished monument. A further three hundred guests had been invited for a display of fireworks after dinner.

"If this doesn't attract the killer nothing will," Alexandre said when Capucine's exposé was finished.

"It better do the trick because it's our last chance until the fall and I could never stand another wait."

As they walked out of Les Editeurs Capucine noticed a bulge under Alexandre's left armpit.

"Hey, what's that? Momo didn't slip you a weapon, did he? Let me see."

Alexandre shied away.

"No. This is serious. You can't go walking around armed without a permit. That's a class-one felony." Using a police hold she pinioned Alexandre's left arm and stuck her hand in his jacket. It was a book.

"What's this?"

"It was the best one of all. Too good to leave where no one will ever read it. Please, Officer, I couldn't help myself. Don't take me in."

The cover of the book was blank. Capucine turned it sideways and read the spine. *Sadomasochism for Beginners.*

"Okay, young man. I'll let you off just this once. But only if I get to read it first."

CHAPTER 38

There was no doubt that Chef Delmas had a flair for extravaganza, Alexandre told himself as he sauntered between two rows of mounted Garde Républicaine—resplendent in their plumed helmets and blue and red uniforms—toward the chrome yellow awning over the door to the restaurant's elevator. He could see a single white police van parked on the quai and told himself that anyone would think it normal for such a celebrity-packed guest list.

At the base of the steps to the elevator a covey of pretty hostesses in short black dresses circulated, bestowing guests waiting for the lift with authentic smiles and flutes of champagne.

Heedful of Capucine's instructions that he was not, under any circumstances, to enter the restaurant without Momo as a chaperone, Alexandre joined the exhilarated swarm, accepted a glass of champagne, and waited for his protector and new best friend. Within a few minutes he was so engrossed in trading smiles of escalating radiance with one of the hostesses that he was oblivious to a large, looming brown mass materializing at his side until it began to grumble. Absurdly, Momo had been decked out in the restaurant's waitstaff livery: Lanvin's adaptation of a Zouave uniform, a tight, brown, buttonless mess jacket over exaggeratedly baggy dark tan pants held at the ankle by leather spats.

"The boss knows I hate these costume gigs," Momo growled in Alexandre's ear. "She also knows I hate tight collars," he said, pulling at the neck of a white collarless shirt. "But still she makes me do this shit."

"You're adorable in Lanvin, sweetie," Alexandre said. "It brings out a whole new you."

"You're not going to be finding it so goddamn funny when someone tries to get at you and I don't have my piece, because there's no place to stash it in this clown outfit."

The door to the elevator slid open. Alexandre moved toward the elevator steps. Momo slid a hand big enough to strangle a sheep under his upper arm and held him back.

"We go in last."

Just as the door began to close, Momo pushed Alexandre roughly into the elevator and sidled in after him. There were refined mumbles of outrage.

As the glass-walled elevator rose four hundred feet through a latticework of steel girders, Paris stretched itself out, a sea of zinc rooftops punctuated by islands of gilt domes. There was a collective buzz of admiration from the passengers.

When the door opened again with a satisfying whoosh, Alexandre found himself face-to-face with Isabelle, also dressed as a Zouave, holding a clipboard.

"May I see your invitation, please?" she asked crisply with a lame attempt at a smile. It was a far cry from the smiles of the hostesses at the elevator's entrance but at least her lips were upturned. Alexandre handed her his elaborately engraved pasteboard card with a grin, which was returned with a scowl.

"Is Capu . . . *Commissaire* Le Tellier wearing one of

these uniforms too?" Alexandre asked Momo. "I really wouldn't want to miss that."

"Yeah, right. She's hanging out in the kitchen, palling with the chef, wearing her usual great clothes, looking like a million euros."

The restaurant's revamped décor fully lived up to the expectations created at the ground level. The area had been divided into four intimate dining rooms, barely lit, placing the spectacular panorama of Paris in dramatic relief. The furnishings succeeded in evoking the Belle Epoque while remaining modern and self-effacing. The only distraction from the view came from the muted luminescence of the tabletops, washed in a delicate glow from small glass globes.

Aping the aplomb of a seasoned maître d'hôtel, Momo showed Alexandre to a four-top up against the glass window and retreated to a dim corner. Out of the corner of his eye Alexandre caught sight of David standing in the opposite corner of the room, also wearing the restaurant livery. Even at a distance it was obvious he was rejoicing in his new outfit. Every few seconds he snaked into a new pose, exploring the costume's possibilities. Alexandre grinned.

The first of Alexandre's dinner companions to arrive were the président–directeur général of the hotel chain that owned fifty percent of the restaurant, accompanied by his wife, a shrewish woman, leathery from excesses of Saint-Tropez sun, who dressed as if she was still nineteen. Her husband, a rotund, jovial bon vivant, was delighted to see Alexandre. "Excellent," he said with a gurgling tobacco laugh as he sat heavily. "Delmas certainly knows how to do things. He's put France's most revered restaurant critic in my care. And who knows better how to show him a good time, right, *chérie?*" His wife frowned sourly.

The next to arrive was an Italian senator long famous for his right-wing populist politics and his fascination with barely pubescent models. He sat down in a flurry of Italian manners and attempted to kiss the hand of the president's wife, which she withdrew in a huff.

A sommelier arrived with the ubiquitous champagne, this time Perrier-Jouët Belle Epoque Blanc de Blancs 2000 in a magnum decorated with Art Deco anemones and eighteen nineties lettering. With an elegant gesture the sommelier poured, holding the bottle with his thumb in the recess at the base and his fingers splayed out on the side.

"We're off to a good start," the hotel president said to Alexandre as the Italian senator craned, casing the room for pulchritude. "But I have to confess I have no idea what we're going to eat. No one tells me that sort of thing."

"The PR firm sent a circular around to the press," Alexandre said. "Apparently we're going to have a tasting menu of four dishes followed by cheese and dessert." Alexandre warmed to the subject. "Their first course is a Brittany lobster with a salad of wild apples and a cold rémoulade spicy sauce made with mayonnaise, gherkins, capers, and mixed herbs. Then there's a dish of country endive cooked with truffles, chicory, raw ham from Bayonne, and Comté cheese."

The hotel president sat on the edge of his chair, his breath quickening, as if he was leaning at the bar of a strip joint. "Then what?" he asked, slightly bug-eyed.

"A pan-sautéed turbot cooked in a flour sauce with shallot, white wine, tomatoes, and parsley. And finally a *grenadin de veau,* pan-seared veal with lightly creamed baby spinach leaves and the veal's *jus.*"

"Doesn't that sound wonderful?" the hotel president asked his wife.

She blew air through her lips and gave an exasperated shake of her head.

The three men chatted, while the president's wife stared moodily out the window. A waiter arrived and removed what looked like porcelain impressionist sculptures of a compressed Eiffel Tower, which had been placed before each diner. Alexandre knew from the press kit that, inverted, they would be the restaurant's dinner dishes. Two other waiters served the lobster with flourishes while a sommelier poured more champagne.

The meal, like the décor, fully lived up to the hype, right down to the cheeses, which came from a famous *affineur* known for aging his wards in a sixteenth-century *cave* as fastidiously as if he was a nanny pampering the children of aristocrats.

But the pièce de résistance was dessert. When all the tables were cleared, the dim background lights were extinguished completely. The diners, ghostly in the up-light from the table lamps, quieted in an expectant hush. Alexandre felt, or imagined he felt, Momo and David stiffen. Six waiters entered, bearing silver platters of beautifully crafted spun-sugar Eiffel Towers in beds of blue, white, and red sorbet, topped with sputtering sparklers and fluttering French flags. The room broke into enthusiastic applause. Momo edged closer, looming at Alexandre's side, darting glances into the room. Alexandre chuckled.

"Are you amused at the scolding Chef will have tomorrow when the management of the tower learns its precious fire regulations were flaunted?" the hotel president asked.

"Hardly. No true gentleman worries about morning-after recriminations,"

The Italian senator smiled broadly and said, *"Questo è certo!"*

The president's wife gave them both a dirty look.

"No, I was thinking of my wife who will be delighted to learn that the dinner has gone off so well," Alexandre said. As he thought of Capucine, no doubt on tenterhooks, peering out through the judas window of the kitchen, his heart went out to her.

"So be perfectly frank with me, my dear Alexandre, if I may be permitted to call you that." Alexandre tuned in to what the president was saying. "If you were sitting on the Michelin committee, what rating would you give this restaurant?"

A hard and fast rule among critics was never to make value judgments, particularly to restaurant owners and staff, before they had written their reviews. But Alexandre was tempted, possibly because of his unaccustomed role that night, to be expansive.

"One star. Unquestionably, one star. The service is perfect, the view obviously without equal, the décor lives up to the view, but the food does not quite have the majesty of two stars." Alexandre paused, waiting for a disappointed frown. "Does that disappoint you?"

The president broke into a broad, toothy smile. "That's exactly what I wanted to hear. You see, dear," he said to his wife. "Delmas is a genius, an absolute genius, just like I told you. I asked him for one star and that's exactly what he produces. No more, no less."

He said to Alexandre, "We undertook very extensive market research before committing our investment. I think we got our product-market segmentation down pat. No stars would have been bad. Two or three would have been equally bad. We want this place to be the big night out on the well-heeled tourist's Paris trip. Too many stars would attract a crowd that would intimidate him. No stars and our target market wouldn't be willing to pay the prices we need to cover our investment." He was genuinely overjoyed. "I sincerely hope you reflect that point of view in your review tomorrow."

"Oh, you can count on that, and, with any luck, I think I can promise you that it will be the best-read restaurant review of the year."

"Really! Do you hear that, dear?"

The president's wife was distracting herself by smashing her spun-sugar Eiffel Tower with a spoon and did not reply.

* * *

In the kitchen, which Chef Delmas had left to receive his accolades from the guests as the coffee service was in progress, Isabelle hissed at Capucine, "See, it's not going to happen tonight. It's because the security is too tight. We overdid it."

"Shuuuuush! We'll talk later."

"And also the access is too limited. It's too dangerous for the killer. We needed a more open location for it to work."

Capucine put her index finger over her lips and breathed, "The evening's not even half over yet. The dangerous part is coming up."

The next phase of the event was the display of fireworks, to be viewed from the roof over the dining room, an area not normally open to the public, which could be reached only by a tight circular iron stairway that exited through a small circular metal hatch that could well have been on a submarine. The PR firm was convinced it would complete the Jules Verne experience by creating a link to the *Nautilus* in *Twenty Thousand Leagues Under the Sea.*

The hundred and twenty guests who had been invited to the dinner would go up first and once they were at their ease sipping champagne, the horde of three hundred B-list guests would be admitted. By then it would be fully dark and the show of fireworks would begin.

Next to the threat of poison, Capucine had been most concerned with the ascension of the tight stairwell. She had ordered Momo to lead the guests up the stairs with Alexandre immediately behind. Isabelle remained on the level below, closely examining the procession of guests, while David had already taken up a position on the roof. Capucine surveyed the scene from the kitchen door judas. The last thing she wanted was to be greeted loudly by one of the guests.

Capucine breathed a deep sigh of relief when the hotel president stepped behind Alexandre to climb the staircase.

He was, in turn, followed by his wife, with the Italian senator behind. Capucine darted out from the kitchen and slipped in after the senator, who broke into a fulsome smile and insisted that she precede him up the stairs. Normally, she would have rewarded his courtesy with a little uplift of her gluteals, but she was far too overwrought for *gamineries*. At the top, Capucine melted into the clutch of waitstaff ready to distribute flutes of champagne.

The roof was a broad, flat, slightly oily metal surface, riveted like the side of a ship, circled by an alarmingly low single rail, only slightly higher than waist level on a good-size man. Even though the sun had slid under the horizon half an hour before, the western sky was still washed in pastel pinks and yellows. As the dark rose into the sky, lights began to twinkle in the city spread out like a Persian carpet below them. Enraptured by the magic of the moment, the crowd fell silent.

Behind them the second wave of guests emerged from the stairwell. By the time they had all been served their flutes of champagne, night had settled and the canvas beneath them had become a luminous gold tracery laid out on a black background. The first rocket soared up lazily from the Champ de Mars and, with a loud, sharp crack, burst into an elegant shower of white sparks. It was immediately followed by two more, the three knocks that announced the beginning of a play in the French theater.

The crowd gravitated to the southern rail. The sky erupted in a blaze of sound and color. Momo locked his muscular hand around Alexandre's arm.

"The boss wants us to stay out of the crowd."

The pyrotechnics continued. The throng exclaimed loudly at each burst.

Capucine scanned the scene, Isabelle by her side. David seemed to have disappeared.

A rocket shot into the sky with a loud shrill whistling, exploding with an almost painful concussion, showering the sky with brilliant red meteors. It was immediately followed by six more. The din was numbing.

Capucine had no idea how it happened so quickly. She looked away for an instant, searching for David, and when she looked back at Alexandre, he and Momo stood clawing at their eyes. A figure in a white chef's outfit grabbed Alexandre by his upper arms and began pushing him toward the west railing, away from the crowd. Alexandre cried out, Momo lurched after him blindly. As they hurtled forward, the white-clad person grabbed Alexandre by the nape of the neck and seemed to squirt something into his mouth with a plastic squeeze bottle. They reached the rail. Alexandre struggled, flailing, coughing, spitting. Momo crashed into them. The squeeze bottle was projected into the void.

As Capucine raced across the roof, she saw the white-clad figure reach under Alexandre's jacket, hauling at his belt to lift him over the rail. Capucine accelerated. Momo staggered like a drunk, helpless. She wasn't going to make it. The figure grabbed Alexandre's thigh and began to push him into the void. Then came the gesture that saved Alexandre. The figure dropped his leg and reached into his jacket. David stepped into the tableau and made a languid, almost caressing gesture over the white-clad figure's head, a priest's benediction. The figure immediately went limp, collapsing on the iron deck of the roof.

As the figure went down, Momo managed to get a hand into Alexandre's collar and pulled him off the railing. They both stood, sightless, tears streaming, gulping air.

Capucine skidded to a halt in front of them. Béatrice lay at Alexandre's feet, inches away from the edge, her arm dangling languidly over the abyss. She looked as tranquil as if she had fallen asleep in the sun at a garden party.

Even blinded, Alexandre had no difficulty maintaining his unrufflable persona. Capucine kissed him on the mouth.

"Ah, what delicious lips," he said. "I'm almost sure I

recognize them. Now, don't tell me whose they are. Let me guess. I love this game."

Capucine kissed Alexandre a second time and gripped his hand. From behind she could hear Isabelle scolding David. "What did you hit her with? That wasn't regulation equipment, was it?"

"Oh, just a little toy Momo brought me from his last trip back home. Effective enough when you know how to use it."

"Still, it's not regulation, now is it?"

Capucine continued clutching Alexandre's hand, her breath coming in short gasps, as the happy staccato of Isabelle and David squabbling behind her reassured her that it really was all over.

Even though the fireworks display was a good five or ten minutes away from the grand finale, the crescendo rose to a deafening level. The crowd was rapt. The entire episode had passed unnoticed.

CHAPTER 39

———————

"I don't see how she could have got up here," Isabelle said.

"I saw her climb off a girder," David said. "She probably came up in the service elevator in the middle of the afternoon. In her cook's outfit no one would have noticed, particularly if she was carrying a tray of something. Of course, you have to have brass balls to spend the afternoon hanging on to a steel strut thirty-five stories off the ground."

"You know," Isabelle said, "when you look at them, those struts are square in section. She could have squeezed inside, put her butt on one of the crossbars and her feet on another. Wouldn't have been all that uncomfortable. If she was below the level of the roof, she would have been completely invisible."

"And her plan must have been to disappear back out there once she'd done the deed and wait until we'd cleared out," David said. "If we hadn't been waiting for her, it might even have worked."

As they spoke, five uniformed *Police Judiciaire* officers emerged from the round stairwell hatch.

At the sight of the uniforms Capucine dropped Alexandre's hand and took charge.

"*Brigadier-Chef,*" she said to an officer with three chevrons on his epaulets. "Handcuff this woman and take her down as quickly as possible. I want absolutely no disturbance."

A beefy officer put his hands under Béatrice's arms and lifted her to a sitting position. Another handcuffed her wrists behind her back.

"*Brigadier-Chef,*" Capucine continued, "radio the men below to tape off the section of the lawn directly under us. Have them search for a plastic kitchen squeeze bottle. Alert forensics, who are to collect it and analyze the contents."

The fireworks display crescendoed to the finale. As four officers carried Béatrice to the hatch, two or three of the guests turned to look but immediately returned their attention to the brilliant pyrotechnics.

It was no easy matter getting Béatrice down the narrow circular stairway. The beefy officer held her by the armpits, her head lolling on his chest, another officer locked his arms around her thighs, above the knees, and they inched down one slow step at a time, followed by the rest of the uniformed officers.

"Now," said Capucine, "Alexandre, you and Momo are next. Alexandre, put your left hand on Isabelle's shoulder and follow her down the stairs with your right hand on the banister. I'll take Momo down. Okay, off you go. David, have a quick look around to see if we missed anything and then clear out and join us downstairs."

Capucine had no idea why she wanted Isabelle to be her husband's Virgil; the order had been given reflexively. However, the impact on Isabelle was manifest. She swelled with pride.

Capucine was sure she would be held to task for not

cordoning off the crime scene and not leaving officers behind to painstakingly collect the names of all the people on
the roof and compare them to their identity papers. Useless or not, police procedure was inviolate. But throwing a
wet blanket on Chef Delmas' opening was out of the question. Without his cooperation there would have been no
arrest.

"Okay, *vieux*," she said to Momo quietly enough so
David wouldn't hear. "This time it's me who's got your
back."

"You always do, *Commissaire*," Momo said, walking in
lockstep behind Capucine, his left arm on her shoulder.

At the bottom of the stairs more uniformed PJ officers
waited with a gurney. The uniforms laid Béatrice out and
handcuffed her wrists to the aluminum struts. It was a
tight fit in the elevator but they squeezed in. On the way
down Béatrice started to writhe. One of the officers unzipped a black shoulder bag and removed a syringe. He
picked up Béatrice's right hand, found a vein, slid the needle in, and squeezed the plunger slowly. Béatrice settled
back into unconsciousness.

Passersby paused to look as the police emerged from the
elevator but then walked on. Some old buffer must have
had a heart attack. The uniformed *brigadier-chef* came up
to Capucine.

"The shot is going to last at least three hours, maybe
more, *Commissaire*. Where do you want her taken?"

"Down to the Quai. Get the duty doctor to come in and
monitor her carefully. Take *Brigadier* Benarouche and my
husband with you and have the doctor look at their eyes.
And have forensics call him once they identify the substance they were squirted with so he can decide if they
need to be hospitalized. Tell the doctor I'll be there in an
hour."

"Sneaking back up for your dinner, are you?" Alexandre asked. "The *grenadin de veau* is worth the detour."

"I need to check out Renaud's apartment. Sometimes confessions come a little more quickly when the suspect is confronted with some hard evidence." As she spoke Capucine realized she had stopped thinking of Béatrice by her given name.

"Aren't you gilding your lily by hoping for a confession?" Alexandre asked.

"*Pas du tout.* We have her in *flagrant délit* for an attempted homicide. I want to make sure she's convicted for the murders, too."

Fifteen minutes later Capucine, David, and Isabelle sat in the Twingo, staring at the green wood door of number twenty-four rue Madame, a few streets away from Béatrice's restaurant, waiting for a contingent of Capucine's officers and the INPS van.

The officers from the brigade were first to arrive. A single officer descended from the patrol car and opened the front door with a passkey. The door open, three more officers emerged with heavy canvas bags and entered the building. Capucine and her two detectives followed. Without a word the three rode up in the elevator to the third floor as the uniformed officers took the stairs two at a time, their boots soundless on the crimson runner held by brass rods over the polished wooden steps.

On the third floor landing they were confronted by two doors, one oak and the other, Béatrice's, covered in green enameled steel plating. High-security doors had been encouraged by insurance companies for decades in Paris.

The officer who had opened the downstairs door examined the locks on the steel door carefully.

"*Commissaire,* this is a Picard seven bar lock. There's nothing I can do with it."

"Does that mean we can't get in?"

There were muted snickers from the officers on the landing.

"No, Commissaire. These richies spend a fortune on burglar-proof doors but they can't be bothered to strengthen the frame that holds the door in the wall. I'll have the frame out in a minute, but there's going to be a little mess." There was open laughter from the other officers. Jobs like this were the reason they had joined the force.

The officer produced a chisel-ended crowbar and explored the wall, tapping gently. At one tap he seemed to hear what he wanted and banged the crowbar into the plaster with a vicious jab. It went in a good four inches.

"*A toi, Jérôme,*" he said.

Another officer jabbed into the other side of the door with an identical crowbar. The two men heaved and threw their weight against the bars. There was a sound of masonry cracking and a large seam appeared at both doorjambs.

"*Attention. Ça vient!*" Everyone pulled back from the door, which fell into the hallway with a resounding crash. A cloud of plaster dust rose in the air.

"*Et voilà!* That's how you do 'er," the *brigadier* called Jérôme said with a happy smile.

The apartment was as tidy as if readied for a fashion magazine to shoot for a profile of the up-and-coming chef. Peach-colored walls were dotted with aged family portraits in elegant gold frames. A handful of delicate antiques punctuated bold leather and steel settees and chairs in brilliant primary colors. A large white enameled bookcase housed a large collection of cookbooks, most by current celebrity chefs but many in the faded back cloth bindings and gold lettering of the nineteenth century.

The *Police Judiciaire* officers milled and peered but did not touch, waiting for the forensics team to arrive.

"Didn't your mamas teach you to knock first?" Ajudant Dechery said in his basso profundo as he walked over the destroyed door. Three of his *agents techniques* peered over his shoulder.

"Sorry I couldn't get here sooner. I've been at the Eiffel Tower. Your people found the squeeze bottle. I sent it to the lab, but I knew from the first sniff what it was, belladonna."

"Belladonna?" Capucine asked. "The stuff the Moroccans use in their *kohl* to make their eyes big?"

"The very same. Deadly nightshade. Grows all over the place in the *Midi*. The berries are loaded with atropine, which is what makes your pupils dilate."

"I have to make a call."

"If it's to the *PJ* duty doctor, don't bother. I already had a chat with him. He knows how to handle it. It doesn't seem like your husband ingested enough to have any effect. But both he and your *brigadier* got enough atropine in their eyes so they won't be seeing much for a few hours."

Capucine felt as if a weight had been lifted from her shoulders.

"And belladonna is a poison?"

"Oh, definitely. The atropine has been used as a pupil dilator since the beginning of time. It's probably what Cleopatra used to snag Mark Antony. But those delicious little berries also contain tropane alkaloids, scopolamine, and hyoscyamine, all of which are deadly. Macbeth, the real one, not the one in the play, knocked out a whole army with the stuff." He paused, proud of his erudition.

"All right, m'dear. What if you let us get going in here?"

As Dechery's team got to work, Capucine, Isabelle, and David continued peering at the contents of the apartment, their hands behind their backs like children who had been warned not to touch.

Of course, it was Dechery who found the piece of evidence needed for a court conviction. He called Capucine over. In the extravagantly fitted and impeccably clean kitchen, the lowest drawer in the least accessible corner was filled with household detritus, supermarket plastic bags, boxes of rubber bands, and menus from Chinese takeaways. At the very bottom of the pile Dechery found an eight-inch turkey trussing needle—its tip flattened into a sharp blade—and a length of neatly coiled kitchen twine.

When the forensic technician had finished an endless series of flash photos of the needle in its habitat, had dusted it for fingerprints, and had taken even more photographs, Dechery picked it up carefully with a pair of long tweezers and examined it closely.

"See these brown stains," he said to Capucine. "That's not turkey blood. From the color, it comes from a mammal. We'll get DNA off this thing for sure, and I'll bet you a month's salary right now this is what was used to stitch Arsène Peroché's mouth shut."

From the living room Isabelle called out, "Hey, *Commissaire,* come check this out!"

In the sitting room a technician was busy at the desk—a lovely Boule piece that must have come from Béatrice's family home—dusting and taking pictures. The desk was littered with books, most with slips of paper marking pages, a stack of bills, a pile of invitations. In the exact center was a mahogany glass-topped case, about seven inches by twelve, containing a single drawer. Through the glass top, most of which had already been obscured by aluminum fingerprint powder, Capucine could see the drawer had been fitted with white foam rubber into which ten grooves had been set. Expensive looking pens had been laid in every alternate groove.

"Can you open this for me?" Capucine asked the technician.

He tugged at the knob with tweezers. Capucine bent over. The drawer contained four fountain pens and, incongruously, a plastic Pilot artist's felt-tip. The gold cap of one of the fountain pens was clearly engraved with the letters AP.

Capucine said to the technician, "This is a critical piece of evidence. It must be treated with the utmost care."

"*Commissaire,* we treat everything with the utmost care. We're not an industrial cleaning service."

Isabelle had wandered off into the bedroom. "It just keeps getting better and better," she shouted. One of the technicians had just found a pair of French Army night glasses. "Momo was right. She must have used this in the blind restaurant. The famous ghostly green glow was the reflection from the eyepieces on her face."

The technician nudged Isabelle away and continued taking flash pictures.

"Five pens, *Commissaire,*" Isabelle said. "That means there are two murders we don't know about. But with all this evidence she's bound to confess, right?"

"We'll see. I'm not so sure about a confession. And I'm even less sure we'll ever find out about the other two victims. But I think we just might have enough evidence for a full conviction."

CHAPTER 40

On her way to the Quai, Capucine called in and learned that Alexandre and Momo had been sent to the small police infirmary in the enormous Hôpital Hôtel-Dieu adjacent to the Quai. Béatrice had been placed in an interrogation cell in the basement of the Quai after she had regained consciousness. She showed no obvious external signs of concussion but had become violent when the doctor attempted to examine her.

Walking down the hall to the infirmary Capucine could hear Momo and Alexandre laughing uproariously. She shook her head in wonder that she had actually thought her husband might experience a post-stress reaction. As she approached the sound she realized she was dreading seeing him. The rush of triumph of the arrest had worn off leaving the bitter realization of the enormity of her actions. She had used the depth of his love for her as a cheap tool in her cheap career, which was really no more than a cheap effort to find a cheap reality for herself. She had actually *used* him.

It was worse than creeping home in the early dawn after having spent the night with another man. Far worse.

A male nurse in dark blue scrubs the same color as a police uniform sat at a desk reading a paperback edition of Jean-Claude Izzo's *Solea*. With his wire-rim glasses and spiky, close-cropped hair the nurse seemed more like a university intellectual than a member of the police force. Wrenching his eyes away from his book, he looked up at Capucine, inquiring with his eyebrows.

"*Commissaire* Le Tellier. I've come to see my husband and *Brigadier* Benarouche."

The nurse stood up out of respect for Capucine's rank and smiled. "*Oui, Commissaire*. They're the ones making all the noise. Good thing the ward's empty. Your *brigadier* had some of his pals from *La Crim'* bring in some beer. They've been at it since the doctor made his last visit. Naturally, I haven't noticed a thing."

"What did the doctor say?"

"Their eyes had been squirted with a concentrated atropine solution."

"I didn't know it was concentrated. Are they in any danger?"

"Good Lord, no. If they were, I wouldn't be letting them get soused. Atropine is just a harmless cycloplegic. It only produces mydriasis."

"Mydriasis?"

"An abnormal dilation of the pupils. It was standard stuff a few years ago when ophthalmologists examined retinas. They don't use it anymore because the patient would be blind as a bat for two to six hours."

"I was told my husband might have swallowed some of the stuff."

"The doctor didn't think so. If your husband had ingested any of it, he'd have a severely upset stomach." In the next room Alexandre sang six bars of *Don Giovanni*, even more painfully off-key than usual. "Of course, that might not have been a bad thing."

Capucine did not smile. She turned toward the ward. The nurse sat down, clearly delighted to be able to get back to his book.

Capucine took two steps and turned back to the nurse. He rose reluctantly, meeting her gaze.

"If atropine's no longer in use, isn't it impossible to get?" Capucine asked him.

The question obviously pleased the nurse. He put his book down on the desk, pages open so he could get right back to it. "No. Nothing could be easier. All you have to do is boil down the juice of belladonna berries. It doesn't need any further processing. Anyone with a kitchen could do it."

In the ward six beds were lined up with military precision, all empty except for Alexandre's and Momo's. They sat on the sides of their bunks, facing each other, their gazes not quite meeting. They each held an infirmary tumbler of beer. A full quart bottle was beside each bed. Two empties had rolled against the wall, and two other bottles were neatly stacked under Momo's cot.

"So," Alexandre said, tapping Momo's knee, "three nuns walk into a bar and—"

"Alexandre," Capucine said sharply.

Alexandre—clearly two, if not all three, sheets to the wind—looked around sightlessly for the source of the sound.

"So you two are having a little party?" Capucine asked.

"*Parfaitement,*" Alexandre said. "We're toasting Momo's bravery and celebrating the fact that I've crossed off the top item on my bucket list—being a murder victim in one of my wife's cases." Alexandre erupted in laughter and poked Momo's upper thigh. "Bucket list, murder victim, get it?" He exploded into peals of laughter again.

Momo looked sheepish. " 'S'cuse me, *Commissaire.* I was assuming I'm not on duty anymore, so it'd be okay if

I rinsed a little of the dust out of my throat. Ale . . . Monsieur de Huguelet is safe here. No more worries. Right?"

Momo reached down to the floor, grabbed the quart bottle and sloshed beer into their glasses. Amazingly, only a small portion wound up on the floor.

"If you're drinking to Momo, you ought to drink one or two to David as well. I seem to recall he had a little more than a mere assist in the play for your salvation," Capucine said.

"By all means. Absolutely. Definitely," Alexandre said, waving his glass in the air, wildly seeking to clink it against Momo's. Failing in his effort, he drank deeply.

"The nurse—he's a great guy, by the way—said that just as soon as our vision comes back, he'll send us home in a squad car. But," Alexandre said, wrinkling his forehead and putting his index finger to his lips to indicate the extreme secrecy of what he was about to say, "we're going to get the car to take us to the Pied de Cochon, near the old Halles. They stay open all night and we're starving. Absolutely ra-ve-nous. You're right. We'll need to get David to come with us. And maybe the nurse too. Did I tell you what a great guy he is?" Alexandre drained his glass of beer and tapped Momo's knee to get him to pour another.

"You two are going nowhere except home. I'll leave orders. Trust me on that. If you want, you can take Momo home with you. And if you're still all that hungry, you can make your truffled scrambled eggs, but that's all you're going to get tonight. Put Momo up in the guest bedroom. He needs some rest."

Capucine kissed Alexandre on the forehead with what she hoped was great tenderness and made for the Quai interrogation rooms. Alexandre smiled at her and turned back toward Momo, anxious to unleash another joke.

When she had worked upstairs in *La Crim'*, the basement interrogation rooms had dismayed her—tangible proof of the brutality for which the *Police Judiciaire* was infamous. The rooms were in the third level basement, well below the level of the Seine, which flowed on the far side of the walls. Imagining the water pressure added to the sense of oppression. The rooms were so damp the green paint on the walls flaked and peeled no matter how frequently repainted. The furniture consisted of old, dented and stained oak tables and gray metal chairs with bent legs. Aluminum dome lamps hung from the ceiling, lighting only the table and whoever was unlucky enough to be sitting at it.

Béatrice was in Room C. Capucine knocked quietly on the ice-cold, ancient, iron door. The judas window in the door opened a crack was closed immediately. The door swung open slowly, screeching on hinges that remained rusty even though they were oiled constantly.

The scene was one Capucine had witnessed far too often while at *La Crim'*. The table had been pushed aside. An unknowable number of people lurked almost invisibly in the shadows. Béatrice sat in a chair directly under the harsh light of the lamp, her forearms duct taped to the arms of her chair, as was done when the suspect's violence threatened wounds from handcuffs.

Only two men were visible in the glow from the cone of light. Capucine had seen them at work many times but had never learned their names. A portly older detective, who—save for the old-style Manurhin three fifty seven in a sweat-darkened leather holster under his left armpit—could have passed for the sort of financial adviser who went to people's homes to sit around the dining table to advise them on their mutual funds—and a young, viperous man, so pallid and rangy he could have been a heroin addict. These were the good and bad cops *de service*.

As Capucine approached the tableau, Béatrice raised her head and spat at her.

"You filthy bitch!" she hissed.

The viperous man slapped her. She hissed at him but then let her head fall on her chest again.

Tallon emerged from the shadows.

"I'm wasting my time down here. These two are getting nowhere. I'm counting on you to produce something. I'm using the conference room upstairs. Call me when you have something to tell me," he said as curtly as if he were still running the *La Crim'*. The door screamed open and clanged shut behind Tallon.

At the sound, Béatrice stood up, arms attached to the chair, and ran at Capucine, attempting to head-butt her in the stomach. Two uniformed officers, of considerably beefier morphology than the average on the force, grabbed the back of the chair and slammed it back in its original position.

The viperous man approached to administer another slap. Capucine stopped him with two raised fingers.

With monosyllables and hand gestures Capucine ordered the two uniformed officers to stand at a distance behind Béatrice and to have a chair brought for herself. She placed the chair so she was diagonally opposite Béatrice, left leg inches away from left leg.

Capucine attempted to recreate the tone of their intimacy.

"You must be exhausted. Would you like some tea? I used to have a selection of tea bags from Mariage Frères in the closet of my old office upstairs and I'll bet they're still there. I can have someone make you a cup of a first-blush Darjeeling."

"*Pute,*" Béatrice spat at her.

"Do you want to talk about it?" Capucine said, maintaining her girl-to-girl cheerfulness.

"There's nothing to talk about. My father will be here soon to take me away. That's what he always does."

"Why were you so angry with Alexandre?"

"Because he's one of them. In fact, I think he may even be their leader."

"Them?"

"Them. Those who judge. Those who command. Those who suck the life out of you."

"Oh, *them*. And they had to be . . . removed? Is that it?"

"Obviously." Béatrice relaxed in her chair. Her breathing slowed. Some color came back into her face.

Capucine inched her chair closer to Béatrice.

"And killing them was the only way of removing them," Capucine said in a whisper.

"I never killed anyone. What the hell are you talking about? You're trying to put words in my mouth. But it's not going to work," Béatrice said loudly.

Capucine needed a long silence. No one in the room moved or even seemed to breathe. They might be brutal but they were definitely very good at the nuances of interrogations.

Just as the silence became unbearable, Capucine said, "I was at your apartment. I saw the pens."

"The pens," Béatrice said wistfully.

"They're important?"

"They're the whole thing. They're what it's about. The distillate of the power. The elixir. The key to the door."

"And you had to kill to get them, didn't you?"

"You bitch! I keep telling you. I never killed anyone. I'm just sitting here waiting for my father to come get me. And he will!"

Another very long silence.

"Tell me about Jean Monteil."

"That fat old buffoon. He knew less about food than my mother, and that's saying a whole lot. I'm talking about a woman who thinks that heating up a few trays of frozen hors d'œuvres for cocktail guests is the culinary achievement of the century. That guy was a serious menace."

"And that's why you had to kill him?"

"Bitch! Shut your fucking mouth. I told you. I haven't killed anybody. I'm just sitting here waiting for my father. So get off my fucking case, *pute!*"

Another very long pause.

"One of the pens had the initials 'A. P.' engraved in the cap," Capucine said.

"Arsène Peroché. What a fucker that guy was. He had taste and he knew what he was talking about. That's true. But he was like all the others. He didn't know how to control his power. He would diss brilliant chefs who were cooking from their hearts. He would suck the life out of them and leave only a hot, sweaty, stinking shell."

"So he had to go."

"Of course he had to go."

"And you needed to kill him."

"You stupid bitch! Will you fucking listen to me? I've never killed anyone in my life. I'm not going to talk to you anymore. So there! Happy now?" She pouted like a child.

"You never killed anyone? Not even your little dog?"

"Who told you about that!!!" Béatrice yelled, attempting to rise from the chair. "It's *so* not true."

"A man who lives under a bridge told me about it."

"What? What man? You're making this up. That's bull-shit. No one knows about Ratafia. No one at all! And it wasn't even me. He fell into the barbecue all by himself. It was an accident. And anyway he deserved it. He never stopped yapping all day long."

"Are you telling me you put your puppy on the barbe-cue?"

"Not at all. Why would you think that? I've never even had a puppy. You know, for a supposedly hot *flic*, you have a very hard time understanding people."

"Tell me about Gautier du Fesnay."

"Gautier? Another one from the evil empire. He had taste but he was vicious. Another wicked judge."

"And he had to die because he judged?"

Béatrice stared at the floor as if she had not heard.

"You had to kill him?"

Béatrice looked unblinkingly into Capucine's eyes as if she had been woken in the middle of the night and was trying to understand where she was.

"I've never killed anyone, ever," she said with chilling sincerity.

After an hour Capucine gave up. She had gone around the track three more times and had got absolutely nowhere. She left the interrogation room with the orders that Béatrice was not to be questioned. She trudged up the famous staircase A to the third floor and went to the conference room. Tallon sat as erect as if on parade reading *Le Monde*. When Capucine walked in, he raised an index finger instructing her to remain silent. After a long wait, he closed the tabloid-size newspaper, smoothed it flat with the palm of his hand, folded it in half, pushed it away on the table.

"Your husband has quite a way with words. He's very amusing. I never go to the places he writes about, but I love his reviews. Was he shaken up by the events this evening?"

"Shaken up? When last seen he was getting sloshed in our infirmary with one of my *brigadiers* and threatening to spend the rest of the night at the Pied de Cochon. I gave instructions to the uniforms who were going to drive him that they were to take him home, even if they had to use force."

"Too bad. I would gladly have joined them. I know it's not the done thing to eat onion soup in the middle of the summer, but I would have made an exception. How did you make out with Mademoiselle Renaud?"

"She's a smart cookie. She's playing a role to set herself up for a plea of insanity and enjoying herself immensely. She talks openly about the murders and why it was oh so necessary for the victims to die, but denies ever having killed anyone. She has a talent for acting."

"So we have a difficult choice, don't we?"

"Yes, sir, we do."

"Sit down. Let's talk. You first."

"Yes, sir." Capucine paused. "This is the first time on this case that I'd have valued the advice of a competent *juge d'instruction.*" She laughed.

"We have two choices," Capucine said. "We apprehended Renaud attempting a homicide. We could take her to the *tribunal correctionnel* and the judge would automatically convict her and she'd begin her sentence immediately. There would be no possibility of appeal. The problem with that is that since no one died in the attempt, she'd get ten years at the outside and be out on parole on in six or less."

Tallon scratched his chin and searched in vain for a window to stare through. "My guess would be an eight-year sentence, with her out on parole in four years. Go on."

"The other thing we could do is prepare a case for all the murders to take to the *cour d'assises.* We have a fair amount of evidence. Some of it very damning."

Tallon frowned.

"The problem, of course, is that Renaud's father would pull out all the stops in hiring a legal team. Even if she's convicted the first time, they would definitely appeal."

"But she'd be in the clink."

"She could be out in a year if we went that route."

"*Commissaire,* you're not thinking like a *flic.*"

"A confession? Please. Of course, you could go down there and whack her into submission and she'd sign anything you wanted. But she'd repudiate it in court and start yelling about police brutality. She'd probably get off scot-free. And can you imagine the press we'd get with her father's money behind it?"

Tallon scowled at her and tapped the table with his middle finger.

"So?"

"So? I just don't know."

They discussed pens, night-vision glasses, turkey trussing needles, and DNA until the small hours of the morning, as Béatrice remained taped to her chair below the level of the Seine. In the end, taking the risk, *faute de mieux*, Tallon remanded Béatrice to La Santé prison, where she would wait until she was transported in a dark cage in a police van to spend her day being scrutinized by a row of men in long black robes with flowing white bibs, to return to La Santé, if the gods of justice were so disposed, to spend the rest of her life behind dark gray walls.

Leaving the Quai, Capucine had a clear vision of Béatrice enclosed in her glass dock, listening to witnesses accusing her from the podium facing the semicircular bench, recoiling from the forbidding, evaluating scowls of the judges. It would be the embodiment of her worst nightmare. Capucine rejoiced at the thought of Béatrice's suffering and hated herself for her pleasure.

CHAPTER 41

Capucine didn't get home until after three. Alexandre was flat on his back on their bed. He snored deeply, rattling from the base of his throat, emitting an almost visible miasma of morning-after beer at each eructation. Nevertheless, Capucine experienced the flood of love she always felt when she saw him asleep. And with the rush came the guilt. There was no getting around it. She had pitted the entirety of what she loved most in life against a single arrest. It was merely one among scores of arrests that were certain to happen in coming years. What kind of person would do that to her husband? What was that telling her about her marriage? What did that tell her about her life?

She walked down the long hall to the guest bedroom. No Momo. She hadn't really expected he would stay the night. Aimlessly, she walked back up the hall and wandered into the living room, far too keyed up to even think of sleep. She poured herself a double measure of vodka and took it into the kitchen, opened the freezer door, and twisted a pink rubber ice-cube tray, hoping to extract two cubes while leaving the others in place. The ice shattered with a noise like a short string of Chinese firecrackers. She stood stock still for a moment listening intently to see if she had woken Alexandre. Silence. She dumped three cubes into the glass and rooted through the lower compartment of the refrigerator for a lemon. She found one, squeezed it in her hand to loosen the juice, and then tossed it back irritably. This was no time for niceties.

She dug into her trousers for her cell phone and pressed in Isabelle's speed dial. Despite the hour Isabelle seemed wide awake. Capucine could hear the murmur of a television in the background.

They spoke for twenty minutes, during which Capucine poured herself another vodka.

"And so how do we know when to make the arrest?"

"I'll be there with you by then."

"What if you're late?"

Capucine snorted a laugh. "That's the one thing you don't have to worry about. Get some sleep. We have a big day tomorrow."

When she hung up, Capucine's exhaustion fell on her all at once like an impossibly heavy coat of chain mail. Making it to the bedroom was an accomplishment. She shrugged off her clothes, leaving them in a pile by the bed, slid under the sheet, and—oblivious to his snores and the stench of beer—pulled Alexandre's outstretched arm over her as if it were an expiating blanket, capable on its own of granting absolution.

It seemed like her cell phone started buzzing the minute her head hit the pillow. She leaned over the side of the bed and groped through the pile of clothes searching for her tan twill trousers. Inexplicably, the yellow light of an advanced morning was visible around the edges of the blind. She extracted the phone from the pocket of her trousers, glanced at the screen, and was astonished that it was noon. The caller was marked "private." She pushed the green TALK button and was greeted with the near-hysterical voice of Martinière.

"Yet another outrage, *Commissaire*. This time I'm definitely going to have to take disciplinary action."

Capucine sighed audibly and contemplated hanging up. There was a long pause.

"*Allô, Commissaire*. Were you asleep? It's after twelve. Are you derelict in your duty as well as insubordinate?"

"All right, *monsieur le juge*, what's the problem this morning?" Capucine sat up, her bare legs dangling over the side of the bed. She made patterns in the rug with her big toes. She bent over and examined her feet closely. No matter what happened, she was going to have a pedicure on Saturday.

"Morning? It's hardly the morning. And the problem? I think it goes far beyond being a mere problem. I just finished reading the magistrates' morning circular, and I see that you have arrested a suspect and remanded her for trial. If I understand the situation, there was the opportunity to have her convicted on the spot *in flagrante delicto* but you—without consulting me—have chosen a full court prosecution for three murders."

"That's exactly right, *monsieur le juge*."

"It is my role to determine judicial procedure, not the police's. As it happens, you did make the correct choice. An on-the-spot delicto conviction would have been a mistake."

Capucine sighed and wrote Alexandre's name in the carpet with her big toe. How could anyone be so long-winded?

"The most serious offense is that I see that Contrôleur Général Tallon has requested a mandate of arrest for someone he seems to believe is the suspected perpetrator of one of the restaurant murders."

"That is also correct."

"That arrest simply must not happen. I will not allow it."

Capucine was amazed. She would never understand the man.

"Why ever not? We arrest guilty people. That's our job."

"Think about it, *Commissaire*. What happens if this person confesses to having committed more than one of the murders?"

"*Monsieur le juge,* I'm just not following you here."

"Don't you see, in that case Béatrice Renaud would no longer be a serial killer? She needs to have committed three murders to be deemed a serial killer."

Without putting on any clothes, Capucine had walked into the kitchen and started making coffee on the Pasquini. She stifled her laughter.

"I think I understand. If she's not officially a serial killer, you couldn't claim you'd apprehended the first serial killer arrested in France in decades."

"Exactly. Do you understand now?"

Her coffee made, Capucine poured some milk into a small metal jug.

"You and the contrôleur général have been precipitate. You made your arrest far too soon. If you'd waited, Renaud would have killed two or three more people. Since you went off half-cocked, it's imperative you don't further jeopardize the situation by making this other arrest. In any event the matter is closed. I've rescinded your arrest warrant and you will be sanctioned if you proceed. Is that clear?"

"Perfectly." Capucine laughed as she fitted the little jug under the steam jet and turned it on. A violent burst of steam blew through the milk, frothing it. She knew an empty threat when she heard one.

"What is that irritating noise?"

"Probably something in the street, *monsieur le juge.* There's no need to be alarmed. The arrest is not planned until next week at the earliest. Why don't I ask monsieur le contrôleur général to give you a call later today? I'm sure he will be very interested in hearing your position." Capucine poured the foaming milk into her coffee, rooted through a small bowl of irregularly shaped Le Perroquet lumps of cane sugar, found one of exactly the right size, dropped it in her coffee. "Will that do, *monsieur le juge?*"

"It will have to, won't it?" Martinière said bitterly and hung up.

Capucine was no more than halfway through her café au lait when her cell phone buzzed again. It was Isabelle with the tight-throated voice, that invariably indicated imminent action.

"I've got them. They've just settled in at the Alsatian restaurant at the end of the Ile Saint-Louis. You know, the one that looks out over the *passerelle* that goes over to the Ile de la Cité."

"Are they having lunch or just a drink?"

"Lunch. They're drinking champagne right now but they're looking at menus. I'm on the rue Jean du Bellay behind a postcard stand in front of a bookstore."

"Good. There's a café across the street from you. Walk up the block, come down on the other side of the street and slip in. If you stand at the bar, you should see them through the window and they won't see you. Get David on his cell phone and tell him to walk down the quai d'Orléans and go into the restaurant at the end. He can say he's waiting for someone. He'll have a perfect view from there. I'll be with you guys in twenty minutes. Don't do anything until I get there."

She got Momo on his cell phone.

"Where are you?"

"At my desk at the brigade, *Commissaire*. I'm on duty today."

"How're you feeling?"

"Fine. I took Monsieur de Huguelet upstairs and the squad car took me to my place. I had a couple of Calvas and went to bed. I was here at eight, no problem."

"Alexandre doesn't have your fortitude. He's still asleep. Anyhow, we need to get going. They're sitting down to lunch. Get one of the squad cars and three uniforms. No automatic weapons. Go to the Ile Saint-Louis. Corner of the rue le Regrattier and the quai de Bourbon. Wait for me there. Do it fast. I need you now."

"Don't worry. I'll drive the car myself."

Fifteen minutes later Capucine pulled up behind the double-parked squad car on the rue Regrattier. The two cars blocked traffic on the street but that was no real inconvenience to the citizenry since the only cars that ever came down the street were delusionally in search of a parking space, something well known not to exist on the Ile Saint-Louis.

Capucine told the three officers they were to wait until called. They nodded, expecting nothing less: waiting was the lot of a police officer. Capucine walked down the quai de Bourbon with Momo and explained the situation. They walked past the rue Jean du Bellay and continued on to the little square at the very stern of the island. There they stopped and Capucine called to give Isabelle and David their instructions.

Capucine rounded the point of the island and walked up the quai on the other side, Momo trailing twenty feet behind.

As she emerged into the little square it was a Paris scene straight from a travel brochure. Tourists cruised boisterously from shop to shop or ogled jugglers and jazz bands on the wide pedestrian bridge. The Seine flowed its stately flow, winking reflections from the sun as huge barges passed, their engines vibrating deep, slow rhythms.

On the terrace of the Ile Saint-Louis' venerable Alsatian restaurant, Sybille and Guy Voisin luxuriated in the sun, surveying the scene and drinking champagne. Voisin placed a proprietary hand on Sybille's thigh as he finished a story. Both of them laughed in bubbly good spirits.

Voisin caught sight of Capucine and stood up.

"*Commissaire,* come have a drink," he said, loudly

enough to be heard twenty feet away. "We're celebrating. Sybille has just signed a fabulous new movie."

Sybille beckoned Capucine enthusiastically.

The juxtaposition of *"commissaire"* and "new movie" was a tonic for both the terrace and the crowd on the bridge, who peered, goggled, gossiped, identified Sybille, and edged closer while trying hard to appear uninterested.

Seeing Capucine advance toward their table, Voisin beamed. But after she took a few steps toward him, his smile evaporated and his eyes darted sharply right and left, a threatened rodent. Capucine had no idea if he'd caught sight of David or Isabelle, but he definitely knew something wasn't right. He jumped out of his chair and ran for the bridge.

As Capucine wheeled to follow she broke a heel, twisting her ankle, nearly falling. She cursed Italian shoemakers. Voisin was already on the bridge, with Momo fifteen feet behind. From the corner of her eye she saw Isabelle and David sprinting from their hiding spots. Capucine took off her shoes and broke into a run.

Momo gained steadily on Voisin. When Voisin reached the middle of the span, he turned, his face contorted in a snarl, produced a pistol, fired once in the air.

Momo continued on without breaking stride.

Isabelle appeared at Capucine's side. "Do I drop him?"

"No. Let it play out. There are too many people on the bridge."

As Momo closed in on Voisin, his eyes widened. He leveled the gun at Momo, taking careful aim. Momo ran on relentlessly. Voisin appeared to lose his nerve, pocketed his pistol, vaulted over the metal railing.

Momo reached the railing a split second after Voisin's leap and clambered over after him. Capucine, Isabelle, and David arrived in the next instant.

As they peered down, the stern of a barge was just disappearing under the bridge, its motor drumming loudly beneath the arch. They ran to the opposite railing. Two shots clanged hollowly, resonating in the steel structure of the bridge.

The bow of the barge emerged almost immediately. Voisin sat drooping in the forward end of the sand-filled cargo hold, a tired child waiting for his mother in the park's sandbox. His right hand clutched his left shoulder. A red stain spread on his suit jacket. Twenty seconds later Momo appeared at the aft end of the hold, kneeling on his left leg in the sand. As he passed under them he struggled to rise and fell back, genuflecting like a worshiper in church bending the wrong knee.

Even though there didn't seem to be any blood, Capucine had the impression Momo had been shot. She flipped open her cell phone and gave a rapid series of orders.

As she spoke into the phone Sybille came up and watched the barge labor its way upriver. When Capucine ended the call, Sybille said, "What an absolutely great exit. And just in time too. That relationship was getting seriously old."

The barge was halfway to the next bridge. A large dark blue police launch sped downstream, its siren wailing the police *pan-pom-pan-pom*, its blue light flashing officiously. The launch slowed as it reached the raised wheelhouse at the barge's stern. The police pilot said something over his loudspeaker that broke up in the breeze before reaching the detectives. The water boiled at the stern of the barge. The captain had thrown his engine in reverse. Undaunted by the interference of her skipper, the barge continued its stately progress upstream. Elegantly, the launch pivoted, advanced to the point where Voisin sat, made fast with boat hooks, and three uniformed officers boarded the barge.

They heard the deep unmuffled growl of large-displacement outboards.

"That's my ride," Capucine said, breaking into a run.

Isabelle followed. "Where are you going?"

"I'm going to get on the launch, arrest Voisin, and have them both taken to the Hôtel-Dieu. You two go to the Quai and I'll meet you there."

A large black rubber Zodiac with two enormous outboard engines and a small lectern-like wheelhouse amidships had nosed up to a stone ramp that led down to the river from the quai of the Ile Saint-Louis. In previous centuries the ramp must have had a commercial use, but now it served only for summer tanning.

Happy to be wearing no shoes, Capucine waded down the ramp into the water and hoisted herself over the fat round tube of the boat's side. A uniformed officer made a move to help her, thought better of it, and saluted once she got on her feet.

No sooner was she upright when the skipper shouted, "*On y va,*" and all the officers except the one at the wheel sat down on the wooden deck, backs to the rubber gunwales. The boat jolted off the ramp violently with a roar of the outboards. The skipper reversed the engines and pressed the two throttles full forward, a Paris policeman showing off for the *Police Judiciaire.* The result was impressive. The boat exploded out of the water and was slammed down again as the skipper trimmed in the outboards. In seconds they were moving faster than the cars on the *voie sur berge.*

Almost instantaneously they reached the launch. Capucine was helped aboard. She gave her instruction to the skipper and went below to see Momo and Voisin.

The launch turned and headed back downstream toward the Hôtel-Dieu. When it came up to the bridge Capucine emerged on deck to signal Isabelle and David that Momo was not seriously hurt: a badly twisted ankle at worst.

The railing of the bridge was thick with people. The tourists had had an epic afternoon. Movie stars, gunshots, French police running right and left, officers on Police boats boarding barges. The works. Isabelle and David were at the rail with Sybille still at their side. Capucine gave them a double thumbs-up sign. Just as the launch reached the bridge, Capucine yelled at Isabelle, "See if you can find my shoes."

Sybille yelled back, "Those fabulous Zanottis you had on, *Commissaire?* I'm going after them right now. Don't worry."

The skipper of the launch darted a sideward glance at his second in command, his thought transparent: shore-based flics were bad enough, but when it came to the *PJ* there was just no understanding them.

CHAPTER 42

At eight o'clock the next morning Capucine walked down the now familiar hallway toward the police infirmary at the Hôpital Hôtel-Dieu. The same nurse she had seen the last time sat at the reception desk, reading just as voraciously. At her approach he stood up and saluted, his finger marking his page with his left hand, Jean-Patrick Manchette's *La Position du Tireur Couché—The Prone Gunman*. Given his penchant for dark noir mysteries, Capucine wondered if he was languishing the way she once had, champing to get into the gritty side of the force.

"Bonjour, *Commissaire*," he said with a polite smile of recognition. "Your prisoner is in the room all the way at the end. The doctor's already been in to see him this morning."

"And?"

"He's stable. No sign of infection. There was a good bit of damage to the muscle. At his age it will take some time to heal and he'll probably loose strength and flexibility in that area. If he were ten years younger he could go home now. But the doctor wants him here for a day or two just to be on the safe side. Anyway, he's on a morphine drip.

He'd be in a lot of pain without it. These wounds are still very painful the day after."

"I need to interrogate him. It would be better if he isn't lying in bed."

"I can have the staff meal room put off-limits for as long as you need it. Will that do, *Commissaire?*"

"Perfectly. And I'd like him off the morphine during the interrogation."

The previous afternoon both Voisin and Momo had been rushed into the hospital's emergency room. Momo had been x-rayed, been diagnosed with a severe ankle sprain, been bandaged, been issued a pair of crutches, been handed a prescription for two weeks' recuperative leave, been given a small envelope filled with painkilling pills, and had finally been delivered to his apartment by a squad car. Voisin's wound was deemed minor. The bullet had traversed the right deltoid muscle without hitting a bone. The wound was cleaned, a single staple had been applied to the entry side and two to the exit, an I/V had been placed in the back of his left hand through which he had received plasma, morphine, and two antibiotics. Since there was clearly no shock reaction, he was sent to the police infirmary section of the hospital where he had spent a peaceful night under guard and under sedation.

Turning the corner toward Voisin's room, Capucine found Isabelle and David bickering in whispers on a wooden bench. After the inevitable handshake for David and air kiss for Isabelle she continued on with the two *brigadiers* in tow. Momo stood in front of Voisin's door, leaning on his crutches, looming over a uniformed officer sitting on a chair, the two chatting quietly.

"Momo, what are you doing here?" Capucine asked. "You're supposed to be on convalescent leave."

"*Commissaire,* I'm here for the interrogation. Wad'ya think? After I pop my ankle jumping off a bridge to catch this fucker, I'm going to stay at home two weeks, watching cooking shows on TV?"

"You're sure you're up for this Momo?" Capucine asked.

"No problem. I threw away those pills they gave me and had a couple of Calvas instead. I feel fine."

In his room, Voisin sat up in bed, to all appearances quite content, eating his breakfast, standard hospital fare of plastic containers of unflavored yogurt and reconstituted orange juice rounded off with an industrial croissant and translucently thin coffee. It looked like a normal hospital scene until one noticed that Voisin's ankles were shackled and the stainless-steel chain ran through the metal bars at the foot of the bed.

Voisin greeted Capucine enthusiastically. "Commissaire, you're an early riser. Good for you! That's the secret for a long and successful life."

"Voisin, I hope you've had enough breakfast. We're going to take you to another room and have a little chat."

Voisin smarted from the change in tone: the "Monsieur" before his name had disappeared and the *vous* had been replaced by the disdainful *tu*, well known in the movies as the standard police address for lowlifes and criminals.

"In that case, I'll need my lawyer present," he said with only partial success at bravado.

Isabelle and David arrived with two uniformed officers and the nurse. Momo stood in the doorway glowering menacingly, imposing on his crutches. The nurse removed Voisin's I/V. One of the uniformed officers pushed a wheelchair up to the bed. The other unlocked one of the shackles, freed the chain from the foot of the bed and reattached it to Voisin's ankle.

As Voisin was helped into the wheelchair, Capucine said, "No lawyer. You were arrested in *flagrant délit* for *refus d'obtempérer*—resisting arrest—and the attempted assassination of a *Police Judiciaire* officer with a firearm. We have up to twenty-four hours to take you to a magistrate, who would convict you on the spot. You would start your sentence immediately. I'm sure you know how people who try to kill police officers are treated in prison. You go to the movies like everyone else."

Voisin paled, either from the thought of prison or from the effort of standing up to get to the wheelchair, possibly both.

"But," Capucine said, "we're not going to worry about those little bagatelles, are we? We're going to talk about other things. I'd like to try to understand your point of view and see if I can help you out. Over the course of the investigation I found you to be very sympathetic. Really very sympathetic. I want to give you every chance I can."

Capucine favored him with her most brilliant smile but persisted with the *tu*. As she expected, he was utterly confused.

The uniformed officer wheeled him down the hallway into the lunchroom. Capucine issued instructions to have the furniture rearranged into a modern interrogation room layout. The central table was pushed to one side and David and Isabelle were seated behind it, symbolically distancing them from the upcoming dialogue. Momo was given a chair in the far corner behind Voisin, whose wheelchair was placed in the exact center of the room. Capucine moved a hard-backed chair to a forty-five-degree angle next to Voisin's and sat facing him, their knees less than two feet apart. The *mise-en-scène* was perfect. The only thing that was missing was the dummy two-way mirror, but you never could have everything you wanted.

Without preamble, Capucine said, "I want to talk to you about Gautier du Fesnay."

"Gautier du Fesnay. Gautier du Fesnay. Rings a little bell. Hang on. Wait. Got it. That poor guy who was killed in that restaurant. Chez Béatrice. Right? What about him?"

"Voisin. If you didn't have this little flesh wound you'd be in one of the interrogation rooms at the Quai, which I don't think you'd find so congenial. After a comment like that, your head would be on the table and blood would be trickling out of your ears because someone would have just hit you very hard on the head with a phone book. Being a smart-ass just doesn't go down in these sessions. *Tu* understand that, I'm sure. Keep this up and I'll have you taken across the parvis, wound or no wound."

Voisin became even paler.

"Now, about Gautier du Fesnay . . ."

"Well, as a matter of fact, he's from Aubagne, the town I was born in, in the Midi. We were at the *école primaire* and the lycée together. That was the last I saw of him. We went our separate ways when we enrolled in our universities. Of course, I read his stuff in the papers. I even used to look at those little film clips of his on the Internet. Who didn't?"

Capucine said nothing. She felt as if she had been doused with a bucketful of ice-cold water. Her initial reports had listed all the birthplaces of the principal players. Fesnay hadn't actually been born in Aubagne but in the same *département*. She hadn't checked more closely because at that point Voisin had seemed no more than an inoffensively comic geriatric sugar daddy who wouldn't harm a fly. This was going to be a lesson to her. A lesson she would never forget. As she brooded, she continued to say nothing.

The pause was no longer than thirty seconds but it seemed infinite. Voisin began to breathe through his mouth and a shine of perspiration appeared on his brow. The morphine was wearing off. His eyes had lost the edge of their focus. The pain had returned.

Capucine edged her chair closer to Voisin, her knee only inches away from his. She reached out and tapped his thigh with her fingertips. His eyes rotated to hers.

"Voisin, I'd like to get you back to your bed and hooked up to your I/V as quickly as I can. I really would. But you're not helping me. You just told me a fib, didn't you?" She spoke as if to a child.

"A fib?"

"Yes. Do you remember when my husband and I ran into you at the Salon du Bordeaux?"

"I think I remember. Maybe not."

"You'd met one of your friends, whom you had taken to Taillevent along with a critic called Druand and Gautier du Fesnay. Does it come back to you now?"

"Oh, that," Voisin said with a little laugh that sounded doubly hollow because of his dry throat. "That was when we were at university together. I think we splurged and had a superb meal at Taillevent. That must have been what he was talking about."

"Voisin, this is just not working, is it? Your friend quite clearly stated that it had been six years before. You're lying and you're taking me for a fool. You've had your chance." Capucine stood up.

"Momo," she said sharply.

Momo swung in from his far corner behind Voisin with long muscular sweeps on his crutches.

"Momo, sit here and take over the questioning. I'm going to take the *brigadiers* out for a coffee. I'm sick of this clown. With no witnesses, I'm sure you can get something out of him before we get back."

She stood up.

"Wait a minute! Just calm down, *Commissaire.*" Voisin looked wildly around the room, desperately wishing himself out of there. The pain had taken five minutes to get him to a level of anxiety that would have required over an hour with verbal techniques. There might be something to these enhanced interviews after all.

She sat down again. Momo swung himself back to his

invisible corner. Now, on top of everything else, Voisin would be fearing the unexpected blow from behind. Beads of sweat formed on his brow.

"Look, *Commissaire,* that guy was right. I *did* have lunch with Fesnay and a bunch of other people at Taillevent. We had just introduced our second wine and I was doing a bit of public relations. That happens all the time. Ask your husband. No need to get shirty about it."

"If it was a routine PR event, why lie about it?"

"Lie? I'm not lying about anything. Look at it from my point of view, *Commissaire.* I go to some restaurant with my girlfriend. Someone gets murdered. Someone I knew vaguely years before. What do you think I'd do? Stand up, waving my hand and saying, 'Over here, Officer. I knew the murdered man. Why don't you take me in for questioning?' Nobody knows anything when the police start asking questions. You know that, *Commissaire.*"

"The stories always come out after a while. But not from you, Voisin. I want to know why."

"*Commissaire,* I told you. I clammed up when your people were asking questions the night of the murder and I wasn't going to admit it when we talked later. After all, it was hardly important. I knew the man from our lycée days and we'd had lunch six years before he was killed. So what? I mean, really."

Voisin was finding the logic of his story convincing. Not something he should be doing. She stood up.

"Momo, keep this lying creep company. We're going for coffee."

Momo swung up at speed, dropped heavily into Capucine's chair, and glowered at Voisin. Momo even glowered when he was trying to be friendly. When he didn't like someone—and he was embarrassed about his ankle—he could be terrifying.

Fifteen minutes later the three detectives returned, laughing happily over the tail end of a story. Capucine carried a thick white porcelain demitasse with the saucer on top to keep the coffee hot. She handed it to Momo.

"I put in three sugars," she said with a smile. The act was designed to show how excluded the interviewee was from the group solidarity of the police. It was wasted on Voisin. His anxiety level had reached a new peak. Capucine knew Momo hadn't said a word and had just stared at Voisin, who must have sat trembling, cowering from a blow that never came.

When everyone was back in his seat, Voisin's anxiety level dropped half a notch.

"Look, *Commissaire*. Let me tell you how it was."

Capucine looked at him stone-faced and said nothing.

"I think you know that when we introduced our second wine, the quality was not as good as it is now. A number of highly critical articles appeared. I needed an ally in the press. When we were children I had been quite close to Gautier, but we really did drift apart when we went off to university. I thought that if I could rekindle our friendship, he would be sympathetic to me. Gautier was already quite famous. He could have done a great deal to bolster the new wine."

"I'm beginning to understand, Guy. This is all about saving the château, isn't it?"

Voisin paused. "Well, that's one way of looking at it, I guess."

"Why was it necessary to kill him?"

"I didn't kill him," Voisin said, but in a voice so timid it sounded like he was trying to convince himself.

"Something happened six years ago that threatened the château, didn't it? I need you to tell me what it was. I know you did what you did to protect the château, but I need to know the details."

Voisin looked confused. He smoothed his hair with his left hand, grimacing in pain as he stretched to reach the right side. He glanced at the door. He shot a look at David and then Isabelle behind the table.

"I made my mistake by trying too hard and being too honest. I invited Gautier to the château for lunch and a complete tour of the brand-new *chai* I had built for the vinification of the new wine. Over lunch we got along quite well, just like old times. But when we toured the *chai* he got aggressive and insisted on sticking his nose into everything and chatting with the workers on his own. It was impossible to stop him without making an unpleasant scene, which was the last thing I wanted. I'm not exactly sure how he did it, but he discovered our little secret."

"Your secret? And exactly what was that?"

Voisin started to shrug his shoulders and winced at the pain. "I was making wine using a viticultural technique that happened to be illegal in France in those days but under current regulations is now perfectly legitimate. I produced a high-yield white wine and brought in some cheap red from one of our neighbors and mixed the two to make rosé." Voisin smirked and shook his head in pleasure at his cleverness. "It's done all over the world. It's not as good as traditional rosé, but it's quite drinkable and extremely cheap to produce. Even the government finally had to admit that it's a viable method."

"And Fesnay threatened to write about what you were doing?"

"Did he ever! And with what he'd found out he had the power to destroy the château."

"So you paid him off."

"He blackmailed me. Not the same thing at all."

"But you kept on making your rosé by mixing red and white."

"What else was I going to do? It was selling well and we desperately needed the money."

"And when your son came to work at the château he also discovered what you were up to?"

"He was supposed to be in charge of marketing but he got interested in the production side as well. He found out how we were making the rosé almost immediately."

"And he was furious. Furious enough to take it to the family board and have you kicked out. And then he started making the second label the way rosé is supposed to be made."

"Exactly."

"So why was Fesnay still a threat?"

"You don't understand the wine business. The fact that we *had* done it was more than enough to demolish the château's reputation. And on top of it all, the way Fesnay would have written about it, I would have come across as the sleazy laughingstock of the industry."

"But that wasn't the important part, was it? You killed him to save the château, didn't you? It's important for us to make that point clear."

"Would"—Voisin hesitated—"that reduce my sentence?"

"Magistrates are human, too."

"You see, he never stopped blackmailing me. In fact, when my son took over, he even increased his demands."

"That must have been difficult for you with your reduced salary."

"Difficult? I was paying him half of what I earned. Half!" Voisin paused. "But you're right. I did it for the château, not for me. I'm counting on you to tell them that. The château is my life."

"How did you kill him?"

"I got lucky. You see, part of Gautier's routine was that we'd meet for lunch and act like we were the best of friends when I gave him his money. Getting money wasn't enough for him. He had to watch me squirm as well. At our last lunch he went on and on about Chez Béatrice. He was reviewing it and was going to give it a fabulous write-up. He even told me the date of his last dinner there before he wrote his piece.

"I had an air pistol at the château I'd use on rats. I've loved shooting the little beggars ever since I was a kid. Got quite good at it, too." Voisin mimed shooting with his index and thumb, smiling nostalgically at a life he knew he would never see again.

"So the next time I went to the château I put the gun in the glove compartment of my car and brought it to Paris. Of course, I wasn't at all sure you could kill a man with an air gun. So when those kids started horsing around at that Brazilian reception I knew it was a gift straight from heaven. I saw them pinch the curare-tipped darts out of the display case and shoot them into the president's portrait along with all the others. When the kids got bored and wandered off I pulled the curare darts out of the picture, broke them in half, and put them in my pocket.

I used my pocketknife to deepen the hole in the front of one of the air gun's pellets, scraped some curare from a dart, and packed it in. Turns out it's damned effective stuff."

"How did you shoot him?"

"It was right out of a James Cagney movie. I cut a little hole in my suit jacket pocket, stuck the air gun in, and shot him in the neck as I walked by. Nobody noticed a thing."

"Weren't you afraid Sybille would see the hole?"

"Sybille?" He shook his head in amazement. "Sybille's only interested in clothes *she* can wear. Anyway, the next day I took the coat to the woman at my dry cleaner's who does reweaving. It was like new after she fixed it."

He paused, pleased with himself after he had told his story. "You have to admit that it was an effective way to kill someone."

"That it was. You had me fooled for quite a while."

CHAPTER 43

Alexandre woke with a start, threw his arm over Capucine's torso, and pulled her close. Capucine tensed. In a few seconds his arm went limp; he had fallen back asleep. Capucine gently slid out of bed and slipped into her silk robe, knotting it tightly.

In the kitchen she dealt with the wiles of the Pasquini, hoping the coffee would remove the bile of guilt from her throat. Alexandre materialized, hugging her from behind and nuzzling her hair.

"What's got into you this morning? You never budge before ten," Capucine asked.

"You escaped. That's what happened," he said, fumbling at the silk cord that held her robe shut.

"We don't have time, *chéri*. Remember, today's the day *I'm* taking *you* to lunch for a change, and we absolutely can't be even a minute late. That would spoil everything."

Alexandre pouted. Something she had never seen him do other than ironically.

As they felt their way down the steep stone steps by the Pont Marie, Jacques chatted easily with Vavasseur, flutes of champagne in hand.

The second Vavasseur caught sight of Alexandre, he retreated to the farthest corner of his stall.

"Just stand here immobile," Capucine whispered in Alexandre's ear. "Let him get used to the sight of you. Pretend he's a scared colt whose confidence you're going to have to gain."

"I forgot my sugar cubes in my other jacket. Could you lend me some?" Alexandre whispered back.

"Docteur," Jacques said fulsomely. "This is Alexandre de Huguelet, Capucine's husband. He's a restaurant critic, a highly poached endangered species. I think you're scaring him."

"The poaching is over, and I doubt the endangerment is defining," Vavasseur said. He was gaining confidence, but he wasn't about to move out of his cubicle.

Jacques went to the riverbank and pulled in a cord, surfacing a squat dark bottle of champagne. He poured out flutes for the two of them and held the bottle up for Alexandre's approval.

"Krug Clos d'Ambonnay nineteen ninety-five," Alexandre said, pursing his lips appreciatively. "I should have lunch here more often."

"You're welcome anytime," Vavasseur said, moving to a position at the edge of his stall but still clearly outside the periphery of the group. "The setting is at its best in the winter, but that's a bit of an acquired taste."

Gradually, with the help of the Krug, they eased into the airy chatter of patrons of a luxury restaurant sipping aperitifs in the garden, letting their appetites blossom before going in to lunch, but Vavasseur continued to remain slightly at arm's length. The usual riverbank dramatis personae came and went, culminating with the perfectly configured Labrador and his owner, who waved cheerfully.

After the third flute of champagne Jacques announced he was starving. "Let's see what they gave us today." There were not one, but two olive drab metal containers as well as a wicker hamper. Jacques opened them all and inserted his nose, sniffing audibly. He then fished out the usual cream-colored menu card and read, proclaiming as if on-stage at the Comédie-Française.

"Voilà. To begin with, it would appear we have a choice. We are offered *cuisses de grenouilles meunières, fine écrasée de racine de persil, sphères fondantes d'ail doux—* frogs' legs meunière with crushed parsley root and melting spheres of sweet garlic. I thought only tourists ate frogs' legs but these do smell delicious." He fanned the aroma toward his nose with an open hand, mocking a gesture dear to Alexandre and most chefs.

"Or," Jacques continued, "we can have an *émincé de coquilles Saint-Jacques sur une betterave jaune assaison-née de caviar, huître en fine gelée de carotte—*scallops on a bed of yellow beetroot seasoned with caviar and oysters in a carrot jelly. You know, indecisive as I am, I'm tempted to have a soupçon of both."

Vavasseur eased cautiously into the perimeter of the group and peered, transfixed, into the two canisters. Food was definitely his opiate.

Jacques continued his reading. "And for the main course, we have a choice of *homard bleu rôti dans sa cara-pace, mitonnée de fruits secs et pomme Granny-Smith—*blue lobster roasted in its shell with a sauce of dried fruits and Granny Smith apples. Or *ris de veau cuit au sautoir, ragoût de légumes oubliés, cappelletti, perles de persil—*sweetbreads with cappelletti, parsley pearls, and a ragout of 'forgotten vegetables.' I love that phrase, sounds like a girl I used to know at the lycée. No, not you, *chère cou-sine,* so stop pouting." His braying cackle echoed under the arch of the bridge.

The festive mood had been created. They arranged the luncheon table using Vavasseur's nightstand, his chair, and another borrowed from the next stall over. Capucine and

Vavasseur sat on the bed, Alexandre and Jacques on the chairs.

They decided to stage a tasting menu and eat all four of the dishes. Jacques delegated the honors of the wine to Alexandre who, ecstatically, discovered three bottles of a 2005 Laville Haut-Brion, at precisely the right temperature in quilted-foil sleeves.

They started with the scallops and moved on to the frogs' legs, which proved to be extremely delicate with the merest hint of sweet garlic and herbs, bearing not the slightest resemblance to the greasy fried horrors reeking of garlic usually served to foreigners.

Elegantly sucking the bones of a frog's leg, Jacques considered Capucine through his eyelashes with his mocking, knowing smile.

"*Cousine*," he said, "the entire purpose of this lunch was for you and Docteur Vavasseur to reveal your legerdemain to the uninitiated. I'm not sure who's the prestidigitator and who's the assistant but you're both going to have to sing for your suppers."

Vavasseur recoiled in alarm.

"I understood I was to be fed twice a day, no matter what. I didn't know there were conditions."

"Of course there aren't. Definitely not! Your meals are as assured as the rising and setting of the sun. That was just an ill-chosen turn of phrase. I'm just keen to find out how you two figured out who the murderers were."

Vavasseur threw up his hands in mock surrender. "All I did was make a few observations. I'm quite sure I learned much more from *Commissaire* Le Tellier than she did from me."

"No, no, Docteur, without you—"

"Let's not have a scrimmage of *politesses, cousine*. I want to know how you knew it was that dykie girl, Béatrice Whatsherface?"

Capucine scowled at Jacques' double-barreled rudeness. A few traces of affection for Béatrice still lingered.

"As it happened, the *juge d'instruction* was quite right. The key to the case *was* profiling. But it took a good bit of flat-footed *flic* work, too.

"Docteur Vavasseur explained that the big Other, the force that prevents the patient from reaching his Mirror Image and attaining his fulfillment, is an authority figure, most often the father, but not necessarily. So it was clear that some sort of conflict with authority was the cornerstone to the profile, quite possibly a rebellion against parental dominion.

"He also pointed out that since the killings were symbolic acts, the audience was key. And what better audience than the police, who are connoisseurs in murder? So from the beginning we were looking for someone who had had difficult relations with his or her parents and was abnormally interested in the police's progress on the case.

"At first we thought it was a locked-room situation and the murderer must be someone who had been both in the dining room of Chez Béatrice and also at the Brazilian reception. Of course, as the murders progressed, it could have been anyone, but there was such a feeling of intimacy about it all that I had a very strong sense it was one of the original suspects."

"Ah, the famous Capucine intuition. What a powerful trump card you have, my dear," Alexandre said. With great concentration he uncorked a bottle of 2000 Château Ausone, which had been provided to accompany the sweetbreads.

"Idiotically, I crossed Voisin off the list almost immediately. Voisin had no problems with his parents whatsoever and not the slightest interest in the case. That left four. It was true Sybille had been abused by her father, but she had learned to use his guilt to manipulate him. She was so satisfied by that situation that it gave her a taste for the sexual manipulation of older men," Capucine said.

Vavasseur nodded in approval. "In fact, of all the suspects, she was by far the most well adjusted."

"Tanguy's relationship with his father was unquestionably flawed," Capucine continued. "So was his view of the entire fabric of social authority. But, somehow, he didn't seem credible as a murderer."

"He had built such an effective temple of imaginary reality to hide in, he had no need of gratification from the real world," Vavasseur said.

They had finished the lobster. Jacques and Alexandre cleared away the dishes, and Jacques opened the thick-bottomed, heat-retaining canisters containing the sweetbreads. The air filled with an aroma that was round and unctuous at the center and pleasantly sharp at the edges. On their plates the half-inch-thick medallions of sweetbreads were surrounded by nubbly little navels of miniscule tortellini, which in turn were surrounded by the muted hues of the "forgotten vegetables." They all fell silent, intent on their meals.

When the dish was half consumed, Capucine sighed, sipping her Saint-Emilion in almost postcoital contentment.

"Where was I?" she asked.

"You were about to reveal the intimate details of your two most luscious suspects," Jacques said.

"Yes, at that stage both Cécile and Béatrice were possibilities."

"You suspected your childhood friend!" Jacques exclaimed in mock horror. "The one you and I spent that long rainy afternoon with in the commons of the château and . . . Oh, sorry. I forgot Alexandre was here."

"Jacques, do you take anything seriously?" Alexandre asked.

"I'm taking this *ris de veau* extremely seriously," Jacques said.

"Cécile was in the middle of a profound *crise*. No doubt about that. But even though it looked like she was trying to escape her parents' paradigm, in fact she was trying to dive even deeper into it."

"Exactly," Vavasseur said. "She had established a life that she thought would be challenging and stimulating, but it turned out to be too easy. Her successes frustrated her. She needed to distance herself from her world so she could focus on her true self, her vision of her Mirror Image. Of course, that's a form of neurosis but it's a very productive one. I'm sure she will have a distinguished career. She will leave a number of broken hearts behind, but she will be fulfilled."

"So it seemed to me that Béatrice was the most likely candidate," Capucine said. "And in one of our final discussions Docteur Vavasseur confirmed the reasonableness of my assumption."

"Yes," Vavasseur said. "And she fitted the profile perfectly. A classic case of the *non du père*—the father's no. In her mirror image of herself she was utterly and completely a chef. But her immensely rich and powerful father opposed that life, which he characterized as 'manual labor.' Worse, he viewed her refusal to join the family business as an act of treason. Even though she was successful, she felt as if she was impotent and losing the battle against her father's power. She needed desperately to protect herself."

"And I thought this psychological stuff was always sexual," Jacques said, pouring himself and Alexandre another glass of Ausone. "What a disappointment."

Both Capucine and Vavasseur looked at him coldly.

"Her only possibility of survival, as she saw it, was a series of symbolic victories," Capucine said.

"Exactly," Vavasseur said. "After each killing her sense of well-being soared and then tapered off gradually until she required a new killing. Early on she must have learned that collecting tangible fetishes from her victims would prolong the feeling of satisfaction. So she gathered pens from her victims. They were very powerful symbols, simultaneously phallic and representative of the restaurant critics' fatherlike power to sanction her."

"I knew sex would come into it sooner or later," Jacques said.

"The pens were critical in the case. They were the tip-off that there were two murderers," Capucine said.

Vavasseur finished his sweetbreads, touched his napkin to his lips, and sighed—a man content with life. "Yes, the pens. But that was all *Commissaire* Le Tellier's work. All I did was underline the probability of the murderer's reliance on fetishes."

"Early on I sensed the first murder was different from the others," Capucine said. "The use of poison was a factor. It was only in the first murder that death resulted from poison. In all the others it was obviously symbolic. Also, all the other poisons were foodstuffs—even belladonna, which was once used as a condiment. Curare certainly isn't edible. And the feel to the first murder was different. It didn't have the same degree of hands-on violence of the other four.

"But it was the pens that were the clincher. It took me a while to see it. Fesnay had his pen in his pocket. Monteil had two plastic pens on him. So at that point they weren't an issue. Peroché had no pen but he might have forgotten it somewhere, so I didn't give it a second thought. It wasn't until I checked and found out he had been taking notes during his dinner in a spiral notebook that the penny dropped. Someone had clearly taken his pen. And then Laroque was found without a pen. So it was clear that the murderer was taking pens as trophies. We found Monteil's plastic pen in Béatrice's trophy case. He'd had three plastic pens in his pocket but Béatrice only took one."

"All that's very well, but how did you know Voisin was the other killer?" Alexandre asked.

"Motive. The most powerful motive of all, money."

"And I thought with those pens we were finally going to get a little sex into this story. Can't you work that teen temptress into this somehow?" Jacques said.

Capucine ignored him.

"From the beginning a lot of little things about Voisin didn't quite add up, the fact that his son had had such an easy time deposing him, the fact that he was so broke his girlfriend had to pay to have his car maintained, things like that. But we were looking for a serial killer and that he definitely wasn't.

"Even when he let drop at the Salon du Bordeaux that he knew Fesnay, it was obvious he'd told us a lie but I still couldn't see him as a serial killer. Of course, when it dawned on me there were two killers the whole thing popped into focus. I could have spent weeks digging into Fesnay's and Voisin's background would have come up with a nice paper trail of the blackmail, but I decided to chance it with a quick arrest and interrogation."

"*Cousine,* get back to the sexy chef and her phallic pens. How did you know it was her?"

"That's the whole point. I was *sure,* but I didn't *know.* You see, we had breakfast a few days after the murder at Dong. She gave herself away with a tiny slip. She was horrified that Laroque had died with 'his *pipi* hanging out,' to use her phrase. We had never released that detail to the press."

Jacques' cackle erupted. "Ah, finally sex rears its ugly little head. I knew that would happen sooner or later." He brayed loudly.

"At the time I was confused. I knew from my first interview that she had a very positive reaction to Gautier du Fesnay. She convinced me she thought he was going to be instrumental in getting her first Michelin star. But when I knew there were two murderers, then she was obviously the serial killer. Her profile was perfect, and she had tipped her hand. But I didn't have a single scrap of evidence."

"So you resorted to entrapment?" Jacques asked.

"It was the only thing I could do. Otherwise, she could have gone on killing for years. We had nothing. Even what we found in her apartment is so circumstantial, we couldn't have made an arrest stick without her attempted murder of Alexandre."

"And other than my boyish good looks, how were you so sure she'd walk into your trap?" Alexandre asked.

"She was already far overdue for her fix and must have been completely strung out. And the setting was just too good to pass up—famous critic, opening of the year, celebrity guests, lots of press. It would have been her most exciting killing. I knew she would bite. And she did."

"So without Alexandre there would be no case at all," Jacques said. "*Fabuleux!* Alexandre is the real hero! Let's drink to him."

They all raised their glasses. Alexandre beamed. It was obvious that for him the attempt at his murder had been far less troubling than a broken cork in a bottle of *grand cru*. Still, Capucine bit her lip. She could just not bring herself to believe that her ambition had not cost her a good bit of her Alexandre.

As if he had read her mind, Alexandre shot her a look. He nodded almost imperceptibly. They rose, walked to the river's edge. Alexandre fished a leather cigar case out of his jacket, eased out a Rey del Mundo robusto, bit off the end, lit it slowly and sensually. The heady aroma of the Cuban cigar floated over the group. Jacques opened his mouth to say something. Vavasseur pursed his lips slightly. Jacques closed his mouth.

Capucine leaned up against Alexandre and took his hand. Slowly they strolled up the stone walkway, their hands swinging slightly with the cadence of their stride.

After a few dozen yards they stopped and looked deeply into each other's eyes. Capucine took the cigar out of Alexandre's hand and cocked her arm to toss it into the river.

Instead she took a deep puff, held it in her mouth for a second, and let it out.

"These things are really quite good. Why didn't you ever tell me?" she said with a giggle and gave the cigar back to Alexandre. He puffed contemplatively for a few beats and returned it to Capucine.

They continued off, hand in hand, down the walkway to the far end of the island, passing the cigar back and forth. In a few minutes the walkway curved to the right and they were lost from sight.